PAUL BOWLES (1965) BY LE GAUNT

PAUL BOWLES was born in 1910 and studied music with composer Aaron Copland before moving to Tangier, Morocco, with his wife, the writer Jane Bowles. He kept Morocco as his home, and it served as the inspiration for *The Sheltering Sky*, which was published in 1949. It was followed by *The Delicate Prey, Let It Come Down, The Spider's House,* and *Without Stopping,* a memoir that describes a life among many of the most important literary figures of the twentieth century. Bowles's prolific career included musical compositions as well as novels, collections of short fiction, books of travel, poetry, and translations. He died in Morocco in 1999.

PAUL BOWLES

THE SPIDER'S HOUSE

With a Preface
by the Author

Introduction by Francine Prose

An Imprint of HarperCollinsPublishers

FIRST ECCO EDITION 2002

The Library of Congress has catalogued a previous edition as follows:

Bowles, Paul Frederic, 1911–1999
   The spider's house.
   Reprint. Originally published: New York: Random House, 1955.
   I. Title.
PS3552.O874S6   1982   813'.54   82-4195
ISBN 0-87685-546-X   AACR2
ISBN 0-87685-545-1 (pbk.)

ISBN 0-06-057891-2

03 04 05 06 07 OS/RRD 10 9 8 7 6 5 4 3 2 1

FOR MY FATHER

I wanted to write a novel using as backdrop the traditional daily life of Fez, because it was a medieval city functioning in the twentieth century. If I had started it only a year sooner, it would have been an entirely different book. I intended to describe Fez as it existed at the moment of writing about it, but even as I started to write, events that could not be ignored had begun to occur there. I soon saw that I was going to have to write, not about the traditional pattern of life in Fez, but about its dissolution.

For more than two decades I had been waiting to see the end of French rule in Morocco. Ingenuously I had imagined that after Independence the old manner of life would be resumed and the country would return to being more or less what it had been before the French presence. The detestation on the part of the populace of all that was European seemed to guarantee such a result. What I failed to understand was that if Morocco was still a largely medieval land, it was because the French themselves, and not the Moroccans, wanted it that way.

The Nationalists were not interested in ridding Morocco of all traces of European civilization and restoring it to its pre-colonial state; on the contrary, their aim was to make it even more "European" than the French had made it. When France was no longer able to keep the governmental vehicle on the road, she abandoned it, leaving the motor running. The Moroccans climbed in and drove off in the same direction, but with even greater speed.

I was embroiled in the controversy, at the same time finding it impossible to adopt either side's point of view. My subject was decomposing before my eyes, hour by hour; there was no alternative to recording the process of violent transformation.

Fiction should always stay clear of political considerations. Even when I saw that the book that I had begun was taking a direction which would inevitably lead it into a region where politics could not be avoided, I still imagined that with sufficient dexterity I should be able to avert contact with the subject. But in situations where everyone is under great emotional stress, indifference is unthinkable; at such times all opinions are construed as political ones. To be apolitical is tantamount to having assumed a political stance, but one which pleases no one.

Thus, whether I liked it or not, when I had finished, I found that I had written a "political" book which deplored the attitudes of both the French and the Moroccans. Much later Allal el Fassi, "the father of Moroccan nationalism," read it and expressed his personal approval. Even coming so late, this was satisfying.

Each novel seems to impose its own particular working regime. *The Sheltering Sky* and *Let It Come Down* were written during travels, whenever the spirit moved and the physical surroundings were conducive to writing. *The Spider's House*, on the other hand, from the outset demanded a rigorous schedule. I began writing it in Tangier in the summer of 1954, setting the alarm for six each morning. I managed to average two pages a day. When winter came I sailed for Sri Lanka. There I adopted the same ritual; early tea was brought in at six o'clock, and I set to work, still meeting my quota of two daily pages. By the middle of March, in spite of visits to distant temples and nights spent watching devil-dances, the book was finished, and sent off from Weligama to Random House.

The tale is neither autobiographical nor factual, nor is it a *roman á clef.* Only the setting is objective; the rest is invented. The focal point of the action is the old Hôtel Palais Jamaï, before it was modernized. I called it the Mérinides Palace because one had to pass the tombs of the Mérinide kings on the way to the hotel. There is now an actual Hôtel des Mérinides, built in the sixties on the cliff alongside the tombs.

The city is still there. It is no longer the intellectual and cultural center of North Africa; it is merely one more city beset by the insoluble problems of the Third World. Not all the ravages caused by our merciless age are tangible ones. The subtler forms of destruction, those involving only the human spirit, are the most to be dreaded.

Paul Bowles
December 1981

INTRODUCTION

"Ten or twelve years ago there came to live in Tangier a man who would have done better to stay away." This wickedly portentous sentence, which begins Paul Bowles's story "The Eye," could—with the medieval city of Fez substituted for the cosmopolitan port of Tangier—just as easily serve as the opening of *The Spider's House* and for most of Bowles's novels and stories, especially if we expand the list of ill-advised travel destinations to include nearly all of Morocco and a virtual Baedeker of hellish jungle outposts in Latin America and Asia. For Bowles's obsessive subject, to which he returned again and again, and which he wrote about brilliantly, was the tragic and even fatal mistakes that Westerners so commonly make in their misguided and often presumptuous encounters with the mysteries of a foreign culture.

One can hardly imagine a more timely theme, one more perfectly suited to the perilous new world in which we find ourselves. Yet, strangely, Paul Bowles's name never (as far as I know) appeared on those rosters of writers one saw mentioned in the aftermath of September 11, classic authors whose work appears to speak across centuries and decades, directly and helpfully addressing the crises and drastically altered realities of the present moment: terrorism, violence, neocolonialist warfare, revolution, and our dawning awareness of the hidden costs of colonialism and globalization. Perhaps it's because the books that were commonly cited (*War and Peace, The Possessed, The Secret Agent,* and so forth) seemed, even at their most pessimistic, to offer some hope of redemption, some persuasive evidence of human resilience and nobility; whereas Bowles's fiction is the last place you would go for hope, or for even faint reassurance that the world is anything but a horror show, a barbaric Darwinian battlefield.

Frequently, Bowles begins his fiction in ways that seem to promise (or threaten) the sort of narrative we might expect from other writers who have focused on the confrontation between East and West, from novelists as dissimilar as Conrad, Naipaul, and Forster, from works in which a naive colonial sightsees his way into one heart of darkness or another—and lives to regret it.

So *The Spider's House* starts off with a prologue that could almost (but not quite) pass for the introduction to an unusually well written political thriller. John Stenham, a writer who has been living in Fez for a very long time, an American who speaks Arabic, who loves the culture with a passion bordering on the delusional, and who understands the locals as well as any Westerner can—which is to say, not at all—is being escorted home from a dinner party. His Moroccan hosts have insisted that the streets are unsafe for him to walk alone, and though Stenham resists with the insulted bravado of the foreigner who has proudly "gone native," he accedes because the mood of the city has lately seemed restive and strange. "Ever since that day a year ago when the French, more irresponsible than usual, had deposed the Sultan, the tension had been there, and he had known it was there. But it was a political thing, and politics exist only on paper; certainly the politics of 1954 had no true connection with the mysterious medieval city he knew and loved." Already, the sentient reader will have predicted that this "political thing" will affect Stenham more than he could have predicted or imagined, and that the shock of his highly unpleasant awakening will give the novel the sort of arc we might find in a book by, say, Graham Greene.

But almost immediately we can watch Bowles part company with his fellow authors and enter territory that he has claimed as uniquely his own, a universe that few, if any, of us would willingly choose to inhabit—which is not to say that Bowles's lifelong residence in that bleak and harsh (though often grimly hilarious) landscape seems voluntary, exactly.

The next long section is written from the point of view of a Moroccan boy named Amar, a complex, intelligent, and intuitive kid from a poor and pious family who, despite his own sharp instincts and good judgment, gets pulled into the very heart of the "political thing" that Stenham would so love to avoid and ignore. It's a convincing and daring portrait—notably few European or American writers have had the courage to write from the perspective of a North African Muslim boy—and one that is absolutely necessary for Bowles's narrative strategy. Because Amar's experience and his view of politics, of religion, of the nature of human existence, and of the way in which the universe operates could hardly be more unlike Stenham's ideas or those of Stenham's chic, decadent American and British friends. This profound and unbridgeable difference creates a tension that underlies—and spikes—the pressure created by the thickening web of conspiracy, and by the growing discord and bloody violence erupting in the souks and streets of Fez.

In his characteristically distanced, clinical, quietly confident and authoritative tone, employing a rigorously unadorned, quasi-journalistic prose style, Bowles approaches his material and his characters in a way that seems relentlessly anthropological, scien-

xii

tific, distanced, unbiased by either contempt and derision on the one hand or sympathy and affection on the other—or by any powerful or particular tribal loyalties of his own. Writing about expatriates and Moroccans warily coexisting in the crowded cities and desert encampments of North Africa, he depicts all these groups acting badly. Even the unusually appealing Amar turns out to be capable of committing murder (manslaughter, really) without suffering much remorse. Every community seems capable of carrying out any crime, no matter how mindless or vile—willing and able to do anything except understand one another.

What mostly (if not entirely) exempts Bowles from the charges of racism that his portrayals of brutal Moroccans have, at times, occasioned is the fact that his dispatches from the various frontiers of savagery are so evenhanded and inclusive. It's not at all clear that the vengeful merchants in his story "The Delicate Prey" or the sadistic bandit tribe in "A Distant Episode" are any worse than the Frenchmen in *The Spider's House*, who round up all the young males in the medina of Fez and bring them into the police station to be tortured and perhaps killed. "As far as I can see," said Bowles in a 1981 *Paris Review* interview, "People from all corners of the earth have an unlimited potential for violence."

Readers accustomed to parsing literature for clues to the personal history of a writer, or for instruction on how to live, may be puzzled by the discrepancies between a body of work that seems to advise against ever leaving home and the facts of Bowles's peripatetic existence. An avid and intrepid traveler, Paul (a dentist's son from Queens) abandoned a promising career as a composer and spent much of his early adulthood in Paris and Germany, North Africa, Mexico, Guatemala, Ceylon, and Thailand. From the 1940s until his death in 1999, he was a more or less permanent resident of Tangier, where he lived with his famously eccentric and fascinating wife, Jane, author of the dazzlingly original novel *Two Serious Ladies*. He also formed a series of intimate relationships with Moroccan men and translated books of Mohgrebi oral narratives.

Bowles was immensely proud and fiercely territorial about his knowledge of North African customs, music, and folktales; about his familiarity with Islam, his fluency in Moghrebi, his ability to understand the North Africans around him or at least (unlike most foreigners) to admit, and know why, he would never understand them. In the prologue to *The Spider's House*, there's a revealing passage in which Stenham (the character who, one might argue, most nearly approaches being a stand-in for the author) admits to "a small sense of superiority to which he felt he was entitled, in return for having withstood the rigors of Morocco for so many years. This pretending to know something that others could not know, it was a little indulgence he allowed himself, a bonus for seniority. Secretly he was convinced that the Moroccans were much like any other people, that the differences were largely those of ritual and gesture . . . "

In fact, *The Spider's House* should top the list of novels that speak to our current condition. Set during the first upheavals that announced a more radical and violent phase of the Moroccan struggle for independence from the French, the book seems not merely prescient but positively eerie in its evocation of a climate in which every aspect of daily life is affected—and deformed— by the roilings of nationalism and terrorism, and by the damage done by colonialism. It's chilling to hear its characters speculate on the root causes of insurrection ("If people are living the same as always, with their bellies full of food, they'll just go on the same way. If they get hungry and unhappy enough, something happens.") and on the grim compensations of terrorism. Listening to his father mourn the widespread sinfulness that, in his opinion, signals the end of Islam, Amar understands why his countrymen are "willing to risk dying in order to derail a train or burn a cinema or blow up a post office. It was not independence they wanted, it was a satisfaction much more immediate than that: the pleasure of seeing others undergo the humiliation of suffering and dying, and the knowledge that they had at least the small amount of power necessary to bring about that humiliation. If you could not have freedom you could still have vengeance, and that was all anyone really wanted now."

Though it would be a reductive oversimplification, a gross injustice to the depth, inventiveness, and psychological complexity

of this novel, it could conceivably be read as a sort of textbook, a
monitory analysis of the sources of anti-American sentiment in
the Muslim world. "The arms used against the Moroccan people
were largely supplied by your government," a nationalist tells
Stenham. "They do not consider America a nation friendly to
their cause." Yet another agitator speculates on the most efficient
means of getting American attention. "Once we've had a few
incidents directly involving American lives and property, maybe
the Americans will know there's such a country as Morocco in
the world . . . Now they don't know the difference between
Morocco and the Sénégal." To make matters even more complicated, Bowles takes a dim view of the opportunism, the cynicism,
the manipulative dishonesty, and the gross irresponsibility of the
insurgent nationalist movement, the people's so-called libera-
tors; this is a coolly reasoned perspective which effectively pre-
vents the reader from forming a simplistic view of the region's
problems, or of their solutions.

What makes this all the more intriguing, all the more persuasive, is that Bowles never thought of himself as a political
writer—and, perhaps as a result, few readers see him that way. In
the preface to *The Spider's House*, he wrote, "Fiction should
always stay clear of political considerations. Even when I saw that
the book that I had begun was taking a direction which would
inevitably lead it into a region where politics could not be
avoided, I still imagined that with sufficient dexterity I should be
able to avert contact with the subject. But in situations where
everyone is under great emotional stress, indifference is unthinkable; at such times all opinions are construed as political ones.
To be apolitical is tantamount to having assumed a political
stance, but one which pleases no one. Thus, whether I liked it or
not, when I had finished, I found that I had written a 'political'
book which deplored the attitudes of both the French and the
Moroccans."

The last sentence is particularly telling. To be a political writer
(as the term is generally understood) suggests strongly held opinions, a polemical agenda, a taking of sides—something that
would have been not merely esthetic anathema but a charactero-

logical impossibility for the exquisitely detached Bowles. The novel's characters (both Moroccan and American) repeatedly express their contempt for those fanatics who would willingly sacrifice individual lives to gain political objectives. Moreover, what Bowles tells us at the start (and what subsequently emerges) is that his initial impulse for writing the book derived from his fear that the city of Fez (and by extension, the rest of Morocco) would be changed and modernized beyond recognition — an anxiety that he wisely mistrusts as stemming from the most self-indulgent species of romanticism. In a startling flash of self-awareness, Stenham realizes, "It did not really matter whether they worshiped Allah or carburetors. In the end, it was his own preferences which concerned him. He would have liked to preserve the status quo because the decor that went with it suited his personal taste." Throughout Bowles's work, you can watch him battling against his own estheticism and cynicism (one of the characters in *The Spider's House* calls Stenham "a hopeless romantic without a shred of confidence in the human race"), and straining to see the world and its denizens as they really are — without sentimentality, without illusions, without blinders.

However unintentional, the political subtext of his fiction provides us with yet another opportunity to note that when one writes accurately and comprehensively about human beings, politics inevitably comes into the story, since — it hardly needs to be said — politics exerts such an enormous influence on every aspect of our lives. Even Chekhov, whom we also tend to think of as a largely apolitical writer (in contrast, say, to Dostoyevsky or Tolstoy) frequently established or clarified the nature of his characters by informing the reader about their political sympathies.

How peculiar it suddenly seems to mention Chekhov and Bowles in the same paragraph, or even the same essay. Were there ever two more dissimilar literary sensibilities? With his sangfroid, his lack of empathy, his chilly refusal to demonstrate an even passing interest in the process of spiritual transformation or individual redemption, Bowles strikes us as the anti-Chekhov. Which may be why he seems, right now, as necessary as

Chekhov, equally valuable in his contribution to the chorus of voices that comprise our literary heritage, and no less essential in his ability to remind us of who we are, of how we live, and of what we can—and inevitably will—do, in accordance with our nature.

In an era in which circumstances much like those that inspired *The Spider's House* force us to enter into a highly partisan and passionate political engagement, we would do well to be aware, and wary, of the dangers and pitfalls of such an engagement: dogmatism, intolerance, the unshakeable conviction of one's own righteousness and innocence, the inability or refusal to admit that other people, in other nations, have hearts and souls, loves and hatreds, that their lives are not so different from ours, that they suffer and die just as we do. What Paul Bowles reminds us of, what he won't let us forget, is that all of us, regardless of nationality or religion, are capable of acting from highly suspect, compromised, "primitive" motives—and of behaving in ways that, we would like to think, we could never even imagine.

—*Francine Prose*

The likeness of those who choose other patrons than Allah is as the likeness of the spider when she taketh unto herself a house, and lo! the frailest of all houses is the spider's house, if they but knew.

—THE KORAN

THE SPIDER'S HOUSE

PROLOGUE

It was just about midnight when Stenham left Si Jaffar's door. "I don't need anyone to come with me," he had said, smiling falsely to belie the sound of his voice, for he was afraid he had seemed annoyed or been abrupt, and Si Jaffar, after all, was only exercising his rights as a host in sending this person along with him.

"Really, I don't need anybody." For he wanted to go back alone, even with all the lights in the city off. The evening had been endless, and he felt like running the risk of taking the wrong turnings and getting temporarily lost; if he were accompanied, the long walk would be almost like a continuation of sitting in Si Jaffar's salon.

But in any case, it was too late now. All the male members of the household had come to the door, even stood out in the wet alley, insisting that the man go with him. Their adieux were always lengthy and elaborate, as if he were leaving for the other side of the world rather than the opposite end of the Medina, and he consciously liked that, because it was a part of what he thought life in a medieval city should be like. However, it was unprecedented for them to force upon him the presence of a protector, and he felt there was no justification for it.

The man strode ahead of him in the darkness. Where'd they get him from? he thought, seeing again the tall bearded Berber in tattered mountain garb as he had looked when he had first caught sight of him in the dim light of Si Jaffar's patio. Then he recalled the fluttering and whispering that had gone on at one end of the room about an hour and a half earlier. Whenever these family discussions arose in Stenham's presence, Si Jaffar made a great effort to divert his attention from them by embarking on a story. The story usually began promisingly enough, Si Jaffar smiling, beaming through his two pairs of spectacles, but with his attention clearly fixed on the sound of voices in the corner. Slowly, as the whispered conversation over there subsided, his words would come more haltingly, and his eyes would dart from side to side as his smile became paralyzed and meaningless. The tale would never be completed. Suddenly, "Ahah!" he would cry triumphantly, apropos of nothing at all. Then he would clap his hands for snuff, or orange-flower water, or chips of sandalwood to throw onto the brazier, look still more pleased, and perhaps whack Stenham's knee playfully. A similar comedy had been played this evening about half past ten. As he thought it over now, Stenham decided that the occasion for it had been the family's sudden decision to provide him with someone to accompany him back to the hotel. Now he remembered that after the discussion Abdeltif, the eldest son, had disappeared for at least half an hour; that must have been when the guide had been fetched.

The man had been crouching in the dark patio entrance just inside the door when they had gone out. It was embarrassing, because he knew Si Jaffar was not a well-to-do man, and while a little service like this was not abnormally expensive, still, it had to be paid for; Si Jaffar had made that clear. "Don't give this man anything," he had said in French. "I have already seen to that."

"But I don't need him," Stenham had protested. "I know the way. Think of all the times I've gone back alone." Si Jaffar's four sons, his cousin and his son-in-law had all murmured: "No, no, no," together, and the old man had patted his arm affectionately. "It's better," he said, with one of his curiously formal little bows. There was no use in objecting. The man would stay with him until he had delivered him over to the watchman at the hotel, and then he would disappear into the night, go back to whatever dark corner he had come from, and Stenham would not see him again.

The streets were completely without passers-by. It would have been quite possible to go most of the way along somewhat more frequented thoroughfares, he reflected, but obviously his companion preferred the empty ones. He took out his little dynamo flashlight and began to squeeze it, turning the dim ray downward to the ground at the man's feet. The insect-like whirring it made caused him to turn around, a look of surprise on his face.

"Light," said Stenham.

The man grunted. "Too much noise," he objected.

He smiled and let the light die down. How these people love games, he thought. This one's playing cops and robbers now; they're always either stalking or being stalked. "The Oriental passion for complications, the involved line, Arabesques," Moss had assured him, but he was not sure it was that. It could just as easily be a deep sense of guilt. He had suggested this, but Moss had scoffed.

The muddy streets led down, down. There was not a foot of level ground. He had to move forward stiff-ankled, with the weight all on the balls of his feet. The city was asleep. There was profound silence, broken only by the scuffing sound he made as he walked. The man, barefooted, advanced noiselessly. From time to time, when the way led not through inner passages but into the open, a solitary drop of rain fell heavily out of the sky, as if a great invisible piece of wet cloth were hanging only a few feet above the earth. Everything was invisible, the mud of the street, the walls, the sky. Stenham squeezed the flashlight suddenly, and had a rapidly fading view of the man moving ahead of him in his brown *djellaba*, and of his giant shadow thrown against the beams that formed the ceiling of the street. The man grunted again in protest.

Stenham smiled: unaccountable behavior on the part of Moslems amused him, and he always forgave it, because, as he said, no non-Moslem knows enough about the Moslem mind to dare find fault with it. "They're far, far away from us," he would say. "We haven't an inkling of the things that motivate them." There was a certain amount of hypocrisy in this attitude of his; the truth was that he hoped principally to convince *others* of the existence of this almost unbridgeable gulf. The mere fact that he could then even begin to hint at the beliefs and purposes that lay on the far side made him feel more sure in his own attempts at analyzing them and gave him a small sense of superiority to which he felt he was entitled, in return for having withstood the rigors of Morocco for so many years. This pretending to know something that others could not know, it was a little indulgence he allowed himself, a bonus for seniority. Secretly he was convinced that the Moroccans were much like any other people, that the differences were largely those of ritual and gesture, that even the fine curtain of magic through which they observed life was not a complex thing, and did not give their perceptions any profundity. It delighted him that this anonymous, barefoot Berber should want to guide him through the darkest, least frequented tunnels of the city; the reason for the man's desire for secrecy did not matter. These were a feline, nocturnal people. It was no accident that Fez was a city without dogs. "I wonder if Moss has noticed that," he thought.

Now and then he had the distinct impression that they were traversing a street or an open space that he knew perfectly well, but if that were so, the angle at which they had met it was unexpected, so that the familiar walls (if indeed they *were* familiar walls) were dwarfed or distorted in the one swiftly fading beam of light that he played on them. He began to suspect that the power plant had suffered a major collapse: the electricity was almost certainly still cut off, because it would be practically impossible to go so far without coming upon at least one street light. However, he was used to moving around the city in the darkness. He knew a good many ways across it in each direction, and he could have found his way blindfolded along several of these routes. Indeed, wandering through the Medina at night was very much like being blindfolded; one let one's ears and nose do most of the work. He knew just how each section of a familiar way sounded when he walked it alone at night. There were two things to listen for: his feet and the sound of the water behind the walls. The footsteps had an infinite variety of sound, depending on the hardness of the earth, the width of the passageway, the height and configuration of the walls. On the Lemtiyine walk there was one place between the tannery and a small mosque where the echo was astounding: taut, metallic reverberations that shuddered between the walls like musical pistol shots. There were places where his footfalls were almost silent, places where the sound was strong, single and compact, died straightway, or where, as he advanced along the deserted galleries, each succeeding step produced a sound of an imperceptibly higher pitch, so that his passage was like a finely graded ascending scale, until all at once a jutting wall or a sudden tunnel dispersed the pattern and began another section in the long nocturne which in turn would slowly disclose its own design. And the water was the same, following its countless courses behind the partitions of earth and stone. Seldom visible but nearly always present, it rushed beneath the sloping alleyways, here gurgled, here merely dripped, here beyond the wall of a garden splashed or dribbled in the form of a fountain, here fell with a high hollow noise into an invisible cistern, here all at once was unabashedly a branch of the river roaring over the rocks (so that sometimes the cold vapor rising was carried over the wall by the wind and wet his face), here by the bakery had been dammed and was almost still, a place where the rats swam.

The two simultaneous sound-tracks of footsteps and water he had experienced so often that it seemed to him he must know each portion by heart. But now it was all different, and he realized that what he knew was only one line, one certain sequence whose parts became unrecognizable once they were presented out of their accustomed context. He knew, for instance, that in order to be as near the main branch of the river as they were now, at some point they had had to cross the street leading from the Karouine Mosque to the Zaouia of Si Ahmed Tidjani, but it was impossible for him to know when that had been; he had recognized nothing.

Suddenly he realized where they were: in a narrow street that ran the length of a slight eminence above the river, just below the mass of walls that formed the Fondouk el Yihoudi. It was far out of their way, not on any conceivable route between Si Jaffar's house and the hotel. "Why have we come out here?" he asked with indignation. The man was unnecessarily abrupt in his reply, Stenham thought. "Walk and be quiet."

"But they always are," he reminded himself; he would never be able to take for granted their curious mixture of elaborate circumspection and brutal bluntness, and he almost laughed aloud at the memory of how the ridiculous words had sounded five seconds ago: *Rhir zid o skout*. And in another few minutes they had circumnavigated the Fondouk el Yihoudi and were going through a wet garden under banana trees; the heavy tattered leaves showered cold drops as they brushed against them. "Si Jaffar has outdone himself this time." He decided to telephone him tomorrow and make a good story of it. *Zid o skout*. It would be a hilarious slogan over the tea glasses for the next fortnight, one in which the whole family could share.

It was a freakish summer night; a chill almost like that of early spring paralyzed the air. A vast thick cloud had rolled down across the Djebel Zalagh and formed a ceiling low over the city, enclosing it in one great room whose motionless air smelled only of raw, wet earth. As they went silently back into the streets higher up the hill, an owl screamed once from somewhere above their heads.

When they had arrived at the hotel's outer gate, Stenham pushed the button that rang a bell down in the interior of the hotel in some little room near the office where the watchman stayed. For a moment he thought: It won't ring; the power's off tonight. But then he remembered that the hotel had its own electric system. It was usually a good five minutes before the light came on in the courtyard, and then another two or three before the watchman got to the gate. Tonight the light came on immediately. Stenham stepped close to the high doors and peered through the crack between them. The watchman was at the far end of the courtyard talking to someone. "*Ah, oui,*" he heard him say. A European in the court at this hour, he thought with some curiosity, trying to see more. The watchman was approaching. Like a guilty child, Stenham stepped quickly back and put his hands in his pockets, looking nonchalantly toward the side wall. Then he realized that his guide had disappeared. There was no sound of retreating footsteps; he was merely gone. The heavy bolt of the gate was drawn back and the watchman stood there in his khaki duster and white turban, the customary anxious expression on his face.

"*Bon soir, M'sio Stonamm,*" he said. Sometimes he spoke in Arabic, sometimes in French; it was impossible to know which he would choose for a given occasion. Stenham greeted him, looking across the courtyard to see who was there with him. He saw no one. The same two cars stood there: the hotel's station wagon and an old Citroën that belonged to the manager, but which he never used. "You came quickly tonight," he said.

"*Oui, M'sio Stonamm.*"

"You were outside, near the gate, perhaps?"

The watchman hesitated. "*Non, m'sio.*"

He abandoned it rather than become exasperated with the man, which he knew he would do if he went on. A lie is not a lie; it is only a formula, a substitute, a long way around, a polite manner of saying: None of your business.

He had his key in his pocket, and so he went directly up the back way to his room, a little ashamed of himself for having started to pry. But when he stood in his room in the tower, look-

ing out over the invisible city spread below, he found that he
could justify his inquisitiveness. It was not merely the watchman's patent lie which had prodded him; much more than
that was the fact of its having come directly on the heels of the
Berber's strange behavior: the unnecessary detour, the gruff in-
junctions to silence, the inexplicable disappearance before he
had had a chance to hand him the thirty francs he had ready to
give him. Not only that, he decided, going further back to Si
Jaffar. The whole family had so solemnly insisted that he be
accompanied on his way home to the hotel. That too seemed to
be a part of the conspiracy. "They're all crazy tonight," he told
himself with satisfaction. He refused to tie all these things together by attributing them to the tension that was in the city.
Ever since that day a year ago when the French, more irresponsible than usual, had deposed the Sultan, the tension had been
there, and he had known it was there. But it was a political
thing, and politics exist only on paper; certainly the politics of
1954 had no true connection with the mysterious medieval city
he knew and loved. It would have been too simple to make a
logical relationship between what his brain knew and what his
eyes saw; he found it more fun to play this little game with himself.

Each night when Stenham had locked his door, the watchman climbed up the steep stairs into the tower of the *ancien
palais* and snapped off the lights in the corridors, one by one.
When he had gone back down, and the final sounds of his passage had died away, there was only the profound silence of the
night, disturbed, if a wind blew, by the rustle of the poplars in
the garden. Tonight, when the slow footsteps approached up the
staircase, instead of the familiar click of the switch on the wall
outside the door, there was a slight hesitation, and then a soft
knock. Stenham had taken off his tie, but he was still fully
dressed. Frowning, he opened the door. The watchman smiled
apologetically at him—certainly not out of compunction for the
lie in the courtyard, he commented, seeing that wistful, vanquished face. In the five seasons he had spent here at the hotel
Stenham had never seen this man wear another expression. If the

world went on he would grow old and die, night watchman at the Mérinides Palace, no other possibility having suggested itself to him. This time he spoke in Arabic. "*Smatsi.* M'sio Moss has sent me. He wants to know if you'll go to see him."

"Now?" said Stenham incredulously.

"Now. Yes." He laughed deprecatingly, with infinite gentleness, as if he meant to imply that his understanding of the world was vast indeed.

Stenham's first thought was: I can't let Moss start this sort of thing. Temporizing, he said aloud: "Where is he?"

"In his room. Number Fourteen."

"I know the number," he said. "Are you going to his room again, to take him my message?"

"Yes. Do I tell him you'll come?"

Stenham sighed. "For a minute. Yes." This would be disregarded, of course; the man would simply tell Moss that Monsieur Stonamm was coming, and disappear. Now he bowed, said: "*Ouakha*," and shut the door.

He stood before the mirror of the armoire, putting his necktie back on. It was the first time Moss had ever sent him a message at night, and he was curious to know what had made the Englishman decide to vary his code of strict discretion. He looked at his watch: it was twenty minutes past one. Moss would begin with florid apologies for having disturbed his work, whether he believed he had caused such an interruption or not, for Stenham encouraged his acquaintances to hold the impression that he worked evenings as well as mornings. It assured him more privacy, and besides, occasionally, if the weather were bad, he went to bed early and did manage to add an extra page to the novel that was still far from completed. Rain and wind outside the window in the darkness provided the incentive necessary to offset fatigue. Tonight, in any case, he would not have worked: it was far too late. Day in Fez began long before dawn, and it made him profoundly uneasy to think that he might not be asleep before the early call to prayer set off the great sound of cockcrow that spread slowly over the city and never abated until it was broad daylight. If he were still awake once the muezzins began their chant, there was no hope of further sleep. At this time of year they started about half past three.

He looked at the typed pages lying on the table, placed a fat porcelain ash tray on top of them, and turned to go out. Then he thought better of it, and put the entire manuscript in the drawer. He went to the door, cast a brief longing glance back at his bed, stepped out and locked the door behind him. The key had a heavy nickel tag attached to it; it felt like ice in his pocket. And there was a strong, chill draft coming up the tower's narrow stairwell. He went down as quietly as he could (not that there was anyone to disturb), felt his way through the dim lobby, and walked onto the terrace. The light from the reception hall streamed out across the wet mosaic floor. No isolated raindrops fell from the sky now; instead, a faint breeze moved in the air. In the lower garden it was very dark; a thin wrought-iron grill beside the Sultana's pool guided him to the patio where on sunny days he and Moss sometimes ate their lunch. The lanterns outside the great door of Number Fourteen had not been turned on, but slivers of light came through from the room between the closed blinds. As he knocked, a startled animal, a rat or a ferret perhaps, bolted, scurried through the plants and dead leaves behind him. The man who opened the door, standing stiffly aside to let him pass, was not someone he had ever seen before.

Moss stood in the center of the room, directly under the big chandelier, nervously smoothing his moustache, an expression of consternation in his eyes. The only feeling of which Stenham could be conscious at the moment was a devout wish that he had not knocked on the door, that he could still be standing outside in the dark where he had been five seconds ago. He disregarded the man who stood beside him. "Good evening," he called to Moss, his intonation carrying a hint of casual heartiness. But Moss remained taut.

"Will you please come in, John?" he said dryly. "I must talk to you."

BOOK 1

THE MASTER OF WISDOM

I have understood that the world is a vast emptiness built upon emptiness. . . . And so they call me the master of wisdom. Alas! Does anyone know what wisdom is?

—SONG OF THE OWL:
THE THOUSAND AND ONE NIGHTS

CHAPTER   1

The spring sun warmed the orchard. Soon it would drop behind
the high canebrake that bordered the highway, for the time was
mid-afternoon. Amar lay beneath an old fig tree, embedded in
long grass that was still damp with dew from the night before.
He was comparing his own life with what he knew of the lives
of his friends, and thinking that certainly his was the least en-
viable. He knew this was a sin: it is not allowed to man to make
judgments of this sort, and he would never have given voice to
the conclusion he had reached, even if it had taken the form of
words in his mind.

He saw the trees and plants around him and the sky above,
and he knew they were there. And since he felt a great disap-

pointment in the direction his short life had taken, he knew the dissatisfaction was there. The world was a beautiful place, with all its animals and birds that moved, and its flowers and fruit trees that Allah had generously provided, but in his heart he felt that they all belonged really to him, that no one else had the same right to them as he. It was always other people who made his life unhappy. As he lay there propped indolently against the tree trunk, he carefully pulled the petals from a rose he had picked a half hour earlier when he had come into the orchard. There was not much more time for him to find out what he was going to do.

If he were going to run away he must go quickly. But already he felt that Allah was not going to reveal his destiny to him. He would learn it merely by doing what it had been written that he would do. Everything would continue as it was. When the shadows lengthened he would get up and go out onto the highway, because the twilight brought evil spirits out of the trees. Once he was on the road there would be nowhere for him to go but home. He had to go back and be beaten; there was no alternative. It was not fear of the pain that kept him from going now and getting it over with. The pain itself was nothing; it could even be enjoyable if he did not wince or cry out, because his hostile silence was in a sense a victory over his father. Afterward it always seemed to him that he was stronger, better prepared for the next time. But it left a bitter flavor in the center of his being, something that made him feel just a little farther away and lonelier than before. It was not through dread of the pain or fear of this feeling of loneliness that he stayed on sitting in the orchard; what was unbearable was the thought that he was innocent and that he was going to be humiliated by being treated as though he were guilty. What he dreaded encountering was his own powerlessness in the face of injustice.

The warm breeze that moved down across the hillsides and valleys from Djebel Zalagh found its way into the orchard between the stalks of cane, stirred the flat leaves above his head. Its tentative caress on the back of his neck sent a fleeting shiver through him. He put a rose petal between his teeth and chewed it into wet fragments. Out here there was no one at all, and no one would arrive. The guardian of the orchard had seen him come in and had said nothing. Some of the orchards had watchmen who chased you; the boys knew them all. This was a "good" orchard, because the guard never spoke, save to shout a command to his dog, to make it stop barking at the intruders. The old man had gone down to a lower part of the property near the river. Except for a truck that went by now and then on the highway beyond the canebrake, this corner of the orchard lay in complete silence. Because he did not want to imagine what such a place would be like once the daylight had gone, he slipped his feet into his sandals, stood up, shook out his *djellaba*, inspected it for a while because it had belonged to his brother and he hated wearing it, and finally flinging it over his shoulder, set out for the gap in the jungle of canes through which he had entered.

Outside on the road the sun was warmer and the wind blew harder. He passed two small boys armed with long bamboo poles, who were hitting the branches of a mulberry tree while a larger boy scooped up the green berries and stored them in the hood of his *djellaba*. All three were too busy to notice his passage. He came to one of the hairpin bends in the road. Ahead of him on the other side of the valley was Djebel Zalagh. It had always looked to him like a king in his robes, sitting on his throne. Amar had mentioned this to several of his friends, but none of them had understood. Without even looking up at the mountain they had said: "You're dizzy," or "In your head," or "In the dark," or had merely laughed. "They think they know once and for all what the world is like, so that they don't ever have to look at it again," he had thought. And it was true: many of his friends had decided what the world looked like, what life was like, and they would never examine either of them again to find out whether they were right or wrong. This was because they had gone or were still going to school, and knew how to write and even to understand what was written, which was much more difficult. And some of them knew the Koran by heart, although naturally they did not know much of what it meant, because that is the most difficult thing of all, reserved for only a few great men in the world. And no one can understand it completely.

"In the school they teach you what the world means, and once you have learned, you will always know," Amar's father had told him.

"But suppose the world changes?" Amar had thought. "Then what would you know?" However, he was careful not to let his father guess what he was thinking. He never spoke with the old man save when he was bidden. Si Driss was severe, and liked his sons to treat him with exactly the same degree of respect he had shown to his own father fifty or sixty years before. It was best not to express an unasked-for opinion. In spite of the fact that life at home was a more serious business than it would have been had he had a more easy-going parent, Amar was proud of the respected position his father held. The richest, most important men of the quarter came to him, kissed his garments, and sat silent while he spoke. It had been written that Amar was to have a stern father, and there was nothing to do about it but to give thanks to Allah. Yet he knew that if ever he wanted anything deeply enough to defy his father, the old man would see that his son was right, and would give in to him. This he had discovered when his father had first sent him to school. He had disliked it so much the first day that he had gone home and announced that he would never return, and the old man had merely sighed and called upon Allah to witness that he himself had taken the child and left him in the *aallem's* charge, so that he could not be held accountable for what might come afterward. The next day he had wakened the boy at dawn, saying to him: "If you won't go to school, you must work." And he had led him off to his uncle's blanket factory in the Attarine, to work at the looms. This had not been nearly so difficult as school, because he did not have to sit still; nevertheless, he did not stay, any more than he had stayed at any one of the several dozen different places where he had worked since. A week or two, and off he went to amuse himself, very likely without having been paid anything. His life at home was a constant struggle to keep from being led off to some new work of his father's devising.

Thus it was that among all his early friends Amar was the only one who had not learned to write and to read other people's writing, and it did not matter to him in the least. If his family had not been Chorfa, descendents of the Prophet, his life no doubt would have been easier. There would not have been his father's fierce insistence on teaching him the laws of their religion, or his constant dwelling on the necessity for strict obedience. But the old man had determined that if his son were to be illiterate (which in itself was no great handicap), at least he was not going to be ignorant of the moral precepts of Islam.

As the years had passed, Amar had made new friends like himself, boys of families so poor that there had never been any question of their going to school. When he met his childhood friends now and talked to them, it seemed to him that they had grown to be like old men, and he did not enjoy being with them, whereas his new friends, who played and fought every minute as though their lives depended upon the outcome of their games and struggles, lived in a way that was understandable to him.

A great thing in Amar's life was that he had a secret. It was a secret that did not even have to be kept secret, because no one could ever have guessed it. But he knew it and lived by it. The secret was that he was not like anybody else; he had powers that no one else possessed. Being certain of that was like having a treasure hidden somewhere out of the world's sight, and it meant much more than merely having the *baraka*. Many Chorfa had that. If someone were ill, or in a trance, or had been entered by some foreign spirit, even Amar often could set him right, by touching him with his hand and murmuring a prayer. And in his family the *baraka* was very strong, so powerful that in each generation one man had always made healing his profession. Neither his father nor his grandfather had ever done any work save that of attending to the constant stream of people who came to be treated by them. Thus there was nothing surprising about the fact that Amar himself should possess the gift. But it was not this he meant when he told himself that he was different from everyone else. Of course, he had always known his secret, but earlier it had not made so much difference. Now that he was fifteen and a man, it was becoming more important all the time. He had discovered that a hundred times a day things came into his head that never seemed to come into anyone else's head, but he had also learned that if he wanted to tell people about them—which he certainly did—he must do it in a way that would make them laugh, otherwise they became suspicious of him. Still, if one day in his enthusiasm he forgot and cried: "Look at Djebel Zalagh! The Sultan has a cloud on his shoulder!" and his friends answered: "You're crazy!" he did not mind. The next time he would try to remember to include their world, to say it in reference to some particular thing in which they were interested. Then they would laugh and he would be happy.

Today there were no clouds on any part of Djebel Zalagh. Each tiny olive tree along its crest stood out against the great, uniformly blue sky; and the myriad ravines that furrowed its bare slopes were beginning to fill with the hard shadows of late afternoon. A threadlike road wound along the side of one of the round hills at its feet; tiny white figures were moving very slowly up the road. He stood and watched them awhile: country people returning to their villages. For a moment he wished passionately that he could be someone else, one of them, with a simple, anonymous life. Then he began to spin a fantasy. If he were a *djibli*, from the country, with his cleverness—for he knew he was clever—he would soon amass more money than anyone in his *kabila*. He would buy more and more land, have increasing numbers of people working on it, and when the French tried to buy the land from him, no matter how much they offered, he would refuse to sell to them. Then the peasants would have great respect for him; his name would begin to be known further and further afield, men would come to him as to a *qoadi* for help and advice, which he would give generously. One day a Frenchman would arrive with an offer to make him a *caïd*; he saw himself laughing good-naturedly, easily, saying: "But I am already more than a *caïd* to my people. Why should I change?" The Frenchman, not understanding, would make all kinds of supplementary, underhanded offers: percentages of the taxes, girls of his choosing from distant tribes, an orange grove here, a farm there, the deed to an apartment house in Dar el Beida, and money in great quantities, but he would merely go on laughing pleasantly, saying that he wanted nothing more than what he already had: the respect of his own people. The Frenchman would be mystified (for when had any Moroccan ever made such a statement?) and would go away with fear in his heart, and the news of Amar's strength would travel fast, until even as far as Rhafsai and Taounate everyone would have heard of the young *djibli* who could not be bought by the French. And one day his chance would come. The Sultan would send for him secretly, to advise him on matters pertaining to the region he knew so well. He would be simple and respectful in his manner, but not humble, and the Sultan would find this very strange, and be a bit resentful at first, until Amar, without saying it in so many words, would let him see that his refusal to prostrate himself was a result only of his realization that sultans, however great, were merely men, all too mortal and all too fallible. The monarch would be impressed by Amar's wisdom in having such an attitude, and by his courage in showing it, and would invite him to stay on with him. Little by little, with a whispered word here and there, he would come to be more valuable to the Sultan than El Mokhri himself. And there would arrive a time of crisis, when the Sultan would not be able to make a decision. Amar would be ready. With no hesitation he would step in and take control. At this point certain difficulties might arise. He would solve them the way every great man solves his problems: by staking everything on his own force. He saw himself sadly issuing the order for the Sultan's execution; it must be done for the people. And after all, the Sultan was nothing but an Alaouite from the Tafilalet—to use plain language, a usurper. Everyone knew that. There were scores of men in Morocco with far more right to rule, including anyone in Amar's own family, for they were Drissiyine, descendants of the first dynasty, the only rightful one in the land.

Slowly the distant figures moved up the hillside. They would probably keep going all night, and arrive home only sometime after dawn. He knew well enough how the country people lived; he had spent long months on his father's farm at Kherib Jerad, before they had had to sell it, and each year they had gone to collect the family's share of the crops. In his case the amused disdain that the city dweller feels for the peasant was tempered with respect. While a townsman was announcing his intentions at great length, a peasant would simply go ahead, without saying a word, and do what he had to do.

Still standing there, looking out over the great expanse of bare sunlit land, his eyes following the little figures that crawled up the face of the slope, he considered the extent of his misfortune. If only his older brother had not happened to turn his head at a given, precise moment three nights earlier in an alley of Moulay Abdallah, Amar could now have been swimming in the river, or playing soccer outside Bab Fteuh, or merely sitting quietly on the roof making tunes on his flute, without the weight of dread inside him. But Mustapha had turned his head, seen him there in that forbidden place among the painted women. And the next day he had approached him, demanding twenty rial. Amar had no money—and no means of obtaining any. He promised Mustapha that he would pay him little by little, as he got hold of small amounts, but Mustapha, being bright as well as merciless, had a plan and was not interested in the future. He did not intend to inform upon Amar; that went without saying. Their father would have been angrier with the informer than with the betrayed. That morning Mustapha had said to Amar: "Have you got the money?" and when Amar had shaken his head: "I'll be at Hamadi's café at sunset. Bring it or look out for your father when you go home."

He did not have the money; he would not go to the café and listen to further threats. He would go straight home and receive the beating so that it would become a thing of the past, rather than of the future. Behind him he heard the warning bell of a bicycle, and he turned to recognize a boy he knew. The boy stopped and he got on, sitting sidewise in front of the rider. Around the curves they coasted, one way and the other, with the sun-filled valley and Djebel Zalagh first on the left, then on the right.

"How are the brakes?" Amar asked. He was thinking that it might be pleasanter to be catapulted into a ditch or down the hillside than to be delivered safely to the gate of his quarter. Whatever he was going to be punished for might be forgiven when he got out of the hospital.

"The brakes are good," the boy replied. "What's the matter? Are you afraid?"

Amar laughed scornfully. They crossed the bridge and the ground became level. The boy began to pedal. As they approached the uphill stretch from the river valley to the Taza road intersection, the work got to be too arduous. Amar jumped off, said good-bye, and took a cross-cut through a grove of pomegranate trees. He had never owned a bicycle; it was not an object the son of an impoverished *fqih* could ever hope to have. Money came only to those who bought and sold. The boys whose fathers owned shops could own bicycles; Amar could only rent one now and then, because the people whom his father treated with his holy words and incantations generally had only coppers to spare, and when an occasional rich man consulted him and attempted to give him a larger sum in payment, Si Driss was adamant in his refusal.

"When your money comes from Allah," his father would tell him, "you do not buy machines and other Nazarene follies. You buy bread, and you give thanks to Him for being able to do that." And Amar would answer: *"Hamdoul'lah."*

At a café just inside Bab Fteuh he stopped and watched a card game for a few minutes. Then he walked miserably home. His mother, who let him in, looked meaningfully at him, and he saw his father standing in the courtyard by the well. There was no sign of Mustapha.

CHAPTER 2

"Come upstairs," said his father, leading the way up the narrow flight of broken steps. He went into the smaller of the two rooms and switched on the light. "Sit on the mattress," he commanded, pointing at a corner of the room. Amar obeyed. Everything within him was trembling; he could not have told whether it was with eagerness or terror, any more than he could have known whether it was a consuming hatred or an overpowering love that he felt for the elderly man who towered above him, his eyes fiery with anger. Slowly his father unwound his long turban, revealing his shaven skull, and while he did this he spoke.

"This time you have committed an unpardonable sin," he said, fixing Amar with his terrible eyes. The pointed white beard looked strange with no turban above to balance it. "Only Hell lies before a boy like you. All the money in the house, that was to buy bread for your father and your family. Take off your *djellaba*." Amar removed the garment, and the old man snatched it from him, looking inside the hood as he did so. "Take off your *serrouelle*." Amar unfastened his belt and stepped out of his trousers, holding one hand in front of him to cover his nakedness. His father felt through the pockets, found them empty save for the broken penknife Amar always carried with him.

"Gone! All of it!" shouted the old man.

Amar said nothing.

"Where is it? Where is it?" The voice rose higher at each syllable. Amar merely looked into his father's eyes, his mouth open. There were a hundred things to say; there was nothing to say. He felt as if he had been turned to stone.

With astonishing force the old man pushed him down onto

the mattress, and ripping the belt from the trousers, began to flail him with the buckle end. To protect his face, Amar threw himself over upon his belly, his hands cupped across the back of his head. The hard blows came down upon his knuckles, his shoulders, his back, his buttocks, his legs.

"I hope I kill you!" his father screamed. "You'd be better dead!"

I hope he does, Amar thought. He felt the lashes from a great distance. It was as if a voice were saying to him: "This is pain," and he were agreeing, but he was not convinced. The old man said no more, putting all his energy into the blows. Behind the swish of the belt in the air and the sound of the buckle hitting his flesh Amar heard a cat on the terrace above, calling: "Rao . . . rao . . . rao . . . ," the cries of children, and a radio somewhere playing an old record of Farid al Atrache. He could smell the *tajine* his mother was cooking down in the courtyard: cinnamon and onions. The blows kept coming. All at once he felt he must breathe; he had not yet drawn breath since he had been thrown upon the mattress. He sighed deeply and found himself vomiting. He raised his head, tried to move, and the pain forced him back down. Still the rhythmical beating continued, whether with less intensity or more he could not tell. His face slid about in the mess beneath it; behind his eyelids he had a vision. He was running down the Boulevard Poëymirau in the Ville Nouvelle with a sword in his hand. As he passed each shop the plate glass of the show window shattered of its own accord. The French women screamed; the men stood paralyzed. Here and there he struck at a man, severing his head, and a fountain of bright blood shot up out of the truncated neck. A hot wave of fierce delight surged through him. Suddenly he realized that all the women were naked. With dexterous upward thrusts of his blade he opened their bodies; with downward thrusts he removed their breasts. Not one must be left intact.

The beating had stopped. His father had gone out of the room. The radio was still playing the same piece, and he heard his parents talking below. He lay completely still. For a moment he thought perhaps he was really dead. Then he heard his mother enter the room. *"Ouildi, ouildi,"* she said, and her two hands began to touch him softly, rubbing oil over his skin. He had not cried out once during the beating, but now he found himself sobbing fiercely. To be able to stop, he imagined his father above his mother, looking on. The ruse worked, and he lay there quietly, submitting to the strong, gentle hands.

He was sick the next day, and the following. As he lay in his little room on the roof, his mother came many times with oil and rubbed his bruises. He was dizzy with fever and miserable with pain, and he had no desire for food, other than the soup and hot tea she brought him from time to time. The third day he sat up and played his *lirah*, the reed flute he had made. That day his mother let Diki bou Bnara, his pet rooster, out of his crate, and the magnificent bird wandered in and out of the room, strutting about, scratching and listening to Amar's songs in his praise. But the third day at sunset, when Diki bou Bnara had been chased back into his cage and the muezzins had finished calling the *maghreb*, Amar heard his father's footsteps approaching as they mounted the stairway to the roof. He quickly turned over to face the wall, pretending to be asleep. Then his father was in the room, speaking.

"*Ya ouildi! Ya Amar!*"

Amar did not move, but his heart beat fast and his breathing was difficult. The mattress moved as his father sat down by Amar's feet.

"Amar!"

Amar stirred, rubbed his eyes.

"I want to talk with you. But first I want to be sure that you have no hatred. I am very unhappy with what you have done. Your mother and your brother and your sister have not had enough food these last days. That is nothing. That's not why I want to talk with you. You must listen. Have you any hatred in your heart for me?"

Amar sat up. "No, Father," he said quietly.

The old man was silent for a moment. Diki bou Bnara suddenly crowed.

"I want to make you understand. *Bel haq, fel louwil.* . . . First, you have to know that *I* understand. Perhaps you think that because I am old I know nothing about the world, how the world has changed."

Amar murmured a protest, but his father continued.

"I know you think that. All boys do. And now the world has changed more than ever before. Everything is new. Everything is bad. We're suffering more than we've ever suffered. And it is written that we must suffer still more. All that is nothing. Like the wind. You think I have never been to Dar Debibagh, never seen how the French have their life. But what if I tell you I have, many times? What if I say I have seen their cafés and their shops, and walked in their streets, ridden in their buses, the same as you?"

Amar was astonished. He had taken it for granted that since the arrival of the French soldiers many years ago, his father had never gone outside the walls of the Medina, save to the country or to the Mellah to buy ingredients for his medicines which only certain Jews sold. Ever since he could remember, the schedule of his father's life had been the same, had consisted of the five trips a day he made to the mosque, together with the hours he spent in conversation at the shops of friends en route to and from the mosque. Outside of that there was nothing, save the administering of his services when they were required. It was surprising to hear him say he had been to the French town. Amar doubted it: if he had been there, why had he never mentioned it until now?

"I want you to know that I have been there many times. I have seen their Christian filth and shame. It can never be for us. I swear they're worse than Jews. No, I swear by Allah they're lower than the godless Jews of the Mellah! And so if I speak against them it's not because of what men like Si Kaddour and that carrion Abdeltif and the other Wattanine have told me. What they say may be the truth, but their reason for saying it is a lie, because it is *politique*. You know what *politique* is? It is the French word for a lie. *Kdoub! Politique!* When you hear the French say: our *politique*, you know they mean: our lies. And when you hear the Moslems, the Friends of Independence, say: our *politique*, you know they mean: *our* lies. All lies are sins. And so, which displeases Allah more, a lie told by a Nazarene, who doesn't know the true faith from the false, or a lie told by a Moslem, who does?"

Now Amar thought he saw where his father's words were leading. He was warning him against associating with certain of his friends, with whom he sometimes played soccer or went to the cinema, and who were known to be members of the Istiqlal. His father was afraid Amar would be put in prison like Abdallah Tazi and his cousin, who had shouted: "*A bas les Français!*" in the Café de la Renaissance one night. How wrong he was, Amar thought with a tinge of bitterness. There was not even the remotest chance of such a thing. That possibility had been ruled out for him from the beginning because he spoke no French and could neither read nor write. He knew nothing, not even how to sign his own name in Arabic. Maybe he'll stop talking now and go downstairs, he thought.

"Do you understand what I'm saying to you?"

"I understand," Amar replied, twisting the sheet between his toes. He felt better; he would have liked to go out and walk a bit, but he knew that if he got up he would no longer feel like going out. Through the iron grillwork of the window he could see the flat rooftops of a distant corner of the city, with a square of darkening sky above.

"It is worse for a Moslem to lie," resumed his father. "And who among all the Moslems commits the greatest sin if he lies or steals? A Cherif. And thanks to Allah you are a Cherif. . . ."

"*Hamdoul'lah,*" murmured Amar, obediently but with feeling. "Thanks to Allah."

"Not only *Hamdoul'lah, Hamdoul'lah!* No! You must become a man and *be* a Cherif. The Cherif lives for his people. I would rather see you dead than growing to be like the carrion you talk with in the street. Dead! Do you understand?" The old man's voice rose. "There will be no more Moslems unless every young Cherif obeys the laws of Allah."

He went on in this vein. Amar understood and silently agreed, but at the same time he could not keep himself from thinking: "He doesn't know what the world is like today." The thought that his own conception of the world was so different from his father's was like a protecting wall around his entire being. When his father went out into the street he had only the mosque, the Koran, the other old men in his mind. It was the immutable world of law, the written word, unchanging beneficence, but it was in some way wrinkled and dried up. Whereas when Amar stepped out the door there was the whole vast earth waiting, the live, mysterious earth, that belonged to him in a way it could belong to no one else, and where anything at all might happen. The smell of the morning breeze moving in across the walls from the olive groves, the sound of the river falling over the rocks as it rushed in its canyons through the heart of the city, the moving shadows of the trees on the white dust beneath, when he sat at midday in their shelter—such things had a particular message for him that they could not have for anyone else, least of all his father. The world where the old man lived, he imagined, must look something like a picture in one of those newspapers that were smuggled in from Egypt: gray, smudged, meaningless save as an accompaniment to the written text.

He listened to his father's words with growing impatience. There were repeated references to his duties as a descendant of the Prophet. To whom could the people turn in times of difficulty, if not to the Chorfa? Every Cherif was a leader. It was true, but he knew there was something wrong with the picture. The Chorfa were the leaders, but they could lead their followers only to defeat, and this was something he could never say to anyone. As if the old man had sensed the emotion, if not the precise idea that was in his son's mind, he stopped talking for a moment, and then began to speak again in a much lower voice, sadly. "I have committed a very great sin," he said. "Allah will be the judge. I should have beaten you day and night, dragged you to school by your hair, until you knew how to write. Now you will never learn. It's too late. You will never know any-thing. And this is my fault."

Amar was shocked; his father had never spoken in such a man-ner. "No," he said tentatively. "My fault."

In the dimness Amar saw his father's arms reach out toward him. A hand was placed on each temple, and the old man bent forward and touched his lips lightly to the boy's forehead. Then he sat back, shook his head back and forth several times in si-lence, rose, and went out of the room without saying any more.

A few minutes later Mustapha appeared frowning in the doorway, obviously having been sent by his father to inquire after Amar's health. The first instant, upon seeing him, Amar had been about to say something bitter; then a strange calm took possession of him, and he found himself saying in the most benign accents: "Ah, *khai, chkhbarek?* It's several days since I've seen you. How is everything?"

Mustapha seemed bewildered; inexpressively he murmured a perfunctory phrase of greeting, turned and went downstairs. Amar lay back smiling; for the first time he felt that he had the upper hand in a situation where he had never dared hope to have it. Mustapha was his older brother; he had been born first, and twenty-six sheep had been sacrificed that day, two of them paid for by his father, whereas when Amar had come into the world Si Driss had bought only one. It was true that there had been another sheep, donated by a friend, but for Amar that one did not count. It was also a fact that Mustapha had been born up in the hills in Kherib Jerad, and the other twenty-four sheep had been brought as gifts by peasants overjoyed to see a Cherif born among them, while Amar had been born in the heart of the city, and only the family had rejoiced, but that did not ever occur to him when he began sifting over his wrongs. The im-portant thing now was that Mustapha was puzzled; he had not expected his father to send him upstairs to inquire after Amar, and he had not imagined that Amar could possibly be in good spirits. Amar knew his brother. Mustapha would go on being troubled by this small mystery until he had solved it. And that

Amar had no intention of allowing him to do. Indeed, he himself could not have told what was in his heart regarding Mustapha, save that on some remote, as yet invisible horizon he divined the certitude of victory for himself, and a total defeat for his brother.

And now there came to his mind an incident which his mother had recounted to him many times. Long ago, when her father had been on his deathbed in this room where Amar now lay, and the whole family was gathered there to say good-bye to him, the old man had commanded Mustapha to approach the bed, so that he might bestow his blessing on the first-born. But Mustapha had been a headstrong, sulky child; whining, he had hidden beneath his mother's skirts, and no amount of cajoling could induce him to go near the bed. It was a shameful moment, miraculously saved by Amar, who for some unaccountable reason had suddenly toddled across the room and kissed his grandfather's hand. Immediately the old man had bestowed his blessing on Amar instead of Mustapha; not content with that, he had gone on to prophesy that the baby would grow up to be a much better man than his brother. A few minutes later he had drawn his last breath. The story had always greatly impressed Amar, but since he was fairly certain that neither of his parents had ever told it to Mustapha, it had not been fully satisfactory as a consolation for the twenty-six sheep. But now he thought of it again, and it began to assume an importance he had not perceived before. What were twenty-six sheep, or, indeed, a hundred sheep, compared to the magic power of a blessing sent direct to him by Allah through the heart and lips of his grandfather? In the darkness he murmured a short prayer for the departed, and an even shorter one of thanks for his own good fortune.

That night in the bowl of soup his mother brought him there were almonds as well as chickpeas. He longed to know whether the whole family was having them too, or whether they had been bought especially for him and for him alone, but he did not dare ask. He could imagine his mother running downstairs in a fit of laughter, crying: "Now Master Amar imagines that we went out and bought the almonds just for him and that nobody else is having any!" There would be even louder laughter from his sister and Mustapha.

"What good soup," he remarked.

CHAPTER   3

The next morning he felt perfectly well. He got up very early and went out onto the roof to look over the wall at the city spread out around him. Fog lay in the valley. A few of the higher minarets pushed up from the sea of grayness below like green fingers pointing skyward, and the hills on both sides were visible, with their raw earth and their rows of tiny olive trees. But the bowl where the center of the city lay was still brimming with the nocturnal, unmoving fog. He stood awhile looking, letting the fresh early air bathe his face and chest, and he said a few holy words as he turned his head in the direction of Bab Fteuh. Beyond the gate was the waste land by the cemetery where he played soccer, and then the village of reed huts where there were many goats, and then the wheatfields leading gently down toward the river, and then the mud villages under the high clay cliffs. And if you went farther there was a sort of canyon-land all made of clay, where in the spring after the rains the water rushed through, often carrying with it drowned sheep and even cows.

In this region there were no plants at all—only the clay with its deep crevasses and crazy turrets made by the rain. Beyond this were great mountains where the Berbers lived, and then desert, and other lands whose names only a few people could tell you, and then, of course, behind everything, in the center of the world, shining in an eternal unearthly light, there was Mecca. How many hours he had spent examining the bright chromolithographs that lined the walls of the barber shops! Some were of historic battles waged by Moslems against demons; some showed magnificent flying horses with women's heads and breasts—it was on these animals that important people used to travel before they discarded them for airplanes—some were of Adam and Eve, the first Moslems in the world, or of Jerusalem, the great holy city where Christians and Jews were still murdering Moslems every day and putting their flesh in tins to be shipped abroad and sold as food; but there was always a picture, more beautiful than any, of Mecca, with its sharp crags above and its tiers of high houses topped with terraces and studded with balconies, its arcades and lamps and giant pigeons, and finally, in the center, the great rock draped with black cloth, which was of such beauty that many men fainted, or even died, on beholding it. Often at night he had stood in this very spot, his hands on the wall, straining his eyes as he peered into the star-filled darkness of the sky, trying to imagine that he saw at least a faint glimmer of the light which streamed up forever into the heavens from the sacred shrine.

Usually from the terrace he could hear the shrill voices and the drums from the market at Sidi Ali bou Ralem. Today, what with the fog, only the sounds from the immediate neighborhood were audible. He went back into his room, lay down on his bed, resting his feet against the wall above his head, and began to play his flute: no particular tune—merely an indeterminate, neutral succession of notes with an occasional long wait—the music for the particular way he felt on this cool, misty morning. When this had gone on for a while, he suddenly jumped up and dressed himself in the only European outfit he owned: a pair of old military trousers and a heavy woolen sweater, along with a pair of sandals he had bought in the Mellah—these last he slipped under his arm, as they were to be put on only when he got into the middle of town, away from the danger of enemy attacks in the streets of his own quarter. It was easier to fight, and to walk, for that matter, barefoot, unencumbered by the weight of shoes. A friend had given him a leather wrist strap which he wore on gala occasions, pretending it had a watch with it. He looked at it for a moment, decided against it, combed his hair carefully, glancing into a pocket mirror which was hung on the wall, and tiptoed down the two flights of stairs into the court-yard. When his mother saw him she called out: "Come and eat breakfast! You think you're going out without eating first?"

He was extremely hungry, but without knowing why, he had wanted to get out of the house immediately, before he had to speak to anyone, and change the way he felt. However, it was too late now. He sat down and ate the boiled oats with cin-namon bark and goat's milk that his little sister brought him. She squatted in the doorway, looking slyly at him now and then out of the corner of her eye. There were streaks of henna on her temples and forehead, and her hands were brick red with the dye. She was old enough to be given in marriage; already two offers had come in, but old Si Driss would not hear of it, partly because he wanted to see her around the house a bit longer (it seemed only last year that she had been born), and partly because neither of the offers had been substantial enough to consider seriously. Amar's mother was in complete agreement with her husband; the longer she could forestall the marriage the happier she would be. It was no pleasure to have sons be-cause they were never home; they bolted their food and disap-peared, and when they grew older one could not even know whether they would return to sleep or not. But a daughter, since she was not allowed to stir from the house alone, even to fetch a kilo of sugar from the shop next door, could always be counted on to be there when one needed her. In any case, each year that passed gave Halima more charms: her eyes seemed to grow larger and her hair thicker and glossier.

When he had eaten, Amar got up and went out into the courtyard. There he petted his two pigeons for a while, watch-ing his mother in the hope that she would go upstairs, so that his departure would be unnoticed by her. Finally he decided to go out anyway.

"It may rain," she called as he reached the door.

"It's not going to rain," he said. *"B'slemah."* He knew she wanted to say more—anything at all, so long as the conversation kept him there. It was always this way when he came to go out. He smiled over his shoulder and shut the door behind him. There were three turnings in the alley before it got to the street. At the second he came face to face with his father. As Amar was stooping to kiss his hand, the old man pulled it quickly away.

"How did you awaken, my boy?" he said. They exchanged greetings, and Si Driss looked penetratingly at his son. "I want to talk to you," he said.

"Naam, sidi."

"Where are you going?"

Amar had no destination in his head. "Just for a walk."

"This is not a world just to go for a walk in. You're a man, you know, not a boy any longer. Think this over, and be home for lunch, because this afternoon you're going with me to see Abderrahman Rabati."

Amar inclined his head and walked on. But the joy of being in the street in the morning was gone. Rabati was a big, loud-mouthed man who often got work for the boys of the quarter with the French in the Ville Nouvelle, and Amar had heard countless stories of how difficult the work was, how the French were constantly in a bad humor and found pretexts for not paying when the end of the week came, and as if that were not bad enough, how Rabati himself habitually extracted small tributes from the boys in return for having found them their jobs. Besides, Amar knew no French beyond *"bon jour, m'sieu,"* *"entrez,"* and *"fermez la porte,"* expressions taught him by a well-meaning friend, and it was common knowledge that the boys who did not understand French were treated even worse, made the butt of jokes not only by the French but by the boys who were fortunate enough to know the language.

He turned into the principal street of the quarter, nodded to the mint-seller, and looked unhappily around him, not even sure any longer that he wanted to take a walk. His father's words had spread a film of poison over the morning landscape.

There was only one way out, and that was to find himself some sort of work immediately, so that when he went home for lunch he would be able to say: "Father, I'm working."

He turned left and went up the dusty hill past the great carved façade of the old mosque, and, further on, the concrete box that had been the scene of so many afternoons of childhood pleasure, the cinema, plastered with shiny photographs of men with guns. Then he turned left again through a narrow street jammed with waiting donkeys and men pushing wheelbarrows, whose downhill course shortly burrowed beneath the houses. Presently he came out into a vast open place dotted here and there with circular towers. It was like a burning village: greasy black smoke poured from the turrets of baked earth. Boys in rags ran back and forth carrying armfuls of green branches which they stuffed into the doors of the ovens. The smoke billowed and hovered in the air close to the ground, not seeming willing to venture upward toward the gray sky. In a further corner, built against the high ramparts of the city, was a section where the ovens had been constructed on two levels. There was a stairway onto the enormous flat mud roof, and he climbed up to survey the scene. Near by in the doorway of a small shed crouched a bearded man. Amar turned and spoke to him.

"Any work for me?"

The man stared at him for a moment without showing any interest. Then he said: "Who are you?"

"The son of Driss the *fqih*," he replied.

The man stared harder. "What's the use of lying?" he demanded. "*You're* the son of Driss the *fqih? You?*" He turned away and spat.

Amar was taken aback. He looked down at his bare feet, wriggled his toes, and reflected that he should have put his shoes on before climbing up here.

"What's the matter with me?" he said finally, with a certain belligerency. "And what difference does it make, my name? I only asked you if you had any work."

"Can you make clay?" the man said.

"I can learn how to do anything in a quarter of an hour."

The man laughed, stroked his beard, and slowly got to his feet. "Come," he said, and he led him to the entrance of another small shed further along the roof. Inside in the dimness was a boy squatting on the floor beside a large tank of water, rubbing his hands together. "Go in," the man said. They stood looking down at the boy, who did not glance up. "You rub as hard as you can," he told Amar, "and if you find even the smallest pebble you take it out, and then you keep rubbing until each handful is like silk."

"I see," said Amar. It seemed like the easiest sort of work. He waited until they got back outside, and then he asked: "How much?"

"Ten rial a day."

It was the normal wage.

"With lunch," added Amar, as though it went without saying.

The man opened his eyes wide. "Are you crazy?" he cried. (Amar merely looked at him fixedly.) "If you want to work, step inside here and start. I don't need any help. I'm only doing you a favor."

Any work that Amar did, even of the simplest kind, such as carrying water at the tannery or holding the long threads with which the tailors made the frogging on the fronts of the *djellabas*, fascinated him while he was doing it; it was sheer pleasure for him to be completely occupied—the sort of delight he could not know when there was room in his mind for him to remember that he was himself. He set to work mixing water with the clay, rubbing, smoothing, washing, removing particles. At the end of the morning the man came inside, looked, and raised his eyebrows. He stooped over, examined the quality of the mixture carefully, dipping the tips of his fingers into it and squeezing them together.

"Good," he said. "Go home to lunch."

Amar glanced up. "I'm not hungry yet."

"Come with me."

They went to the end of the long roof, down the stairs, and across a stretch of bare ground to where great bundles of branches had been piled. Here another stairway had been cut into the earth. The astringent smell of wet clay was tempered with a sweeter, musky odor which came from several fig trees down below, beside a channel of the river where the water flowed by very quickly and without a sound. In the cliff at the bottom of the steps was a door. The man removed the padlock and they went in.

"Let's see if you can run the *mamil*."

Amar let himself down into the opening in the floor, made himself comfortable on the seat which was on a level with the man's shoes, and began to turn the large wooden wheel with his foot. It took a certain strength and dexterity, but none that he had not already used while playing soccer.

"Do you understand how it works?" the man asked, pointing to a smaller wheel that spun near Amar's left hand. He piled some clay on the turning disc, squatted down. With manipulating and sprinkling of water the shapeless mass soon took the form of a plate.

"Just keep turning the wheel," he said, apparently expecting Amar to tire and stop. "I'll take care of this part." But it was clear to Amar that the apparatus was arranged so that one man could do everything by himself, using his hands and feet at the same time. After a bit the bearded man stood up. "You'd better go home for lunch now," he said.

"I want to make a jar," said Amar.

The man laughed. "It takes a long time to learn how to do that."

"I can do it now."

The other, saying nothing, removed the plate he had been making, and stood back, his arms folded, an expression of amusement on his face. "*Zid*. Go on, make a jar," he said. "I want to see you."

The clay and the water were at his right hand, the revolving wheel at his left. There was no light in the room save that which came through the door, so that he had necessarily missed the finer points of the man's work; nevertheless, he did exactly as he had seen him do, not forgetting to maintain a continuous sideward pushing with the flat of his bare foot on the big wheel.

Slowly he modeled a small urn, taking great care to make its shape one that pleased him. The man was astonished. "You've worked a *mamil* plenty of times before," he finally said. "Why didn't you say so? I'm always ready to pay ten rials and lunch to a good workman, somebody who knows something."

"The blessing of Allah be upon you, master," said Amar. "I'm very hungry." Even though he would not be home for lunch, his father would be pacified by the good news he would give him at dinner time.

CHAPTER 4

A certain rich merchant, El Yazami by name, who lived in the quarter and had once sent his sister to Si Driss for treatment, was leaving for Rissani that afternoon. Already his servants had carried seven enormous coffers to the bus station outside Bab el Guissa, where they were being weighed and hoisted to the top of the vehicle, and there were many more crates and amorphous bundles of all sizes constantly being carried from the house to the terminus. El Yazami was making his annual pilgrimage to the shrine of his patron saint in the Tafilalet, from which he always returned many thousands of rial the richer, given the fact that like any good Fassi he was in the habit of combining business with devotion, and knew just what articles could be transported to the south and sold there with the maximum of profit. And it occurred to him as he stood looking up at the workers loading his merchandise on the top of the big blue bus that about five hundred medium-sized water jars would be a remunerative addition to his cargo. Allowing twenty percent for breakage, he calculated, the gain could still be about one hundred fifty percent, which would be worth while. And so, accompanied by one of his sons, he set out for Bab Fteuh to make a quick purchase. When he came within sight of the village of mud ovens and smoke, he sent his son to examine the wares on one side of the road while he went to investigate the other side. So large a quantity was not always available at such short notice. The first person his son ran into was Amar, up from his damp workroom under the fig trees for a breath of air and furtive cigarette. Amar knew the boy by sight, although they had never been friends. After greetings had been exchanged, the young Yazami told him what he was looking for.

"We can supply them all for you," said Amar immediately.

"We need them now," said El Yazami.

"Of course." He had no idea whether such a large number could be furnished or not, but it was important that he be the one to communicate the order to his employer, who would surely reward him.

The man with the beard was incredulous. "Five hundred?" he cried. "Who wants them?" He knew he could get the jars from his colleagues; what interested him was to know whether this was a serious offer or some fantasy of Amar's.

"Over there." Amar indicated the young Yazami, who was idly chinning himself on the underside of a ladder. The potter was not impressed. The youth did not look like someone who was going to buy even one water jar.

"*Son of sin,*" began the man under his breath. Amar had run over to the boy, taken him by the arm.

"Fifty rial for you tomorrow if you buy them here," he whispered.

"I don't know . . . my father . . ." He pointed in the direction of the elder Yazami, who was inspecting jars on the far side of the thoroughfare.

"Bring him over here fast, and come by for your fifty rial tomorrow." There was no guarantee that the potter would give him anything if he put the sale through, but he had decided simply to leave if he did not. The world was too big, too full of magnificent opportunities, to waste time with unappreciative masters.

The boy went across the road to the other side and talked a-while with his father. Amar could see him pointing in his direction. The potter returned to his crouching position outside the shed. "Go back to work," he called. Amar stood, hesitating. Then, risking everything, he ran across the road, and presently returned with El Yazami and his son. The potter stood up; as the three approached, he heard the portly gentleman saying to Amar: "I remember you as a boy no bigger than a grasshopper. Don't forget to greet Si Driss for me. May Allah preserve him."

The purchase was made quickly, and Amar was dispatched to round up a group of boys who could carry the baskets of jars to Bab el Guissa. When the last load had departed, the potter went down the steps into the dark little room where Amar sat.

"*Zduq*," he said, looking at him with bewilderment, "you really are the son of Si Driss the *fqih*."

Amar stared at him in mild mock surprise. "Yes. I told you that."

The man fingered his beard meditatively. "I didn't believe you. Forgive me."

Amar laughed. "Allah forgives," he said lightly. Without looking up he went on working, pretending to be completely absorbed in his gestures, and wondering if the potter were going to offer him his reward now. Since the man said no more on the subject, but began to talk about a load of clay that was due, he decided that it would be necessary to take action. Hoisting himself out of the hole in the floor, he seized the man's arm and kissed the sleeve of his *djellaba*. The man pulled back.

"No, no," he objected. "A Cherif—"

"An apprentice to a master potter," Amar reminded him.

"No, no—"

"I am only a *metallem*. But I can make a prophecy. From this day on, your life will prosper. My gift tells me that. Allah in His infinite wisdom has granted me the knowledge." The potter moved backward a step, looking at him with wide eyes. "And I'd tell you even if at this moment you were raising your hand to strike me." The potter made a gesture of puzzled protest. "Allah is all-powerful, and knows what is in my heart. Therefore how can I withhold it from you? He knows that this moment my father is lying ill at home without the money to buy a keg of buttermilk which would make him well. He knows that you have a generous heart, and that is why He sent the rich man here this afternoon to buy from you, to make it possible for you to use your heart."

The man was looking at him now with mingled wonder and suspicion. Amar saw this, and decided to come to the point.

"With five days' pay in advance I would leave here this evening the happiest man in the world."

"Yes," the potter said, "and have I got my own policeman to go and find you tomorrow and drag you here? How do I know you'll ever come back? I'd probably find you down in Dar Debbagh carrying hides to the river, trying the same trick on them there."

Amar was convinced the man would give him the money; without further words he turned away and climbed back down to his sunken seat to resume his work. When he had the wheel going, he looked up and said: "Forgive me, *sidi*."

The man stood perfectly still. Finally he said, almost plaintively: "How do I know you'll come back tomorrow?"

"*Ya, sidi*," Amar said. "Since the world began has any man ever been able to know what would happen tomorrow? The world of men is today. I'm asking you to open your heart today. Tomorrow belongs to Allah, and *incha'Allah*"—he said the words with great feeling—"I shall come back tomorrow and every day after that. *Incha'Allah!*"

The man reached into his *choukra* and pulled out the money.

"Here is your father's buttermilk," he said. "May he get well quickly."

The waste land at the foot of the cemetery opposite Bab Fteuh was not on his way home, nevertheless Amar contrived to pass by it when he had finished his day's work, on the slim chance that the younger Yazami might possibly be among the two dozen or more boys practicing there with a football. He did not find him, but he found a student who claimed to know where he was, and in his company began a quest which led through the damp

streets of El Mokhfia and across the river to a small café he had
never seen before. El Yazami was here, seated among a group of
boys his age, playing checkers. When he saw Amar his face fell:
the only reason Amar could have for seeking him out so soon was
to tell him the money was not to be forthcoming. After urging
Amar to have a Coca-Cola, which he politely refused—for, this
being an expensive café with tables and chairs instead of mats,
he did not want in any way to get involved—El Yazami took his
arm and propelled him outside, where they stood in the dark under a high plane tree and talked.

Amar's principal interest was in keeping the other away from
his place of work, where the boy's presence would immediately
arouse the suspicions of the potter. He wondered how he could
have been so foolish as to have made that the meeting-place.

"It would be better if you didn't come tomorrow," he said.
Then he added: "He only gave me twenty-five rial." In the darkness he handed over the coins; the other went to the doorway to
count them by the dim light that came from within. It was an
agreeable surprise because he had expected nothing.

"I still owe you twenty-five," Amar was saying, "and you'll get
them as soon as I do. But try and bring in some more business,
yes? You'll get the rest sooner." This seemed sensible enough to
El Yazami, and he agreed to do what he could. They parted,
each one reasonably pleased with the outcome of the meeting.

Surprisingly enough, during the days that followed, El Yazami
did make efforts to find customers for Amar's employer, and
these were not in vain. Indeed, they were so successful that one
evening at the end of the week the potter came down into
Amar's little workroom. He stood a moment looking at the boy
before he spoke. When he did begin to speak, it was with satisfaction and a slight awe in his voice. "*Sidi,*" he said. (Amar
smiled inwardly: he had never addressed him thus before.)
"Since you have been here with me Allah has favored me with
more success than I had ever thought was possible."

"*Hamdoul'lah,*" said Amar.

"Do you like your work?"

"Yes, master."

"I hope you'll stay with me," the man said. It cost him an effort to go on, but he managed it. After all, he told himself, it was surely Allah who had made him take the boy on; he had not believed he was a Cherif and had the *baraka*, and he could not remember now what had prompted him to be friendly to him. If Allah were involved it would be safer to be generous. "Suppose I double your wages."

"If it is Allah's will," said Amar, "I should be very happy."

The man pulled a small ring from his pocket and held it forth to Amar. "Put this on your finger," he said. "A little gift. No one can ever say that Saïd is not grateful for favors shown him by Allah."

"Thank you very much," said Amar, slipping the ring on to various fingers to try the size and appearance. "There's one thing I'd like to know. When does the new wage go into effect? Beginning today or beginning the first day I came to work for you?"

The man stared at him, was about to say something harsh, but decided not to, and instead shrugged his shoulders.

"It can begin at the beginning if you like," he said; in spite of the fact that he did not particularly like Amar, he was determined to keep him on with him if possible. It was not only the divine favor of which the boy seemed to be a symbol, but also the fact of the sales. Although the two could be considered facets of the same thing, he preferred to try to think of them separately: it was more acceptable to Allah.

"If it's not worth it to you . . ." Amar began.

"Of course it is. Of course it is," he protested.

"The day you have no money, I'll work for you without pay, twice as hard, so that Allah may favor us with money again."

The potter thanked him for his generosity and turned to go out.

"Six days at twenty rial," Amar was thinking. "He gave me fifty. He still owes me seventy. And twenty-five still for Yazami . . . *bel haq*, not yet . . . Why doesn't he just pay, instead of talking so much?" And he determined to get the money that night.

"Master!" he cried, to stop the man from going through the

door. The potter looked at him, surprised. Now Amar had to go on. It was an unheard-of thing, but he was going to ask his employer to sit with him in a café. And the words he heard himself saying probably astonished him more than they did the older man.

"All right," said the potter. When the day was finished they went together to a café near Bab Sidi bou Jida, where there was a small garden in the back, through which one of the myriad channels of the river had been directed. Weeping willows and young plum trees edged the stream, and one small light bulb hung from a trellis overhead, almost buried in grape leaves. The mat where they seated themselves was only a few centimeters from the swift surface of the water.

Amar ordered the tea with dignity; he was bursting with a pride and a delight which he took pains to conceal. It occurred to him that he would be still happier if he did not have ahead of him the problem of finding the right chink in the conversation where he could gain a foothold for reasonably requesting the money, and he was momentarily tempted to let it go for this time, and relax in the pleasure of the occasion. But then he reminded himself that the only reason for the invitation was to get his wages, and sighing, he steeled himself to go through with the business at hand.

The potter told him about his two sons, his altercation with a neighbor which had amounted almost to a feud, and finally about his great dream, which was to make the *hadj*, the pilgrimage to Mecca. Amar became enthusiastic; his eyes shone.

"To go there by Allah's grace, and then die happy in your heart," Amar whispered, a beatific smile on his lips. He leaned back, closed his eyes. "*Al-lah!*"

"Not this year," said the potter meaningfully.

"Perhaps next year there will be enough money. *Incha'Allah.*"

The man snorted. Then he leaned forward, putting his lips close to Amar's ear. "It's all right here. There's no one listening."

Amar did not understand, but he smiled and looked around the dim little garden. How peaceful it was, with the light evening breeze stirring the small leaves of the grapevine that clustered around the electric bulb, making the shadows move and change on the yellow mat below. For a moment he pushed aside the thought of money. From time to time the dark water beside them rippled audibly, as if a tiny fish had come to the surface for an instant and then darted beneath. It was in peaceful moments such as this, his father had said, that men were given to know just a little of what paradise was like, so that they might yearn for it with all their soul, and strive during their time on earth to be worthy of going there. He felt utterly comfortable and happy; soon the hot mint tea would be carried out to them, and he had asked for a sprig of verbena to be put in each glass. And when he had the money he would begin looking for real European shoes, and sell his Jewish sandals. . . .

"No, not this year," the man resumed, a wicked light suddenly in his eyes. "May their race rot in Hell."

Amar looked at him in surprise. If anyone said that, he could mean only the French, but he was not aware that the man had made any previous allusion to them. As he turned the subject over in his mind, he was conscious that the potter was staring at him with a nascent suspicion.

"Don't you know about Ibn Saud?" he asked suddenly. "Have you never heard of him?"

"Of course," said Amar, stung by the tone of the other's voice. "The Sultan of the Hejaz."

"*Huwa hada*," said the man, "but I can see you don't know anything about what's going on in the world. You should wake up, boy. There are great things happening. Ibn Saud is a man with a head. This year not a single *hadji* from Morocco has got into Mecca. They all got as far as Djedda and had to turn back."

"Poor things," said Amar, commiserating immediately.

"Poor things?" the man cried. "Poor donkeys! They should have stayed home. Is this a year to go off to Mecca, when that filthy carrion of a dog they gave us is still sitting there on the Sultan's throne? No, I swear if I had power I'd shut the doors of every mosque in the country until we get our Sultan back. And if that doesn't bring him, you know what will."

Amar did indeed know. The man meant *jihad*, the wholesale

slaughter by every Moslem of all available unbelievers. He sat silent, a little stunned by the man's violence. By no means was he unaware of the fact that the French had put a false monarch on the throne of his country; he assumed that everyone in the world knew that. He resented the indignity the same as anyone else, but he did so without giving the matter any thought. In his experience the substitution of Ben Arafa for Sidi Mohammed had not altered anything; the reason was that he had not come in contact with anyone who had strong political convictions. His father had fulminated against unbelievers and their evil work in Morocco ever since he could remember, and this new bit of malevolence on their part—to kidnap the Sultan and hold him prisoner on an island in the sea, replacing him with a doddering old man who might as well be deaf, dumb and blind—was merely the most recent in a long list of hostile acts on their part.

But now he saw for the first time that there were men who gave it much more than a passing glance, for whom it was more than a concept, a string of words about a distant happening; he saw the symbolic indignity turn into a personal affront, disapproval transformed into rage. The man sat there glaring at him, a vague shadow, that of a grape leaf, played across his wrinkled forehead. An owl suddenly uttered an absurd, melancholy sound in the canebrake across the stream, and Amar was made conscious in an instant of a presence in the air, something which had been there all the time, but which he had never isolated and identified. The thing was in him, he was a part of it, as was the man opposite him, and it was a part of them; it whispered to them that time was short, that the world they lived in was approaching its end, and beyond was unfathomable darkness. It was the premonition of inevitable defeat and annihilation, and it had always been there with them and in them, as intangible and as real as the night around them. Amar pulled two loose cigarettes out of his pocket and handed one to the potter. "Ah, the Moslems, the Moslems!" he sighed. "Who knows what's going to happen to them?"

"Who knows?" said the man, lighting the cigarette. When the qaouaji brought their tea they drank it without speaking, slowly.

The breeze blew harder, bringing with it the chill odors of the higher air on the mountains. It was not until after they had separated in the street that Amar realized he had forgotten to ask the man for his money. He shrugged his shoulders and went home to dinner.

CHAPTER   5

The young spring grew, wheeled along toward summer, bringing drier nights, a higher sun and longer days. And along with the numberless infinitesimal natural things that announced the slow seasonal change, there was another thing, quite as impalpable and just as perceptible. Perhaps if Amar had not been made aware of it by the potter, he could have continued for a while not suspecting its presence, but now he wondered how it had been possible for him to go on as long as he had without noticing it. One might have said that it hung in the air with the particles of dust, and settled with them into the pores of the walls, so completely was it a part of the light and atmosphere of the great town lying sprawled there between its hills. But it expressed itself in the startled look over the shoulder that followed the tap on the back, in the silence that fell over a café when an unfamiliar figure appeared and sat down, in the anguished glances that darted from one pair of eyes to another when the family, squatting around the evening *tajine*, ceased chewing at the sound of a knock on the door. People went out less; at night the twisting lanes of the Medina were empty, and Friday afternoons, when there should have been many thousands of people, all in their best clothing, in the Djenane es Sebir—the men walking hand in hand or in noisy groups among the fountains and across the bridges between the islands, the women sitting in tiers on the steps or on the benches in their own reserved bamboo grove—there were only a few unkempt kif-smokers who sat staring vacantly in front of them while urchins scuffed up the dust as they kicked around an improvised football made of rags and string.

It was strange to see the city slowly withering, like some doomed plant. Each day it seemed that the process could go no further, that the point of extreme withdrawal from normal life had been reached, that an opening-up would now begin; but each new day people realized with a kind of awe that no such point was in sight.

They wanted their own Sultan back—that went without saying—and in general they had faith in the political party that had pledged to bring about his return. Also, a certain amount of intrigue and secrecy had never frightened them; the people of Fez were well known to be the most devious and clever Moslems in Morocco. But scheming in their own traditional fashion was one thing, and being caught between the diabolical French colonial secret police and the pitiless Istiqlal was another. They were not used to living in an *ambiance* of suspicion and fear quite so intense as the state of affairs their politicians were now asking them to accept as an everyday condition.

Slowly life was assuming a monstrous texture. Nothing was necessarily what it seemed; everything had become suspect—particularly that which was pleasant. If a man smiled, beware of him because he was surely a *chkam*, an informer for the French. If he plucked on an *oud* as he walked through the street he was being disrespectful to the memory of the exiled Sultan. If he smoked a cigarette in public he was contributing to French revenue, and he risked a beating or a knifing later in some dark alley. The thousands of students from the Medersa Karouine and the College of Moulay Idriss went so far as to declare an unlimited period of national mourning, and took to walking morosely by themselves, muttering a few inaudible syllables to each other when they met.

For Amar it was difficult to accept this sudden transition. Why should there be no more drums beaten, no flutes played, in the market at Sidi Ali bou Ralem, through which he liked to pass on his way home from work? He knew it was necessary to drive the French out, but he had always imagined that this would be done gloriously, with thousands of men on horseback flashing their swords and calling upon Allah to aid them in their holy mission as they rode down the Boulevard Moulay Youssef toward the Ville Nouvelle. And the Sultan would get an army from the Germans or the Americans and return victorious to his throne in Rabat. It was hard to see any connection between the splendid war of liberation and all this whispering and frowning. For a long time he debated with himself whether to discuss his doubts with the potter. He was earning good wages now and was on excellent terms with his master. Since the night several weeks ago when they had gone to the café, he had attempted no further consolidation of intimate friendship, because he was not sure that he really liked Saïd. It seemed to him partly the man's fault that everything was going wrong in the town, and he could not help feeling that had he never known him, somehow his own life would be different now.

He decided finally to take the risk of speaking with him, but at the same time to make sure that his real question was masked with another.

One afternoon he and Saïd had locked themselves into the upper shed to have a cigarette together. (No one smoked any more save in the strictest secrecy, because the Istiqlal's decision to destroy the French government's tobacco monopoly provided not only for the burning of the warehouses and all shops that sold tobacco, but also for the enforcement by violence of the party's anti-smoking campaign. The commonest punishment for being caught smoking was to have your cheek slashed with a razor.) Being shut into this small space with his master, and sharing with him the delightful sensation of danger which their forbidden activity occasioned, gave Amar the impetus to speak. He turned to the older man and said nonchalantly: "What do you think of the story that the Istiqlal may sell out to the French?"

The potter almost choked on his smoke. "What?" he cried.

Amar invented swiftly. "I heard that the Resident, the *civil* they have there now, offered the big ones a hundred million francs to forget the whole thing. But I don't think they'll take it, do you?"

"What?" the man roared, again. Amar felt a thrill of excitement as he watched his reaction. It was as if until this moment he had never seen him save asleep, and now were seeing him awake for the first time.

"Who told you that?" he yelled. The intensity of his expression was so great that Amar, a little alarmed, decided to make the report easily discreditable.

"A boy I know."

"But who?" the man insisted.

"Ah, a crazy *derri*, a kid who goes to the College of Moulay Idriss. Moto, we call him. I don't even know his real name."

"Have you repeated this story to anyone else?" The potter was glaring at him with a frightening fixity. Amar felt uncomfortable.

"No," he said.

"It's lucky for you. That's a story invented by the French. Your friend was paid by them to spread it. He'll probably be killed soon."

Amar was incredulous; it showed on his face. The man tossed his cigarette away and put his two hands on the boy's shoulders. "You don't know anything," he declared. "You're only a *derri* yourself. But be careful and don't spread stories, about the Istiqlal, about the French, about politics at all, any kind of story, or you'll get us both thrown in the river. And when you go into the river you're already taken care of. *Fhemti?*" He made a quick horizontal movement with his forefinger across his throat, then returned his hand to Amar's shoulder and shook him slightly.

"What do you think's going on here, a game? Don't you know it's a war? Why do you think they killed Hamidou, that fat one, the *mokhazni*, last week? Do you think it was for fun? And the thirty-one others here in Fez, this month alone? Or did you never hear about them? All just a game? It's a war, boy, remember that. A war! And if you haven't got the sense to have faith in the Istiqlal, at least keep your mouth shut and don't repeat the lies you hear from *chkama*." He stopped a moment and looked at Amar incredulously. "I thought you were brighter than that. Where have you been all this time?"

Amar, used to a much more gentle and respectful attitude on the part of his employer, went back to his workroom feeling injured and resentful. He sensed that the potter would like to change him, to see him become otherwise than the way he was; his rancor was largely a continuation of what he had felt that night when they had sat in the café together, save that now there was an added grievance. The man had awakened his sense of guilt. Where, indeed, had he been all this time? Right there with everyone else, only he had been so intent on his own little childhood pleasures that he had let it all go by without paying any attention. He knew that bombings by the Istiqlal had been a daily occurrence in Casablanca for the past six months, but Casablanca was far away. He had also heard all about the riots and assassinations in Marrakech, but these things might almost as well have been happening in Tunis or Egypt, as far as their ability to awaken his interest was concerned. When the first bodies of Moslem policemen and *mokhaznia* had been found in his own city he had seen no connection whatever with the events in other places.

Fez was Fez, but it was also synonymous with Morocco to him and his friends, and they used the words interchangeably. Since crimes were always committed for personal reasons, each new murder had automatically been attributed in his mind to a new enemy with a new grudge. But now he saw how overwhelmingly right the potter was. Every man whose body had been found at dawn lying in an alley or at the foot of the ramparts, or floating in the river below the Recif bridge, beyond a doubt either had been working for the French or had inadvertently done something to anger the Istiqlal. Then that meant the Istiqlal was powerful, which did not at all coincide with his conception of it, nor with the picture the organization painted of itself: a purely defensive group of selfless martyrs who were willing to brave the brutality of the French in order to bring hope to their suffering countrymen.

This was a discrepancy, but he felt it was only a small part of a much greater and more mysterious discrepancy whose nature he could not for the moment discover. Had it been Frenchmen they were killing he would have understood and approved unquestion-ingly, but the idea of Moslems murdering Moslems—he found it difficult to accept. And there was no one he could talk with about it; his father would never say more than he had already said, that all politics was a lie and all men who engaged in it *jiffa*, carrion. But the French worked ceaselessly with their politics against the Moslems; was it not essential that the Moslems have their own defensive organization? He knew his father would say no, that everything is in the hands of Allah and must remain there, and ultimately he knew that this was true; but in the meantime, how could any young man merely sit back and wait for divine justice to take its course? It was asking the impossible.

Now since this new problem had begun to ferment in his head he no longer experienced the same pleasure when he worked. For him to have felt the accustomed happiness, the work would have had to continue to occupy his consciousness entirely, and that was no longer possible. He felt that he was merely waiting, mak-ing the hours pass forcibly by filling them with useless gestures. It was his first indication of what it is like to be truly aware of the passage of time; such awareness can exist only if something is go-ing on in the mind which is not completely a reflection of what is going on immediately outside. Also, for the first time in his life he found himself lying awake at night, staring up into the dark-ness, turning the problem over and over in his head without ever arriving at any further understanding. Sometimes he would be still awake at three, when his father always rose, dressed, and went to the mosque, first to wash and then to pray, and only after he had heard him go out and the house was quiet once more would he fall suddenly asleep.

One such night, when his father had closed the door into the street and turned the key twice in the lock, he got up and stole out onto the terrace. Mustapha stood there in the gloom, leaning against the parapet, looking out over the silent town. Amar grunted to him; he was annoyed to see him there in what he con-sidered his own private nocturnal vantage point. Mustapha grunted back.

"*Ah, khai, 'ch andek?*" said Amar. "Can't you sleep, either?"

Mustapha admitted that he could not. He sounded miserable.

It was not thinkable that he could confide in Mustapha; nevertheless there was an absurd note of hope in Amar's voice as he said: "Why not?"

Mustapha spat over the edge into the alley below, listening for the sound of its hitting before he answered. "My *mottoui's* empty. I didn't have any money to buy kif."

"Kif?" Amar had smoked on many occasions with friends, but a pipe of kif meant less to him than a cigarette.

"I always have a few pipes before I go to sleep."

This was something recent, Amar knew. On various occasions when they had had to share the same room there had been no kif, and Mustapha had slept perfectly well.

"*Ouallah?* Can't you sleep without it? Do you have to smoke it first?"

Now Mustapha's initial burst of confidence was over, and he was himself once more. "What are you doing out here, anyway?" he growled. "Go in to bed."

Reluctantly Amar obeyed; he had one more thing to think about as he fell asleep.

BOOK 2

SINS ARE FINISHED

You tell me you are going to Fez.
Now, if you say you are going to Fez,
That means you are not going.
But I happen to know that you are going to Fez.
Why have you lied to me, you who are my friend?

— MOROCCAN SAYING

Ramadan, the month of interminable days without food, drink or cigarettes, had come and gone. The nights—which in other years had always been sheer pleasure, with the Medina brightly lighted, the shops kept open until early morning, the streets filled with men and boys sauntering happily back and forth through the town until it should be time to eat again—were dismal and joyless. It is true that the *rhaitas* sounded from the minarets as heretofore, the drums were beaten and the rams' horns blown to call sleepy people to the final meal, the same as always, but they caused no pleasure to those who heard them. The whole feeling of Ramadan, the pride that results from successful application of discipline, the victory of the spirit over the flesh, seemed to be missing; people observed the fast automatically, passively, without bothering to make the customary jokes about the clothing that was now too big, or the remarks about the number of days left before the feast that marked the end of the ordeal. It was even whispered around that many of the Istiqlal were not even observing Ramadan, that they could be seen any noon, brazenly eating in the restaurants of the Ville Nouvelle, but this was generally believed to be French propaganda. Then the rumor had begun to circulate that there would be no Aïd-es-Seghir, no festival when the fast was finished. This grew in volume until it had acquired sufficient stature to be able to be considered an established fact. And indeed, when the day arrived, instead of finding the streets full of men in new clothes—since that day out of all days in the year everyone was supposed to wear as many new garments as he could afford—early strollers discovered that hundreds of respectable citizens were already out, clad in their shabbiest *djellabas* and suits; and many who had not placed credence in the rumors had to hurry home through back streets to change, before they dared appear in public. A few new outfits had been ruined by deft razor slashes, but there had been no fights. And with this inglorious exit the month of Ramadan had made way for the month of Choual.

Now the heat had come in earnest. Amar rose at daybreak, worked until mid-morning, when he stretched out on a mat he had spread along the floor of his cave, and slept through the unbearable hours of the day until late afternoon; after eating he resumed his work and continued until dark. Then he would wander listlessly homeward through the breathless streets, sometimes stopping to listen for the sound of distant cries coming from another quarter of the town, the noise made by a mob, something to announce that the tension was taking a physical form. Everyone had this strange compulsion, to stand still a moment in the street and listen, because everyone was convinced that the tautness could not go on indefinitely. Some day something had to happen—that much was certain. What form the release might take could only be guessed at. And lying out on the roof at night under the stars—for it was too hot to sleep in the room on the mattress—he would strain his ears, trying to imagine he could hear, perhaps in the direction of Ed Douh or the Talâa, the faint sound of many voices calling. But it was always silence that was there, broken now and then by a sleepy rooster crowing on some distant housetop, or a cat wailing in the street below, or a truck far out on the Taza road, backfiring as it coasted down the hill toward the river.

There came an early morning, when even as he stepped out of his room onto the roof he knew that he was not going to work that day. The idea of doing something else, anything else, filled him with a great excitement. It seemed years that he had been going every day to the village of mud huts, greeting the potter, getting the key to the cave from him, climbing down the steps and going into the damp room where the *mamil* was, letting himself down onto the seat in the floor, and beginning to turn the wheel. Each day was like the day before; nothing changed, and the forms of the jars and vessels he made no longer interested him. None of it meant anything—not even the money, half of which he gave regularly to his father and some of which he saved, carrying it with him in a knotted handkerchief wherever he went. Each day he would untie the handkerchief and count the contents again, perhaps adding a little to them, and wondering what he could buy with what he now had. There was not yet enough to buy a pair of real shoes, but that was because he had had other expenses.

He was hungry, but the house was still. His father, back from the mosque, had returned to bed, and the family slept. Quickly he dressed and went downstairs. The pigeons were making their soft noises on the shelf by the well. In the street the air smelled like the beginning of the world. Most of the stalls were closed, and the few that had opened still harbored the dark air of night in their recesses. He bought a large disk of bread, six bananas, and a paper of dates, and went on his way along the Recif. Here the fish shops were all open and the powerful medicinal odor of fresh fish was like a knife in the air. Little by little the streets were filling, as people came out their doors. When he got to the newer houses of El Mokhfia there were trees here and

there behind the walls where birds sang. He went out of the city
through Bab Djedid and across the bridge. The dusty road led
between two high walls of cane that leaned in all directions.
When he reached the main road he stood a moment trying to
decide which way to go. It was then that a soft voice called:
"Amar!" from very near by. He turned his head and recognized
Mohammed Lalami, a boy somewhat taller than he, and perhaps
a year or two older. He was emerging from the thicket on the
bank of the river, his hair dripping with water. They exchanged
greetings.

"How's the water?" Amar asked.

"No good. Too low. You can't swim. It's all right if you just
want to rub off the dirt." He kept shaking his head vigorously,
like a dog, and sleeking his hair back, to get the water out of it.

"Why don't we go to Aïn Malqa and swim?" said Amar. Although they had been friendly in the past, it was several months
since he had seen Mohammed, and he was curious to talk with
him and see what was in his head.

"Ayayay!" said Mohammed. "And how do we get there?"

"We can get bicycles in the Ville Nouvelle."

"Hah! They're giving them away now?"

"Ana n'khalleslik," Amar said promptly. "It's on me. I've got
some money."

Mohammed, showing mock embarrassment, accepted by not
refusing, and they started out. When the city bus came by, on
its way from Bab Fteuh to the Ville Nouvelle, they boarded it
and stood on the back platform bracing themselves against the
curves, and joking with a one-legged man in a military jacket who
claimed to be a veteran of the war.

"What war?" Amar demanded, belligerently, because he was
with Mohammed.

"The *war*," said the man. "Didn't you ever hear of the war?"

"I've heard of a lot of wars. The war of the Germans, the war
of the Spanish and the *rojos*, the war of Indochine, the war of
Abd-el-Krim."

"I don't know anything about all that," the man said impatiently. "I was in the war."

Mohammed laughed. "I think he means the war of Moulay Abdallah. He got into the wrong bordel and somebody caught him with the wrong girl. Is that all he cut off, just your leg? You're lucky, that's all I can tell you." The man joined the two boys in their laughter.

In the Ville Nouvelle the Frenchman who rented bicycles inspected their *cartes d'identité* with prolonged care before he let them ride off.

"The son of a whore," muttered Mohammed as they pedaled down the Avenue de France under the plane trees, "he didn't want to let us have them. The Frenchman who came in while we were waiting, you noticed he let him take the bicycle and didn't even ask to see his card."

"He was a friend of his," said Amar. It would have been a good opportunity to start a conversation about what was on his mind, but he did not feel like it yet; it was too early and he felt too happy.

Once they had left the town and there was no more shade, they realized how painfully hot the sun was. But it only made them more eager to get to Aïn Malqa. They were on the plain now; the fields of cracked earth and parched stubble rolled slowly by. There was a narrow channel on each side of the long straight road, filled with water that ran toward them. Twice they stopped and drank, bathing their faces in the cold water and letting it run down their chests. "A piece of bread?" asked Amar; he was dizzy with hunger. But Mohammed had already breakfasted and did not want anything, so he decided to wait until they got to where they were going.

About a kilometer before Aïn Malqa the road led into a eucalyptus grove and began to curve round and round, going downward toward the lake. Mohammed coasted ahead, and Amar, looking at the back of his neck and legs, found himself wondering whether he would be able to hold his own, should he ever get into a fight with him. As he was watching, he saw that Mohammed had gone a bit to the side of the road and was expecting him to come abreast of him, but he pressed a little more on the handbrake to remain behind. He decided that although Moham-

med was taller, he himself was stronger and lither, and could
probably even come out the winner. He had once seen a film
about judo, and he liked to imagine that when the moment came
he would know how to use some of its tricks successfully against
his adversary. You moved your wrist suddenly, and the man fell
powerless at your feet. Now he released the brake, allowing the
bicycle to spurt ahead and catch up with the other. "It's cooler
here," he said.

It was as if they were making a slow descent down one side of a
gigantic funnel. The sloping ground beneath the trees was brown
with a deep mass of the dried long leaves from other years; the
light, a constantly shifting mixture of filtered sun and shade, had
become gray. The grove was completely silent, save for the sound
of the wheels on the fine gravel.

When they arrived at the bottom, they got down and walked,
for the ground was soft. Through the willows ahead they could
see the still surface of the tiny lake.

"Ah," said Mohammed with satisfaction. "This is paradise."

There was no one in sight. He propped his bicycle against a
tree and before Amar had even arrived at the spot, he had
stripped off his shirt and *serrouelle*. He had no underwear.

"You're going to swim like that?" said Amar, surprised. Since
he had been working with the potter he had bought himself two
pairs of cotton shorts, one of which he was now wearing under
his trousers.

Mohammed was hopping up and down, first on one foot and
then on the other, in his eagerness to get into the water. He
laughed. "Just like this," he said.

"But suppose someone comes? Suppose women come, or some
French?"

Mohammed was not concerned. "You can come and get my
trousers for me."

It did not seem like a very practical arrangement to Amar, but
there was nothing else to do; if Mohammed were going to swim
at all he would have to swim naked. Together they ran out into
the sheet of icy water, splashing ahead until it was up to their
shoulders. Then they swam back and forth violently, exaggerating

each gesture because of the cold. When they had used up their first spurt of energy they climbed onto a small concrete dam that had been built at one end of the lake, and rested in the sun on the dry part of the construction that was above the spillway. Here they told jokes and chuckled until the sun became so hot on their bodies that the dark world beneath the surface of the water again began to seem a desirable place to be. However, it appeared to have been tacitly agreed that they would wrestle to keep from being the first one to go in. They soon stopped, because they had both realized simultaneously that the drop from the dam's far side down onto the dry rocks below was a good deal too high to risk in case one of them slipped. Standing up, they caught their breath, and as if at a signal, dove into the water. By this time Amar had only one thing in his mind, and that was his breakfast. In the middle of a series of gasps, bubbles and flying water-drops he announced the fact to Mohammed; the shoreward trip became a race.

Amar arrived at the muddy bank first, loped under the willows to where his bicycle was, and unstrapped the parcel tied to the back of it. They took the food to a rock up the shore a bit and sat there in the sun eating. It was while they were sitting here that they became aware of the presence, among the rocks on the opposite shore, of another boy, who was carefully washing his clothes and spreading them on the rocks to dry. Shading his eyes with his hand, Mohammed watched for a while. "*Djibli*," he announced presently. It was of no interest to Amar whether the boy was from the mountains or the city, and he continued to munch on his dates and bread, looking out over the water, around at the small cactus-studded hills that ringed the lake basin, and occasionally up at the sky, where at one point a hawk came sailing into the range of his vision, plunged, glided, and moved off behind the high curved horizon.

"Where are you working now?" asked Mohammed. Amar told him. "How much?" Amar cut the true figure in half. "How is it? Good *maallem*?" Amar shrugged. The shrug and the grimace that went with it meant: Is anything good now? and the other understood and agreed. Mohammed, Amar knew, worked on and off in one or another of his father's shops. He settled back; his position on the rock was comfortable, and all he wanted was to recline there for a few minutes in the sun and enjoy the feeling of having eaten. But Mohammed was fidgety and kept shifting around and talking; Amar found himself wishing that he had come alone.

"Another big fire near Ras el Ma last night," said Mohammed. "Eighteen hectares."

"When the summer's over, there won't be any wheat left in Morocco," Amar remarked.

"Hope not."

"What'll we do for bread next winter?"

"There won't be any," said Mohammed flatly.

"And what'll we eat?"

"Leave that to the French. They'll send wheat from France."

Amar was not so sure. "Maybe," he said.

"Better if they don't. The trouble will start sooner if people are hungry."

It was easy for Mohammed to talk that way, because he was reasonably certain that he himself would not ever be in need of food. His father was a merchant, and probably had enough flour and oil and chickpeas stored in the house to last for two years if the need should arise. The middle-class and wealthy Fassi always had enormous private provisions to draw on in the event of emergency. To be able to weather a siege was part of the city's tradition; there had been several such situations even since the French occupation.

"Is that what the Istiqlal says?" Amar asked.

"What?" Mohammed was staring across at the country boy, who had finished his laundering and now was squatting naked atop a large rock, waiting for the garments to dry.

"That people should be hungry?"

"You can see that yourself, can't you? If people are living the same as always, with their bellies full of food, they'll just go on the same way. If they get hungry and unhappy enough, something happens."

"But who wants to be hungry and unhappy?" said Amar.

"Are you crazy?" Mohammed demanded. "Or don't you want to see the French get out?"

Amar had not intended to get caught this way on the wrong side of the conversation. "May the dogs burn in Hell," he said. That was one of the troubles with the Istiqlal, with all politics: you talked about people as though they were not really people, as though they were only things, numbers, animals, perhaps, but not really people.

"Have you been in the Zekak er Roumane this week?" Mohammed asked.

"No."

"When you go through, look up at the roofs. Some of the houses there have tons of rocks. *Ayayay!* You can see them. They have them piled so they look like walls, but they're all loose, ready to throw."

Amar felt his heart beat faster. *"Ouallah?"*

"Go and look," said Mohammed.

Amar was silent a moment. Then he said: "Something big's going to happen, right?"

"B'd draa. It's got to," Mohammed said casually.

Suddenly Amar remembered something he had been told about the Lalami family. Mohammed's father, having discovered that Mohammed's elder brother was a member of the Istiqlal, had put him out of the house, and the brother had gone off to Casablanca and been caught by the police. He was now in prison, awaiting trial along with some twenty other youths who had been apprehended at the same time for their activity in terrorist work, particularly in smuggling crates of hand grenades over the frontier from Spanish Morocco. He was something of a hero, because people said that he and another Fassi had been singled out by the French press as being particularly dastardly and brutal in certain of the murders they had committed. Then probably Mohammed knew a good deal more than he would say, and he could not even be asked whether the story about the brother were true or false; etiquette forbade it.

"What are you going to do when the day comes?" he finally said.

"What are *you* going to do?" countered Mohammed.

"*Ana?* I don't know."

Mohammed smiled pityingly. Amar looked at the shape of his mouth and felt a wave of dislike for him.

"I'll tell you what I'm going to do," Mohammed said firmly. "I'm going to do what I'm told."

Amar was impressed in spite of himself. "Then; you're a—"

Mohammed interrupted. "I'm not a member of anything. When the day comes everybody will take orders. *Majabekfina.*"

Amar tried not to think of the scene that would ensue were he to say what was on the tip of his tongue at the moment. This was: "Including rich men, like your father?" It was too much of an insult to utter, even in fun. Then for a moment, like a true Moslem, he contemplated the beauties of military discipline. There could be nothing, he reflected, to equal a government which was simply the honest enforcement, by means of the sword, of the laws of Islam. Perhaps the Istiqlal, if it were successful, could bring back that glorious era. But if the party wanted that, why had it never mentioned it in its propaganda? While the true Sultan had been in power the party had talked about the rich and the poor, and complained about not being able to print its newspaper the way it wanted to, and indirectly criticized the monarch for little things he had done and other little things he ought to have done. But ever since the French had taken the Sultan away, the party had spoken of nothing but bringing him back. If he returned, everything would be the same as it had been before, and the Istiqlal had certainly not been pleased with the state of affairs then.

"*Yah,* Mohammed," said Amar presently. "Why does the party want to see Sidi Mohammed Khamis back on the throne?"

Mohammed looked at him incredulously, and spat over the edge of the rock into the water. "*Enta m'douagh,*" he said with disgust. "The Sultan will never come back, and the party doesn't want to see him back."

"But—"

"It's not the party's fault, is it, if all the people in Morocco are *hemir,* donkeys? If you can't understand that, then you'd better begin eating a different kind of hay yourself."

Mohammed's head was tilted far back, his eyes were closed; he looked very pleased with himself. Amar felt his own heart suddenly become pointed in his chest. It was fortunate, he thought, that Mohammed could not see his expression at that moment, as he looked at him, for he surely would not have liked it. Some of his anger was personal, but most of it was resentment at having been allowed a sudden unexpected glimpse of what was wrong with his native land, of what had made it possible for a few Nazarene swine to come in and rule over his countrymen. In a situation where there was everything to be gained by agreement and friendliness there could be nothing but suspicion, hostility and bickering. It was always that way; it would go on being that way. He sighed, and got to his feet.

Mohammed sat up and looked across the water. The country boy was wandering among the rocks over which he had spread his pieces of clothing, feeling them to see if they were dry. Mohammed went on looking, his eyes very narrow. Finally he glanced up at Amar.

"Let's swim across and have some fun with him," he suggested. And as Amar did not respond, he continued: "If you'll hold him for me I'll hold him for you."

The words that came out escaped from Amar's lips before he had formed them in his mind. "I'll hold your mother for you," he said viciously, without looking down at him.

Mohammed leapt to his feet. *"Kifach?"* he cried. "What was that?" His eyes were rolling; he looked like a maniac.

Now Amar looked at him, calmly, although his heart had more sharp points than ever, and he was breathing fast. "I said I'd hold your mother for you. But only if you'll hold your sister for me."

Mohammed could not believe his ears. And even when he reminded himself that Amar had said it twice, so that there could be no doubt, he still had no immediate reflex. There seemed to be no possible gesture to make: they were standing too close together, their faces and bodies almost touching. Accordingly Mohammed stepped backward, but lost his balance, and fell into the shallow water at the foot of the rocks. Amar sprang after him, conscious of being still in the air as Mohammed's back hit the surface of the water, and conscious, an instant later, of having landed more or less astride Mohammed's belly, which was only slightly submerged. Mohammed was bubbling and groaning, trying to lift his head above the water; the water was so shallow that he had hit the stones. Amar stood up; Mohammed staggered to his feet, covered with mud, and still wailing. Then with a savage cry he lunged at Amar, and the two fell together back into the water. This time it was Amar's turn to have his head pounded upon the bed of the lake. Pebbles, stiff, slippery leaves and rotten sticks were ground against his face; the world was a chaotic churning of air and water, light and darkness. He felt Mohammed's hard weight pushing him down —an elbow here, a knee there, a hand on his throat. He relaxed a second, then put all his effort into a rebound which partially dislodged Mohammed's grip. Twice he drove his fist up into Mohammed's belly as hard as he could, managing to lift his head above the water and breathe once. Drawing his leg back, he delivered a kick which reached a soft part of Mohammed's body. A second later they were both on their feet, each one conscious only of the eyes, nose and mouth of the other. Now it was merely a matter of perseverance. Amar's fist went well into the socket of Mohammed's left eye. "Son of gonorrhea!" Mohammed bellowed. Almost at the same instant Amar had the impression that he had run headlong into a wall of rocks. The pain was just below the bridge of his nose. He choked, knew it was blood running down his throat, recoiled and spat what he had collected of it into Mohammed's face, hitting him just below the nose. Then he rammed his head into Mohammed's stomach, knocking him backwards, and following through with another, better planned blow with the top of his head which sent Mohammed sprawling on the muddy ground of the shore. He leapt, sat once more astride him and pounded his face with all his might. At first Mohammed made powerful efforts to rise, then his resistence lessened, until eventually he was merely groaning. Still Amar did not stop. The blood that poured from his nose had run down his own body onto Mohammed's head and chest.

When he was positive that Mohammed was not merely playing a trick in order to lunge at him unexpectedly, he got unsteadily to his feet and gave the boy's head a terrific kick with his bare heel. He had to keep sniffing to keep the blood from coming out his nostrils; the thought came to him that he had better wash himself.

He squatted a few meters out from the shore and bathed hurriedly, constantly glancing back to be sure that Mohammed was still lying in the same position. The cold water seemed to be stanching the bleeding, and he continued to splash handfuls of it into his face, snuffing it up his nose. When he went back to dress he stopped and knelt down beside Mohammed. Seen this way, his features in repose, the downy tan skin of his face looking very soft where it showed among the smears of blood and dirt, he was not hateful. But what a difference there was between what Amar could see now of Mohammed and what Mohammed was like inside! It was a mystery. He had been going to bang his head against the ground, but now he no longer wanted to, because Mohammed was not there; it was a stranger lying naked before him. He got up and went to dress. Without looking back again, he led his bicycle out to the road, got on, and rode away. When the gradient got too steep he had to walk.

The eucalyptus grove seemed even more silent than it had a while ago. At the top, as he was about to emerge onto the long straight road across the plain, he imagined he heard a voice calling from below. It was hard to tell; what would Mohammed be calling him for? He stood still and listened. Certainly someone was shouting in the grove, but far away. The voice sounded hollow and distorted. And he still would have said that it was saying his name, save that it was inconceivable under the circumstances that Mohammed should do such a thing. Or perhaps not; perhaps he had no money and was more frightened of

facing the Frenchman in the bicycle shop than he was ashamed
of calling out to Amar. In any case, Amar was not going to wait
and see. Feeling perverse and unhappy, he mounted the bicycle
again and sped off under the noonday sun, back toward the city.

CHAPTER   7

Like most of the boys and younger men who had been born in
Fez since the French had set up their rival Fez only a few kilometers outside the walls, Amar had never formed the habit of
going to a mosque and praying. For all but the well-to-do, life
had become an anarchic, helter-skelter business, with people
leaving their families and going off to other cities to work, or
entering the army where they were sure to eat. Since it is far
more sinful to pray irregularly than not to pray at all, they had
merely abandoned the idea of attempting to live like their elders, and trusted that in His all-embracing wisdom Allah would
understand and forgive. But often Amar was not sure; perhaps
the French had been sent as a test of the Moslems' faith, like a
plague or a famine, and Allah was watching each man's heart
closely, to see whether he was truly keeping the faith. In that
case, he told himself, how irate He must be by this time, seeing
into what evil ways His people had fallen. There were moments
when he felt very far from Allah's grace, and this was one of
them, as he pedaled at top speed through the dried-up fields,
with the huge sun above his head sending down its deadly heat
upon him.

He knew that Mohammed had been at fault, but only in a
way he could not help—only for being Mohammed; whereas he
himself was truly to blame for wanting Mohammed to be some-

thing other than what it had been written that he must be. He knew that no man could be changed by anyone but Allah, yet he could not prevent himself from feeling resentful that Mohammed had not turned out to be the possible friend he was looking for, in whom he could confide, who could understand him.

Djebel Zalagh was there ahead of him, behind the invisible Medina, looking not very imposing from this angle—merely a higher part of the long ridge that seemed to continue indefinitely from one side of the horizon to the other. And in the heat haze today, it had no color but gray, a dead color, like ashes. The Arab city of course could not be seen because it was built in what was really a wide crevasse below the plateau of the plain; its position made it warmer in the winter, because it was sheltered from the icy winds that swept across the plain, and cooler in summer, because the merciless rays of the sun did not strike it with quite so much force. Then, too, the river coursed in countless channels through the ravine on whose slopes the Medina was built, and that helped to cool the air. The inhabitants were fond of pointing out to one another, as well as to visitors, the insufferable climate of the Ville Nouvelle, for the French had built their city squarely in the plain, and as a consequence it was open to all the excesses of the intemperate Moroccan weather. Amar could not understand how anyone, even the French, could be so stupid as to waste so much money building so large a city when it could never be any good, since the land on which it was built was worthless in the beginning. He had been there in the winter and felt the blasts of bitterly cold wind that rushed through the wide streets; nowhere in the world, he was sure, could the air be more inhospitable and unsuited for human beings to live in. "It's poison," he would report when he returned to the Medina from a trip to the Ville Nouvelle. And in the summer, in spite of the trees they had planted along their avenues, the air was still and breathless, and at the end of each street you saw the dead plain there, baking in the terrible sunlight.

Far ahead he could see the white spots that were the new

city's apartment houses; they looked like bird droppings piled in the immensity of the plain. "All that will disappear in one night," he thought, to reassure himself. It had been written that the works of the unbelievers were to be destroyed. But when? He wanted to see the flames soaring into the sky and hear the screams, he longed to walk through the ruins while they were still glowing, and feel the joy that comes from knowing that evil is punished in this world as well as in the next, that justice and truth must prevail on earth as well as hereafter.

This was the hour when no one was abroad; he had not met a soul since leaving Aïn Malqa. One would have said that the earth had been deserted by mankind and left to the insects, which screamed their song in praise of heat as he sped along— one endless shrill fierce note that rose on all sides, perpetually renewed.

His nose had started to bleed again, not so profusely as before, but dripping regularly every three or four pedals; it was beginning to feel as wide as his head, and painful. He stopped, knelt down by the channel of water beside the road, and bathed his face. The water was cold; he did not remember it as being that deliciously cold. He took a deep breath, bent far over, and submerged his head; the force of the current made the flesh of his cheeks vibrate. When he had finished his ablutions and immersions he felt refreshed and relaxed. Feeling that way made him want to rest a bit. He stood up and scanned the plain for a tree, but there was none, and so he went on. A few kilometers further ahead he caught sight of a mass of green a good distance away on his left. It looked like a small fruit orchard, and there was a lane leading across the fields toward the spot. He turned off. The lane was bumpy and hard to ride on; he managed however to make slow progress without having to get down. If he had had to walk, he would have considered that it was not worth his while to make the side trip. The orchard proved to be larger and more distant than he had thought. It lay in a slight depression; what he had seen from the road was only the tops of the trees, and as he approached they grew taller. Such a wealth of green meant the presence of underground springs. "Olives, pears, pomegranates, quinces, lemons . . ." he murmured as he entered the orchard.

At that moment he heard ahead of him the sound of an approaching motorcycle. The idea had not crossed his mind that the land might have a house on it, that the house might be inhabited, but now it did occur to him, the hypothesis made more unpleasant by his suspicion that the inhabitants were likely to be French, in which case they would either beat him, shoot him, or turn him over to the police, the last possibility being the most fearsome. It was a very bad thing to be caught on a Frenchman's farm at any time, but particularly now, when for the past few weeks hundreds of *domaines* had been raided by the Istiqlal and the crops set afire.

Quickly he leapt to the ground, and lifting the bicycle, began to run clumsily with it among the trees, looking for a place to hide. But it was a well-tended orchard, without bushes or undergrowth, and he could see that his project was absurd: he would have had to run very far in order not to be seen, if the cyclist happened to be looking his way as he passed. And the noise was already very loud, almost upon him. He turned, set the bicycle down, and walked slowly back. When the motorcycle appeared he had almost reached the lane. The rider, a small, plump man wearing goggles and a visored cap, was bouncing uncomfortably as the machine veered from one old rut to another, hitting clods of earth that were like rocks. As he came along, he was looking straight at Amar; he stopped, let the motor idle an instant, then turned it off. The sudden silence was astonishing, but then it proved not to be silence at all; there were the cicadas singing in the trees.

"*Msalkheir*," the man said, carefully removing his cap, then his goggles, and never taking his eyes from Amar's face. "Where are you going, and where are you coming from?"

"Taking a walk," said Amar. "Looking for a tree to lie under." He had decided that the man was a Moslem (not because he spoke perfect Arabic, for some Frenchmen could do that, but because of his manner and the way in which he spoke), and that relieved his anxiety to such an extent that he found himself telling him the simple truth.

"Taking a walk with a bicycle?" The man laughed, not unpleasantly, but in a way that meant he did not believe a word Amar had said.

"Yes," Amar said. Then a drop of blood fell from his nose, and he realized that his shirt was decorated with red spatters of it.

"What's the matter?" asked the man. "What happened to your face? Did you fall off the bicycle?"

It was too late to do any lying now, Amar reflected ruefully. "No, I had a fight. With a friend," he added quickly, lest the man might suppose that his fight had been with one of the workmen or one of the guards on the property.

The man laughed again. He had a round face with large mild eyes, and he was growing bald. "A fight? And where's the friend? Lying dead somewhere in my orchard?" In the man's eyes Amar could distinguish nothing beyond an interested amusement.

"At Aïn Malqa."

Now the man frowned. "Excuse me, but I think you're crazy. Do you know which way Aïn Malqa is?"

Amar sniffed, to keep another drop of blood from coming out his nostril. "I haven't touched any of your fruit," he said aggrievedly. "If you want me to get out, tell me and I'll go."

The man's face assumed a pained expression. "*La, khoya, la,*" he said gently, as if he were soothing a skittish horse. "Where do you get such foolish ideas? Nothing of the sort." He started up his motor. "He's leaving," thought Amar hopefully. But then his heart sank as the man, one foot on the ground, made a U-turn with the machine and brought it to a halt facing back the way he had come.

Above the clamor of the motor, he shouted: "Get on your bicycle!" Amar obeyed. "Ride ahead of me!" He pointed, and Amar set off, going deeper into the orchard, the roar of the slowly moving cycle behind him.

They kept going. There seemed to be no reason for turning his head around, because the man kept at an unvarying distance behind him. Amar was miserable. It was absurd to think of trying to escape; such a thing was manifestly impossible. But he was frightened: he had never before met a Moslem like this, one whose intentions were so difficult to guess that he might as well have been a Nazarene.

The road curved suddenly to the right, and there was an old house, standing in a clearing of the orchard. A path led up to its door; it was bordered by high rose-bushes that had been left to grow wild. For the country the house was enormous, its long expanse of windowless wall being fully ten meters high. There were cracks zigzagging down from the top; plants and bushes had grown in them, but they were all dead save for a tiny gnarled fig tree whose gray trunk thrust itself through the wall like a fat snake. The roar of the motor behind him stopped, and Amar at last looked back with some nervousness. The man had jumped off his motorcycle and was letting down the standard that would keep it upright. He caught Amar's eye and smiled briefly. "Here we are," he said. "The door is open. Walk in."

Amar, however, went only as far as the doorway and stood waiting for his host, who, when he came, pushed him ahead impatiently. Inside the door was a long staircase which they climbed, coming out at the top onto a covered gallery which ran around three sides of a large square courtyard. In places the railing had rotted away, and several of the great beams overhead sagged precariously. In the air there was the humming of innumerable wasps.

"In here," said the man, and he pushed him gently through a doorway into a long room whose light came from a series of small windows placed above the roof of the gallery. At the far end, seated on the cushions that went the length of the room, were three boys, all of them older than Amar by two or three years. The man led him over to them and he shook hands with each one, noticing as he did so that they all greeted him in the European fashion, without bothering to lift their fingers to their lips after touching his hand. And for that matter, they were all

dressed completely like Frenchmen, not only in the choice of
the garments they wore, but in their way of wearing them. One
boy had been reading a book and the other two had been talking while one of them rubbed the sleeve of a jacket with a cloth
soaked in gasoline, but now they all politely ceased what they
had been doing and leaned forward expectantly as Amar sat
down.

The man seated himself on a high hassock facing them and
held out his arm to indicate Amar as though he were a rare
animal he had run to earth. "Look at this, will you?" he cried.
"Here I was going to the city to meet Lahcen, who's waiting at
this minute at the Renaissance, and I come across this gazelle
in the orchard. Not in the lane, you understand, but coming
from the mill."

"What mill?" interrupted Amar. The blood had finally managed to run down to his lip.

"Then he says," the man went on imperturbably, "he's coming from Aïn Malqa." The boy who had been reading laughed.
"Oh, he has a bicycle," the man assured him. "It's completely
possible. But what's happened to him? Look at him. He won't
talk. He says he had a fight with a friend."

The boys needed no invitation; they were studying Amar
carefully but without insolence. To avoid their scrutiny, which,
however civil and unhostile, embarrassed him, Amar began to
look nonchalantly around the strange room. He had never seen
a room remotely like it. It was, by his standards, extremely disorderly, with no sign of the scrubbed neatness that characterized
the rooms in his own house, although he could not have said
that it was precisely dirty. There were great crooked piles of
books and magazines everywhere on the floor, and fat leather
hassocks that looked as though they had been tossed purposely
here and there, with no attempt to place them in a row, the
way they should have been placed. On three small coffee tables,
also just put down anywhere in the middle of the room, there
were huge baskets of peaches; the air was thick with their rich
odor. The walls, which one would have expected to bear large
gold-framed photographs of relatives—for this was obviously a

rich man's house, even though it was old—were empty of any kind of picture or adornment, save for a very large map of Morocco printed in pastel colors; he had seen one like it when he peeked through a window at the Bureau du Contrôle Civil one day. And in whichever direction he looked he saw bowls of cigarette stubs and ashes, and there were ashes on the floor as well. He decided that this was a typical French room, and that the man wanted people to think he was French.

"This isn't the Tribunal," said the man, smiling at Amar. "Still, the fact is, I caught you on my property and I want to know what you were doing here. Do you blame me?"

Amar had never heard his own tongue spoken quite in this way before: the man used all the local expressions, but at the same time he interspersed his sentences with words which showed that he knew true Arabic, the language of the mosque and the *medersa*, the *imam* and the *aallem*. And the manner in which he mixed the two languages was so skillful that its result sounded almost like a new tongue, easy and sweet to the ear.

"No," said Amar. "But I told you the truth." He was uncomfortably aware that his own speech was hopelessly crude, the language of the street.

"Perhaps, but you didn't tell me enough. *Zid*. Go on. Tell us the whole story. Maybe you'd like a drink."

Amar was thirsty, and so he said: "Yes." One of the boys jumped up and stepped to the other end of the room, returning with a tall bottle and several very small glasses. Amar looked at the bottle suspiciously. The boy caught his glance, said: "Chartreuse," and poured a little out for him. Then he served the others. This was not at all what Amar wanted, but he sipped it and proceeded to recount the happenings of the day. When he got to the fight, the man stopped him. "*Essbar*," he said. "What were you fighting about?"

He wanted to say: "I don't know," for he did not know how to put into words the real reason why he had felt like proffering the insult to Mohammed. Certainly it was not the suggestion Mohammed had made; there was nothing unusual in that, nor would there have been anything extraordinary in his accepting it. It had more to do with Mohammed's smug sureness of being right—he was simply the kind of person you feel a need of hitting. But he knew he could scarcely hope to make his listeners understand that, without going into a long digression which would lead them into politics, and even if he had been mentally equipped to engage in such a discussion with them, the thing was unthinkable. He did not even know where his audience's sympathies lay; they could easily all be with the French.

"I didn't like him," said Amar. "He was the kind of *ouild* that needs a good punch now and then."

"I see," the man said seriously, turning his head and taking in the three boys with a glance which seemed to be warning them not to laugh. "So you punched him. *Zid.*"

Amar was a little more relaxed now; he felt that the man believed him, and this set him enough at his ease so that he could remember all the details of the fight, which he told minutely. The man was frankly amused now—Amar could see it in his eyes—but he remained sitting solemnly listening while Amar brought the story up to the moment when he had heard a motorcycle coming through the orchard and had tried vainly to escape among the trees, only to turn back and be discovered before he had reached the lane. The man reached over and clapped him on the shoulder, laughing. "Very good, very good," he said. "I think we can take that story just as it comes. Now I've got to go to the city for a little while, but I'll be back. You stay here, and the house is yours. If you want anything, just ask for it."

He got up; Amar automatically jumped to his feet. He had heard and understood the man's invitation, but he considered it mere urbane politeness. Besides, he wanted to be off; the house and the boys and his host were somehow all unexplained, like a dream, and he was overwhelmed by uneasiness. He looked up and saw almost wistfully the patches of blue sky through the windows at the top of the wall.

"Sit down," the man said. This was certainly a command, and he obeyed. The man stepped lightly to the door and disappeared. An instant later the motorcycle roared, and then its sound slowly became fainter.

CHAPTER   8

As if it were part of a ritual, everyone sat perfectly quiet until the hum of the motor had died away completely, and it was no longer possible for them to hear anything, even by listening with great attention. Then the boy who had been reading turned to Amar and said: "Have some peaches. There are thousands of them."

Amar rubbed his hand across his face. "I'm very thirsty." He looked at his hand and saw dried blood and fresh blood, and the day suddenly seemed endless. "I ought to go," he said tentatively.

The three immediately murmured polite protests. He could see that they would prevent him from leaving, perhaps even by force if they had to. "I ought to go home," he said again. "My nose—"

The boy who had spoken got up and stood looking down at him. "Look," he said. "You lie down here and I'll take care of you." He went to the doorway and called: "*Yah, Mahmoud!*" An elderly man in a slightly soiled white *gandoura* appeared presently; the boy stepped out onto the gallery and conferred briefly with him. Then he returned, knelt in front of Amar, and began to remove his sandals. Embarrassed, Amar pushed his hands away and took them off by himself. "Now lie down here," the boy commanded, indicating the place where he had been sitting. The other two watched while he helped Amar to make

himself comfortable, stuffing pillows under his head, Amar feebly protesting the while, ashamed at having such a fuss made
over him. But it felt good to be stretched out. He was very tired.
No one spoke until the servant came in bearing a tray, which he
set down on the floor beside the cushion where Amar lay. Raising himself on one elbow, Amar drank the glass of cold water.
There were storks on the glass, embossed in bright red outline.

"Perhaps I can come back and visit your father some other
day," he began. He was certain the man was not the father of
any one of them, but he wanted to hear what they would reply.
There was silence for a moment; it was clear that the others were
not sure what they ought to say.

"Moulay Ali will be back very soon," said the boy who had
taken charge of him; apparently he was to be spokesman. "Lie
down. I'm going to put some *filfil* on your face." Amar lay back.
"Close your eyes, tight." This was unnecessary advice, as Amar
did not intend to let any of the red pepper get into his eyes,
whatever happened. The boy gently smeared the paste over his
forehead and across the bridge of his nose. "You ought to go
to a doctor," he said, when he had finished. "I think your nose
is broken."

Mektoub, thought Amar, mentally shrugging. He had no
desire to consult a doctor; he was going to keep his money for
shoes.

The boy sat down somewhere further along on the cushion,
beyond the other two, who Amar felt were merely sitting there
watching him. It was very silent in the room; now and then
there was the sound of the page of a magazine being turned, or
one of them cleared his throat. He could hear the steady hum of
the wasps on the gallery, and beyond, an occasional cock crowing, out in the afternoon sunlight. He had been pressing his
eyes very tightly shut, but slowly the facial muscles relaxed and
he felt himself in danger of falling asleep. That could certainly
not be done here in this house, with strangers looking at him;
the idea of it terrified him. He decided to talk, about anything at
all, so long as he remained awake. It was imperative that he
open his mouth and say something. It seemed to him that he

was sitting up, having a long, serious discussion with the three boys, and they were listening and agreeing with him. And somewhere, very far away, there was the booming of thunder in the sky. Suddenly someone coughed, and he realized that he was not sitting up at all; that meant that he had very nearly fallen asleep.

"Tell me," he said aloud. "Did Moulay Ali really think I had come to set fire to his place?"

Unexpectedly all three boys laughed. "You'd better ask him about that," said the one who had helped him. "How do I know what he thought? He'll be here in a minute."

"Do you all live in Fez?" It did not matter what the others thought of his foolish questions, if only he could keep from falling asleep.

"They do. I live in Meknès."

"Are you staying here now?"

"*Sa'a, sa'a*, sometimes I come and stay a few days. Moulay Ali is a great friend. I've learned more from him than from any *aallem*." The other two murmured in agreement.

This seemed a strange statement to make. "But what does he teach you?"

"Everything," the other said, almost fervently.

"I want to sit up," said Amar. "Could you wipe off the *filfil*, please?"

"No, no. Lie still. Moulay Ali will be coming. I want him to see that I've taken care of you."

Amar had succeeded in rousing himself sufficiently so as to be no longer afraid of sleeping. Again the thunder rolled in some far-off part of the world. He lay still. Fairly soon there was the sound of the motorcycle in the distance, coming along the road, turning into the lane, arriving in the orchard among the trees, and finally, in a blast of noise, drawing to a stop before the house. In the stairway there were voices, and Moulay Ali entered the room, accompanied by another man with an extraordinarily resonant, deep voice. "This is Lahcen," said Moulay Ali. The three boys acknowledged the introduction. "Aha! I see our friend is asleep! What's that you've smeared over his face? *Filfil?*"

"I'm not asleep," said Amar. He would have liked not to be obliged to take part in the conversation, but obviously he could not merely lie there saying nothing.

"He'd better sit up," said Moulay Ali. The boy from Meknès held Amar's head and began to scrape the dried paste from his forehead and eyebrows with a knife. When he had cleaned it all off, he bathed the places with a damp cloth. Lahcen and Moulay Ali were holding a conversation which made no sense whatever.

"This?" "Yes, nine." "I have that." "I thought you said eleven." "No! Not that. This, this!" "Oh, yes." "This one, five." "*Ouakha.*" "Now, this, I was telling you about. You see, you can't be sure." "I'm sure." "It's impossible to be sure. Take my word for it." "All right, leave it open." "Put six plus and leave it." "And what about . . . ?" "We'll get to that later. Have a peach. The best in the Saïs."

When he thought the area around his eyes was dry, Amar opened them and sat up. "Ah, there he is!" cried Moulay Ali. "*Kif enta?* Better now?"

In the center of the room a tall man with a soft gray *tarbouche* on his head was bending over, eating a peach and trying to keep it from dripping onto his clothes. Eventually he straightened, pulled out a handkerchief and wiped his mouth and hands. Then at Moulay Ali's request he stepped over and greeted Amar. The iris and pupil of his left eye were completely white, like a milky marble. Straightway Amar guessed that he was not of the same social condition as the three boys and his host. Assuredly he had not had the same education: his language was scarcely more distinguished than Amar's. So this is Lahcen, he thought, and he could not imagine why Moulay Ali had rushed into the Ville Nouvelle to fetch him.

"We'll leave our buying and selling until later," Moulay Ali remarked pointedly, "and get Mahmoud to make us some tea." He went to the door and called the servant.

Amar had been dreading the mention of tea; it meant that he could not leave until he had drunk at least three glasses with his host. He sat back disconsolately and looked at Lahcen, who

was picking his nose. The *tarbouche* on his head was the only
article of Moslem clothing in the entire room, and it looked
strangely out of place, both in its surroundings and on that
bullet-shaped head. It was the sort of hat you would expect to
see on an elderly, slightly eccentric gentleman of means, who
might be taking his grandchildren out for a Friday stroll.

"Sit down," said Moulay Ali to his new guest. "Talk to our
friend here." To one of the boys he said: "Chemsi, come over
here. I want to show you something." Lahcen smiled at Amar
and sat down.

"I hear you went swimming at Aïn Malqa today," he said.
"How's the water these days? Still cold?"

"Very cold."

"Been to Sidi Harazem lately?"

"No. I work. It's too far."

"Yes. It's far." He was silent a moment. Then he said: "You
work in the Ville Nouvelle?"

"No, at Bab Fteuh."

"That's my quarter."

Amar did not recall ever having seen him, but he said: "Ah."

"Have you ever been to Dar el Beida?" Lahcen asked him.
Amar said he had not. "That's a place to swim. At the beach,
the sea. Nothing better."

"French women by the million," Amar said.

Lahcen laughed. "By the million."

They talked on for a time about Casablanca, Amar wondering anxiously all the while how soon the daylight would begin
to fade. It seemed to him that he had been shut into this room
for a week. But since tea was coming, he could not even mention the fact that he wanted to leave.

"It says: *dans la région de Bou Anane*," Moulay Ali was saying. "Does that mean anything to you?"

Chemsi hesitated, and said it did not.

Moulay Ali snorted. "It does to Ahmed Slaoui."

"Oh!" exclaimed Chemsi.

Moulay Ali nodded his head slowly up and down, looking
slyly at Chemsi. "Do you see what I mean?" he asked him at

length. "Use the whole article word for word, put Maroc-Presse
and the date, and then add what you know about the *région de
Bou Anane.*"

"Poor Slaoui," said Chemsi.

"He may not be there now," Moulay Ali reminded him.

Mahmoud arrived carrying an enormous copper tray, with a
silver teapot and glasses. The two returned from the corner
where they had been talking, and Moulay Ali tossed the folded
newspaper he had been holding in his hand to the two other
boys. He sat down and began to fill the glasses. The tea bubbled
and steamed, and the odor of the mint came up.

"What's your name?" he said suddenly to Amar.

Amar told him. Moulay Ali raised his eyebrows. "Fassi?" he
asked.

"My family has always lived in Fez," Amar answered proudly;
he was aware that the boys were scrutinizing him afresh. Perhaps they had thought he was a *berrani,* an outsider.

"What *haouma?*" Moulay Ali was passing out the glasses of
tea.

"Keddane, below the Djemaa Andaluz."

"Yes, yes."

Amar was waiting for his host to say: "*Bismillah,*" before he
tasted his tea, but he said nothing at all. Nor did anyone else.
Usually Amar murmured his prayer under his breath, so that it
was scarcely audible, but this time, seeing that the others all had
been so remiss, he said it in a normal voice. Lahcen turned his
head to look at him.

The boy who was reading the newspaper put it down slowly
and took his glass. There was consternation on his face. "Bubonic plague," he said. "That's a terrible disease. You burst."

"*Eioua!*" agreed Moulay Ali, as if he were saying: "I told
you."

Lahcen took a noisy sip of tea, licked his lips, said:
"Laghzaoui—I mean, Lazraqi says Algeria's full of it now."

"It must have come across the border," began the boy.

"Rumors!" snapped Moulay Ali, looking fixedly at Chemsi.

"We don't know anything about Algeria." Chemsi nodded his head in agreement.

They went on discussing remote towns in the south of the country, "as though they were important places," thought Amar. It was perfectly clear to him that the conversation was being made around a central point which they all saw but were taking pains that he should not see. After he had drunk his third glass of tea, he stood up. "It's very late," he said.

"Of course, you want to go," said Moulay Ali, smiling. "Very well. But don't forget us. Come back some day and we'll have a party, with music. Now you know where the house is."

Lahcen grinned. "Our friend Moulay Ali plays the flute and the violin."

"And if I'm not wrong our friend Lahcen plays the liter bottle," added Moulay Ali archly. The boys laughed. "Especially Aït Souala rosé," he added.

"But he's very good on the flute," went on Lahcen. "Play a little," he urged.

Moulay Ali shrugged. "Amar wants to go. Another day. And Chemsi'll bring his *oud* from Meknès." Chemsi protested shyly that he played badly. "What do you play?" Moulay Ali asked Amar, taking his hand without rising from the hassock.

Amar was embarrassed. "The *lirah*, a little."

"*Baz!* That's perfect! You can take my place when I get tired. Good-bye. Take care of your war scars." His face grew serious. "And don't wander into any more private roads, do you understand? Suppose I hadn't been me? Suppose I had been Monsieur Durand or Monsieur Blanchet? *Eioua!* You wouldn't be going home on your bicycle now, would he?" He turned to the boys for corroboration. They smiled. Lahcen said: "*Ay!*" with great feeling.

Amar stood there, searching in his head for something to say that would show them he was not a fool, not a child, that he was aware that all their words had an inner core of meaning which they had kept hidden from him. He decided that the best thing was to be mysterious himself, to let them think that perhaps he had understood them in spite of all their precautions, but not in such a way that they might imagine he bore any resentment toward them for playing what was, after all, no more than a rather childish game.

"Thank you for your trust in me," he said gravely to Moulay Ali.

It had its effect; he saw that in Moulay Ali's eyes, although Moulay Ali did not move a muscle. Perhaps precisely because he did not move; he seemed to freeze for a fraction of a second, eyes and all. And so did everyone else, if only for that short instant. But before the instant was over, Amar had pushed ahead, taking momentary command. He held out his hand and said: "Good-bye," and then moved on to the three boys, one by one, and finally Lahcen. And bowing again briefly to his host, he turned and walked to the door. As far as he could tell, no one said anything as he went down the stairs.

He was convinced that before he could get well away from the house someone would call him back; it seemed too good to be true that he should at last be out in the open again. Quickly he hopped on the bicycle and in a great burst of energy began pedaling along the bumpy lane. The sun was still fairly high in the sky; it was not quite so late as he had thought. The light in the orchard was golden; the shadows of the tree trunks made straight black stripes along the earth. Cicadas still whirred their song in the branches above his head, but the sound was less intense than it had been at noon. He continued to ride as hard as he was able, to get sooner onto the main road. Once out there, he felt, he could refuse to return to the house if Moulay Ali should come roaring after him on the motorcycle. He was sweating and panting by the time he reached the road, but then there were no more ruts and clods and bumps, and he relaxed into an easy, steady speed. The hundred-meter slabs sped past; he began to feel happy again. There were shadows in the back of his mind, questions that needed to be answered, matters that had to be faced, and they were imminent, all around him, but for the moment the strength of the present was great enough to keep them all there at bay, backed up against the wall of eventuality.

CHAPTER 9

The sun was rapidly retiring from its vague position in the bowl of the sky overhead, toward the definite remotenesses of the Djebel Zerhoun; the dark mass of peaks at the extremity of the plain had been brought nearer by the intense light behind them. Somewhere there in the heart of the mountains nestled the holy city of Moulay Idriss, built by his own family many centuries ago when Haroun er Rachid was still alive. He knew how it looked from the postcards he had seen—draped like a white cloth over its escarpments, and surrounded by whole forests of giant olive trees, forests that stretched in all directions through the valleys and up the slopes. He was whistling as he passed the first small farms that were scattered at the outskirts of the town. The odious little dogs that French people seemed to like so much rushed out at him as he rode by, barking furiously. He pretended they were Frenchmen, tried to run them down, and called out: "*Bon jour, monsieur!*" to them when he had gone by.

The daytime air with its hot smell had made room for the new evening air that was rolling down from the heights ahead. The difference between them was the difference there is between a boulder and a flock of birds flying, or, he thought, between being asleep and being awake. "Perhaps I've been asleep all day," he said to himself as a joke. No dream could have been more senseless than his day had been; that was certain. But because the events of the day had really taken place, he was troubled by

their possible meaning in the pattern of his destiny. Why had
Allah seen fit to make him meet Mohammed Lalami as he came
up from his bath in the river, and why had He directed his bicycle to the hidden house of Moulay Ali in the fruit orchard?
Since nothing in all existence could ever be counted as accidental, it had to mean that his life was fated to be linked with
Mohammed's and Moulay Ali's, and this he did not want at all.
Perhaps by saying the proper prayers he could persuade Allah
to direct the path of his life in such a way that he could miss
seeing them again, all of them, including Lahcen and the three
boys. It was always the entrance of other people into his life that
made it difficult. But then the happy thought occurred to him
that it was possible Allah had given him his secret strength precisely in order to enable him to protect himself in these en-
tanglements with other people, which were, after all, inevitable.
If he could learn to trust it, use it when it was needed, was it
not likely that he could win out over them? He pondered the
question. Surely that was what Allah had meant by making
Amar Amar, by giving him the gift of knowing what was in the
hearts of other men. The problem was to make this gift strong
and absolutely sure, as he had done to his body during his childhood, while the other boys were sitting in classrooms; he had
done that not by imposing any conscious discipline, for he had
no conception of discipline (save that he had watched athletes
training, and felt sorry for them) but by a process opposed to
discipline—by simply allowing his body to express itself, to take
complete command, and develop itself as it wished.

He pedaled past the suburban villas with their plots of green
lawn, through small streets that were short cuts to the side of
town where he was going. The last open space before the beginning of the city proper was the botanical garden. Part of the
land was a nursery enclosed by a fence of barbed wire; the rest
was an uncultivated wilderness veined with well-trodden paths.
If you wandered quietly in here at twilight you sometimes came
upon surprising scenes, for it was the only place near the town
where the French boys and girls could find any degree of privacy. On several occasions Amar had discovered couples lying

tightly embraced in the bushes, oblivious of his passage, or merely indifferent to it. What puzzled him was why they did not do their kissing and love-making in the brothels. The girls obviously worked as prostitutes, otherwise they would not be out walking with the boys. Why then did they leave the brothels and carry on their work in the open air, like animals? Was it that all the rooms were full at the moment, or that they were doing this without the knowledge of the *batrona*, so that they could keep all the money themselves and not give her any? Or were they merely evil, vicious creatures that had lost all shame, whose hearts Allah in His wrath had changed to the hearts of dogs? This was perhaps the facet of Nazarene life which shocked him most profoundly, but still, it amused him to walk silently along the paths until he came upon a couple, and then to cough loudly as he passed near them.

When he arrived opposite the entrance to the garden, he turned in and bumped along the path for a while, until it became so rough that he had to get down and walk. As he jumped off the bicycle there was an ear-splitting clap of thunder overhead; he felt the sound in the earth under his feet. Fearfully he looked up and saw that a great, black curtain had been stealing across the sky from the south, following him as he rode; and a huge cloud that looked like a fist was thrusting itself outward from the blackness behind it into the clear sky above.

There was no point in going back to the road: the rain would be arriving any second. Its smell was already in the air. He looked up again. The strange fat cloud was billowing like smoke. Ahead there were several greenhouses, and if no Frenchman were around one of these would be his shelter. Any Moslem who might be working on the grounds would surely let him go in; it was unthinkable to refuse a person protection from a storm. He tried to go faster, but with the bicycle it was impossible. At last he got to the opening in the wire fence. Beside it there was a sign written in both Arabic and French characters; this, he supposed, was a warning to people that it was forbidden to enter. But which was worse, he asked himself, an angry man or the wrathful spirits in the air at the moment? There was no doubt as to the answer. One could go mad just from being brushed against by a storm demon, and the air was swarming with them. When the first drops fell he leaned the bicycle against a tree and ran swiftly ahead to the door of the nearest greenhouse. It was not locked. He stepped inside: the sweet vegetable odor was very strong in the heavy air, and the fading light that came through the dusty panes of glass seemed old, as though it had been in here for many years. He closed the door and stood against it looking out. Some distance down the path he could see the rear wheel of the bicycle sticking out from behind a bush. He watched it fixedly. It would be a terrible thing for him if anyone should make off with the bicycle, but when the rain began to pour down so heavily that he could no longer see anything but a rapidly darkening blur beyond the streaming windowpanes, he knew that no matter what happened he would not go out there now.

The inside of the greenhouse had grown almost as dark as night. It seemed to him that he felt the damp hot breath of the silent plants at the back of his neck, and he could not bring himself to turn his head, or even to move his eyes in one direction or the other. The thunder crashed and the rain fell against the thousand panes of glass over his head. Soon the water was running through and splattering on the floor somewhere back there in the dark. He pressed his forehead against the cold glass and waited. Perhaps there had been someone in the greenhouse when he came in, hidden behind the plants—a Frenchman with a pistol. Even now he might have it pointed at him, at any moment he might speak, and when Amar turned around or opened the door to escape he would shoot. The great ambition of every Frenchman in Morocco was to kill as many Moslems as possible. But a moment later it occurred to him that it was likely that Allah was protecting him today with His blessing. First there had been his victory over Mohammed, then his adventure with Moulay Ali, which had begun ominously but terminated well, and now his steps had been directed into the park so that he might find shelter from the rain. If he had continued to ride, he would have been caught in the storm. Why should he now lack faith in Allah's willingness to continue to hold him in His favor at least until the end of the day? *"Hamdoul'lah,"* he whispered.

And an instant later the rain's wide voice was still; it merely ceased falling, all at once, and there was nothing but the diminishing sound of its dripping from the trees.

Without looking around even now, he opened the door and ran down the path. It was almost completely dark, but he could distinguish the wheel of the bicycle ahead. He led the vehicle quickly to the outer part of the garden, and continued to the road. Then he hopped on, wet seat and all, and went triumphantly toward the town.

It was a pleasure to ride along the smooth-surfaced streets in the evening. The lights in the shops were doubly bright with their reflections shining from the wet pavements; the sidewalks were crowded with French people and Jews, most of them adolescents, who joked with each other as they met and passed. It was the hour when everyone who was able came out and walked up and down the Boulevard Poeymirau, covering only the few blocks between the Avenue de France and the Café de la Renaissance. At last it was cooler in the street than inside the houses and apartments.

Amar knew he had run up an enormous bill for the rental of his bicycle, for he had added the hours in his head, but still he was loath to give it up; only the fear that the shop might close, so that he would have to pay an extra twelve hours for the night, forced him now to the side street where the Frenchman stood smoking outside the door of his shop. He got down and led the bicycle across the sidewalk. The man looked at him suspiciously, took it from him and without saying anything began to inspect it with great care. Not being able to find any broken or missing parts, he wheeled it inside, and with a piece of chalk on a blackboard calculated the sum that Amar owed him. It was even more than he had expected. In his chagrin at hearing the figure, he forgot how he had arrived at his own estimate, so that he could not discover where the discrepancy lay. It was clear to him that the man was cheating him, but it was worth paying the difference to avoid an argument which could have got him nowhere but the *commissariat de police*. He was curious to know whether Mohammed had come back with the other bicycle, and, if he had, how he had paid for it, but even had he known how to speak the man's language, he would have thought it wiser to be silent. He untied his handkerchief, counted out the money and gave it to the man; the latter was watching him with an infuriating sneer which was only partly covered by the cloud of smoke that rose from the cigarette hanging at the corner of his mouth. It was only after he had left the shop and was walking along under the trees that he noticed how fast his heart was beating, and from that fact realized how badly he had wanted to hit the Frenchman. He smiled to himself; he had escaped from that trap, at least. The Ville Nouvelle was a succession of such traps. If you kept out of one you were likely to fall into another. It was not for nothing that the biggest and most imposing building on the Boulevard Poeymirau was the police station, or that outside it there was always a long line of jeeps and radio patrol cars that stretched around the block. That was why it was best not to come here at all. If you minded your own business in the Medina you were reasonably safe, but here, no matter what you did, you could suddenly be informed that it was forbidden, which meant that you disappeared for a month or two, and worked on the roads or in a quarry somewhere during that time. And if this had happened to you once, it was that much easier for it to happen a second time; your dossier always worked against you.

The nearest bus stop was on the corner opposite the police station. As he waited in line he observed with interest the abnormal activity in front of the main entrance. There was a great amount of coming and going of men both in and out of uniform. What was missing, however, was the usual contingent of Arab youths who were generally to be seen outside the door; these were petty (that is, non-political) informers and errand-runners, procurers of black-market cigarettes and other commodities for the police. He wondered what had happened to them.

When his bus finally came, he stood on its back platform.

The next stop was at the corner of the Avenue de France and the Boulevard du Quatrième Tirailleurs. From here you could see some of the lights of the Medina down in the valley. He watched the people crowding onto the bus: a Berber in a saffron-colored turban who acted as though he had never seen a bus before, a very fat Jewish woman with two small girls, all of them speaking Spanish rather than Arabic (the more presumptuous dwellers of the Mellah conversed in this archaic tongue; it was frowned upon, considered almost seditious, by the Moslems), an Arab woman wearing a *haik*, in whom Amar thought he discerned a prostitute from the *quartier réservé*, and several French policemen, two of whom had to hang to the railing outside because there was no possible way for them to squeeze themselves further. He expected the vehicle to continue straight ahead to the Taza road and go down the hill; instead it swung to the left and followed the Boulevard Moulay Youssef. "Ah, *khaï*, where does this bus go?" he asked of a workman covered with whitewash who was standing pressed against him. "The Mellah," said the man. "But the last one went to the Mellah," Amar protested. "This one should be going to Bab Fteuh." The man turned his head one way and then the other. Amar saw his face briefly in the light of a passing street lamp; he would have said it bore an expression of fright. "*Skout*," the workman said in a low voice. "There aren't any buses going to Bab Fteuh. Don't talk."

CHAPTER 10

Amar hesitated. If what the man said were true, then it was useless to get out and walk back to the corner to wait for the

right one. It would be quicker to go on to the Place du Commerce outside the Mellah and catch a bus going to Bou Jeloud
than to walk all the way to Bab Fteuh, and besides, the Taza
road was outside the walls in the darkness of the country. It was
not at all the kind of walk that he relished making: there were
far too many trees and streams along the way, places where evil
spirits, *djenoun* and *affarit* abounded, not to speak of Moslem
bandits and French police. It was better to continue this way,
even though he had to walk the length of the Medina afterward.

Before the bus roared into the Place du Commerce he realized that something quite extraordinary was going on there. At
first it was hard to tell just what: there was a great amount of
light, but it was light which was constantly changing and moving, so that the trees and the buildings appeared to be in a state
of flux. And the noise was unidentifiable: giant raspings that
seemed to be being dropped down into the square from the balconies—mass upon mass of meaningless, buzzing sounds that
reverberated between the walls. As the bus moved through the
open space that swarmed with people, the sound shifted, and he
could hear that there were other focal points of wild racket; each
loudspeaker was giving forth different noises, and the mechanisms were such that the noises had long ago ceased to bear any
resemblance to what they originally had been intended to sound
like. In front of the Ciné Apollon a samba might easily have
been pieces of scrap iron falling from a great height onto a
metal floor. In the corner between the public latrines and the
subcommissariat of police, the voice of a young man describing
a set of china that could be won in a lottery sounded like an
express train crossing a trestle. The young man may have been
conscious of this, for now and then he limited his message to
the simple, rapid reiteration of the one word *tombola*. A candy
stand whose machine was playing an Egyptian selection might
have been a range for machine-gun practice, and a soft-drink
bar whose concessionaire had chosen a pile of Salim Hilali records was making a series of sounds that would not have been
unusual coming from a particularly brutal abattoir. For this was
a *fechta*, a traveling fair, each of whose booths boasted a separate

gramophone and loudspeaker, and some were lucky enough to be furnished with microphone as well. The fair had come from Algeria, where its equipment had been bought second-hand, the purchaser rightly assuming that the uncritical audience of Morocco and the border towns of the Algerian desert, where it was destined to travel, would not hold it against him if paint were chipped and metal rusted and paneling patched. The important thing was to make it as loud and as bright as possible. Both these things had been done; where the lights were concerned, the impresario had managed even more than brightness. He had arranged it so that all the bulbs massed on the façades of the booths and strung through the branches of the trees continually flashed on and off, slowly, regularly, in great groups that worked independently of each other; the studied purpose of this was to induce first vertigo, and then euphoria.

Amar got out of the bus, surrendered his ticket to the inspector, and stood still for a moment, letting the chaos soak in. Then, already a little exalted, he moved toward a stand where some youths were pounding a platform with an enormous mallet. At each crash a vertical red bar shot up to what was assumed to be a height corresponding to the force of the blow, and a stout man with black teeth unenthusiastically pushed the bar back down to zero, crying either: *"Magnifique!"* or *"Allez, messieurs! Voyons, on est des enfants?"*

Amar wandered on to where a great crowd was gathered around two legionnaires shooting at a long procession of white cardboard ducks that moved jerkily in front of a panorama of palm trees and minarets. This place stood in the crossfire of two equally powerful loudspeakers. He moved ahead to the lottery: holding the microphone, the young man was bellowing: ". . . *bolatombolatombolatombola* . . ." Among the spectators, he recognized a boy from his quarter. They grinned at each other; it was all they could do under the circumstances. Further along, standing on a platform, an ape-like man with a two-day beard, wearing a red satin dress and long dangling earrings, his hands folded behind his head, was making the rudimentary motions of a *danse du ventre*. Seated on his right, gazing out with empty eyes over the heads of the crowd toward the invisible mountains at the east, was a girl wearing a kepi and a Spahi uniform, listlessly beating a snare drum. On his left stood a middle-aged woman, flashing an entire mouthful of gold teeth at the public as she smiled, crying into her microphone in a voice of iron: "*Entrez, messieurs-dames! Le spectacle va commencer!*"

The friend also had drifted here, and now stood next to Amar. "*Hada el bourdel,*" he shouted to him; Amar nodded sagely. The platform had been erected at the entrance of what he supposed must be a very expensive traveling brothel, and presently he was much astonished to see several Jewish women among those buying entrance tickets.

Now he moved ahead, to a kind of shed in front of which three mechanical dolls jiggled on a high pedestal. They were as large as children and wore real clothes. To Amar there was something indefinably obscene in the idea of putting good wool, cotton and leather on these dead, jittering objects; it outraged his sense of decorum. He stood watching their spasmodic movements, feeling a mixture of repugnance and indignation. One figure was playing a violin and opening and shutting a very wide mouth. A second banged together a pair of tin cymbals soundlessly, its senseless head turning from side to side atop its elongated neck. The third swayed back and forth from the hips as it pushed and pulled on a miniature accordion. The shifting light made their hesitant movements more plausible, at the same time removing them wholly from the world of reality and making them somehow believable inhabitants of another world that was all too possible, a pitiless world whose silence would be this crackling inferno of noise, and whose noon and midnight would shine with the same shadowless glare. "*Le Musée des Marionettes!*" cried an Arab boy at the door. "*Dix francs, messieurs! Dix francs, mesdames! Juj d'rial! Juj d'rial! Juj d'rial!*"

After a prolonged inner debate on the seemliness of his being observed entering such a place, since almost all the people who were going in and coming out were country folk and Berbers, he decided that not too much opprobrium would attach to his buying a ticket and going in. The museum consisted of a Ushaped corridor with a row of glass exhibit-cases along the inner wall. It was brightly lighted, and crowded with Moslem women in various stages of mirthful hysteria. Why they found the exhibits funny to such a degree he could only guess; to him they were only mildly amusing. All of them were crudely caricatured scenes of life among Moslems: a schoolmaster, ruler in hand, presiding over a class of small boys, a fellah plowing, a drunk being ordered out of a bar. (This last he considered a gross insult to his people.) The scenes which delighted the women so much that they could scarcely move away from them were those showing Moslem females. One was a domestic drama, in which the wife sat with a mirror in one hand and a whip in the other; her husband was on his knees scrubbing the floor. Back and forth twitched the woman's head: she would raise the mirror and gaze into it, and then she would turn to the man and deliver a blow with the whip. At that instant without fail there would be a renewed scream of laughter from the white bundles clustered in front of the glass. The other scene was the interior of a bus, where a man sat next to a woman in a *djellaba*. Here she would lower one side of her veil, disclosing a hideous face, and replace it just as the man's head swung around toward her. It was a less complicated game than the other, but being highly improper it evoked equal merriment on the part of the feminine spectators. Amar stood for a while watching, and thought: "This is the way the Nazarenes corrupt our women, by teaching them how whores behave." He wanted to say it aloud, but the prospect of having so many women turn and stare at him intimidated him, and he strode out into the street with as intense an expression of disgust on his face as he could muster.

"... *latombolatombo* ..." cried the young man of the lottery. Now he held an alarm clock in his hand, now a great, fat doll dressed in pink satin, whose eyes, Amar noted with interest, opened and shut when she was bent forward or backward. "Like a cow's eyes," he thought, and he wondered what made them work, even as he was conscious of hating the idea that he should be interested at all in such childish nonsense. They would forbid things like this, he was certain, when the Moslems took power. By what right did the French assume that such absurdities would amuse the Moroccans? The fact that they *were* amused by them was beside the point; they would have to change. He could imagine the French coming here from the Ville Nouvelle, not to look at the exhibits, but to be entertained by watching the Moslems look at them. Is it my fault, Mohammed Lalami had said, if the people of Morocco are donkeys? There he was right.

He found himself being pushed from behind toward the long counter where the prizes were displayed. There were sets of shining aluminum cooking utensils, tablecloths and mantillas draped over the counter, umbrellas hanging by their crooks, fountain pens arranged by the score in designs on sheets of painted cardboard, table lamps with red bulbs in them, flashing on and off, along with all the other lights, and even a small radio, which the young man now and then announced would be given as a special prize to anyone who picked the winning number three times in succession. This detail was lost on Amar, who was thinking that it would be a wonderful thing for a man to have his own radio right in the room with him. So far he had seen them only in cafés. "For thirty francs," the young man was crying, "you can have this magnificent apparatus." That much Amar did understand, and at the risk of being laughed at by the onlookers (for one never knew quite what was happening in the world of the Nazarenes) he worked his way ahead to the edge of the counter and held out thirty francs. Of course, it was wrong; he saw that immediately in the expression on the young man's face. "Only one number at a time!" he shouted to the crowd, as though they all had made the same mistake. "Only ten francs!" He took one coin from Amar's hand. "*Messieurs-dames!* This time it will be Monte Carlo! Players will choose their own numbers! Only five players! One more?" Someone at the far end of the counter raised his hand; a girl working at that end took his coin. "*Les numéros?*" The players called their choices.

The only number Amar was certain of pronouncing correctly was *dix*. He said the word clearly; the young man seemed satis-

fied, turned and spun the disk that was affixed to the wall, moving
the microphone so that it picked up the clicking sound made by
the metal flange as it hit the large pins that marked the numbers.
The clicking slowed down, the wheel stopped, and Amar saw
with more terror than satisfaction that the indicator was without
a doubt directly over a thin yellow slice of the disk which bore
the number ten. "*Numéro dix!*" shouted the young man without
emotion. The girl at the other end reached out nonchalantly and
took up a strange-looking object which she tossed to the an-
nouncer. The Christians and Jews, and doubtless some of the
Moslems watching, recognized it as a rag doll which was meant
to be a comic representation of a French sailor. It had a pot-belly
and a hideous painted face, but its uniform and headgear had
been made with an eye to detail. The young man held it up so
everyone could admire it; then he handed it to Amar.

For Amar this was a minor crisis: he did not want to accept
the thing, but he knew it was the only possible procedure. If he
refused it, there would be roars of laughter from the onlookers,
the loudest and most derisive of whom would be the Moslems.
He reached up, seized the doll by its neck, and without paying
any attention to the young man's question as to whether or not he
wanted to take another number, burrowed through the crowd
until he reached its outer edges. He stood still for a moment in a
comparatively deserted space outside the entrance to the school.
The problem was to find a sheet of paper in which to wrap his
prize; he could not very well walk through the streets carrying it
this way. It would be worth the money, he decided, to buy a
newspaper; that would certainly be the quickest way to hide it.

There were usually two or three newsboys on the other side of
the *place*, in front of the large café where the bus drivers got their
quick glasses of coffee or wine. As he was making his way around
the periphery of the square under the trees, all the lights and
loudspeakers went off. For a second there was complete silence
and darkness, as if a giant breath from above, extinguishing the
light with one puff, had also blown everyone away. Then on all
sides a great sound rose up—the sound a thousand or more people make when they all say: "Ahhh!" at once. Even when that

sound had died down, everything was different from what it had been a minute before; it was like being in another city. Now Amar saw that it was not really dark. Through the leaves of the trees overhead the stars were very bright, and here and there at the far side of the square was a food stall lighted by the single spurting flame of a carbide lamp. When he had got across to the other side he stood still, listening through the vast babble for the high voice of a newsboy crying: *Laa Viigiiie!*, but the sound did not come. In the breeze that blew by his face he was conscious of the heavy smell of wet earth and the smoke of burning oil from ten thousand kitchens behind the walls of the nearby Mellah. Suddenly he was extremely hungry. He determined to go home now, taking the first bus that left for Bab Bou Jeloud. It would not do to arrive back home too late, in any case: they might suspect that he had not been to work.

Again he stood on the back platform, as the bus rolled through the dark Mellah. There was more light crossing Fez-Djedid, perhaps because the proprietors of the cafés and shops had had time to bring out candles, oil lamps and tin cans filled with carbide. A good many legionnaires got off at Bab Dekakène, to pass the evening in the *quartier réservé* of Moulay Abdallah.

When the bus got to Bou Jeloud, he waited until everyone had left the vehicle, and then stepped inside the dimly illumined interior. There on a seat was what he was looking for—a newspaper. Quickly he snatched it up, before the driver should see it. He was still wrapping the doll as he walked under the great arch of the gate. Emerging on the other side, he was unpleasantly startled to collide with a figure that had stepped in front of him, its arm raised to halt him. He recognized a *mokhazni* in uniform.

"What's that?" The *mokhazni* pulled the bundle out of Amar's hands and ripped the paper off. The doll fell limply forward against his arm; he held it out and fixed the beam of his flashlight on it. Then he shook it and squeezed it between his fingers systematically, all over its body. Finally with a grunt he tossed it to Amar, who, fumbling in the darkness, dropped it. "*Cirf halak,*" said the *mokhazni*, as though it were Amar who had done the bothering. "Get out of here." And he returned to the shadows where he had been waiting.

"Son of a dog," Amar said between his teeth, but so softly, he knew, that his words were covered by the sound of the voices of passers-by. He had heard of other people's having similar experiences recently, but the world in which he moved was so circumscribed, even geographically, that he had never until now come in contact with the new vigilance that was being exercised. He turned left into the covered *souks* of the Talâa el Kebira, now holding the doll by its feet, and so intent upon giving a semblance of variety to the string of curses he was muttering under his breath that he was not immediately conscious of the person walking beside him. Suddenly he turned his head, and in the flickering light from one of the meat stalls saw the older brother of Mokhtar Benani, a boy he often played with on the soccer field.

"*Ah, sidi, labès? Chkhbarek?*" he said, embarrassed, hoping first that the boy had not heard his private tirade, and next that he would not look down and see the absurd thing he was carrying. At the same time, his intuition told him that there was an element of strangeness, if not in the fashion of this salutation, in its very fact. There was no possible reason for the older Benani, whose first name he did not even know, to be stopping at this moment in the Talâa el Kebira to speak with Amar. Until now they had never exchanged a word; on various occasions this boy had come to the soccer field to fetch his younger brother, there often had been an argument involved in the fetching, and Amar remembered the older brother because he had never lost his temper or raised his voice during the discussions. Now that he heard that voice again, he marveled fleetingly. It had a rich, burnished quality which made it not quite like any other voice he had ever heard, and its mellifluousness was heightened by the fact that the boy used a large complement of Egyptian words in his phrases and pronounced the "*qaf*" perfectly. This last feat Amar considered wholly remarkable in itself; like most Fassiyine he was incapable of pronouncing the letter.

Amar was neither analytical nor articulate, but he generally knew exactly why he was following a particular course of behavior. If he had been asked at this moment why he did not utter a simple " *'Lah imsik bekhir"* and go on his way, he would have replied that Benani's voice was something pleasant in the world, and that he enjoyed listening to it. On his side, Benani may have been dimly conscious of this, for he seemed disposed to talk at some length, making discreet inquiries as to Amar's health and that of his family, as well as to his work and his general state of mind. "And the world," he said, at several junctures in the conversation. Amar was quite aware that he was referring to the political situation in Morocco, but he had no intention of showing that awareness here, nor, he imagined, did the other expect him to.

"Where are you going?" Benani finally inquired, shifting his position and glancing downward at Amar's hand, which he was holding as far behind him as he could.

"Home." Amar also turned imperceptibly, trying to keep the doll behind him in the dark.

"Why don't you eat with us? I'm meeting a few *drari* in the Nejjarine, and we're going to eat somewhere."

Amar ignored the question for the moment. "And Mokhtar?" he said. "Where's Mokhtar? Will he be there?"

Benani's lip curled scornfully before he said: "No. He won't be there. He has to study. These are older *drari.*"

He's trying to flatter me, Amar decided. He knows I'm Mokhtar's age. Still, he was curious to see why, and so he stood there.

"I've got to go home," he said. He knew that if his suspicion were correct, now would begin the cajoling, the pressing of the arm, the faint tugs at the sleeve and lapel.

He was quite right: all this did happen, and presently he found himself wandering slowly along the interminable dark street with him, downhill, downward, down, firm now in his conviction that Benani wanted something very definite from him.

CHAPTER 11

The café was like any other large street café in the Medina: bare and uncomfortable, with tables that rocked on their unequal legs, and chairs that threatened to collapse under the weight of the sitter. The plaster on the walls had been clumsily splashed with pink and blue paint to give a marbled effect; in many places it had cracked and fallen, and the mud of the outer wall was visible.

There were six of them. They had brought bread and olives with them, and now they sent out for skewers of lamb. At first they sat at a table near the *qaouaji's* booth, where the charcoal fire occasionally showered them with sparks. When the skewers of *qotbanne* arrived, they moved in a body to a small niche in the back which had no table and no chairs—only a width of matting on the floor and another strip around the walls. They exactly filled the niche, with two sitting along each side, and a newspaper spread out in the center.

The shameful problem of the sailor doll had been settled while Amar and Benani were still alone together. Mercifully Allah had decreed that Benani was to stop at a latrine halfway down the hill; Amar had seized that moment to fling it up into the network of rafters in the ceiling of the edifice, and it had flopped over one of them and stuck there. It was certain Benani had noticed that he had been carrying something, for Amar caught him looking surreptitiously toward the hand which he still held behind him as they emerged from the latrine. But now Benani could surmise as much as he liked; it did not matter.

The others were indeed older than Amar by a few years, all of them being seventeen or over. However, from the beginning they had been civil with him and had made an obvious effort to put him at his ease—an effort which was not entirely successful, since he could not help feeling out of place among them, yet being both flattered by and suspicious of their attention. It was Benani who sat beside him and joked with him; he seemed to have taken it upon himself to play the role of apologist for Amar that evening. If Amar made a remark with which the others appeared not to sympathize, he would either question Amar in order to get him to go on and be more explicit, or he would give them his own explanation of Amar's words. Unfortunately this seemed destined to happen again and again; although they all understood and spoke the same dialect, and used the same symbols of reference, it was as if they had come from separate countries.

The difference was principally in the invisible places toward which their respective hearts were turned. They dreamed of Cairo with its autonomous government, its army, its newspapers and its cinema, while he, facing in the same direction, dreamed just a little beyond Cairo, across the Bhar el Hamar to Mecca. They thought in terms of grievances, censorship, petitions and reforms; he, like any good Moslem who knows only the tenets of his religion, in terms of destiny and divine justice. If the word "independence" was uttered, they saw platoons of Moslem soldiers marching through streets where all the signs were written in Arabic script, they saw factories and power plants rising from the fields; he saw skies of flame, the wings of avenging angels, and total destruction. Slowly Benani became aware of this vast disparity, and secretly began to despair. However, his task for the evening was not that of trying to reconcile two points of view; it was something quite distinct from that. He knew that the others had completely lost patience with him for bringing them together with this ignoramus, this anomalous shadow from the world of yesterday; they felt that he should have taken care of him by himself. But he was convinced that it was his duty to conduct the gathering in the way he believed best.

"*Yah*, Abdelkader!" he called. "Let's have a Coca-Cola."

The *qaouaji* arrived with a bottle.

"Is it cold?" demanded Benani.

"Hah! It's cold and a half," the *qaouaji* informed him.

Benani took the bottle and offered it first to Amar. "Have a little," he urged him. As Amar tipped the bottle to his lips, Benani said to him casually: "Played any soccer recently?" Amar swallowed and said he had not. "Been swimming?" pursued Benani. "Today," Amar said, passing the bottle back to him. "A lot of people at Sidi Harazem?" Benani inquired. Amar said he had not been there. He decided to sit back and enjoy himself. The others with their sudden silence and watchful eyes had given the show away. He would offer no information except that explicitly demanded by Benani, and then he would confuse him by telling the truth. Nothing could be more upsetting, because one always judiciously mixed false statements in with the true, the game being to tell which were which. It was axiomatic that a certain percentage of what everyone said had to be disbelieved. If he made nothing but strictly true statements, Amar told himself, Benani would necessarily be at a disadvantage, for he would be bound to doubt some of them.

As he had foreseen, the casual conversation quickly turned into a grilling as Benani lost first his poise and then, at least partly, his temper.

"Oh, so you went to Aïn Malqa. I see."

"Yes."

"Then you came back."

Amar looked surprised. "Yes."

"You were just getting back when I met you?"

"No. I was at the *fechta.*"

"That doesn't start until eight," Benani said in an accusatory tone.

"I don't know. I wasn't there very long."

"You must have stayed late at Aïn Malqa."

"Not very. The sun was on top when I left."

Benani took a gulp of Coca-Cola and passed the bottle on to the boy on his right. Then he whistled for a moment, as if that little interlude might give the scene a semblance of naturalness.

"You must have stopped to sleep on the way back," he said presently.

Amar laughed. "No. I was looking for a place, but I couldn't find one. I got into somebody's orchard by mistake."

"Ay! That was dangerous. The French are shooting fast these days."

If he lied and pretended to have met no one and seen nothing, they would be convinced that he had understood more than he really had. The important thing was not to seem to have noticed anything very unusual about Moulay Ali.

"It wasn't a French orchard. It belonged to a Moslem."

"A Moslem?" echoed Benani in a tone of disbelief. "On the Aïn Malqa road?"

"You know, a Moslem with a motorcycle. Moulay Somebody. A little bald, and walks like an owl."

One of the boys laughed briefly. Benani winced with annoyance, but did not turn his head. Instead, he shut his eyes, as if he were trying to place the man.

"Moulay Somebody," repeated Amar.

Benani shook his head. "I don't know him," he said uncertainly.

"He lives in an old house."

"With his family?"

"I don't know."

"Did you go inside?"

"Oh, yes. He invited me in. . . . Look," said Amar suddenly. "If you want to know who was there and what they were doing, why don't you go and ask him?"

"Who, me?" Benani cried. "I don't know him. Why would I know him?"

"*Khlass!*" said Amar, smiling tolerantly. "You know him better than I do." And taking an even greater chance, he continued. "And you saw him tonight."

The others all sat up just a little straighter at that instant. Amar was delighted. He decided to try to clean up the disorder of the conversation.

"I can't tell you anything about your friend because I don't know him. But you don't want to know about him, anyway. You want to know about me. *Zduq*, ask me more questions."

"Don't be angry," said Benani. Amar laughed. "We're all friends. What difference does it make whose orchard you went into? He wasn't French and he didn't shoot you. That's the important thing."

It was as though Amar had said nothing; he saw that they were not going to be honest with him, and he wondered if it would give him a greater advantage to go on being honest with them, or whether he should stop and begin to play the game their way. He decided to go on a little further.

"At first I thought you spoke to me because you'd heard what I was saying in the Talâa, when I was talking to myself."

"Would that be a reason?" asked Benani.

So he did hear me, thought Amar, feeling more satisfaction at having discovered the truth about that. "It might be," he replied.

"*Enta hmuq bzef*," Benani said disgustedly. "You're crazy." One of the boys was whispering in the ear of another. The latter, whose face was bursting with very red pimples, suddenly spoke up. "At first you thought that, you say. But what do you think now?" Benani looked angrily at him; Amar hazarded the guess that it was because he had not managed to ask him that himself. He glanced out into the café. The place was empty. The *qaouaji* had shut the door and lay asleep in front of it. He looked at the faces of the five older boys and saw no friendliness in them.

"*El hassil*," he said slowly. "I don't know what to think."

He could not go on being truthful now; it was out of the question, because what he saw with complete clarity was that not only had Moulay Ali sent Benani after him to investigate him— he had instructed him to do it in the manner of the police; that is, without divulging anything on his side and using any means he saw fit, as long as he extracted the information. Benani had played his part too crudely for there to be any room for doubt. Probably more than anything Moulay Ali wanted to know what he had heard out there in the orchard house, how much he had understood and deduced, and whether he was going to hold his tongue.

He had not told them very much, he reflected, but perhaps he should have told them nothing at all. He looked down at his hands, saw the ring the potter had given him, and remembered the potter's warning. It was quite possible that some of these very *drari* sitting here with him had stabbed or shot an *assas* or a *mokhazni*; there was no way of knowing.

They were still looking at him expectantly.

"*El hassil,*" he said again. It was no use; he could not pretend innocence. "I think you want to know if my heart is with your hearts."

Benani frowned, but Amar could see that he approved of his reply.

"We're interested in your head, too," he said. "It's no good having a heart if you haven't got a head. You haven't got much of a head. That didn't matter until today. But now—" he looked at Amar fixedly—"you've got to have a head, you understand?"

He did understand perfectly. Benani was saying that since he had stumbled onto Moulay Ali he was necessarily involved; there was no way of pretending otherwise.

"I have a head, but no tongue," he said.

Benani laughed shortly. "I know, I know. They all say that. But after the first five minutes in the *commissariat* they have a tongue that would reach from Bab Mahrouk to Bab Fteuh. Until you get to the *commissariat* you need a head. It's only when you get there that you find out what sort of heart you have, and know what's more important to you, your own skin or your Sultan's faith in you."

Benani was watching him closely, probably to trace the effect of his words on Amar's countenance. This seemed scarcely the moment to recall Mohammed Lalami's words: "The Sultan will never come back, and the party doesn't want him back," but he could not help hearing them again in his mind's ear, as well as what Mohammed had said immediately afterward: "It's not the party's fault, is it, if the people of Morocco are all donkeys?" Benani was taking him for one of the donkeys, was telling him, in fact, that he had got to be one. The lie had to be at the center of any understanding he could have with these people. He nodded his head slowly, as if he were pondering the profound wisdom of Benani's statement.

"We're your friends," Benani said, leaning forward and wrapping the debris of the meal in the newspaper, "but you've got to prove that you know how to have friends."

What bad luck, Amar thought. He did not want any of them as friends. "*B'cif*," he said, "of course." He looked at them. There was the pimply one who seemed to consider himself Benani's henchman, a yellow-skinned, sickly one with thick glasses, a rather fat one who looked as though he had never walked farther than from the Kissaria to the Medersa Attarine, and a tall Negro whom he seemed to remember having seen at the municipal swimming pool in the Ville Nouvelle.

Benani sat up straight again, holding the folded paper in his hand. "*Rhaddi noud el haraj men deba chouich*," he said sententiously. "It's going to be war this time, not just games." Amar felt a thrill of excitement in spite of himself. "Do you know what's happened?" Benani went on, his eyes suddenly blazing dangerously. "Tonight five thousand partisans are sleeping outside Bab Fteuh. Did you know that?"

Now Amar's heart was beating very fast, and his eyes were wide open. "What?" he cried.

"It's no secret," said Benani grimly. He called to the *qaouaji*, who got sleepily to his feet and staggered to where they sat. "We're on our way," Benani told him. The *qaouaji* shuffled back to the door, opened it, and peered out. Then he shut it again. The four others rose, shook hands solemnly with Amar and Benani, and went to the door; the *qaouaji* let them out. Benani remained seated where he was, silently staring at the mat on the floor, and Amar, not knowing whether the audience was over or not, also merely sat, until the other, who was taking the precaution of waiting until those who had left should be completely dispersed, finally rose to his feet.

"You'd better not go outside the walls tomorrow," he said, "or you may not see your family for a long time. I'm going to walk home with you."

Amar protested politely, although he knew that Benani's decision had not been made through solicitude for his safety.

"*Yallah*," said Benani paying no attention to him. "Let's go." He paid the *qaouaji*, said a few words to him, and they stepped into the street. The arc-lights in the Medina were so sparsely placed that they had to walk awhile before they could tell whether the electricity was still cut off. It was, but Benani had a flashlight which he used from time to time. The wind was damp and the sky was still covered over. So far they had not met a single passer-by.

"It's going to rain," said Benani.

"Yes."

"But it won't last. Not at this time of the year."

Amar thought this a useless sort of thing to say. Only Allah could know whether it would rain and for how long. He held his tongue, however, and continued to walk along beside Benani. When they got to the entrance of his alley Amar said: "Here's my *derb*," and began to thank him and bid him good night. But apparently Benani wanted to see exactly where Amar lived. "I'll take you to your house," he said. "It's nothing."

"You'll have to come all the way back. There's no way out," Amar warned him.

"Nothing."

Even when Amar had knocked on the door, Benani did not leave. He stood against the wall where he would not be seen by whoever opened to let Amar in. It was Amar's father who called out: "*Chkoun?*" and who eventually, with a good deal of banging about and clinking of keys, swung open the door, shielding his candle from the wind with his key hand. Seeing Amar, sensing that there was someone with him, he held the candle up and out, trying to see beyond. "Where have you been?" he demanded querulously. "Who's with you?" Amar could not answer. Benani, now convinced that this house was not a false address, and, from the genuineness of the scene, that the old man was indeed Amar's father, darted off into the night, leaving Amar to cope with the situation. For once Si Driss's relief at seeing his son was greater than his anger at having waited for him.

"*Hamdoul'lah,*" he said several times, as he bolted the door and padded across the courtyard to wash his hands in a pail by the well. The doves shivered and fluttered once, startled at having been wakened.

Amar's principal desire was to get upstairs quickly, before the old man's mood changed. He stooped and kissed the sleeve of his father's *gandoura,* murmured: "Good night," and started up the first steps.

"Wait," said Si Driss. Amar's heart sank.

A minute later they both went slowly up the stairs, the old man first, carrying the candle, and Amar following. When they got to the top of the second flight Si Driss was panting, and reached for the support of Amar's arm. Inside his room Amar fixed the candle to the floor, and they sat down on the mattress.

His father leaned toward him, to see him better.

"*Yah latif!* What's the matter with your face?" he cried. "It looks like a rotten peach. How did that happen? Who hit you?"

"One," said Amar quietly. He did not expect his father to press the point, and he was right. The old man merely said despairingly: "Why do you fight?" The question that Amar was expecting: "Where have you been?" did not come. Instead, after a pause, his father asked him: "Have you seen anything?"

There was to be no punishment. Amar was astonished. "No," he said uncertainly.

"Tomorrow, *incha'Allah,* we must get up very early and buy whatever we can get. Who knows when it will begin? We have nothing in the house. Si Abderrahman will sell me fifty kilos of flour. That we can be sure of. The rest is in the hands of Allah."

"Yes," said Amar. He did not know what else to say.

The old man was shaking his head back and forth. "This time it will be very bad. The French have sent the Berbers to make war on us. May Allah save us all. Who knows what will become of us? There's not one gun in the Medina; they saw to that."

Amar comforted his father with inadequate phrases, secretly amazed that Si Driss should at last be taking politics so seriously, and uncomfortable to see that the calm he had always thought adamant was now shattered.

"You must sleep a little," said his father at last. "We have work to do tomorrow."

When he had gone, Amar lay wide-eyed, staring into the empty night. A light rain had begun to fall; beyond its soft sound there was only silence.

CHAPTER   12

The next day was not the day that Si Driss had feared it would be. The Berber troops outside Bab Fteuh stayed where they were, making their temporary quarters more comfortable for themselves. Rain fell quietly in the morning, but at noon it suddenly cleared, and a curtain of rising mist over the city made the light painful. Amar and his father had gone out at dawn, leaving Mustapha at home with the womenfolk, and had brought back the flour from Si Abderrahman's house, which was near by. Then they had scoured the Medina to find sugar, chickpeas, candles and oats. Almost all the shops had been boarded up, and at those which were doing business there were clusters of agitated men trying with cajolery, threats and pleas to buy food at normal prices. The food was there, but the few shopkeepers who were courageous enough to have remained open (for roving bands of young vigilantes were reported to be wrecking the shops in the center of the city) hoped to profit quickly by their daring. Tramping through the streets were groups of glum-faced French policemen who looked straight ahead with hard eyes. No children were visible, and there was a noticeable absence of young men.

Amar arrived at work only about an hour late. The potter was squatting on his terrace as usual, but there was no sign of his merchandise lying about; all the water jars, bowls and dishes had been stacked inside the shed. There was an unaccustomed silence lying over the mud village below, and the smoke rose from only a handful of ovens.

"*Sbalkheir*," said the potter, looking up at him unhappily. "I was afraid they'd caught you."

Amar laughed. "*Sbalkheir*," he replied. For a moment he was not sure whether Saïd meant the French or the Istiqlal, then his own doubt struck him as absurd; he could only have been referring to the French. "No, I had a lot of work to do for my father," he said, hoping that the potter would let it rest there and not press him for details.

"It doesn't matter," said the other, fingering his beard. "I'm going to close up anyway, until *they*—" he gestured with his head toward Bab Fteuh—"go back where they came from. Allah! There's a city of them out there. This is just the beginning. There'll be more tonight, and they'll be at Bab Guissa and all the other gates. They put them there first because of the sheep market. Only four days to the Aïd."

Amar's face fell. If that were the case, it meant that they would surely have no sheep to sacrifice this year at his house, because all the money had gone to buy the staples he and his father had just lugged home. He had not realized the time was so short; vaguely he had hoped that somehow between now and the festival there would be a way of amassing enough money to buy a sheep, even if it were a small one. The prospect of having no sheep at all was a social disgrace of enormous proportions, and one which the family had never yet had to face. "Four days," he said sadly. The warm rain suddenly fell with more force, spattering their legs with the mud from the roof. They shrank against the wall.

"There are a lot of fools out there buying sheep anyway," Saïd went on. "There'll be trouble. Wait; you'll see. In my *derb* this morning they beat up an old man who was leading his sheep home. They beat up the sheep too, left them both lying there against the wall in a heap." He grinned at the memory. Amar was listening incredulously.

"It's the only thing to do," Saïd continued. "What right has anybody got to make a feast when the Sultan is in prison in the middle of the ocean?"

"But it's a sin not to have the Aïd el Kebir," said Amar slowly. "Which is greater, the Sultan or Islam?"

The potter glared at him. "Sin! Sin!" he cried. "Is there any sin worse than living without our Sultan? Like dogs? Like heathens, *kaffirine?* There are no sins any more, I tell you! It doesn't matter what anyone does now. Sins are finished!"

Secretly Amar agreed with him, but he would have preferred to say all that himself. Coming from Saïd, it sounded a little silly. He was too old to feel that way, Amar thought.

Saïd's rancor had been aroused; his expression was distinctly unfriendly now. He seemed to think he was having an argument with Amar.

"At any rate," he grumbled, "I don't need you around here. I've let the others go. I don't need anybody. Who's going to buy jars now?"

Amar was thinking of the money the potter owed him. It was not much, but it was something. "And afterward?" he said.

"Afterward, come back. If there is any afterward," he added with a harsh laugh.

"We'll leave the money until then, Si Saïd." Amar looked at him dreamily; it was the soft, veiled look which is meant to hide the scheming behind the eyes, but no Fassi could mistake it. The potter jumped to his feet and dug into his pocket.

"No!" he shouted, holding out some bills. "I don't do things that way. Here."

Amar took the money with bad grace. He had hoped to gain two things by letting it go until later: prestige in the eyes of Saïd, and possibly a greater sum when the time for collection came, in the event that Saïd had forgotten the exact amount.

"Very good," he said hesitatingly, pocketing the money. "I'll be around now and then, to see you."

"*Ouakha,*" replied Saïd without enthusiasm. And as Amar moved away he called after him, possibly remembering the prosperity the boy had brought to his establishment, and feeling that he had been abrupt with him. "These are bad days, Si Amar. We're all unhappy. We speak quickly."

Amar turned, stepped over to the man, and kneeling, kissed the sleeve of his *djellaba*. "Good-bye, master," he said.

The potter looked down at him distraughtly and pulled him to his feet. "Good-bye," he said.

So now he was free again, Amar reflected, as he wandered back through the wet streets. On the one hand he was happy to feel that the world was open, that once more anything might happen; at the same time, he had enjoyed the sensation of building up his power and prestige, the feeling of moving toward something which he had had while he had been working at Saïd's. Now it had all been destroyed at one blow. But no man has the right to lament the arrival of the inevitable.

A string of donkeys came plodding through the narrow street, their panniers bulging with sand. "*Balek, balek,*" chanted the man at their rear. He wore a slit sugar sack over his head as a *djellaba* to protect his face from the rain. As he passed by, Amar for some reason looked down at the ground. There, directly in front of him, lay a twenty-rial coin in the mud. Swiftly he bent over and picked it up, murmuring: "*Bismil'lah ala maketseb Allah.*" And suddenly he was reminded of a similar occasion long ago, when he had been working at the brick factory in the Taza road. That time it had been more than a hundred rial that he had come upon, lying in the street unnoticed. Since he had been on his way to work, he had taken the money directly to his master. The man had flown into a rage, and flinging the money on the ground, had struck him in the face, a blow whose unexpectedness made it only more painful. "Is that money yours?" the man had demanded. Amar had said it was not. "Then why did you pick it up? Next time when you see something in the street, leave it there and go on your way." Then the man had sent a boy to Amar's home to fetch his father. When Si Driss had arrived, the master had given him the money and advised him to beat his son, but Si Driss had taken exception to the man's counsel and gently led Amar home, telling him that the man was right about the money, but wrong in his desire that

Amar be punished, and that he would find a new master else-where. A few days later he had installed him as a shoemaker's apprentice in the Cherratine. How many times, he wondered, had his father gone to protest the unjust treatment of his son by his employers? A great many times, certainly; Si Driss could not countenance even the smallest infraction of his conception of the Moslem code of justice, and on this account primarily Amar bore him an intense, undying love. Beyond the gates of justice lay the world of savages, *kaffirine*, wild beasts.

When he got home, his father and Mustapha were there, sit-ting quietly in the room off the courtyard, waiting while his mother and Halima prepared tea in the corner. His father was not surprised to hear that he was no longer working; he took the money that Amar handed him without saying anything more than: "Sit down and drink tea." (The twenty-rial piece, the gift from Allah, remained in his pocket, but he had given him all that he had collected from the potter.)

Mustapha sat there, looking even glummer than usual. He had not had any work in several weeks, and it had secretly irked him to see that Amar had stayed on at the potter's so long; now he could meet his brother's gaze with equanimity. The center of his life seemed to be elsewhere than at home—in the cafés of Moulay Abdallah most likely, Amar thought; around the house he was merely a hollow shell, grunting a reply if he were spoken to, but never coming to life.

"It's still swollen," said his mother, looking up at the bridge of Amar's nose from where she sat on the floor fanning the charcoal.

Si Driss sighed. "His nose is broken," he said gently.

"Ay, *ouildi, ouildi!*" she began, and burst into tears.

"It's nothing, woman," the old man said, looking at her sternly. But she was inconsolable, and abandoned herself to a fit of weeping. Halima continued the tea-making. When she had served the others, she handed her mother a glass and induced her to sip a little.

"Listen!" said Si Driss, raising a silencing finger. In the dis-tance there was the sound of strenuous chanting, as if the people who were doing it were walking very quickly. "The students," he said. It was hard to tell how far away they were, because there were none of the usual neighborhood noises. "Our soldiers," the old man added with bitterness.

"May Allah preserve them!" sobbed Amar's mother.

Mustapha spoke up unexpectedly. "Every tobacco store in the Medina is smashed."

"Good," said Amar.

Mustapha glared at him. "Good in your head," he growled.

Si Driss overlooked the impropriety of this exchange of conversation in his presence, motioning to Halima to refill his glass. Amar rose and went upstairs to his room. He sat on his mattress, thinking of what a useless and unpleasant man his brother was going to be. It seemed certain that Mustapha's present ill-humor was due solely to the fact that he had not been able to get any kif in the past few days. Probably his usual source of supply had been cut off by the trouble.

Now that there was a stock of food in the house, so that although they might not eat particularly well, it was unlikely that they would go hungry even if the trouble became very bad, Amar should have been relieved and felt more or less at ease. Not at all—he had never been more nervous and restless. He wanted to go out and be everywhere in the town at once, but it was still raining a little, and in any case he had the feeling that no matter where he went the streets would be empty, and that the sounds of activity would be coming from some distant, un-locatable spot.

He tried playing his flute for a few minutes, but it made an unreasonably loud noise in the middle of this quiet morning, an absurd and sour sound that finally made him toss it up onto a shelf between the broken alarm clock and the colored picture of Ben Barek the soccer idol, in his red and blue uniform. Then he stepped out onto the roof and tried to see beyond the nearby housetops, but the fine drizzle that was falling obscured everything. However, the sky was brightening. He went back in and lay down. The air was hot and breathless. Today even the roosters of the neighborhood seemed to have agreed to observe the general silence. And with only four days to go before the Aïd, it was incredible that there should be no sign or sound of sheep on the terraces. Never before had such a strange thing happened; in other years you could hear the bleating coming from every direction during the ten or fifteen days before the feast. Some families bought their animals as much as a month ahead of time, to be able to fatten them properly for the sacrifice. This year—silence, which was why he had not realized that the day was so close. If his father had been alone downstairs, he would have taken the unusual step of going down and discussing it with him. But Mustapha was there, and it was, after all, an affair between his father and Mustapha, in which he had no part. When the old man died, it would be Mustapha who would attend to the buying and killing of the sheep, not Amar.

And now he began to wonder what the outdoor ceremony of the Aïd at Emsallah would be like, with the Berber soldiers spread out there just below. It was the most important event of the year, upon which the prosperity and well-being of the city depended. There were always at least a hundred thousand people there, swarming through the cemetery and ranged across the hillside above it, come to watch the *khtib* slit the throat of the sheep sent by the Sultan, and to see whether the runners, who operated in wonderfully organized shifts, would arrive opposite the Andaluz mosque with it while it still breathed. This was essential, for if the sheep had expired before they threw it down at the feet of the *gzara*, it was a very bad omen for the coming year. But with Bab Fteuh blocked by the soldiers, how were the runners going to get through? Allah was watching them, each one of them must exert himself to the utmost; if their teamwork were faulty in passing the sheep from one group of four to the next, if one of them fell, if the way were not completely cleared, the sheep might breathe its last while they were still on the way, and although the final group might arrive in the courtyard with each man holding one of its legs in the most perfect position, it would all be in vain, and the city would suffer the displeasure of Allah for the entire year to come, until the fault could be obliterated at the next Aïd el Kebir.

It was intolerable that the gate should be barred by the presence of all those soldiers; the French could only mean it as a provocation. "They want us to try and break through, so their Berbers will shoot," he thought with sudden fury. Just as they had taken the Sultan away on the very day of the Aïd a year ago, to make sure that there could not possibly be any good fortune or happiness, so they were going to try and prevent the Moslems from finding favor with Allah again this year. The thought, once it had occurred to him, was too awful for him to keep it to himself. He bounded up from the mattress and ran down the two flights of stairs.

The family had finished tea, but they were still sitting just as before, save that his mother had moved onto the small mattress beside Halima. Her face was pink with weeping, and she looked scarcely older than the girl. Si Driss had married her when she was thirteen; she still had the flesh and force of a young woman. Amar looked at her now as he came into the room, saw the traces of tears on her face, knew that she had shed them for him because it hurt her to think of his becoming other than the way he was (even if were only a bone in his nose that had changed its shape) and felt a terrible urge to take her in his arms, kiss her cheeks and eyes. He sat down quietly, letting his arms hang at his sides. What he had it in his mind to say retreated from him for a short moment. When the awareness came that he and his mother had in some strange manner become the two focal points of attention on the part of the others, he forced himself out of his brief stupor, turned to his father, who was watching him with an uncomprehending expression on his face, and said: "What's going to happen at Bab Fteuh?"

"Who can know? With those devils there—"

"How are they going to get the sheep through?"

His father looked surprised. "There's not going to be any sheep. Don't you know that?"

Amar stared at him wildly. "But there has to be."

"There has to be, yes, but there's not going to be. It's the end of Islam, all this. Just as it was written. By the Moslems' own will."

Amar was aghast. "The Moslems'!" he cried. "The Moslems' own will!"

"Of course. Who forbade us to buy sheep, threatened to kill us if we did? The Wattanine. The friends of Si Allal, the Istiqlal, whatever you want to call them. Who goes snooping around to be sure nobody has a sheep on his roof? The boys from the Karouine with their schoolbooks under their arm, the friends of freedom. Who beats and stabs the people trying to carry out Allah's commandments? The same boys. Why? They say the *khtib* can't accept a sheep from Arafa because he is a French Sultan. They say there must be no rejoicing until Mohammed ben Youssef comes back."

"Arafa's not our Sultan," said Amar hesitantly.

"And was Si Mohammed?" asked his father, his eyes bright with excitement. During the Sultan's quarter of a century on the throne, Si Driss had never allowed a portrait of him to be hung in the house. Now that it was a prison offense to possess such portraits, although there were countless thousands of them hidden in the Medina, he felt somehow doubly righteous. "Remember *Hakim Filala*." And he proceeded to quote the saying that had been popular among malcontents ever since the beginning of the Alaoui dynasty three centuries back. " 'The reign of the Filala: it's not costly but it's not cheap. It's not noisy but it's not quiet. You have a king but you have no king. That's the reign of the Filala.' And that's the truth. Who let the carrion French into Morocco in the first place? A Filali. Don't ever forget that when you're listening to your friends tell you about the Sultan, the Sultan, the Sultan. . . ."

Amar knew all this perfectly, but to him it seemed a most inopportune moment to go over it. His father was really getting old. "But the soldiers at Bab Fteuh," he began. That at least was a hostile act which had clearly been instigated by the French.

"Use your head," said the old man. "The friends of freedom don't want the festival, and they'll stop it anyway, all by themselves. Don't you think the French know that? But the French can't afford to let *them* stop it. Then everyone would know how strong the Istiqlal is. If someone is going to do something, the French have got to be the ones to do it. They want just what the Istiqlal wants, but they want the credit. They have to make it look as though they were the ones who did it. They're all working together against us. In five years the children of Fez will be saying: 'Aïd el Kebir? What's the Aïd el Kebir?' No one will remember it. This is the end of Islam. *Bismil'lah rahman er rahim.*" He sat, staring vacantly ahead of him for a moment. No one spoke. "The fault is all our own," he went on presently. "Because Satan stands next to you, you don't make him your friend. There is sin everywhere now." Si Driss shook his head sadly, but his glittering black eyes looked dangerous.

Listening, Amar could not help hearing again the potter's words of only a few short hours ago: "Sins are finished." In some hideous, perverse fashion the two statements coincided. If there were no sins, then everything was necessarily a sin, which was what his father meant by the end of Islam. He felt the imperative and desperate need for action, but there was no action which could possibly lead to victory, because this was a time of defeat. Then the important thing was to see that you did not go down to defeat alone—the Jews and the Nazarenes must go, too. The circle was closed; now he understood the Wattanine whom the French called *les terroristes* and *les assassins*. He understood why they were willing to risk dying in order to derail a train or burn a cinema or blow up a post office. It was not independence they wanted, it was a satisfaction much more immediate than that: the pleasure of seeing others undergo the humiliation of suffering and dying, and the knowledge that they had at least the small amount of power necessary to bring about that humiliation. If you could not have freedom you could still have vengeance, and that was all anyone really wanted now. Perhaps, he thought, rationalizing, trying to connect the scattered fragments of reality with his image of truth, vengeance was what Allah wished His people to have, and by inflicting punishment on unbelievers the Moslems would merely be imposing divine justice.

"*Ed dounia ouahira,*" he sighed. "The world is a difficult place." He looked out into the courtyard: the drizzle had ceased entirely, and the sun was beginning to break through the mist. He decided to go out, but at the very moment he was making the decision his mother spoke.

"You mustn't go out again today. This is a bad day."

Amar turned hopefully to his father. "Let him go," the old man said. "He's not a woman. Tomorrow will be worse."

"I'm afraid," she complained. Amar smiled.

CHAPTER   13

In the street he walked along looking at the mud that oozed up around his toes at each step; the covered stretches were dry, and there the dust lay thick on the ground. Wherever there was a pile of fish heads or some donkey manure, the flies were innumerable; they rose in black swarms and settled again quickly. What good was it to have the *baraka,* he was thinking, and to be different from everyone else, if you could do nothing for your people? Something terrible was going to happen—of that he was convinced—yet it was of no help to know it. The tautness that had been going on for so long was at last going to break, the blood was ready to come out and spill on the ground. And no one wanted to prevent it; on the contrary, the people were eager to see it, even if it was to be their own blood.

Each shop-front along the way was boarded up and padlocked. The narrow alleys seemed hotter for being deserted. Occasionally a man passed, walking quickly, the rustling of his garments audible in the silence. "As though it were late at night," Amar thought. He stood still suddenly. The long empty vista of the

Souk Attarine, with its pale sunlight filtered into thousands of small squares by the latticework overhead, looked like a dried river bed stretching off into the dusty distance. The strong smell of all the spices was there as always, but the small squares of sunlight that should have been moving up and down hundreds of *djellabas* and *haiks,* as their wearers wandered beneath the trellises, lay flat on the ground in still, regular patterns.

From the street of the lawyers' booths at his left came the long mechanical whine of a beggar. Again and again he heard the sound, repeating exactly the same words in exactly the same way. "Poor man," Amar said to himself. "He'll starve today." He started to walk again, more deliberately, as though he were beginning to derive a small amount of pleasure from it. The street bore to the left, became very narrow, and opened upon a tiny square lined with shops where the students of the Karouine bought their textbooks. The beggar's voice was still clearly audible. He turned back and down the alley where he knew the man would be sitting. He found him further along than he had expected, squatting with his back against the wall, a crude staff in one hand, his face with its two purplish eyeless sockets raised toward the absent multitude, chanting his endless song. He was a young man with a full, pointed black beard and very white teeth. Amar stopped walking and stood watching him for a moment. Someone had given him a fairly new *djellaba,* but beneath it, around his legs, nameless rags emerged, and his turban was yellow with dust. In the direction from which Amar had just come, above the man's sharp litany, he now heard the confused sound of voices and cries. As he debated whether to go toward them or away from them, he realized that they were approaching rapidly, and that mixed with the shouts were other less usual noises, the indefinite scufflings that accompany a struggle. For a moment he considered stepping over to the beggar, seizing his turban, putting it on his own head so that it would cover part of his face, and sitting down beside the man. But then it occurred to him that the beggar, being blind, might not understand quickly enough, in which case he could still be demanding an explanation as the others came into view. Instead, he turned and rapidly scaled the façade of the stall behind him, using the iron bolts as rungs for his bare feet. It took a big effort to hoist himself to the roof, because there was nothing to grasp at the top, but he made it, and silently. Up here, and on the other formless roofs of the shops in the alley, everything was a jumble of packing cases, broken iron bedsteads, waste paper and rags. A gaunt cat stared at him malevolently from atop a roll of rotten matting a few roofs away. Carefully he lay face downward, his head behind a battered washtub, and peered around its crooked edge, up the alley.

Soon they came into view, surrounded by a cloud of dust. About twenty young men were walking with comparative swiftness in a tight group; in their midst, struggling to break through to the outside, and being propelled ahead with the aid of shoves and blows, were two powerfully built *mokhaznia*, their navy blue uniforms hanging from them in strips, so that parts of their bare chests and shoulders showed through. As they heaved themselves desperately against the living wall that imprisoned them, strange sounds like sobs came from their mouths, and their eyes rolled back and forth in their heads like the eyes of madmen. Their faces and necks ran with blood from the blows they had received. In fact, everyone was spattered with it, the captors scarcely less than their prisoners. The dust that was in the air around them they had raised a few paces back, where the alley was covered; now they slid clumsily in the mud. If one of the men began to fall, he was kicked into an upright position by a dozen feet around him. From the corner of his eye Amar saw the cat flatten itself to the roof and, sliding away like a serpent, disappear.

Above the chaos the beggar's voice continued its hopeful chant, louder than before. He must be crazy, Amar thought, not to realize what was going on right in front of him. But now, when they were directly below him, so that Amar could have spit into their midst, there came the sound of shouts and police whistles from the brighter end of the alley, toward Ras Cherratine. It was as if an electric shock had passed through all of them at the same instant. Everything happened with lightning speed. The two *mokhaznia* made two final, superlative lunges in opposite directions. The circle gave momentarily; several of the young men lost their balance. Amar felt the impact of their bodies against the wall below him. But at the same time the knives briefly mirrored pieces of the sky; those left standing closed in. One *mokhazni* screamed: "Ahhh!" and the other fell soundlessly. The young men stumbled over each other as they fled back the way they had come. Amar saw the faces of some of them as they panted their final curses above the two figures lying on the ground. They too looked like madmen, he thought, but he had a powerful and senseless desire to be one of them, to know what they had experienced as they had felt the blades of their knives going inside the enemy's flesh.

Now they were gone, and the beggar was still singing, like some insect in a summer field; if he had moved his right leg forward he would have kicked the head of one of the *mokhaznia*. But he did not move; his face remained tilted upward at the same angle, and his mouth continued to move, forming the holy words. The French would be there in a minute, and they would doubtless drag the poor blind man off to jail as a witness; they were capable of such incredible stupidity.

Amar had raised his head now, and was rapidly examining the topography of the rooftops. It would not be good to be caught up here, but if he jumped down into the alley it was likely that he would fail to get to either end of it before the police arrived. He scrambled to his feet, and carefully stepping over the objects whose contact would give off sound, made his way along the string of roofs until he came to the wall of a higher building. A ledge built the length of this led back from the alley and became a narrow wall dividing two courtyards. Feeling no dizziness and keeping his eyes fixed firmly on his feet, he moved along the top of the wall to its end, and hoisted himself onto another roof there. Looking backward for an instant, he saw that an old woman in the courtyard immediately below was watching his progress with interest. That was bad. "Look the other way, grandmother," he said, glancing about the clean-swept surface of the cube-like structure on which he stood. There must be a street somewhere near by.

The old woman's voice came up from below: "May Allah bless you." Or had she said: "May Allah burn you?" He was not sure which: the two Arabic words sounded so much alike. At the edge he peered down; there was another wide roof considerably lower than the one where he was at the moment. Further down at the side he saw a marble-paved court, with a small orange tree in each corner, but the angle was such that he could not tell whether or not the street lay beyond. If he jumped down onto the roof it would make a noise; he would have to continue quickly, and it was too far to climb back up to where he stood now. Even had there been no trouble in the city, for him to be caught on the roofs would have meant being taken to jail: the roofs were for the women. A man climbing from terrace to terrace could be only one of two things: a thief or an adulterer. Today of course it was worse. They would simply shoot at him. He said a short prayer, let himself hang down as far as he could, and dropped the rest of the way. If there were people inside the building, they had certainly heard the noise he made when he hit. He ran to the other end of the roof, saw the empty street below, and dropped again, landing very hard with his bare feet flat in the mud. It was a small complicated alley with a great many dead ends where there were merely doors on all sides, and he had to follow several false leads until he had found the exit passage, a little wider than the others, which, after rounding three corners, at last led out into another alley that in turn gave on a through street. Unless one knew a particular *derb* by heart, one could always be fooled. He had come out into the basket *souk*, but how strange it looked, completely boarded up and deserted! If only one among its several dozen shops had been open, it would still have been itself, but this way, only its distinctive shape, its steeply sloping floor and the hundreds of bunches of tiny green grapes that hung from its lattices above made it recognizable.

He decided that for the moment he was safe, that no one had

seen him jump down, and he began to walk. When he turned
the corner of the small street that led to the gate of Moulay
Idriss, he realized that he would have done better to go in the
other direction. A group of French police stood by the gate
ahead of him. He hesitated, started to turn around.

"*Eh, toi! Viens ici!*" one of them called. Reluctantly he
walked toward them. If he had gone the other way, he could have
got up through Guerniz, he reflected, but he had come this way.
Visions of torture flitted across his mind. They put you between
vises and turned the screws until your bones cracked. They covered the floor of your cell with pails full of slippery soap and
then smashed bottles on it, then they made you walk back and
forth naked, and you kept falling, until you had pieces of glass
sticking out of you all around, like the top of a wall. They horse-
whipped you, burned you with acids, starved you, made you
curse Allah, put strange poisons into you with needles, so that
you went crazy and answered whatever questions they asked
you. And always they laughed at you, even at the moment when
they were beating you. They were laughing now, looking at him,
perhaps because it was taking him so long to get to them, for he
felt that he was scarcely moving at all. When he got fairly near,
the one who had called to him began to speak in a loud voice,
but Amar had no idea what he was saying. He stopped walking.
The policeman roared: "*Viens ici!*" That he did understand. He
moved ahead once again. The man stepped toward him and
grabbed him roughly by the shoulder, talking angrily all the
while. Unexpectedly he pushed him against the side of a stall
behind him, banging his head on the long iron bolt. His movements were sudden, unforeseeable, violent. Now with one enormous red hand across Amar's throat he pinned him against the
wall, while another man lazily approached and looked at him,
smiling. This one also spoke to him. He stuck his hands into
Amar's pockets, felt everywhere in the creases of his clothing—
silently Amar gave fervent thanks to Allah for having directed
him to leave his folding knife at home—and then struck him
once on the cheek with the back of his hand. At this point he
walked away, as if he were disgusted, either at the contact with

Amar's flesh or at not having found what he had been looking
for. The first man removed his hand from across Amar's neck,
hit him once on the same cheek, exactly as the other had done,
and gave him a violent push which sent him sprawling. Amar
looked up at him, expecting to see the man's boot approaching
to kick him or stamp on him, but he had turned away, and was
sauntering back toward the others. "*Allez! Fous le camp!*" said
one who was leaning against the side of the archway. Amar sat
up in the muddy street and looked at them; something about his
expression—perhaps its mere intensity—displeased one of the
other men, for he called the attention of the man beside him to
it, and they both came forward toward him, slowly and menacingly. Now his intuition whispered to him that the safe thing
to do was to get up and run as fast as he could, that that was what
they wanted to see. But he was determined not to give them that
satisfaction. With exaggerated care he picked himself up, and not
looking at any of them, took a few steps away from them.

Out of prudence he decided to compromise on a limp. And so,
clutching at the door of a shop now and then for support, he
made his slow progress down the street, sure that from one second
to the next a blow would come from behind. When he finally
looked back, at a point beyond the exit into the basket *souk*,
the walls of the passageway had curved sufficiently to hide the
men from his view. He stopped limping and went on to a public fountain, where he laboriously washed the mud from the
legs of his trousers. There was not much he could do about the
seat of them. The sun was strong now; he sat awhile by the fountain letting it dry the large wet patches he had made on the
cloth.

Merely sitting still this way, gazing down the empty street,
helped to calm the churning he felt inside his chest. He had just
seen two Moslems killed, but he had not felt even a stirring of
pity for them: they were in the pay of the French, for one thing,
and then they had surely committed some unspeakable crime
against their own people to have been singled out that way for
annihilation. Although he was grateful for having been vouchsafed the spectacle of their death, he wished it might have been

slower and more dramatic; they had fallen so quickly and unceremoniously that he felt a little cheated. Under his breath he began to invent a long prayer to Allah, asking Him to see to it that every Frenchman, before he was dragged down to Hell, which was a foregone conclusion in any case, might suffer, at the hands of the Moslems, the most exquisite torture ever devised by man. He prayed that Allah might help them discover new refinements in the matter of causing pain and despair, might show them the way to the imposing of hitherto undreamed-of humiliation, degradation and agony. "And drop by drop their blood will be licked by dogs, and ants and beetles will crawl in and out of their shameful parts, and each day we will cut away one more centimeter from each Frenchman's entrails. Only they must not die, *ya rabi, ya rabi.* Never let them die. At each corner of the street let us have one hung up in a little cage, so when the lepers come by they can use them as latrines. And we will make soap of them, but only for washing the sheets of the brothels. And one month before a woman is to give birth we will pull the child out and make a paste of it and mix it with the flesh of pigs and the excrement from the bellies of the Nazarenes' own dead, and feed their virgins with it."

It took energy to invent these fantasies; soon he tired of it, and with a final impassioned invocation, to make his impromptu prayer more formal, he rose and started on his way once more. By taking back streets he might be able to get all the way up to Bou Jeloud. The emptiness of the city spurred him on; he wanted to be in the midst of people. Up there, in the large cafés, there was sure to be at least someone.

CHAPTER 14

He went ahead, up the long steep hill through Guerniz with its great high houses on either side of the street. Here there was always the sweet smell of cedar wood and the gurgling of water behind the walls. A goat stood under an arch and looked out at him with its questioning yellow eyes. Through these streets and squares an occasional well-dressed man hurried, on his way to some nearby house for lunch, and looking askance at Amar, with his battered face and muddy European garments. Each time he caught this expression of fastidiousness mixed with fear he smiled to himself: the ones who wore it were not friends of freedom. It was a sure way of telling. They had what they wanted in this world, and they shared no desire with the students and other youths to see the world change. At the same time it was dangerous to try to judge people's sympathies by their appearance: there were many wealthy men who gave their money and time to the Istiqlal, and by no means all of the poor agreed with, or even understood, the party's program, although the party made constant bids for the favor of the lower classes.

But he would have staked all he possessed on his conviction that these few men he saw now taking their quick dainty steps along the streets of Guerniz were afraid—afraid of what might happen as a result of the present crisis. France might lose part of her power to protect the system under which they lived and prospered. Then thoughtfully he asked himself how he would feel if his father still owned the land at Kherib Jerad, and the orchard by Bab Khokha, and the three houses in the Keddane, if all of that, as well as the oil press and the mill, had not long since been sold and the money spent. While he was posing this question to his conscience and waiting for a reply to come out, his attention was distracted by the sound of wild cheering from the direction of the Talâa. Where there was a crowd, that was where he wanted to be. Abandoning his decision to use only the back streets, he cut through the nearest alley that led off to his right, and was almost running when he came up against the first by-standers, trying to witness things from a safe distance. He zig-zagged ahead until he reached a point where there were so many men packed into the narrow alley that he was unable to push his way further. He could see nothing at all, but he could hear the shouting and singing. Occasionally the men beside him, from whom the procession was likewise hidden, took up a chanted refrain, and filled the small space around them with resonant sound. Not Amar: it would have embarrassed him to open his mouth and shout or sing along with them. It was part of his nature to push his way to the inside and yet at the last mo-ment to remain on the outside. When the time came he always found it difficult to participate; he could only grin and be thrilled by the others. His friends had long ago given up trying to instill in him a sense of teamwork on the soccer field. His principal in-terest there was in the brilliance of his own plays. Sometimes they would ask him if he thought he were playing alone against both teams. When they complained he would say impatiently: "*Khlass!* Was that a good pass or wasn't it? Do you want me to play or don't you? Just tell me that much and then shut up. *Khlass men d'akchi!*"

Now he stood here awhile, listening and looking at the men around him. They were ordinary people: small shopkeepers, arti-sans and their apprentices, all of them carried away by the excite-ment of the moment. The students marching in the Talâa were carrying portraits of the former Sultan; they were bound to meet the police when they got to Bou Jeloud, if not before, and there would be a fight. But that was what they wanted. They were un-armed, and they knew the French would attack. Each one se-cretly hoped to become a martyr; it would be almost as glorious as death on the battlefield. Amar wanted to see their faces and admire them, but being shut off from them he could feel only an abstract sympathy which was easily replaced by impatience. Soon he fought his way out of the crowd and returned the way he had come. It was possible that further up the hill he could double back to the Talâa above the head of the procession and catch it there. But each alley he chose was equally crowded, and he had to keep turning around and continuing upward on the parallel thoroughfare. When he got to Ed Douh he took a way that not everyone knew about, going down a flight of steps, across a public latrine, and out the other side, along a passage so narrow that if two people were to meet each other, one had to stand flat against the wall while the other squeezed through. The sun was very strong now, and the mud had dried almost completely. Down in here the stench was terrible; he hurried along, trying to breathe as seldom as possible until he arrived at the Talâa a little below the house of Si Ahmed Kabbaj. The cortege had not yet arrived, no police were in sight, and people were lined up along the sides of the thoroughfare or dashing excitedly from one side to the other. Amar knew where he wanted to go: it was a café one flight up, above a grocery store, a little way inside the Bou Jeloud gate.

The place was full, everyone was talking very loud, and there was not a single place to sit. Disappointed, he resigned himself to staying in the back room. If something happened outside, he could always run through and watch from one of the windows.

Even in the inner room there was not much choice in the way of places to sit. He found a table in the corner furthest from the main room; two men were already seated there playing dominoes, probably because all the cards and chess sets were in use, but there was space on the bench for another. When the boy came by, Amar ordered half a bread and a salad of tomatoes and turnips.

The conversation around the café, although it never touched on the situation of the day, was louder and more animated than it would have been normally. A sizable group of men stood at each window that gave on the street, merely waiting. When Amar's food came, he murmured "Bismil'lah" and ate it ravenously, sopping up the almost liquid salad with small pieces of bread. Then he sat awhile quietly, prey to a growing impatience; it spread from his chest upward and downward, so that he drummed with his fingers on the bench and the table, and jiggled his feet. The domino players looked up from their game now and then, and stared at him, saying nothing. Even if they had spoken he would not have minded. The day was important and glorious; he felt that much with a conviction which increased every moment. Whether it presaged joy or misery was unimportant; it was different from all other days, and by virtue of that fact alone, it deserved to be lived differently.

Then suddenly he made an important decision: to leave here and have tea at the Café Berkane, which was just outside the walls, beyond the bus stop. Benani had warned him to stay inside the walls today, but after all, Benani was not his father. He called the boy, complained about the food, refused to pay, then did pay, joked awhile with the proprietor, and left smiling. It was excessively hot in the open square, and there was still no sign of the demonstration. Slowly he walked up to the big gate and passed under its main arch, out into the world of motors and exhaust fumes. He had never seen so many policemen; they were lined up all around the outer square, against the walls, along the waiting room for the buses, in front of the Pharmacie de la Victoire, and as far up the road as he could see—many more than there had been the year the Sultan had come on a visit. This was very fine, and he was delighted that he had taken the courageous step of coming outside the Medina. They were all enemies, of course—he did not lose sight of that fact—but they looked admirably impressive in their uniforms, massed this way around the periphery of the square, and they had various models of guns with them which he had not seen before. It was decidedly worth seeing.

The Café Berkane, a fairly new establishment, had made use of a long, narrow strip of land between the ramparts of the Casbah Bou Jeloud and one of the branches of the river. The entrance to the building was reached by going across a small wooden footbridge, but there were generally tables on the outer side of the stream as well, scattered here and there under the delicate vertical fronds of the pepper trees. Today, however, the tables had not been put out, and the space usually given over to them was empty save for a few policemen who had been stationed there out of the glare, glad to be even in the thin, powdery shade that was half sunlight. Amar expected them to stop him as he approached the little bridge and perhaps search him again, or forbid him to enter, as if he were crossing a frontier, but they seemed not even to notice him.

The interior here, in contrast to the place he had just left, was almost deserted, and the few clients who occupied tables, if they spoke at all, conversed quietly, almost in whispers. This was most unusual; Amar quickly decided it was because they realized that they were outside the walls, and consequently felt less sure of themselves with regard to what this strange day might bring forth. Then, of course, there was the fact that those who sat near the windows and door had a clear and sobering view of the policemen standing out there in the sun. There were several rooms in the Café Berkane, all but one of which had windows on the front, directly over the water; if you spat or dropped a cigarette butt out, it landed in the river and was rapidly rushed downstream. The other room, a small afterthought tacked on to the back of the building, had an entirely different atmosphere: instead of facing north it faced south and east, and its view consisted of a section of the massive rampart walls and a square basin of still water—nothing more. The water in the pool was not deep—perhaps a meter—nor was it stagnant, since it was connected with the stream by a channel which went under the café. The owner had meant to plant bamboo and iris around its edge and to have water lilies floating on its surface; it had seemed such an excellent idea at the time he had built the café that he had been willing to spend the money for the cement to make the basin. Once he had opened the establishment, however, he had forgotten his original intention, and now the edges of the pool were ragged with masses of dying weeds, encouraged by the proximity of water but weighted down with the constantly descending dust from the nearby square. The small back room was the one Amar preferred, because it was the quietest, and the still water seemed to him more desirable and rare than the moving stream: in Fez rushing water was no novelty.

He knew just which table he wanted. It was behind the door, beside the window, all by itself. Often when he was not working he had come here and sat an entire afternoon, lulled by the din and music from the other rooms into a stage of vague ecstasy, while he contemplated the small sheet of water outside the window. It was that happy frame of mind into which his people could project themselves so easily—the mere absence of immediate unpleasant preoccupation could start it off, and a landscape which included the sea, a river, a fountain, or anything that occupied the eye without engaging the mind, was of use in sustaining it. It was the world behind the world, where reflection precludes the necessity for action, and the calm which all things seek in death appears briefly in the guise of contentment, the spirit at last persuaded that the still waters of perfection are reachable. The details of market life and the personal financial considerations that shoot like rockets across the dark heavens of this inner cosmos serve merely to give it scale and to emphasize its vastness, in no wise troubling its supreme tranquillity.

He passed through the first two rooms of the café, and into the small back one, where he was relieved to see that the table he wanted was unoccupied. In fact, there was no one in the room at all, which made him decide that he would stay only long enough to drink one tea, and then move to a more populous spot in another room. This was a small ceremony that he was inventing, for his feeling about the day demanded the observance of some sort of ritual. When he paid for the tea, he would change the twenty-rial piece he had found that morning in the street. It would be a most acceptable way in the eye of Allah, he thought, to use the money.

Today, without the customary hubbub, and without the usual unceasing noise of the radio (for the electricity had not yet been turned back on), the room in the rear seemed less a refuge than a small dungeon. He could hear the chugging sound of the buses' idling motors out in the square. He ordered his tea. While he was waiting, a boy came through the café carrying a huge tray of pastries, and stuck his head in the door. For some reason, perhaps because the boy looked vaguely like the friend who had

ridden past that day on his bicycle and given him a ride, or perhaps because a man had just walked through the outer room
whom he had often seen in cafés selling small amounts of kif
clandestinely, Amar found himself thinking of the day he had
determined to run away. Each time he reviewed that incident in
his mind, he was conscious of a still active desire to avenge himself. At the same time he knew that he would never lift a finger
against Mustapha, any more than Mustapha himself had done
against him. It had to be done some other way. Allah had decreed that Mustapha should be born first. Therefore it was
Mustapha's duty vis-à-vis his brother to compensate for that
superiority with extra kindnesses. Mustapha had never understood that; on the contrary, he had used his position tyrannically,
always to extort further offerings. Injustice could be redeemed
only by successful retaliation. He stood up and peered around
the doorway into the next room: the kif seller was talking in a
corner by the window. The man had to be extremely careful in
establishing the identity of his customers, or he could fall into
the hands of an agent for the police. It was well known that the
French had suppressed the sale of kif in the hope of getting the
Moslems into the habit of drinking spirits; the revenue for
the government would be enormous. The fact that the religion
of the Moslems expressly forbade alcohol was naturally of no interest to them: they always befriended those who broke the laws
of Islam and punished those who followed them.

At this moment something strange happened: a man and a
woman, both Nazarenes, came across the footbridge and went
into the first room. An instant later they appeared in the second
room, staring about shamelessly for a table at which to sit. For
a moment they seemed to have found one that pleased them,
then the woman said something and the man walked over to the
doorway where Amar stood and peered inside the small room. It
was when he looked out the window and saw the pool that he
seemed to be deciding to install the woman in the inner room.
Amar sat down quickly at his table, for fear they might choose
that one to sit at. The *qaouaji* arrived with his tea. As he was
leaving, the man called to him in Arabic, and ordered two teas

and two *cabrhozels*. Now Amar looked closely at the man, decided he was not French, and felt the wave of hatred that had been on its way recede, leaving a residue of disappointment and indifference tinged with curiosity. When after a moment he realized that the man and the woman were both aware of his scrutiny, he turned quickly away and stared out at the pool, sipping his tea slowly. A little later he looked back at them. They were talking together in low voices and smiling at each other. The woman was obviously a prostitute of the lowest order, because her arms and shoulders were completely uncovered, and the dress she wore had been cut shockingly low in the neck. As if to confirm Amar's verdict, she presently took from her handbag a small case containing cigarettes, and put one in her mouth, waiting for the man to light it for her. Amar was astounded at her brazenness. Even the French women in the Ville Nouvelle did not go to quite such extremes in their lewd dress and behavior. And even the most disreputable prostitute would have taken the care to keep herself from being so badly burned by the sun. This woman had obviously come from working in the fields: she was completely brown from having been out in the open for a very long time. Yet here she was, wearing gold bracelets. His intuition now told him that he had made a mistake in his evaluation of her. She was probably not from the fields at all, but had had some misfortune which had obliged her to walk for many days in the sun's glare, and now she was ashamed, and wanted to hide herself from the crowd until she should be white again, which was why she had sought out the empty back room in which to sit. If this were the case, she would not be pleased to catch him staring at her. He sipped his tea assiduously and looked out the window. Soon he rose again and glanced through the doorway into the corner where the kif seller had been. The man had sat down, evidently on the invitation of a client, and was having a glass of tea. Amar walked over and spoke to him. The man nodded, handed him a little paper packet. Amar paid him, returned to his seat, and resumed his surreptitious examination of the two tourists. (Not being French, they fell perforce into that category.) What peculiar people they were, he reflected; the most foreign of all the foreigners he had seen. Their clothing was unusual, their faces were different, they laughed almost constantly, yet they did not seem to be drunk, and the most unaccountable detail to Amar was the fact that although, judging by all the small external signs by which one can judge such things, these two were interested in each other, the man never once seized even the woman's hand, never leaned toward her to touch her or smell her, nor did she, in spite of her otherwise lax conduct, once lower her eyes, find it impossible to meet his gaze. She merely sat there, as though she were unconscious of the difference in their sex. At the same time Amar divined an intensity in the air, as it were, between the two, a factor that for him weighed more heavily than their outward demeanor, which, after all, could have been entirely simulated. He had watched a good many French couples together, and while their definition of accepted public deportment included certain excesses which were unthinkable with Moslems, the two over-all patterns did not differ radically; French behavior contained no glaring disparities. But he found this couple basically incomprehensible.

When he had finished his tea, he decided to go outside and walk around the pool, but the small door had not been opened for a long time, and the bolt was rusty. This occupied him for a while, until he had succeeded in hammering it back with a stone which lay in the corner near by, perhaps kept there for that purpose. Then he opened the door, breaking all the spiderwebs, and stepped out. The sun was painfully hot in the airless space here between the café and the high city wall, and the pool was a malignant mirror magnifying its white light. He knelt down to feel the water: it also was hot. A dragonfly had skimmed too close to the surface and wet its wings; it made desperate contortions in its struggle to rise from the water. He watched it for a moment with interest, then, feeling sorry that it was about to die, he rolled his trouser-legs up as high as he could and lowered himself into the pool. It was rather deeper than he had imagined; the water came up to his thighs. The floor felt slippery and unpleasant on the soles of his feet, but he waded out, put his hand under the dragonfly and lifted it up. Then he stood there in the water looking at it and grinning, because its two enormous eyes seemed to be returning his stare. Perhaps it was thanking him. "How great are the works of Allah," he whispered. When the hot sunlight had dried its wings, it moved them a few times, and suddenly flew off into the air toward the ramparts. Amar climbed out of the pool, rolled his trouser-legs down, and wrung them out. Then he sat by the edge of the pool in the sun letting them dry. It seemed to him that in the distance, coming up over the roofs out of the dusty city, he could distinguish the clamor of human voices. But it was far away, and it sounded a little like the wind blowing through a crack in the door. If the procession came through Bab Bou Jeloud he wanted to be in the outer room to watch, and if there were a fight, a few of the French police were bound to be knocked down; that was what he wanted to see. It was always the Moslems who were pushed about, beaten and killed, even, as had happened today before his eyes, when it was Moslems who did the beating and killing. For a moment he felt a belated surge of sympathy for the two *mokhaznia* back in the alley near the lawyers' booths. Perhaps they had not known when they accepted their jobs with the French that they would be required to inform against their own people, and when they discovered it, it was already too late, they knew too much for the French to let them go free, and they were caught fast.

But in that case, he argued, it was their duty, even under pain of death, to refuse to carry out orders. How much more heroic it would have been for them to die as martyrs at the hands of the French than to be shot down shamefully like animals, their bodies cursed and spat upon by their brothers! He knew that a Moslem who died on the battlefield went directly to Paradise, without waiting for judgment, but he was not well documented on the fate of traitors. However, it seemed logical that they should be consigned straightway to the jurisdiction of Satan. He shuddered inwardly at the thought of what awaited anyone who landed in Hell. It was not the idea of the suffering that seemed fearful, but the certainty of its eternal continuation, no matter how repentant the victim might be. Suppose a man's heart changed, and he longed for Allah with all his might. The pain would lie, not in being forever roasted on a spit like a *mechoui* of lamb, or in being torn limb from limb the way the friends of freedom said the French had done to the Moslems at Oued Zem, but in the knowledge that never under any conditions could he be vouchsafed the presence of Allah. Death is nothing, he told himself, looking between his almost closed eyelids at the blinding sun reflected in the pool; the fortunate man is the one who can make of his death a glorious event that people will not forget. It occurred to him that perhaps that was why Mohammed Lalami had been so smug yesterday: he might already have known that his brother was going to be executed by the French. Some day, he thought, Mohammed would lie in wait for him and catch him unawares, and he would have a real fight on his hands. It might be a good idea, if ever he should catch sight of Mohammed, to go up to him and offer him his hand in apology. Probably Mohammed would not accept, but it might soften his heart and prepare the ground for a future reconciliation.

The sounds of shouting and singing were coming louder, and his trousers were nearly dry. He got up and went inside.

BOOK 3

THE HOUR
OF THE SWALLOWS

*To my way of thinking, there is
nothing more delightful than to be
a stranger. And so I mingle with
human beings, because they are
not of my kind, and precisely in
order to be a stranger among them.*

—SONG OF THE SWALLOW:
THE THOUSAND AND ONE NIGHTS

CHAPTER   15

Mornings, Stenham and Moss were in the habit of sending little
notes to one another via the servants. Since his apartment gave
on the garden, Moss would hand his missives to old Mokhtar,
the man who swept the walks and tended the flowers outside his
door; Mokhtar would go up to the main lobby and pass them
to Abdelmjid, who had charge of vacuum-cleaning the rugs of
the public rooms. The year before, it had been Abdelmjid himself who would climb up into the tower and deliver the envelopes
at Stenham's door, but recently he had married Rhaissa, a jolly
black girl whose mother had been a slave in the house of a
former pacha, and since she cleaned the three rooms of the tower
every day, it was now she who came and knocked at his door

when there was a note that had been sent up from **Room Four-teen** for him.

The heart's desire of every modern Moroccan girl is to have her incisors and canines capped with gold. Originally Rhaissa's teeth had been healthy enough, but when her mother had found a husband for her, she had naturally taken her to have the necessary embellishments installed in her daughter's mouth before the marriage. The work had been done by a native specialist in the Medina, and ever since, poor Rhaissa had suffered a great deal. Each day she insisted on showing Stenham her inflamed gums; in her opinion the dentist had worked an evil spell on her during the treatment because her mother had demurred at paying the price he had asked. But now, out of her own earnings, she had paid every franc herself, and still she had pain. Stenham came to dread her morning invasion of his quiet; he had bought her a packet of sodium perborate, and she was using it regularly, first having emptied the powder from the pharmacist's envelope into a special paper covered with magic symbols she had got from a *fqih*. She thought it was doing some good, but she intended to go back to the *fqih* soon and get another paper with a different set of symbols.

"I want to help the poor girl," he told Moss, "but I can't go on looking into that red crocodile mouth every damned time she comes in to make the bed."

It was one of those mornings when the city steamed quietly under the strong sun. A haze of wood smoke and mist hung above the flat terraces, enclosing and unifying the sounds that rose from below, until when they reached his window they were as monotonous and soporific as the uninterrupted humming of bees. Between ten and eleven o'clock in such weather the city sounds always took on this strange character. He wondered if perhaps it had to do with the direction of the wind, since the one recognizable noise was that of a distant sawmill somewhere over toward Bab Sidi bou Jida. A few sluggish flies would sail into the room and go to sleep on the tile floor in the sun. During this hour or so, Stenham would abandon his work and, putting two chairs together face to face in front of the windows, would stretch out voluptuously in the hot sunlight, from time to time raising himself to scribble a few words in a notebook he kept lying beside him. He had to be sure to lock the door first, to prevent Rhaissa from bursting in on him and finding him naked; she had not completely mastered the difficult task of remembering to knock before turning the door handle.

Today however she did knock, and he struggled up and into his bathrobe, muttering: "Who the hell?" Any disturbance before lunch, other than the arrival of his breakfast tray, infuriated him. He flung the door open and Rhaissa tendered him the note she held in her hand. He thanked her gruffly, saw that she was eager to discuss the state of her gums, and shut the door in her face.

The note, from Moss, read: "What a beautiful day! Hugh has promised to join me for lunch at the Zitoun. Bastela has been ordered. Will you come too? May I expect you here in my room at half past twelve? My new model is a monster!!! Affly., Alain."

He lay down again in the sun, but found it impossible to go on inventing details in his description of the court of the Sultan Moulay Ismail. Soon he sprang up, shaved and dressed, and went down to Moss's room, hoping to catch him in the act of painting. But the model, an extremely gnarled old man, was just shuffling across the patio when he arrived, and Moss was cleaning his brushes. "This is most unusual," he said. "You've come early. You'll have to wait while I change. There's a new *Economist* on the table behind you; it just came this morning. Why don't you take it out into the garden with you? Or do you think you'd find it too dull after the incredible excesses of your creative imagination?"

Stenham snorted; he was tired of having to react to Moss's banter. "Excesses?" he said, picking up the magazine and stepping back out into the sunlight. "Excesses?" Down here there were sparrows twittering, and the air was strong with the scent of datura blossoms. Moss was bright; he knew fairly well where to stick the needles, but now the spots that had been tender were leathery, and Stenham, when he reacted at all, did so only out of courtesy and laziness. It made conversation easier, for Moss would simply have gone on, poking about, looking for other vulnerable points in his friend's character which so far he had not exploited.

He liked Moss because he was an enigma, and he was certain Moss enjoyed playing the magician, the mystery man with a thousand unexpected eccentricities up his sleeve. "I'm a simple businessman," Moss would declare piteously, "and I don't understand this mad jungle that seems to be the natural habitat of all you Americans." . . . "Don't take anything for granted when you talk to me. I must have everything explained. Your American ethical system is so utterly fantastic that my simple brain is quite at a loss trying to contemplate it."

But other times he would forget himself and complain: "After all, the English are really too much. One can't live in that constipated fashion forever. The world is a very lovely place. Have you ever been to Bangkok? I rather think you'd approve. Delectable people." . . . "The only thing that makes life worth living is the possibility of experiencing now and then a perfect moment. And perhaps even more than that, it's having the ability to recall such moments in their totality, to contemplate them like jewels. Do you understand?"

Stenham would bait him, saying very seriously: "No, I don't think I do. I'm afraid perfection doesn't interest me. It's always the exception; it's outside everything, outside reality. I don't see life that way."

"I know," Moss would say. "You see life from the most unattractive vantage-point you can find."

Stenham had long ago seen through the simple businessman pose; Moss had even confided on one occasion that he was writing a book, but without going further to say what kind of book it was going to be. And once from London, enclosed along with a rather pointless letter whose purpose was patently that of making the enclosure seem an afterthought, he had sent him a sheaf of short lyric poems, not very original but sufficiently well fashioned to convince Stenham that their author was by no means new to the muse. "He's as guilty as I am," Stenham liked to remind himself.

The sun down here in the garden was hot; the moist black earth exuded a sweetness, the heavy and disturbing odor of spring. Old Mokhtar came along the walk, his spent *babouches* scuffing the mosaics beneath. His turban always gave the impression of being about to come unwound. Not that it mattered how presentable he looked; ill health and overwork had drained all character from his soft, small face, and the turban, firmly or loosely wound, could do nothing for his woebegone appearance. Stenham always felt vaguely uneasy in his presence: the gentle vanquished expression he wore awoke a distant sense of guilt.

Moss moved out onto the terrace, adjusting his dark glasses, dressed as always for a stroll along Piccadilly. "I think I'm about ready to go, if you are. Shall we start?"

In the courtyard they looked to see whether Kenzie's MG were there, but it was not. Moss frowned.

"He's gone. We shall have to walk. And do let's go the short way."

"There are a dozen short ways," Stenham objected.

"The least labyrinthine, the least tiring. The quickest! Really, you are so difficult."

Stenham leading, they turned into the street to the left, making their way around the donkeys loaded with olives that were being carried to the press. "What do you mean, difficult? Why do you say that?" Stenham never could quite decide why it pleased him to lure Moss into a particular vein of querulousness; it was a game that could go on for hours, Moss playing the part of the simple, ingenuous soul, mystified and complaining, to Stenham's patient, mundane mentor, and it added pungency if Stenham occasionally made a direct accusation, such as: "Why do you insist on pretending this crazy unworldly innocence? What are you trying to discover?" It increased the savor because he said these things in such a way that they fell far short of the truth, of what he would have said had he really wanted to put an end to the game. Moss was quite aware of this, and knew that Stenham knew he was aware, and thus the game continued, growing always more ramified, more complex, more subtle, and taking up more of the time they spent together. Some day, thought Stenham, there would come a moment when it would no longer be possible to pull Moss out of it; whatever he said or did would only be in character, and the words would be uttered, the gestures made, no longer by Moss, but by this absurd creation of his that had nothing in common with the man it was meant to mask. I started him on this, he told himself, but he was there waiting to respond. And he picked the role of imbecile. And here I am, as usual, leading him, and he's pretending he doesn't know the way.

Here a public fountain dribbled in its niche; women and girls waited with their pails under its blue and green tiled vault. 1352, read the smaller tiles under the florid Arabic script that, praising the institution of monotheism, warned against substitutes for the one and only variety of it. "1352; that makes it a little over twenty years old," he thought. The constant slopping of water from the pails had made a cloaca of the street at this point; the clay had turned to viscid and slippery gray mud, and milky water bubbled up to fill each new footprint.

"Now, really, I say!" cried Moss. When he was pretending to be outraged, his voice became sharper, his accent more exaggeratedly Oxonian. "*Where are you taking me?*"

"You've been through here half a dozen times before," Stenham shouted over his shoulder.

Eleven hundred years ago the city had been begun at the bottom of a concavity in the hills, a formation which had the contours of a slightly tilted bowl; through the centuries as it grew, a vast, eternally spreading construction of cedar wood, marble, earth and tiles, it had climbed up the sides and over the rim of the bowl. Since the center was also the lowest part, all the passageways led to it; one had to go down first, and then choose the direction in which one wanted to climb. Except the paths which followed the river's course out into the orchards, all ways led upward from the heart of the city. The long climb through the noonday heat was tiring. An hour after they had started out they were still struggling up the crowded lanes of the western hill. The mist had been totally dissipated, the sky had gone blue, hard and distant. The street widened, was suddenly filled with small boys on their way home from school. Moss and Stenham were finally able to walk abreast. Through the din of childish voices Moss said: "Will you tell me where we're coming out? I should have said there was no way of getting through the walls this far down. Don't you think we should have tried to get to Bab el Hadid?"

"D'you think so?" Stenham made his voice deliberately vague. He knew perfectly well where he was going, but the fun consisted in seeming to be wandering until the last minute, and then making a sudden virtuoso turn which would bring Moss out into a place that would be all the more startling for being completely familiar.

"I expect you've got one of your impressive conjurer's tricks up your sleeve," murmured Moss with a false air of resignation, "but I must say that this time I don't quite see how you can."

"No trick at all," Stenham assured him simply. "We're merely taking the most direct route to the Zitoun. Or, at least, I think we are. As soon as we get to the next turn I can tell you."

The next turn took them along a short dusty lane. Under an archway ahead a native policeman in a fez stood talking to a Senegalese soldier. As they stepped beneath the arch the breeze hit their faces, and there was the sound of a fast-running torrent. A panorama of hills lay before them.

"You *are* extraordinary!" said Moss delightedly. "I think you broke the doorway through the wall yourself. What's it called? Or has it a name?"

Stenham crossed the road and stood at the edge of the parapet looking over the narrow valley to the green slopes beyond. "Of course it has a name. They call it Bab Dar el Pacha."

"Oh, do shut up!" cried Moss. "You *know* there's no such gate. I've learned them all by rote, from Bab Segma to Bab Mahrouk and back again, and there's no such gate in the list."

"You'd better amend your list. Bab Dar el Pacha's a new gate they hacked in the wall twenty or thirty years ago so the Pacha could get a car up to his door."

"Vandalism," Moss remarked.

There was a short climb from here up to the hotel. Students from the College of Moulay Idriss came coasting down the hill on bicycles, going home to lunch, most of them wearing horn-rimmed spectacles, and all of them clothed in formless European suits that had never seen an iron or a sponge since the day they had been made.

Less spectacular than the tall trembling poplars that lined the road, but of more interest to the small boys who swarmed there, were the mulberry trees growing by the stream. The boys swished their long bamboo poles violently through the foliage above: the leaves sailed down and the green berries fell. Kenzie's yellow MG was parked in front of the Zitoun's entrance. It was covered with children; they were standing on the headlights and bumper, climbing over the doors and fighting on the front seat for the honor of sitting at the steering wheel. When Stenham and Moss arrived abreast of the car, the youth who stood beside it, studiously inscribing the word MOHAMMED with a ball pen on the gray canvas top, did not move. Probably he did not consider his contribution to the collection of scribblings which the car bore to be of much importance; there were so many others more showy and startling. Grinning faces, hands of Fatima, and various devices in both Roman and Arabic script had been scratched into the paint with nails and pebbles.

"Watch this," said Stenham. He went up close to the youth, who glanced at him and continued his careful work.

"*Chnou hada?* What are you doing?" he asked the boy.

The boy smiled. "Nothing," he answered simply.

Stenham pointed at the letters written on the cloth. "And that? What's that?"

"An automobile." The coldness that had come into his voice was doubtless due to the fact that he thought the Nazarene gentleman was taking him for an ignorant country boy.

"No, that word."

"Mohammed."

"Why did you write it?"

"Because it's my name."

"But why did you write it on the car?"

The youth shrugged, making it apparent that he considered this inquisition without cause or interest, and raised his hand again to complete the flourishes he was designing around the already written name. But Stenham seized the hand and pulled it away with some force. Some of the smaller children had drawn near and were watching. "Get out of here!" he yelled at them. They retreated to a safer distance.

"What's the matter with all of you?" He addressed his words to the adolescent, who still held the pen in his hand as if he were determined to finish what doubtless seemed to him a fine example of his signature. There was, of course, no answer, and so he was forced to continue. "That won't come off. Don't you know that?" Still there was no answer.

Moss came nearer, and beaming at the boy, said in his mellifluous if slightly English-sounding French: "Automobiles are very expensive. You shouldn't spoil them."

Now the boy reacted. "I haven't spoiled it at all," he said with dignity.

"But look!" exclaimed Moss, pointing to the disfigurations everywhere on the yellow paint. "See what the boys in this town have done! All that was done since this gentleman came here two weeks ago. It's going to cost him a lot of money to repair all that."

"How much?" said the youth impassively.

Moss thought quickly. "Perhaps fifty thousand francs. Or more."

The youth's face brightened. "He could sell it and buy a new one."

Stenham could not contain himself. "*Mahboul!*" he yelled. "You're an idiot! Get away from the car, you and all the rest of you! Go on! Go on!" He pushed the youth roughly out into the road, returned and lifted two of the smaller boys out of the front seat. The rest ran silently off and joined a group of berrywhackers.

The garden was a level square of ground which lay protected by the high embankment and the masses of unkempt vegetation along its side; the light wind that stirred the tops of the trees did not at the moment reach it. Tables were here and there, and canvas deck chairs to loll in. The place was deserted save for Kenzie, sitting in a far corner near the tea-house, having an animated discussion with a waiter in a white jacket, who crouched beside his chair. He had seen them come into the garden, but he affected not to be aware of their presence until they had arrived at his very feet. Then he glanced up and smiled casually, as if he had just left them only five minutes earlier. The waiter pulled up chairs for them and disappeared into the tea-house, from which now issued the scratching and clicking that in an Arab café marks the beginning of a phonograph record. "*Bilèche tabousni fi aynayah?*" complained Abd el Wahab in an enormous, dusty voice. "Why do you kiss me on my eyelids?"

"I've got a guest coming," Kenzie said suddenly.

CHAPTER   16

Kenzie had been sitting with no glass in front of him, and he appeared to have no intention of ordering anything, either for himself or for those who had just joined him. Stenham knew that Moss had observed this, and he was waiting to see what he proposed to do about it; he himself never drank, nevertheless he would have liked a glass of mint tea to wash down the dust he felt he had swallowed during the climb up through the Medina. But he was determined not to do the suggesting or the ordering: he did not intend to have the drinks charged to him. For one thing, he was living on a strict budget at the moment, hoping to make the advance on his present book last until he had completed it. And then, he felt that he, as the only American present, ought not to be expected to pay for everyone's drinks. Besides this, he had noticed on similar occasions during the past fortnight a certain sparring between Moss and Kenzie, as if each one had decided that the other should be forced to disburse a little more than his share; neither one ever seemed to have any small change on hand. Kenzie had confided to him that if he and Moss took a carriage together from Bou Jeloud to the Ville Nouvelle in the afternoon, Moss always rushed forward to pay, so that Kenzie would have to pay the return trip. "Well," Stenham had said, "why not?" "Because at six o'clock the tariff goes up," Kenzie had explained, with perfect seriousness. Now he felt that the situation might actually come to a head, if he merely sat still and waited. All that seemed destined to happen, however, was a mutual offering and refusing of cigarettes, with each man settling back to smoke one of his own brand.

"She's staying here at the Zitoun," Kenzie said presently, continuing the conversation of a moment ago.

"Curious," Moss observed, breathing out a thick cloud of smoke which he watched a second before going on. "An American staying here. You wouldn't expect it to be comfortable enough for her."

Stenham held his tongue, certain that Moss was trying to bait him.

"She's rather a good sort, and not at all stupid," Kenzie went on. "Yesterday I found her sitting all alone here in the garden reading. We got to talking, and I told her you were here"—he looked at Stenham—"and she's heard of you. I thought it might be fun if the only four English-speaking people in Fez had a grand reunion."

"Don't forget the missionaries and the Consul and his wife," advised Stenham.

"But I said people." Kenzie was an avowed enemy of the British Consul: there had been unpleasantness over the mislaying of a pile of mail. Stenham and Moss were well informed on the subject.

"I rather wish you'd told me she was going to eat with us," Moss said; he sounded aggrieved. "And the reason is"—he raised

his voice—"that I'm jolly hungry and I'd have eaten more breakfast if I'd known. Where is she?"

"She'll be along in a minute," Kenzie assured him.

"Incidentally," said Stenham, "you'll find a new addition to
the collection of graffiti on your car when you go out. The word
'Mohammed' nicely written in indelible ink on the hood, just
behind the strut. I caught him in the act."

"I hope you gave him a good buffeting," said Kenzie.

"Well, no, as a matter of fact, I didn't."

"A good clout on the head works wonders. They don't forget
it."

"Maybe," said Stenham, "but then another one comes along
who hasn't had the benefit of a clout. You can't discipline the
whole country."

"Still," Moss said dreamily, "that's what must be done before
they can ever accomplish anything."

Stenham bridled. "What d'you want them to accomplish? You
sound like a leader of the Istiqlal. Why have they got to accomplish something? Can't they just be let alone and go on as they
are?"

Moss smiled. "No, my dear fellow. You know very well they
can't."

Stenham looked around the garden and thought: It's too nice
a place to spoil with an argument. To Moss he said pleasantly:
"My question was rhetorical. You're worse than my wife. She always thought everything needed an answer."

Moss cleared his throat and signaled the waiter, who had come
out of the tea-house and was pulling dead leaves from one of the
vines that covered its sides.

"A bottle of Sidi Brahim rosé, and set the table, please, and
bring a big bowl of ice to cool the wine in. We'll have the *bastela* first. How is it today?"

"*Magnifique, monsieur*," said the waiter gravely.

"*Magnifique*, eh?" Moss echoed, amused.

The waiter hurried off. Stenham glanced at Kenzie, to see how
he was taking Moss's petulance. Kenzie smoked blandly. A stork
sailed slowly past overhead, not moving its wings, but balanced,

soaring on some invisible air-current. From the loudspeaker in the tea-house came the enigmatic phrases of a Chleuh dance: rasping *rebab*, excitable *guinbri*, high childish voices making their long, throaty mountain calls above the hopping accompaniment.

Moss was really very pro-French, Stenham was thinking. Like them, he refused to consider the Moroccans' present culture, however decadent, an established fact, an existing thing. Instead, he seemed to believe that it was something accidentally left over from bygone centuries, now in a necessary state of transition, that the people needed temporary guidance in order to progress to some better condition, "So that," Stenham had bitterly remarked, "they can stop being Moroccans." For the French had basically the same idea as the Nationalists; they quarreled only over externals, and even there he was beginning to wonder if these supposed disagreements were not part of a gigantic Machiavellian act, put on under the combined auspices of the French and Moroccan Communists in governmental positions, who, knowing better than anyone that before there can be change there must be discontent, were willing to drag the country to the verge of civil war in the process of manufacturing that discontent. The methods and aims of the Istiqlal were fundamentally identical with those of Marxism-Leninism; that much had been made abundantly clear to him by reading their publications and talking with members and friends of the organization. But wasn't it possible that any movement toward autonomy in a colonial country, especially one where feudalism had remained intact, must almost inevitably take that road?

He was always hearing the complaint: "America has not helped us." That was only the first sentence of a long and fearful indictment whose final import was, to him at least, terrifying. And time passed, with hatred of France and America growing each day, being artificially inculcated in every segment of the population by the clever young cynics sent out for that purpose. Yet it was impossible for him to take sides in such a controversy, because whenever he thought it all through to some sort of conclusion, the controversy always seemed to evaporate: it was as though the two sides were working together to achieve the same sinister ends.

"Or is Moss right, and am I a hopeless reactionary?" The key question, it seemed to him, was that of whether man was to obey Nature, or attempt to command her. It had been answered long, long ago, claimed Moss; man's very essence lay in the fact that he had elected to command. But to Stenham that seemed a shallow reply. To him wisdom consisted in the conscious and joyous obedience to natural laws, yet when he had said that to Moss, Moss had laughed pityingly. "My dear man, wisdom is a primitive concept," he had told him. "What we want now is knowledge." Only great disillusionment could make a man say such a thing, Stenham believed.

For protection, to follow out his train of thought, he closed his eyes and tilted his head upward so that he might appear to be listening to the conversation. Perhaps thus he could be assured of a few extra seconds alone. But it soon became evident that his very resolve to escape for a moment was on the contrary a sign that he had been absent and was being drawn back. The words of Kenzie and Moss began to penetrate to his hearing; he was on his way back to consciousness of the canvas chair, the sun in the garden, the trembling poplars.

"Are you asleep, by any chance?" Moss inquired. Stenham forced himself to smile indulgently before he opened his eyes.

"No, just content."

"I believe you're invited tonight to Si Jaffar's for one of those interminable dinners, aren't you?"

"Now I'm not content. Why did you remind me?" Stenham asked.

"I didn't suppose you had forgotten it, and I mentioned it because I intend to talk about Si Jaffar, and I want to caution you against repeating any of what I'm going to say." Moss now ceased looking seriously over his spectacles and smiled. "It's a perfectly absurd tale, but I think you and Hugh would enjoy it. Yesterday the old man and I met by chance in the Ville Nouvelle, and I invited him to sit with me at the Versailles. He ordered one of your ghastly American drinks—one of those outlandish medicinal mixtures called Tipsy Kola or some such thing, and then proceeded to hug the glass as though it were at least Armagnac. An hour later he was still taking tiny sips, and talking, talking, of course, all the while, in his incredible French."

"What about?" asked Kenzie.

"Oh, scandal of various sorts, juicy bits about the French, mostly. And a little about the Moroccans. They *are* extraordinary people, these Fassiyine."

"I expect he told you some amusing things."

"Some were most amusing," Moss answered absently. "Toward the end of our interview I managed, only God knows how, to take enough control of the conversational reins to steer us into the highly delicate subject of Moulay Abdallah. I began by asking him if he knew how many prostitutes the quarter housed. His little eyes became even more pig-like than usual, and he began to wring his hands, but so violently I thought the skin would come off any minute. 'Oh, *là*, Monsieur Mousse!' he wailed. 'This is a very difficult problem. It is so many years since I have paid a visit to our renowned quarter, you understand—' The old reprobate! I'm told he's there every week at least once. But I asked him if he'd say it was nearer five thousand or twenty thousand. By this time he was rubbing his hands in the other direction to ease the pain. 'Ah, Monsieur Mousse! None of my acquaintances has ever attempted to count the unfortunate girls!' This is merely to illustrate the difficulties and hazards that one can't escape if one wants to converse with the old fox."

Stenham did not feel that Moss's caricature did Si Jaffar justice, even though it was recognizable; there was a whole other side upon which it did not touch at all.

"But I'm nothing if not persevering," Moss continued. "I went ruthlessly ahead, as you can imagine, in the hope of getting to my point before some friend of his came by and ruined everything. I was finally able to get down to age groups, and mentioned little Khémou and my divine baby Haddouj, making it quite clear that anything over fifteen was not for me. At this point his smiles were dripping like treacle from his old face, and he was merely caressing his fingers rather lecherously. 'Ah, you are so right, Monsieur Mousse! It is the little ones who are the precious pearls. Among us it is said that they are like the first tender shoots of wheat that spring up to announce the return of life to the earth,' or some such balderdash. I can't possibly remember all he said, because he went on and on, absolutely delighted with the turn the conversation had taken, singing praises of budding trees, early adolescence, swollen streams, young doves learning to fly, and keeping it all, now that I think of it, quite general and impersonal, so that actually in the end it was I who had said everything and he nothing—but nothing at all. Wherever I was able, I dropped a hint, you know, how it was jolly difficult for a painter to get a model, and how I realized it was out of the question even to dream of getting one anywhere *except* from some house in Moulay Abdallah, and how even there I knew it was almost impossible. And each time he would nod understandingly and agree: 'Oh, yes, out of the question, naturally.' . . . 'Ah, yes, Moulay Abdallah.' . . . 'Ah, of course, almost impossible. You are quite right.' And so eventually I had to put it to him. I said: 'Si Jaffar, do you think you could use your influence to get me a model?' At this the old monster merely closed his eyes like a cat. He had on both pairs of glasses by this time, and he made a most peculiar-looking cat, I can assure you, with his white silk hood up over his fez. When he opened his eyes, he said: 'Monsieur Mousse, I understand your difficulties. I am able to sympathize with you. I sympathize even very strongly, and I assure you that no matter what hardship it may cost me, you will have a model at your door at nine o'clock tomorrow morning.' That sounded more like what I wanted to hear, and I thought it would be only politic to let the subject drop."

Stenham listened apathetically. For one thing, whenever the two Englishmen talked together in his presence, he felt, unreasonably enough no doubt, that he was in some subtle fashion being left out of the conversation. And then, since it was he who originally had brought Moss and the Moroccan family together, he did not wholly approve of Moss's efforts, however roundabout they might be, to enlist the old gentleman as a procurer. However, a story told by Moss never became downright boring, because its course followed a carefully plotted graph. And so he listened. Suddenly, before the tale was anywhere nearly finished, he knew how it was going to come out. "My new model is a monster!" Moss's note had read. And he remembered the bent and misshapen old man he had met in the patio. A feeling akin to admiration for Si Jaffar awoke in him, and he began to chuckle. Moss turned reproachful eyes upon him. "You beast!" he cried. "Don't you spoil my story!"

"I won't. I'm sorry." He ceased laughing aloud, and merely smiled. It ended exactly as he had foreseen: the ancient gentleman was indeed the model Si Jaffar had sent.

"Priceless," said Kenzie.

"That seems to me a rather civilized way of having a good time," Stenham said. He did not want to see enmity develop between Moss and Si Jaffar: in a place where the circle of acquaintances was so small, a feud could complicate everyone's life no end. "It's a practical joke, I'll admit, but about a thousand percent more subtle than our kind, don't you think?"

"No," Moss objected, turning around in his chair to look for the waiter, "I rather fancy it's more than a mere joke. They don't go in for jokes, you know. My feeling is that it was meant decidedly as a rebuff. But there you are; you can cudgel your brains about it for the next ten years, but you'll get nowhere. The old fox will be as innocent as a newborn babe the next time I see him. What can you do? It's rather devastating, I must say."

"But what amuses me," insisted Stenham, "is the note of madness they can inject into any situation at the drop of a hat. Like the other day when I met the hotel manager in the Medina and stopped to talk for a minute. You know I never go into the office, so I never see him except in the street somewhere, and then's when I have to pass the time of day, which means a little dissertation on the weather. Which is what we were doing, when suddenly a very dignified gentleman approaches and says in French: 'Pardon, messieurs, but I believe you were discussing amber? May I ask if you were referring to cut pieces, or to amber in its natural state?' What do you say then?"

Moss did not appear to see any connection between this story and his own experience. "What, indeed?" he said distraughtly, craning his neck again to catch sight of the waiter.

At the far end the gate opened; the day, the garden acquired sudden meaning as she skipped down the steps. All of what a moment ago had seemed a complete cosmos now retreated instantly into the background to become nothing more than the décor in front of which the principal character was to move. She was in her early or middle twenties, and she wore a white silk shirt and white slacks. The men rose as she came lightly toward them, turning this way and that among the tables and chairs.

"Ah, charming," Moss murmured, but in a very low voice.

Her form and face were such that she belonged to the happy category of women who can always be sure they are attractive under any circumstances, even the most adverse; her carriage and manner of walking made it clear that she knew this. Also, Stenham felt, she took it so much for granted that she did not attach very great importance to it. He had a brief vision of windswept sunny places as she came near. Then Kenzie said: "And this is Mr. Stenham, a compatriot of yours. Madame Veyron."

The waiter had come into the garden behind her, and stood at a respectful distance during the first moments of conversation. Again it was Moss who called him over and impatiently told him to set the table.

"If I've kept you waiting," she said, "you must blame it on this town. I suppose it's an old story to all of you, but when I get wandering around down in those *souks* I just can't leave. It's fascinating."

"It never gets to be an old story," Stenham assured her. "At least, not to those who like it. Of course, not everybody likes it."

She put her elbows on the table and leaned forward. "Now, really. How could anyone help loving it?"

Kenzie laughed. "A great many people seem to be able. It's not one of the favorite tourist spots, by any means. A bit overpowering, I should think, on first contact."

She seemed to be considering; the serious expression enhanced the straightforward beauty of her features. "Overpowering. Of course it is. But don't we all like to be overpowered, one time or another?"

"Oh, yes," agreed Moss. "For a while it's pleasant. But once one ceases to be awestruck by the complexity of the streets or the completeness of the still medieval society, unless one has discovered other virtues in a town like this, it can become most *un*overpowering—a bloody bore, as a matter of fact, I should think. So the tourists come, stay a day or two, and go on somewhere else. For which I confess I give thanks."

"Well," she said, in a suddenly very flat, American fashion (as she spoke it came and went, Stenham noticed, that small reminder of the part of the world in which she had grown up, and which had formed her), "I've been here all of three days, and so perhaps you can believe me when I say I think, I *think*, anyway, that I've found enough unspectacular aspects around the town to qualify me as a potential Fez-lover." She folded her hands together and squeezed them, hunching her shoulders at the same time; the gesture seemed that of a small girl. "It's so *exciting!*" Then she fished in the pocket of her slacks and pulled out a pack of Casa Sport.

"Here," said Kenzie. "Have one of these."

She shook her head vehemently. "No, I like this black tobacco. It goes with the place. I'll always associate the smells here—the cedar wood, the mint, the fig trees, all the other mad, wonderful smells—with the taste of this tobacco. At home in Paris I always smoked Gauloises anyway, but these are very different, somehow. Not the same taste at all." She took two puffs and turned completely to face Kenzie. "I have a confession to make. I've ticked off that guide you got me, and found myself another who can at least walk. Your old Santa Claus couldn't keep up with me. He was always straggling miles behind, panting and rolling his eyes like a lunatic. He hated me, anyway. I *had* to get rid of him."

Kenzie's expression was one of displeasure, but he merely said: "Oh? You want to be careful."

She looked to Stenham for confirmation of this opinion. "Do

you think so, Mr. Stenham? I know you know the place inside out."

He did not want to pique Kenzie by assuming the omniscient part she had assigned him. "A girl can't be too careful," he said with a grin.

"And you, Mr. Moss, what do you say?" she went on, making a game of it.

"Oh, I should think if he was an authorized guide he'd be safe enough."

"No. I mean in general. Do you think it's dangerous for me to go around alone?"

"I should say that in normal times the place was absolutely safe, but of course now— Well, they *are* dreadfully fanatical, you know."

"You're all a bunch of old fuddy-duds," she complained.

Moss and Kenzie seemed to stiffen imperceptibly, and turned their heads toward Stenham, as if to discover from his expression whether she were seriously annoyed. Her remark obviously was not one to be expected during the first few minutes of an acquaintanceship. He decided not to enlighten them, and changed the subject.

While they ate the *bastela*, over which Mme Veyron continued to enthuse (and it was very good; the pastry was flaky and the little pieces of steamed pigeon-breast were perfectly cooked), Moss held forth upon the deviousness of the native mind, as illustrated by his previous anecdote. Then the question of wine arose. Moss wanted more rosé, but of a different brand; Kenzie thought some white would be better. "You don't *drink* wine with *bastela*," objected Stenham.

"What nonsense!" Moss snapped. He clapped his hands, and this time the waiter came running. "*Une bouteille de Targui rosé*," he told him. "You'll see," he assured Mme Veyron. "It goes perfectly." To Stenham he remarked: "You have a rather unpleasant puritanical strain."

"Say puristic. I just can't see wine with Arab food."

"Really?" said Mme Veyron with the interest of one being told a fact not generally known. Moss ignored her.

"No, I say puritanical, because I mean that. I've observed you, my dear man, over a period of time, and I've come to the conclusion that you simply don't want to see anyone enjoy himself. You don't even like to see people eat well. You're happiest when the food is tasteless and insufficient. I've watched you, my boy. Whenever we happen to get a really miserable little meal your spirits soar. Disgusting trait."

"You're so wrong," Stenham said, attempting to give his voice the proper ring of sincerity. However, he was troubled. There was at least an element of truth in what Moss said, but it was not that simple; a reason came in between. It had to do with a sense of security. He could not feel at ease with gourmets and hedonists; they were a hostile species.

"Why *don't* you ever drink?" Kenzie asked him gently.

"Because it makes me sick. Can you think of a better reason?"

"I don't believe it," Moss said flatly.

Stenham was annoyed with himself; he felt it was his fault that the conversation had taken this inquisitorial turn. It seemed to him that if he had been going to answer such a question at all, he should have taken a more belligerent and irrational tack, and not exposed himself this way in front of her. It was as though he had shown them his biceps and they had said: "You need the exercise." For years people had been asking him this same question, and he considered it a private matter, one which could not possibly interest anyone but himself. "You don't drink! Not even wine? Why not?"

"Don't get me started on it," he said, raising his voice slightly. "Let's say that for me it's what we Americans call a low-grade kick. You understand that?" He was looking only at Moss.

"Oh, quite! And may I ask what you consider a high-grade kick?"

"There are plenty of those," he replied imperturbably.

His tone may have nettled Moss, for he pressed on. "Such as—?"

"You're on the carpet, Mr. Stenham," said Mme Veyron.

Stenham pushed away his plate; he had finished anyway, but he liked the dramatic gesture as an accompaniment to the words he was going to say. A sudden gust of wind from the south swept through the garden, bringing with it the smell of the damp river valley below. A corner of the tablecloth flapped up and covered the serving dishes. Kenzie lifted it and dropped it back where it belonged.

"Such as keeping these very things private. After all, one's thoughts belong to oneself. They haven't yet invented a machine to make the human mind transparent."

"We're not discussing thoughts," said Moss with exasperation. "You're more English than the English, my dear John. I find it most difficult to understand you. You have all the worst faults of the English, and from what I can see, very few of the virtues we've been led to expect from Americans. Sometimes I feel you're lying. I can't believe you really are an American at all."

Stenham looked at her. "Won't you vouch for me?"

"Of course," she said smiling, "but I'll bet you're from New England."

"What do you mean, *but?* Of course I'm a New Englander. I'm American *and* a New Englander. Like a Frenchman I met once in a jungle town in Nicaragua. He had the only hotel there. 'Are you French, monsieur?' I asked him. And he answered: '*Monsieur, Je suis même Gascon.*' I'm *even* a Gascon, and I like to keep the state of my finances private. And my politics and religion. They're all high-grade kicks as far as I'm concerned. But only if they're kept private."

"The world's not going in that direction," said Moss dryly. "You should be flexible, and prepare for what's coming." He had finished peeling an orange and now, splitting it into sections, he began to eat it. "You're preposterous," he added, but without conviction, as if he were thinking of something which might or might not be connected with the conversation.

"I know just what Mr. Stenham means," announced Mme Veyron, rising suddenly. "Excuse me a second. I'm going to my room for a minute. I'll be right back. I don't want to miss any of this."

They stood up, holding their napkins in their hands. "It's all over," said Stenham meaningfully. "You won't miss anything."

Moss shook his head slowly back and forth. "I dislike to see anyone so ill equipped for the future. The difference between us, my boy, is that I believe in the future." (That and God knows how many million dollars, thought Stenham.) "One of these days the future will be here, and you won't be ready for it."

Mme Veyron returned to the table; she had put on a little white canvas hat with a crush brim. "I'm a little afraid of this sun," she explained. "It's awfully treacherous, and I've had some horrible experiences."

"Sunburn can be pretty bad," Stenham agreed.

"No, I can take any amount of it on my skin. But I get sunstroke so easily. It wasn't so bad when I had Georges with me —my husband—but when I left him and began batting around alone, it wasn't funny. It's frightening to be all alone and have a fever and be delirious, and know there's not a living soul within a thousand miles who gives a damn whether you live or die. And I nearly did die last year in Cyprus. The doctor I called in gave me aspirins, one after the other, and when they didn't seem to have any effect he went off to consult an old woman, and I found out later she was the local witch."

"But at least you came out of it all right," Stenham said.

"It looks like it." She smiled. "Anyway, her treatment was all done over her own fire in her own hut somewhere on the edge of town. I never even laid eyes on her."

Kenzie was laughing, a little too enthusiastically, Stenham thought. "Priceless!" he exclaimed. An instant later he rose, saying to her: "Would you like to see the inside of the tea-house? It's quite attractive. Order coffee, will you, Alain?" The two moved off, she stooping every few steps to examine a flower or a leaf.

Stenham arranged his chair so that he could lie far back in it, staring into the blue afternoon sky. "*Bastela's* an indigestible dish," he said heavily. The inevitable languor that followed on the heels of such a noonday meal was announcing itself. He was not sleepy, but he felt an utter disinclination to move or think. In his mind's eye he began to see vignettes of distant parts of the town: arched stone bridges over the foaming river, herons wading in shallow places among the reeds and cane, the little villages that the very poor had recently built at the bottoms of the ancient quarries—you could stand at the top and look down vertically upon their houses made in building-block patterns; the people were not so impoverished that their terraces could not be spread with orange and magenta rugs being aired, and women sat in tiny courtyards that were pools of shade, out of the venomous sun, thumping on their drums of clay. Now he saw the entrances to the vast caves in the further quarries, hidden by the wild fig trees that had grown up; inside the huge rooms and long corridors it was cool, and the greenish light came down through deep shafts, filtered by the vegetation that choked their openings. The silence of centuries was in here; no one ever entered but an occasional outlaw who did not fear the *djenoun* that inhabited such places. It was all these strange and lonely spots outside the walls, where the city-dwellers unanimously advised him not to walk, that he loved. Yet their beauty existed for him only to the degree that he was conscious of their outsideness, or that he could conjure up the sensation of compactness which the idea of the Medina gave him. It was the knowledge that the swarming city lay below, shut in by its high ramparts, which made wandering over the hills and along the edges of the cliffs so delectable. *They are there, of it,* he would think, *and I am here, of nothing, free.*

Soon Kenzie and Mme Veyron came out of the tea-house, chatting affably. The waiter appeared with coffee (although Stenham could not have told when Moss had ordered it), and the general conversation was resumed feebly, with isolated remarks and distraught if polite rejoinders. It was dying because everyone wanted nothing better than merely to sit in silence. But of course silence was unthinkable, and so they talked.

Interesting things would be happening in the not-too-distant future, Kenzie promised. Although Casablanca was the present theatre of activity, Fez was the fountainhead of resistance to French rule, and the government was nearly ready to crack down on the rebellious elements there. But it would be extremely serious because it would mean mass arrests on a gigantic scale. The concentration camps were being enlarged at the moment, to have everything in readiness for the day. This was all being recounted for Mme Veyron's benefit, but it was not eliciting the response which it should have; from time to time she said: "Oh," or "I see," or "My God!" and that was all. And Stenham thought sadly: "He enjoys all this. He wants to see trouble." For Kenzie was making it very clear that he sided wholly with the Moroccans. Stenham, for his part, could find no such simple satisfaction. There was no possible way, he felt, of telling who was right, since logically both sides were wrong. The only people with whom he could sympathize were those who remained outside the struggle: the Berber peasants, who merely wanted to continue with the life to which they were accustomed, and whose opinion counted for nothing. They were doomed to suffer no matter who won the battle for power, since power in the last analysis meant disposal of the fruits of their labor. He could not listen to Kenzie's excited recounting of arms discoveries by the police in the homes of wealthy citizens of the Medina, or of what the followers of Si Mohammed Sefrioui were rumored to be plotting in some stinking cell of the Medersa Sahrij at that very moment, because it was all of no importance. The great medieval city had been taken by force and strategy innumerable times; it would be taken again some day, the difference being, he feared, that on that day it would cease for all time being what it was. A few bombs would transform its delicate hand-molded walls into piles of white dust; it would no longer be the enchanted labyrinth sheltered from time, where as he wandered mindlessly, what his eyes saw told him that he had at last found the way back. When this city fell, the past would be finished. The thousand-year gap would be bridged in a split second, as the first bomb thundered; from that instant until the later date when the transformed metropolis lay shining with its boulevards and garages, everything would have happened mechanically. The suffering, the defeat or victory, the years of reconstruction—none of it would have had any meaning, it would have come about all by itself, and on a certain day someone would realize for the first time that the ancient city had been dead since the moment the first bomb had gone off.

Moreover, no one would care. Perhaps one could say it was already dead in one sense, for most of those who lived in it, (and certainly the younger ones without exception) hated it, and desired nothing more than to tear it down and build something more in accordance with what they considered present-day needs. It looked too impossibly different from any city they had ever seen in the cinema, it was more exaggeratedly ancient and decrepit than the other towns of Morocco. They were ashamed of its alleys and tunnels and mud and straw, they complained of the damp, the dirt and the disease. They wanted to blast the walls that closed it in, and run wide avenues out through the olive groves that surrounded it, and along the avenues they wanted to run bus lines and build huge apartment houses. Fortunately the French, having declared the entire city a *monument historique,* had made their aims temporarily unattainable. The plans for every new construction had to be submitted to the Beaux Arts; if there was any departure from the traditional style it could not be built.

"One thing you must give the French credit for," he was fond of saying, "is that they've at least managed to preserve Fez intact."

But often he felt there was a possibility that this was true only architecturally, that the life and joy had gone out of the place a long time ago, that it was a city hopelessly sick.

Suddenly Mme Veyron stood up. "I'm sorry, gentlemen," she said, stifling a yawn. "This has been very nice, but I'm simply overcome with sleep. I've got to lie down and have a little siesta."

Kenzie was disappointed. "I'd hoped to take you to the gardens later," he said. They were strolling toward the gate.

"Why don't you give me a ring about five-thirty from your hotel? Would there still be time?"

"It would be a good deal quicker if I called by here for you then."

She assumed an expression of dubiousness, but not before Stenham had caught a flash of resentment in her eyes.

"Well," she said slowly, "you may have to wait awhile for me to get myself ready."

He would do some waiting, too, thought Stenham; she'd see to that. Then he decided to try his hand. "Why don't you all have tea tomorrow with me? We can go to some out-of-the-way little café."

They had climbed the steps and were standing in front of the entrance door. Kenzie stood to one side with the waiter, paying the check.

"I think it would be wonderful. Let's," she said.

CHAPTER 17

Stenham awoke the next morning with a slight headache. The food at Si Jaffar's had been unusually heavy, and as a result he had passed a night of fitful sleep during whose frequent moments of wakefulness he was leadenly conscious that he was suffering from indigestion. *Bastela* at noon, and then at night lamb with lemon and almonds, drowned in hot olive oil, and that glutinous bread, helped down by six glasses of mint tea that was so sweet it stung the throat. . . . The more honor they wanted to pay you, the more inedible they made the food, weighing it down with sugar and oil.

It was a day of violent clarity, throbbing with sunlight. Any part of the sky he stared at from his pillow blinded him. The doves that had their nests somewhere outside his windows gurgled beatifically, and he had the feeling that they were some sweet substance melting out there in the fierce morning sun;

soon they would be nothing more than a bubbling syrup, but the sound would go on, the same as now. He yawned, stretched, and got slowly out of bed. The telephone was attached to the opposite wall. Moss found this an insufferable inconvenience. "I shouldn't like to have to stagger across the room to order breakfast," he had said when he first saw it. "Do take a comfortable room, and with a proper bath," he had urged him. "Like yours?" Stenham had said. "Yours happens to be just four times as expensive as this. Have you thought of that?" "Come, now, John. When things are as cheap as they are here, such mathematics don't mean anything," Moss had objected. "And you have dollars. I with my poor pounds have some excuse for trying to make my money stretch." This was another facet of the little game they played together. Stenham knew perfectly well that Moss had one of the largest fortunes left in England, and that moreover he owned apartment houses, cinemas and hotels in places that dotted the globe from Havana to Singapore, including several cities of Morocco, to which he made constant little trips, referring to these as "tours of inspection." But he also knew that it gave Moss intense pleasure to play poor, to pretend that the security which his several million pounds gave him was not there in the background, because, as he had exclaimed one day when he was in a confiding mood, "it's a stifling sensation, I assure you; every consideration is dictated by the existence of that *thing* there behind you. You have no freedom—none." At the time Stenham had replied rather tartly that you had whatever freedom you really desired. But he was willing to abet him in his pretense.

He took the receiver off the hook; it began to make a loud, tinny purring which continued until there was a small explosion as a man's voice said: "*Oui, monsieur.*"

"I should like to order breakfast."

"*Oui, monsieur, tout de suite.*"

The man hung up and the noise began again. Furious, Stenham jiggled the hook until the voice returned and spoke again with some asperity. "*Vous désirez, monsieur?*"

"I want breakfast," said Stenham with exaggerated clarity,

"mais ce matin j'ai envie de boire du thé. Au citron. Vous avez compris?"

"But I have already ordered coffee for you, the same as every day," the voice objected.

"Change the order."

"I shall do my best," the voice said with dignity, "but it will be somewhat difficult, since the coffee is at this moment being prepared in the kitchen."

"I won't drink the coffee," announced Stenham severely. "I want tea." He hung up, certain that he was going to find it impossible to work this morning. Any small incident at this hour could prove a barrier. And now the blood seemed to be pounding harder in his head. After swallowing two Empirins with a glass of cold water, he unlocked the door into the corridor and lay back to relax. He knew it was absurd to think so, but a day which did not provide at least some progress to his book seemed a day completely lost. In vain he argued with himself that a man could scarcely make his writing a reason for living unless he believed in the validity of that writing. The difficulty was that he could find no other reason; the work had to be it. At the same time he was unable to attach any importance to the work itself. He *knew*, no matter what anyone said to the contrary, that it was valueless save as a personal therapy. "Life has to be got through some way or other," he would tell himself. To others he said: "Writing is harmless, and it keeps me in dinners and out of trouble."

The tea came, brought by Rhaissa, who had a new tale of woe. Her relatives from the country had arrived without warning and deposited themselves in her house, seven of them, and being, of course, wildly envious of her good fortune as a city-dweller, had set about making her life miserable. They had appropriated her clothing, some of which they had sold in the Joteya; the rest they were wearing on their persons at the moment. They had broken several of her dishes, and let the children gouge holes in her walls. And worst of all, they had either stolen or destroyed her precious sodium perborate, because in an unguarded moment she had been foolish enough to tell

them of its magic properties. Her eyes blazed with indignation when she came to this part of the recital. Stenham lay back
against the pillows watching her, sipping his tea, thinking that
at least the two disturbances had come simultaneously, that it
would have been worse had the tea difficulty been today and
Rhaissa's saga tomorrow. When she had stopped he said, with
the inflection of outrage he had learned from years of speaking
with these people: "*Menène jaou? O allèche?* And why don't
you put them out?"

She smiled sadly. Of course that could not even be considered. They were relatives. One had to put up with them. In another two weeks or so they would be gone, if Allah willed it
so. Until then she would have to feed them and bear their depredations in silence.

"Don't you ever go to visit them?" he asked her.

She shook her head with contempt. Why should she? They
lived in the country, far away, and you had to walk or go on a
donkey after you got off the bus, and their village was several
hours away from the road.

"But if you did go, wouldn't you do the same thing, just sit
down and eat their food and make yourself at home?"

Rhaissa began to laugh gently. Such ingenuousness touched
her sense of the ridiculous. In the first place, she explained, they
hid all their food when they saw you coming. And then, you
never went to visit the people who lived in the country unless
there was an important marriage or a death which involved a
possible inheritance, because why would anyone go to the
country otherwise? It was empty, there was nothing to see. And
if for some reason you did have to go, then you took all your
food with you from the city.

"But that's crazy," objected Stenham. "The food all comes
from the country."

"*Hachouma,*" said Rhaissa, shaking her head. (It was the classical Moroccan reply, which, along with "*Haram,*" provided an
unanswerable argument that could end any discussion; Shame
and Sin were the two most useful words in the common people's vocabulary.) If you were lucky enough to live in the city,

you had to pay for that privilege by being an uncomplaining, if not eager prey to the greed of your rustic relations; any other course of behavior was shameful, and that was that.

"I'll give you another paper of powder tomorrow, *incha'Allah*," he told her.

A flood of blessings poured forth. Grinning, Rhaissa went out. Presently he heard her singing as she scrubbed the floor of the corridor.

His headache was going away. At the back of his mind there was expectation: he was looking forward to the tea later in the day with the American girl. "Madame Veyron" was the most inapposite name that fate could have provided for her. She should be called something like Susan Hopkins or Mary Williams. He found himself wondering what her name really was, and what she was really like. But if he allowed himself to dwell on such conjectures he would do nothing all day. Was it a foregone conclusion that he would not be able to work? With the prospect in mind of seeing her, it should be possible for him to discount the telephone scene and Rhaissa's interruption. He sprang out of bed and shaved. Then he sat and worked quite well until half past twelve, when he dressed and went down to the dining room for an early lunch, having decided to write letters afterward.

If there happened to be many tourists staying in the hotel, the restaurant proved to be slightly understaffed. These last few weeks, however, the news of unrest in Morocco had apparently frightened away all but the most hardy prospective visitors: there had been only a handful of transients, so that the waiters spent most of their time standing along the walls talking together in low voices. The Europeans stood by the entrance door and the Moroccans lined up near the door that led into the kitchen.

The three most desirable tables were those in front of the windows, looking over part of the hotel garden, the crenelated walls of the former palace, and the Medina beyond. Recently Stenham had been able to sit here when he pleased. Today he was annoyed to see that all three tables were occupied by groups

of Americans. He sat down at a small table where the light was
fairly good, and began to read. The waiters were used to his
eating habits; sometimes he took two hours to complete a meal,
turning page after page before he signaled to them that he was
ready for the next course.

The Americans nearest him were discussing their purchases,
made that morning in the *souks*. Eventually they shifted to the
subject of a woman acquaintance who had been present at the
bombing of a café in Marrakech; she still had pieces of shrapnel
in her, they claimed, and the doctor had told her it was quite
safe to leave them there. A man's voice then declared that such a
procedure was dangerous, that they could work their way to the
heart. Stenham tried without success to cut the sound of their
talk from his consciousness and isolate himself in his book. He
went on listening. When the people left the table, he managed
to read a bit; this was interrupted by an unexpected tap on his
shoulder. He looked up angrily into the amused face of Mme
Veyron.

"That's a good way to get indigestion," she said as he got to
his feet. "Reading at mealtime."

"How are you? I didn't see you come in."

"Of course not. I saw *you* come in. I was sitting over there in
the corner." Today she wore a simple tailored suit of powder-
blue sharkskin worsted; the severity of its lines were negated by
her mannequin-like figure, whose presence the suit emphati-
cally proclaimed.

"Won't you sit down a second with me?" he asked her.

She looked hesitant. "My friends are outside waiting. We're
going to have coffee on the terrace."

"Sit down anyway," he said firmly, and she did.

"But really, I can't stay."

"Who are your friends?" he inquired, conscious of a faint
envy: they had had her with them all during lunch.

"An American couple and a friend of theirs I met this morning in the *souks* down below. They're stationed at one of the
air bases near Casablanca somewhere. They asked me to have
lunch with them." She cast a quick glance around the dining-

room. "How does it happen you're all alone? Where's Mr. Kenzie? And the other one? I forget his name."

"Oh, I never eat with them," he said, as if eager to vindicate himself for having been with the two Englishmen the day before. "Yesterday was a special occasion, unusual. I don't know where they are." He looked at her. The flesh could not have been molded more artfully around her cheekbones and the corners of her mouth. Actually it was that, he decided, and nothing else, which made her beauty. It was a face to be sculpted, not painted. The eyes were of a neutral color, grayish hazel, the hair was medium light, halfway between blonde and brunette, perfectly straight and worn quite short in a coiffure that looked too anarchic to have been planned, and too smart to be accidental. It was all in those strange, perfect, multiple curves that led the vision upward from the lips over the cheek to the temple. He knew she was aware of his appraisal and that she felt no self-consciousness or resentment. "It's nice to see you," he said after a moment.

"I really can't sit here. They want to get started back to Casablanca in a few minutes and they've been awfully nice to me."

"Why don't you join me after they've gone? I'll be sitting over at the end of the terrace at one of the tables under the big palm tree."

"Well," she said doubtfully, "they offered to drop me at my hotel on their way back. I don't know."

"Remember, you're due to see me at five, you know, anyway. You hadn't forgotten?"

"Of course I hadn't forgotten," she said indignantly.

"If you have to go home, I'll take you back in a cab, but stay and have another coffee with me after your friends leave."

"All right." She smiled very briefly, but radiantly, and walked out.

He ate the rest of his lunch at what for him was an uncommonly rapid pace; he did not really believe she might change her mind and leave with her friends, but there was, after all, the possibility of it, and the fact that she was now out of sight made it seem more real. But when he went outside he saw her there in the sun with the others, looking a little grave and nodding her head. In order not to cross the terrace where she sat, he went through the bar and down the dark corridor that led toward the main entrance hall, then out into a small shady courtyard where goldfish swam in a pool beneath a group of tall banana plants. From there he came out upon an extension of the terrace and took a table at the remote end, against the wall, and almost hidden by the huge green fan of spears made by a palm branch that waved in front of his face. When the Americans had left he intended to wait a decent interval, perhaps five minutes, and then go and join her. However, she rose almost immediately and came to his shady corner.

"They've gone," she announced. "I'm thinking of moving to this hotel. I didn't realize it was as reasonable as it is. They told me they had a double room without bath last night for twelve hundred francs. I'm only staying over at my little horror because I have to watch the pennies these days. But the difference is so little. Do you realize I have to pay seven hundred for my closet, and they don't even sweep it out? There's still a big piece of bread under the bed that was there the day I came."

"Seven hundred!" he exclaimed. "But I have a fine room for eight. You're being royally rooked." It was too good to be true, that she might move here. He decided to say no more, for fear she might sense his eagerness and change her mind.

"I'd like to talk with the manager and see what they have, at least."

"The place is pretty empty. Which brings me to a question I've been wanting to ask you. How does it happen you're wandering around Morocco alone, this year of all years?"

She looked at him fixedly, as if debating the wisdom of entering the conversational room whose door he was holding open for her. A second later she seemed to have made her decision, but he could not tell whether it had been made with full confidence in him or with certain reserves. And the fact that the question of confidence had arisen at all in his mind reopened an airless chamber of his past where suspicion had been mandatory and trust in others a matter open to hourly question.

"This year of all years," she echoed. "That's the answer. I'd always wanted passionately to see Morocco, and I had an awful premonition that I'd better come now or I'd miss it altogether."

"Why?" He thought he knew what she meant, but he wanted to be sure.

"Well, my God, look at the papers!" she cried. "It doesn't take any great brain to see what's happening." Now he felt almost certain that she had divined his thought, and was on the defensive. "There's a little war in progress here. There won't be anything left of the place if it goes on at this rate." (But it's hard to feign innocence if you've eaten the apple, he reflected.) "And it looks to me as if it *is* going to go on, because the French aren't going to give in, and certainly the Arabs aren't, because they can't. They're fighting with their backs to the wall."

"I thought maybe you meant you expected a new world war," he lied.

"That's the least of my worries. When *that* comes, we've had it. You can't sit around mooning about Judgment Day. That's just silly. Everybody who ever lived has always had his own private Judgment Day to face anyway, and he still has. As far as that goes, nothing's changed at all."

A little Algerian waiter, who sometimes served as assistant barman, had come up to the table.

"*Vous prenez que'que chose, Monsieur Stenhamme?*" he inquired.

"Coffee?" Stenham asked her.

She shrugged her shoulders. "Yes. I might as well. I'll be hopped up all afternoon, but it doesn't matter."

"Or have a liqueur."

"Cointreau, Chartreuse, Pippermenthe, Crème de Cacao, Grand Marnier, Whiskey, Benedictine, Armagnac, Gin, Banania, Curaçao—" the waiter intoned.

"Stop him!" she cried. "He'll have Pilsner in there any minute. No, no, no! Coffee was the suggestion, and coffee it is."

"*Deux cafés.*"

She lighted a cigarette. "Before I was married, I worked in

Paris for UNESCO awhile. Just a secretarial job—nothing important. But I did get around, and it did give me a new kind of interest in things. I wouldn't say I'm fascinated by politics, but at least I know they exist." (Her least intelligent remark to date, he thought; very much on the defensive.)

"And before, what did you know?"

She laughed. "Not very much, I'm afraid. Dances, dates, art school, even dramatic school." She was silent a moment. The terrace was completely deserted now, and the only sounds were the sporadic twittering of sparrows down in the lower garden and the steady clicking of a typewriter at the reception desk across the terrace.

Stenham was dissatisfied; he felt he had bungled things. He had not got the answer he had been wanting; perhaps he had not put his question properly. Not the great question, which it was of no use to ask anyway, since the information had to be volunteered, but the first, vague, general query which might lead the way. Again, maybe it was not one question, but many. Why was she interested in Morocco? What did she want to see here? What was she doing here all alone, when most people refused to come even with large groups? Why was she not afraid, where had she been, how long was she staying? His intuition told him that an inquisition was not in order at this stage of the acquaintanceship, that if he put questions now, she would not take offense, would not so much as show by any word or gesture that she minded them, but would merely disappear without a word of warning, and then she would take good care that he never saw her again. This was certainly not the way he wanted things to happen.

"I don't know what you've seen here in Morocco," he said, "but I don't think you're likely to see anything greater than this town."

"Oh, I know. I'm sure of that. That's why I decided to stay awhile. Originally I was only going to give it a day. Can you imagine? I decided that even if I miss certain other things it'll be worth it, to see more of Fez. But I've only got a given amount of energy. I can't keep going night and day."

"There are a lot of questions I'd like to ask you," he said suddenly, in spite of himself, and a little scandalized at his own lack of control. (But perhaps this was the right way to intimacy —the neutral approach. Had not everything been completely natural so far? And what did he want, in any case, but intimacy, in the final analysis?) "The sort I can't expect to get any intelligible answers to from our English friends."

Her expression had not changed at all. "What sort of questions?" she said.

"About your—our—reactions to this place. Just what it means to you or to me. It's sort of important, don't you think? I mean, what do we see in it, why do we like it, what have we got in us that responds to such a city? Or perhaps you don't respond completely, the way I do."

"Oh, I love it! I love it!" she protested.

This was not the kind of answer he wanted, and he wondered fleetingly if she were, after all, only a very pretty American tourist, if he were not making a novel of a simple meeting. Later, he told himself; he could never get further than she was willing he should. The problem was not to discover who she was, but rather to assume that he knew, and make her willing to confirm the identification. She must never feel that his conversation was attempting to enfold her. Later, at some still unforeseeable moment, if he were lucky, he would be granted that necessary glimpse into her mind that would tell him what he wanted to know. Forget it all, he said to himself. Beyond the trees the day was hot and clear, waiting to be used.

"It's a shame to be sitting here," he told her.

She looked surprised. "What's the matter with here? It's delightful."

"Wouldn't you like to hire a carriage, and be driven by two clodhopping old horses all the way around the Medina? It's a beautiful drive, if you don't mind the sun."

"Oh, I love the sun," she said.

"But you have to have your head covered," he reminded her; he felt that if it were he who made the objections for her, she might be more likely to accept.

"It's not so bad if you're in motion. It's lying still on the beach that's fatal. Anyway, I have an enormous handkerchief in my handbag I could wrap around. But—"

"Ah, you wanted to look at rooms, of course. Let's do that now. Then afterward, if you still felt like going, we could call a cab."

"I thought you said a carriage."

"I know, but the nearest carriage-stand is at Bab Bou Jeloud. It would be about an hour and a half before they got here. Perhaps not quite that long," he quickly added, fearful that she might come to the correct conclusion that the complete tour would take a very long time indeed. "It's getting the message to the driver, and so on. You know how slow they are. What you have to do is go in a car to Bou Jeloud and take your carriage there."

"Well, I think it would be wonderful. But you've probably done it ten thousand times."

"Not that many. And certainly I've never done it with you."

She laughed.

"Why don't you look at the rooms now, and I'll call for the taxi. It'll be on its way while you're looking." He wanted to make the decision irrevocable.

"Fine, fine." She got up, and they went across the terrace to the desk. When he came out of the telephone booth she and the receptionist had gone upstairs, up *his* stairs, to the tower. This was where he had been almost positive the man would take her, because it was there in the old wing where the cheapest rooms were. The regular tourists inevitably preferred the spacious modern bedrooms of the other parts of the hotel. He hoped the receptionist would be tactful enough not to point at his door as they went past, and say: "Monsieur Stenham's room"; it would be like him to do something stupid like that. Then she would undoubtedly decide on another floor, or perhaps the new wing or a room down in the garden near Moss, or she might even give up the idea entirely. He walked back across the terrace and stood looking over the balustrade down into the lower garden, feeling almost jittery and not at all pleased with himself. This unpleasant condition he attributed to the sense of failure he felt with regard to the little conversation they had carried on during coffee. Whatever happens with her, he thought, will be my fault a hundred percent. Usually when he had discovered the reason for his perturbation, the understanding sufficed to mitigate it somewhat; this time it changed nothing. "Wrong explanation," he decided. He stood there, his eyes fixed now on one branch of trembling poplar leaves, keeping his mind a blank, because he heard voices coming down the stairs to the lobby, and he had renounced trying to discover the reason for his momentary depression. It was they; they stood a moment in the lobby talking. Then, smiling, she came out and joined him.

"Well, what's the verdict?" he said.

"I'm calling him tonight to let him know definitely. I've got to do a little bookkeeping first, and see just where I am financially, before I step into high life."

"How'd you like the rooms?"

"Oh, well, of course they're charming. There's one, especially, that looks like something out of Haroun er Rachid's palace. And the views are so wonderful."

They went up the main stairs and waited at the gate for the taxi. It came, an incredibly battered old vehicle; the driver kept the motor running while he poured water into the radiator, but as they got in it stalled. "Patience is all we need," murmured Stenham. After a good deal of violent cranking and advice volunteered by a slowly collecting crowd of hotel employees and interested passers-by, the chauffeur managed to start the engine shuddering again, and they jounced out through the two arched gates onto the steep serpentine road that wound upward through the cemeteries and olive groves. At Bou Jeloud they stepped from the running-board of the cab into the creaking carriage. It took Stenham a while to arrange the price with the driver, an enormously fat man who wore a crimson cummerbund to match his fez, and even the final agreement was for more money than it should have been. However, he thought, a little recklessness often made him feel more satisfied with himself; it might do that now.

"Let's go!" he cried. "*Yallah!*"

CHAPTER   18

They moved slowly through the throngs of people who were on their way to and from the Joteya carrying mattresses, worn clothing, broken alarm clocks and hammered brass trays from the Seffarine. "This is their coliseum," Stenham told her. "This is where they really enjoy themselves. A man may have a brand-new shirt or pair of shoes and be delighted with whatever it is, but in a few days the urge will get too strong, and he'll come up here and spend a day trying to see what he can sell it for. Then he'll sell it at a loss, of course, and buy something second-hand to take its place. He's had his money's worth, though: the pleasure a whole day of haggling has given him. And he goes back home happy, with an old shirt or an old pair of shoes instead of a new one. The French have caught on; they charge them admission just to get into the market, and look at the waiting-line."

When they were finally outside the ramparts in the country, going between the dusty walls of cane, the horses established their rhythm, jangling the brass bells of their harnesses, and the carriage lurched crazily. To brace themselves, they put their feet up on the worn black leather seat facing them, their legs out straight in front of them.

"This is absolute heaven," she said happily. "Just the right speed for seeing this landscape."

At each new curve the vista changed: sand-colored hills, rows of green-gray olive trees, distant glimpses of the eroded country to the east, with its bare mesa-topped mountains hard in the afternoon sunlight, a sudden view of the vast oyster-gray Medina at their feet, formless honeycomb of cubes, terraces, courtyards, backed by the groved slopes of Djebel Zalagh. "There just isn't a straight stretch anywhere on this road. It's all curves," she said as he lighted a cigarette for her. Still the landscape went on unfolding, the countryside revealing its graceful variations on the pastoral theme. Small, hot ravines of bare yellow earth where only agaves grew, like giant stalks of asparagus, sudden very green orchards where people sat smiling in the shade (and the musky, almost feline odor of the fig trees was like an invisible cloud through which the carriage had to pass), an ancient, squat, stone bridge, cows standing in the mud, now and then a motionless stork sailing on a high air-current above the city. The road had dipped down to the river and climbed up again, it had gone near to the ramparts, past the arches of Bab Fteuh, veered off into the country, still descending through deserted terrain, as though it would never stop. When it flattened out, the pace slowed a little, and later, when it began to wind upward once more, the driver occasionally cracked his whip, calling a lengthy, falsetto: "Eeeee!" to the tired horses.

"Don't let him whip them, please," she implored, as the long leather thong descended with the sound of a firecracker for the fifth or sixth time.

Stenham knew the uselessness of arguing with an Arab about anything at all, and particularly if it had to do with the performance of his daily work, but he leaned forward, saying in a tone of authority: "*Allèche bghitsi darbou? Khallih.*" The fat man turned halfway around and said laughing: "They're lazy. They always have to be beaten."

"What does he say?" she inquired.

Taking a chance, he replied: "He says if you don't want him to whip them he'll stop, but they go faster if they hear the whip."

"But he's actually hitting them with it. It's awful."

To the driver in Arabic he said: "The lady is very unhappy to see you beat the horses, so stop it."

This did not please the fat man, who made an involved speech about letting people do their work the way they always did it; if the lady knew a great deal about horses he expected to see her driving a carriage one day soon. Stenham secretly sympathized with the man, but there was nothing to do save forbid the use of the whip—if he could manage it.

"Put it away, please. *Khabaeuh*."

The man was now definitely in bad spirits; he went off into a muttered monologue, addressing it to the horses. The latter continued to go ahead with decreasing speed, until the carriage was moving approximately at the pace of a man walking. Stenham said nothing; he was determined that if there were to be any further suggestions for the driver, they should be made by her.

They could never have got back to the hotel by five o'clock in any case; that he had known from the beginning. And at this rate it would be dark before they completed the tour. Stones and bushes moved past in leisurely fashion. The air smelled clean and dry. He turned to her. "This is a strange situation," he said, smiling.

She looked a little startled. "What do you mean?"

"Do you realize that I don't even know your name?"

"My name? Oh, I'm sorry. It's spelled V-e-y-r-o-n."

"Oh, I know that," he said with impatience. "I mean, your own name. After all, you're not living with your husband, are you?"

"Actually, the idea of using George's last name only occurred to me here in Morocco. And I've found it makes everything so much easier. I don't know why I didn't do it before. My maiden name is Burroughs, and the French can't get anywhere near it, either in spelling or pronunciation."

"You have a first name, I suppose." He smiled, to offset the dryness of his remark.

She sighed. "Yes, unfortunately. It's Polly, and I loathe it.

You know it's impossible to take anyone named Polly seriously. So I've always used just the last syllable."

"Polly Burroughs," he said reflectively. "Lee Burroughs. I don't know. I think I like Polly better."

"Well," she said firmly. "You're not going to call me Polly. I can tell you that right now. If you want to send me into an emotional tailspin, all you have to say is 'Hello, Polly,' and I'm gone. I can't *bear* it!"

"I promise never to do the awful thing."

They drove on with painful slowness, upward round the innumerable curves, each bend bringing new vistas of empty, sun-flooded valleys to the north and a wider expanse of the flat lands to the east where the river made its leisurely meanders. The light became more intense as the afternoon progressed. Now that he knew her first name he felt closer to her, and several times in the conversation he called her Lee, watching her to see if she minded. She appeared to take it for granted.

It was six o'clock when they came to the little café atop the cliff overlooking the city, and he told the driver to stop. The place was deserted.

"We've committed a *faux pas* of major proportions, I'm afraid," she said as they got down from the carriage. "Our English friends will never forgive us. They were expecting us at five. But it's all been so beautiful I must confess I don't care."

They sat in the late sunlight at the very edge of the precipice and ordered tea. The vast city, made more remote by its silence, lay spread out below.

"What's very hard to believe," she said presently, "is that this can be existing at the same moment, let's say, that people are standing in line at the information booth in the Grand Central Station asking about trains to New Haven. You know what I mean? It's just unthinkable, somehow."

He was delighted. "Lee, you understand this place better than anybody I've ever met. You're so right. It's a matter of centuries, rather than thousands of miles." He was silent a moment thinking: Even the smallest measure of time is greater than

the greatest measure of space. Or is that a lie? Does it only seem
so to us, because we can never get back to it?

"It's very, very strange and disturbing, this place," she was
saying, as if to herself. "I don't quite see how you can stay in it.
It would be like being constantly under the influence of some
drug, to live here. I should think going out of it could be terribly painful, when you've been here a long time. But then of
course, perhaps after a while the effect wears off. That's probably
it. It must."

A man in a turban brought the tea. Small, furry bees began to
appear and to balance themselves on the edges of the glasses.
Their movements were slow and clumsy, but they were determined to get to the sweet liquid. Stenham proceeded to describe
a series of complicated flourishes in the air with his glass, in the
hope of putting them off the scent long enough to raise it to
his lips, but when he was about to drink he saw that one had
fallen in and been scalded to death. He fished it out with his
finger and flipped it away; others had now arrived and were
crawling down the inside of the glass.

"It's sort of hopeless," she said.

"Do you want the tea?" he asked her.

"Of course I do."

"Then we'll have to go inside the café. It's the only remedy."

They carried their glasses into the tiny room and sat down.
The air smelled musty. There was no window.

"Now, aren't they funny people?" she demanded. "Wouldn't
you think that with this fantastic view outside they'd have at
least some sort of peep-hole, instead of shutting themselves into
a cell this way? Or don't they even know there *is* a view?"

"Oh, I think they know, all right. Sometimes they'll sit for
hours looking at a view. But my guess is that they still think in
terms of tents. Any building's a refuge, something to get inside of and really *feel* inside, and that means it has to be dark.
They hate windows. It's only when they've shut themselves in
that they can relax. The whole world outside is hostile and
dangerous."

"They can't be that primitive," she objected.

"Will you give me one of your Casa Sports? I'm all out of mine." The taste of the black tobacco reminded him of the *souks*, and for a second he had an image of the slanting rays of sunlight that filtered through the latticework above, each ray blue with a mixture of smoke and dust-motes. Or was he being reminded of something she had said in the garden the day before?

"They're not primitive at all. But they've held on to that and made it a part of their philosophy. Nothing's ever happened to change that."

She sighed. "But has anything ever happened to change anything? I wish I knew what makes them tick. They're such a mixture, such a puzzle."

They would have to be leaving, he thought. Night came down quickly, and he wanted to get inside the ramparts before it was completely dark. But he did not intend to alarm her by saying such a thing, and in any case she had drunk only a little of her tea.

"There's one thing I've found that helps," he said. "And that is that you must always remember it's a culture of 'and then' rather than one of 'because,' like ours."

Frowning, she said: "I don't think I follow."

"What I mean is that in their minds one thing doesn't come from another thing. Nothing is a result of anything. Everything merely *is*, and no questions asked. Even the language they speak is constructed around that. Each fact is separate, and one never depends on the other. Everything's explained by the constant intervention of Allah. And whatever happens had to happen, and was decreed at the beginning of time, and there's no way even of imagining how anything could have been different from what it is."

"It's depressing," she said.

He laughed. "Then I've said it wrong. I've left out something important. Because there's nothing depressing about any of it. Except what the place has become under the Christians," he added sourly. "When I first came here it was a pure country. There was music and dancing and magic every day in the streets.

Now it's finished, everything. Even the religion. In a few more years the whole country will be like all the other Moslem countries, just a huge European slum, full of poverty and hatred. What the French have made of Morocco may be depressing, yes, but what it was before, never!"

"I think that's the point of view of an outsider, a tourist who puts picturesqueness above everything else. I'm sure if you had to live down there in one of those houses you wouldn't feel the same way at all. You'd welcome the hospitals and electric lights and buses the French have brought."

This was certainly the remark of a tourist, and an ignorant tourist, too, he thought, sorry that it should have come from her.

"At least you can say you were in on the last days of Morocco," he told her. "How's your tea? Finished? I think we ought to be going."

The driver glowered at them as they climbed into the carriage. From the café the road was downgrade all the way. The horses needed no prodding to make them go along briskly. A cool breeze swept across the hillside as they came down toward Bab Mahrouk, and the day had almost faded from the sky.

Twilight is an hour which, by subtly making them conscious of the present, can bring two people together, or it can set each one digging among his own private memories. Stenham was thinking of an evening more than twenty years before, when, as a college freshman on vacation, he had driven down this same road, more or less at the same hour (and possibly even in the same carriage—who could tell?). His state had been one of unquestioning happiness. The world was beautiful and life was eternal, and it was not necessary to think further than that. Now he had changed of course, but he was convinced that the world also had changed; it seemed unthinkable that any youth of seventeen today could know the same light-heartedness, or find the same lyrical sweetness in life that he had found then. Sometimes for the space of a breath he could recapture the reality, a delicious pain that was gone almost as it appeared, and it provided him with proof that there was a part of him which still lay bathed in the clear light of those lost days.

She too had gone back into memory, but all the way to her
childhood. What is there, she thought, that's missing now, and
that I had when I was little? And a second later she had the
answer. It was the sense of timelessness that had been there
inside her and was gone forever. She had been robbed of it the
day her aunt had come to her and said: "You will never see
your mother and father again." The fact that there had been a
plane crash had meant nothing to her, and even the knowledge
that her parents were dead had been only a mysterious, awe-
some abstraction. Mingled with her feeling of loss she had experienced a strange sense of liberation. But now she knew that
what had happened was that time had begun to move inside
her. She was alone, therefore she was herself, and at last on her
way. And ever since then she had been on her way, moving
toward the end. There was nothing tragic or even pathetic
about it, any more than there is anything tragic or pathetic
about the rotation of the earth. It was merely the difference
between being a child and being an adult. She had become an
adult early, that was all. The long ride had shaken something
loose in her spirit; she felt now rather the way she often felt
at the end of a concert—a little battered, but emotionally refreshed.

Suddenly he reached out and took her hand. "How are you?"
he said gently, forcing his fingers between hers. They had gone
through the gate, were in an open space where a few feeble
flares guttered on the counters of stalls; shadowy figures moved
by very close to the carriage, almost brushing its wheels with
their garments as they passed. She laughed shortly, not returning his pressure. "I'm fine," she answered. "Perhaps a little
tired."

"Shall we take a cab to my hotel? How about having dinner
with me?"

"It's awfully sweet of you, but I just don't feel up to it."

"Are you sure?"

"Yes, really. All I want is to lie out flat in bed and have a
little something to eat, right in bed, I mean, and then sleep,
sleep, sleep!"

"Perhaps it's just as well," he said, determined not to sound disappointed. "Mr. Kenzie and Mr. Moss would probably be in the dining-room, and we'd have to face them. If you go to your hotel I'm going to eat at an Arab place here near Bou Jeloud. Sure you wouldn't like to join me?"

"I'd love to," she said, carefully disengaging her hand to light a cigarette, "but I'm not going to tonight. May I take a rain check on it?"

"Any time. The place'll always be there." He was saying exactly the wrong things; surely she was going to detect the degree of his chagrin. But his effort to mask it seemed to leave no margin of energy for conversation. How difficult it is, he thought, to hide the fact that you really care about a thing, and how right people are to distrust suavity. "I'll make our excuses tomorrow when I see our friends," he went on, casting about for any subject to talk about. "I'll say you weren't feeling well—"

"You certainly won't!" she exclaimed indignantly. "If you do that I'll call Mr. Kenzie myself and tell him the truth. After all, I didn't know we were going to be gone all afternoon. I wasn't feeling well, indeed!"

The carriage had drawn up and come to a halt at the end of a long line of other carriages; the driver, in a good humor at last, because he was about to be paid, called out: "*Voilà, messieurs-dames!*" When Stenham handed him the money he demanded considerably more, citing the wait and the speed at which he had been required to move. After a short altercation he gave him half the supplementary sum. That appeared to be sufficient, for the fat man shouted "*Bon soir!*" in a jovial voice, and jumped down from his seat, hoisting a small boy up to guard the vehicle while he went across the square for tea.

They walked in the dark through the street that smelled stronger than any stable; the stars overhead were there in such quantity and brilliance that they looked artificial. In most places of the world the sky was not completely powdered with them —there were also dark patches. He wanted to call her attention to the fact, but something in him would not move, and he remained silent. When they came to the Café Bou Jeloud, where there were always a few old taxis waiting, he said: "Remember, you have work to do tonight."

"Work?" she inquired, not understanding.

"Or so you said. You were going to make financial calculations and call the hotel in the morning."

"Yes." Her voice had no expression. They got into a cab, and were off, around corners and through crowds, with an incredible racket of banging metal, wheezing motor and constantly bellowing horn.

"Thank God there are no cars in the Medina," he said. "The casualty list would be something."

"I'm really awfully tired," she answered, as if he had inquired how she felt. He did not believe her.

In front of her little hotel with its single light over the door they got out, and he paid the cab. "Aren't you keeping it?" she said, surprised.

"My restaurant's a ten-minute walk through the Medina."

"Well, thanks again," she said, holding out her hand. "It's been delightful. At the moment I'm just knocked out."

"I'll call you tomorrow," he told her.

"Good night." She went through the door into the office. He stood outside in the dark a moment, and saw her pass the doorway with her key in her hand. Then he turned and went up the quiet road to Bab el Hadid.

The next morning as he lay in bed working, Abdelmjid came up from downstairs with a telegram in his hand. It read: THANKS JOING MEKNES LEE.

He stared at it and worked no more that day.

CHAPTER 19

It had been a shock, her sudden departure. On the one hand it obviated the necessity for an explanation to Moss and Kenzie of his failure to keep the rendezvous, for she had sent similar telegrams to both of them, and that permitted him to lie vaguely, saying that he had been around to her hotel and found her already gone; they put the incident down to feminine caprice and American ill-breeding. But on the other hand it set in motion a whole machinery of self-questioning and recrimination. He was completely convinced that he had somehow frightened her off. The question was: at what point had she taken alarm?

A good many times he went back over, in as much detail as his memory allowed, the sequence of their conversations, trying to force himself to recall her expression and tone of voice at each point. It was a difficult task, above all since, obviously, even though he might arrive at isolating the precise moment when he suspected that she had been put on her guard, there was no possible way of being certain that he was right, or, indeed, of knowing whether he had had anything at all to do with her bolting from Fez. Nevertheless, he continued with his attempt at recall and analysis of the afternoon and arrived at the conclusion that the whole thing had taken place at the very beginning, before they had ever left the hotel.

What brought him to this, was, of course, his very clear memory of leaning against the balustrade looking down into the garden, the feeling that everything had gone wrong, and the inability he had met with in his effort to explain to himself the sense of nervousness and frustration to which he had been prey. "I was right about her!" he would think with triumph. All the tortured little turnings of her mind that he had imagined he had observed had actually been taking place, then; her replies and remarks had been a welter of subterfuge. But a moment later he would return to doubt. A few days of this went on, and then he determined to talk to Moss about it.

"Alain," he said one day as they sat at lunch in a restaurant of the Ville Nouvelle, "What did you feel about Mme Veyron? What was your impression of her?"

"Mme Veyron?" said Moss blankly. "Oh, that rather intelligent, pretty American girl that Hugh had us to lunch with. You ask my impression? Well, I had no particular impression. She seemed pleasant enough. Why?"

"But you did have the impression that she was bright. So did I. And yet, if you think back, I'll bet you can't remember her making one intelligent remark, because she didn't."

"Well, really," Moss said, "I can't say that I remember very much at all about the conversation. Certainly it wasn't brilliant, if that's what you mean. It seems to me that it was Kenzie who did most of the talking that day. In any case, Mme Veyron made no shining contributions, there's no doubt about that. But I must say, I did have the distinct feeling she was not at all stupid."

Stenham beamed. "Exactly. The reason I'm saying all this, and you're going to laugh your head off at me, is that I've been thinking a lot about her. I think she's a Communist."

Moss did laugh, but discreetly. "I should think it was *utterly* unlikely," he said. "But do go on. How extraordinary you are, really! No, really, how extraordinary! Why on earth would you imagine such a thing about that poor girl?"

"Well, you know my history," Stenham began, feeling his heart beat faster, as it always did when he began to refer to this particular episode in his past. "I was with them night and day when I was in the Party, and you get so you can recognize them almost infallibly."

He suddenly wondered what had prompted him to talk about all this; Moss could not possibly have anything helpful to say, could throw no light on the dark sections of the subject, could not even share his interest. "As far as I know," he went on, "I haven't met a Communist in fourteen years, ever since I got out. But my sense of smell is still acute, and I'm convinced I'm right about her. And if I am, she's a lot brighter than either of us thought, because she put on a magnificent little act for herself."

"Really," complained Moss, "how can you believe a person's political convictions will change him to such an extent? Why shouldn't she be like everyone else, even if she is a Communist? I daresay I've met dozens and never been aware of the fact."

"You've got a lot to learn about them, then. That's all I can say. A real Communist, a consecrated one, is as different from us as we are from a Buddhist monk. It's a new species of man."

"Oh, balls, my dear John, balls." Moss signaled the waiter. "*La suite*," he said. "For a normally intelligent man you have some of the *most* unconsidered opinions. And you? I suppose you were a new species of man for the term of your adherence to the Party?"

Stenham frowned. "I never was a believer. I joined just for the hell of it. When I found out what it really was, I got out fast." He stopped for a second, then corrected himself. "That's not quite true. I don't think I remember my exact motives for getting out, but I do know I stopped being interested the day we became Russia's ally, in the summer of 1940. And a month or so after that I went around and told them I was leaving. The crowning touch was that they told me I couldn't leave on my own initiative."

Moss had listened to this with obvious impatience. "It wouldn't be, by any chance, that you admire her and suspect she has the constancy of mind and purpose that you lack? It couldn't be that?" He looked at Stenham with a droll expression, reminiscent of a robin listening for a worm.

"Good God! Are you mad?" Stenham cried. He waved away the platter that Moss tendered him. "No, none of those cardboard string-beans. I'd rather go without vegetables. All I can say is, you're absolutely, completely wrong."

"It's always possible, I admit," Moss said complacently. "But my personal conclusion is that the very instability that originally made it possible for you to go to such extremes—and it is an extreme, joining an organization like that—now makes you suspect everyone of being equally capable of such fanaticism. And of course, the world isn't like that for a moment. Good heavens, John, stop seeing life as melodrama. From the moral viewpoint you're fundamentally a totalitarian; you realize that, I hope?"

Stenham smiled. "That's the last thing I am, Alain, the very last thing."

The unpleasant accusation remained in his mind, however, and on his walks he thought about it. What disturbed him, he told himself, was not the fact that he believed there was any truth in it, but that Moss should have known so well exactly which dart to throw and where the unprotected spot lay. He was not sure that Moss himself had known what he meant when he had made the indictment, but that had slight importance beside the fact of his obsession with the meaning which he himself had unconsciously chosen to read into Moss's words: the imperfections in his character which once had caused him to open his arms to the Communists were still there; he still saw the world in the same way. That in essence was what he imagined the other had meant, and if it were true, then he had made no progress whatever through all the years.

In his mind he followed his retreat from where he had been to where he was now. First he had lost faith in the Party, then in Marxism as an ideology, then slowly he had come to execrate the concept of human equality, which seemed inevitably to lead to the evil he had renounced. There could be no equality in life because the human heart demanded hierarchies. Having arrived at this point, he had found no direction in which to go save that of further withdrawal into a subjectivity which refused existence to any reality or law but its own. During these postwar years he had lived in solitude and carefully planned ignorance of what was happening in the world. Nothing had importance save the exquisitely isolated cosmos of his own consciousness. Then little by little he had had the impression that the light of meaning, the meaning of everything, was dying. Like a flame under a glass it had dwindled, flickered and gone out, and all existence, including his own hermetic structure from which he had observed existence, had become absurd and unreal.

Accepting this, he had fallen back upon the mere reflex action of living, the automatic getting through the day that had to be done if one were to retain any semblance of sanity. He had begun to be preoccupied by an indefinable anxiety which he described to himself as a desire to be "saved." But from what? One hot day when he was taking a long walk over the hills behind Fez he had been forced to admit to himself with amazement and horror that there was no better expression for what he feared than the very old one: eternal damnation. It was a shocking discovery, because it revealed the existence of a mysterious, basic cleavage somewhere in him: he had not even the rudiments of any sort of faith, nor yet the memory of a time in childhood when such faith had been present. He had been shielded from faith. Religion in his family had been an unmentionable subject, on a par with sexuality.

His parents had told him: "We know there is a force for good in the world, but no one knows what that force is." In his child's mind he had come to think of the "force" of which they spoke as luck. There was good luck and bad; that was the extent of his religious understanding. There were also millions of people in the world who still practiced some form of religion; they were to be considered with a spirit of tolerance, like the very poor. Some day, with the necessary education, they might advance into the light of rationalism. The presence of a religious person in the household had always been regarded as something of an ordeal. He had been carefully coached ahead of time. "Some people in this world have strange beliefs, like Ida with her rabbit's foot, and Mrs. Connor with her crucifix. We know those things don't mean anything, but we must have respect for everyone's beliefs and be very careful never to offend anyone."

But even at that early age he knew that his parents didn't really mean *have* respect; they meant that it was good manners to pretend to have it in the presence of the person concerned.

Above all else, any reference to the doctrine of the immortality of the soul was regarded as the acme of bad taste; he had seen his parents shudder inwardly when a guest innocently touched on it in the course of the conversation. As a child of six he had known that when the physical organism ceased to function, consciousness was extinguished, and that was death, beyond which there was nothing. Until this minute the idea had been there, one of the pillars in the dark at the back of the cave of his mind, as much an axiom of practical life as the law of gravity.

Nor did he have any intention, if he could help it, of letting it change its status. His first reaction, that day, when he had identified his fear, was to sit down on a rock and stare at the ground. You've got to get hold of yourself, he thought. He could usually discover the origin of a state of anxiety; as often as not it was traceable to some precise physical cause, like insufficient sleep or indigestion. But what he had experienced in that flash had been almost like a momentary vision: he had seen consciousness as a circle, its end and beginning joined so that there was no break. Matter was conditioned by time, but not consciousness; it existed outside time. Was there then any valid basis for assuming that it was possible to know what went on inside the consciousness at the moment of death? It might easily seem forever, that instant when time ceased to function and life closed in upon itself, therefore it could prove to be inextinguishable. The immediacy of the experience had left him with a sensation of nausea; it was impossible to conceive anything more horrible than the idea that one was powerless to stop existing if one wanted, that there was no way to reach oblivion because oblivion was an abstraction, a fallacy. And so he sat, trying to shake off the nightmare feeling that had settled on him, thinking: What strange things happen in the mind of man. No matter what went on outside, the mind forged ahead, manufacturing its own adventures for itself, and who was to know where reality was, inside or out? He thought with passing envy of the people down in the city below. How wonderful life would be if they were only right, and there were a god. And in the final analysis what more commendable and useful thing had mankind accomplished during its whole existence, than the inventing of gods in whom its members could wholly believe, and believing, thereby find life more bearable?

When he had sat awhile, smoked three cigarettes, and let the intensity of his vision pale, he got up and went on his way, reflecting ruefully that if he had not originally had the senseless impulse to confide his suspicions concerning the girl to Moss, Moss might never have made the particular remark which, no matter how indirectly, was responsible for the mental agitation that had finally produced the unpleasant vision of a few minutes ago.

And then it occurred to him that if his suspicion about her were correct, then almost certainly she knew all about him. Kenzie had said: "She's heard of you." That could have been either merely the innocent reference to his books that it was meant to sound, or it could have been something else. Certainly the Party never forgot the names of those who had been of it. But nothing provided a satisfactory explanation of the manner of her departure.

That week the political situation in the region worsened considerably. A wave of arson spread over the land; everywhere the fields of wheat, gold, dry, ready to be harvested, caught fire, went up in flame and heavy blue smoke. The fire-fighters, French volunteers from neighboring farms, and from Fez and Meknès, were often shot at, sometimes hit. The express train on its way to Algier through the valleys of the waste land to the east of Fez was derailed and wrecked, then strafed. A bomb exploded in the post office of the Medina, just five minutes' walk from the hotel. Because a dozen Jews had been burned alive in a political manifestation at Petitjean, a monstrous little town some sixty miles back of Fez, there were riots in Fez between Jews and Moslems, and the police threw a protective cordon around the Mellah.

"If we catch a Jew alone in the street at night now, we treat him like a Moslem woman," Abdelmjid had said one morning when he came to get the breakfast tray.

"What do you mean?" Stenham had asked him; he expected a

shocking revelation, a new, lurid sidelight on the socio-sexual deportment of the Moroccans.

"Why, we throw stones at him until he falls down. Then we throw more stones and kick him."

"But surely you don't do that to Moslem women," Stenham protested; he had seen examples of unparalleled brutality to women, but there had always been some motive.

"Of course we do!" Abdelmjid had replied, surprised that the Christian should not be acquainted with such a basic tenet of public behavior. "Always," he added firmly.

"But suppose you were sick," Stenham began, "and your wife, Rhaissa, had to go out and get medicine or help for you?"

"At night, alone? Never!"

"But if she did?" he insisted.

Abdelmjid, used to the Europeans' futile fondness for playing with possibilities, humored him in the elaboration of his improbable fantasy. "Then she would run the risk of being killed, and it would serve her right."

Stenham had no more to say. Sometimes the senselessness of their violence paralyzed him. They were like maniacal robots; perhaps once there had been some reason for their behavior, but the reason was long since gone, no one remembered what it had been, and no one cared.

For the past few days not a single guest had arrived at the hotel. Outside the entrance gate there were always four or five French policemen standing; Stenham imagined they looked accusingly at him as he passed. At the outer gate, hidden in among the buses, they parked their command-car, but only during the day; at night the place was empty. An army could have assembled there undetected. Kenzie had twice been called to the Prefecture and been solemnly advised to drive his MG out of the city and back to wherever he had come from. "Is that an order?" he had inquired. "If so, the British Consul will be most interested to hear about it."

"What cheek!" he had snorted when he returned to tell Moss of his experience. "My visa's in order. Just trying to scare me out, the bloody bastards."

Moss, however, was inclined to take a more serious view of it. "I think you should go about on foot and in public conveyances, like the rest of us," he counseled him. "You're so conspicuous there in your solitary splendor, riding through the mob in Fez-Djedid. I noticed it the other day when I was sitting in one of the Algerian cafés there and you passed, and I thought: What a patient race they are, really. I wonder they haven't attacked you."

"Attacked me!" Kenzie cried indignantly. "Why should they?"

"Yes, attacked you," Moss repeated imperturbably. "Any situation like this is largely a matter of the have-nots versus the haves, you know. You're only tempting Providence, I assure you."

"But the car has English plates," objected Kenzie.

Moss was shaken by laughter. "I daresay those people are aware of that! The few who've ever heard the word probably would tell you England was a town somewhere in Paris. Why don't you have an enormous Union Jack made and spread it over the hood? Then they might think you were advertising a circus."

"They haven't bothered me yet. It's the French I have to look out for."

From day to day they were following the situation by reading the papers from Casablanca and Rabat, and this gave the events a character that was official and at the same time vaguely legendary, removing them a little from reality. Sometimes they felt that they were living in the middle of an important moment of history, although they had to remind themselves and each other of it from time to time. Also, the news sources, all French, gave a firm impression that the authorities were completely in command of things, that nothing serious had happened or was going to happen. Even if one made allowances for the natural tendency of the government-controlled press to play down the gravity of the events, one still felt confidence in the ability of the French to keep the situation from getting out of hand. The closing off of the Mellah seemed somehow an unreal event, an absurd and arbitrary precaution. One could determine how people felt only by observing their faces, and to Stenham those faces looked the same as always. So that he was forced to suppress a smile when Rhaissa came bursting into his room one morning with the news that a certain *mejdoub* had been murdered in the Zekak al Hajar by the French only an hour ago, and that before the day was out very bad things would happen. She was in a state of excitement bordering on hysteria; this made it difficult for him to get any sort of clear picture of what had happened.

He knew that the only difference between a *mejdoub* and an ordinary maniac was that the *mejdoub* was a Cherif. It was impossible for a Cherif to be crazy; by virtue of his holy blood his madness was automatically transformed into the gift of prophecy. For this reason, no matter how outrageous a person's behavior in public might be, it was dangerous to attribute it to a mere derangement of the mind. Unless one knew the person and his family, one might commit the sinful mistake of imagining he was a madman when in reality he was a man directly in touch with the truth of God. Many times Stenham had observed this attitude on the part of the common people. If a man were rolling in the dust of some foul alley, half latrine, or addressing the sun in the middle of the crowd, or screaming unintelligible insults to a café-ful of card-players, the others carefully ignored him. If he offered them violence, they met it with determined gentleness, and even though Stenham was aware that their reaction was motivated by fear rather than kindness, he often had admired the restraint and patience they showed in dealing with these obstreperous creatures.

"The French shot a *mejdoub?*" he repeated incredulously. "They couldn't have. There's a mistake somewhere."

No, no, she insisted, there was no mistake. Everyone had seen it. He had been calling maledictions upon the French, crying: "*Ed dem! Ed dem!* The Moslems must have blood!" the way he always did, and two policemen on their way down to the Nejjarine had stopped and watched him for a moment. And when he had seen them, he had identified them as emissaries of Satan, and shrieked louder for Allah to exterminate their race, and suddenly the two Frenchmen had spoken a few words with each other, gone over to him and pushed him against the wall. Then he had rushed at them and struck them and scratched them, and they had reached for their pistols and shot him down, each with one bullet. And the *mejdoub* (the blessing of Allah be upon his head) had fallen down, still howling: "*Ed dem!*" and died right in front of all the people, and more police had come and taken the body away, and hit the people in the street to make them keep walking along. And it was a terrible, terrible sin, one which Allah would not find it in His heart to forgive, and one which the Moslems would be obliged, whether they wished it or not, to avenge. Today was an accursed day, *bismil'lah rahman er rahim.* "And my husband and I, who work for the Nazarenes here in the hotel, who knows what will happen to us? The Moslems are very bad. They may kill us," she finished tearfully. There was always that element of ambivalence in the mind of a Moslem when he talked to a Christian about his own people. For a while it was "we," then suddenly it shifted to "they," and as likely as not out came some sort of bitter criticism or condemnation.

"No, no, no," said Stenham. "They might kill *me*, because I'm a Nazarene, but why should they kill you? You're a good Moslem. You're just earning your living."

Rhaissa was not consoled. She could think of too many good Moslems who had been earning their living working for the Nazarenes, and who had been shot down or stabbed without a chance to defend themselves; the fact that they had been working for the police was not relevant in her mind. "*Aymah!*" she wailed. "This is a very bad day!"

When he had finally got rid of her he went to the window and listened. The day was like any other day, the same sleepy sounds rose up from the Medina: the distant droning of the sawmill, donkeys braying, here and there a snatch of Egyptian song from a radio, and the cries of children. In the garden sparrows chirped. He sat down to work, found it impossible, and silently cursed Rhaissa. Then he tried lying in the sun for a while, with the hope that it might relax him, or start the flow of thought, or whatever it was he needed. But for the past week or ten days the weather had been too hot for sunbathing, and surely it was too hot today. The sweat ran down all the creases of his flesh, wet the cushions of the chairs. So he began to type letters at the table in the center of the room, lifting his gaze at frequent intervals to let it run unthinkingly across the panorama of hills and walls. After an hour or so, he slowly became conscious of the fact that he was spending most of his time looking out at the Medina. He incorporated the discovery in the letter, in one of those apologetic passages a person is wont to include when he feels that the missive he is engaged in writing, as a result of inattention or interruptions, is not going to be as well composed as it should be. "This is the damnedest place for trying to concentrate. It's quiet, but that seems to count for nothing. Even while I'm writing this I find myself stopping every other minute to stare out the window. It isn't to admire the view, because I don't even see it. I know it by heart. You can imagine how much worse it is when I'm trying to work. . . ."

He stopped again and reread what he had typed. It was absurd; he would have done better to try to find out *why* he kept staring out at the Medina. What did he think of that vast object out there, shining in the morning sun? He knew it was a medieval city, and he knew that he loved it, but that had nothing to do with what went on below the surface of his mind as he sat looking at it. What he really felt was that it was not there at all, because he knew that one day, sooner or later (and more likely sooner), it would not be there. And it was the same with all objects, all people. The city was, in a rough sense, a symbol; that was easy to see. It represented everything in the world that was subject to change or, more precisely, to extinction. Although this was not a comforting point of view, he did not reject it, because it coincided with one of his basic beliefs: that a man must at all costs keep some part of himself outside and beyond life. If he should ever for an instant cease doubting, accept wholly the truth of what his senses conveyed to him, he would be dislodged from the solid ground to which he clung and swept along with the current, having lost all objective sense, totally involved in existence. He was plagued by the suspicion that some day he would discover he always had been wrong; until then he would have no choice but to continue as he was. A man cannot fashion his beliefs according to his fancy.

When he had finished four letters he shaved, dressed, and went out the back way into the courtyard. There was no one there; even the tall Riffian *huissier* who watched the cars was not in sight, perhaps because there were no cars at the moment to watch. On the other side of the gate in the street, life went on as usual. The proprietor of the antique shop that operated exclusively for guests of the hotel bowed low when he saw Stenham. For the first three or four years he had persisted with tenacity in the belief that this tourist could be persuaded to buy *something*; many times he had lured him into the shop and offered him tea, cigarettes and pipes of kif, all of which Stenham had accepted with the warning that he was there solely as a friend, not as a customer. This had not hindered the man from going to the trouble of unfolding Berber rugs to spread across the floor, calling his sons and bidding them act as models to show off the ancient brocaded kaftans in front of the Nazarene gentleman, or opening the studded chests covered with purple and magenta velvet to bring out daggers and swords and powder horns and snuff boxes and chapelets and fibulae and a hundred other obsolete items in which Stenham had absolutely no interest.

Now, after all this time, the man had finished by being a little in awe of this inexplicable foreigner who had withstood so many onslaughts without once succumbing; the two were on the politest of terms. Nevertheless, Stenham did not like the man's unctuousness, and he knew him to be an unofficial informer for the French. That was almost inevitable, of course, and was not the man's fault. Any native who came in regular contact with tourists was obliged to tender reports to the police on their activities and conversation (although it was hard to understand what importance such superficial information could have for those who kept the records of the Deuxième Bureau). On several occasions the proprietor had attempted to engage Stenham in conversations that were, if carried through to their natural conclusion, obviously going to come out into the realm of politics, but Stenham, in accepted Moroccan fashion, had gently led them in other directions and left them dangling in mid-air, impaled on the hooks of *Moulana* and *Mektoub*, from which no man could decently remove them.

"I hope the health is fine this beautiful day," said the man, in French, as Stenham came near. Even his insistence on using the despised language annoyed Stenham; he liked Moroccans to speak to him in their own tongue. Then, without changing his facial expression or the debonair inflection of his voice, he added: "*Un mot, monsieur.*"

"What?" said Stenham, startled.

"Don't wander today." The man smiled vacuously. "*Ah, oui,*" he went on, as if in answer to a remark by Stenham. "*Ah, oui, il fait très beau.* The sun is a little warm, of course, but that's normal. It's the summer now. Better to stay in the hotel. And Monsieur Alain? Is he well? Give him my salutations, please. I have some very fine Roman coins now, a perfect merchandise for a great *connoisseur comme Monsieur Alain.* Tell him, please. You see, the front of my shop is closed. I am about to go inside and lock the door. *Bon jour, monsieur! Au plaisir!*"

He bowed again and stepped into his shop. Stenham stood quite still for a moment, fascinated by this unexpected performance. The entire front of the store was indeed boarded up, with heavy iron bars running diagonally in both directions across the shutters. He had not noticed it until now. And the man did, even as he watched, close the door, lock it, and noisily slide its three bolts, one after the other.

He walked on to the outer gate and stood there in the midst of hurrying porters, peering up and down the winding road. For once there were no policemen visible, and so he continued along the open space between the city walls and the cemetery where the native buses stood, looking, out of curiosity, for the command-car. It was not there. He began to suspect that there might be some truth in Rhaissa's tale, that the police had been ordered to potential trouble spots down in the city. But here the work of loading and unloading the buses and trucks was going

on as always, and there was no intimation that the day had anything unusual about it. Bored and hot, he strolled back to the
hotel, met the receptionist on the main terrace.

"It's hot today," he said.

The tall man glanced up at the sky. "I think we may have
thunder showers later this afternoon." In his striped trousers
and cutaway jacket he looked like a distinguished undertaker.

"Tell me," said Stenham, "there are no other guests in the
hotel now, besides the two English gentlemen and me, are
there?"

The man looked startled, hesitated. "We are expecting others
this evening. Why? If you wish to change your room, there is a
choice, yes."

Stenham laughed. "No. I'm delighted with my room, and
also delighted to have the hotel empty. Not for your sake, of
course," he added. "But it's more agreeable this way."

The receptionist smiled thinly. "A question of taste, *bien
entendu.*"

"All your European help sleep here in the hotel, don't they?"

Now the man permitted himself to draw his head back slightly
and stare into Stenham's face. "I think I know what is in your
mind, Monsieur Stenham. But allow me to reassure you. There
is nothing to fear. Our native help is completely reliable."
(Stenham smiled to himself: the man had come out to Morocco
for the first time four months ago and was already speaking like a
colon.) "Most of them, as you know, go home at night. The few
who are stationed here have long records of loyal service, and
with the exception of the watchman, all are locked into their
rooms by the major domo, who keeps the keys on his person."

To Stenham this was both ludicrous and shocking. He said:
"Really? I didn't know."

"Besides," pursued the other, thinking he had made his point,
"there is absolutely no cause for anxiety here in Fez."

"Oh, I realize that," said Stenham. "But this has been a bad
season for you, even so."

"The hotel is losing some fifty thousand francs a day, monsieur," the man announced gravely. "The season will show an

enormous deficit, naturally. We keep the quantity of our food purchases down to the minimum, but I believe you will have noticed no lowering of the quality?"

"Oh, no, no," Stenham assured him. "The food is always excellent." This was not true, and they both knew it; at their best the meals were only adequate.

Suddenly Moss appeared on the stairs coming up from the lower garden. He was swinging a cane. The receptionist greeted him, excused himself, and disappeared.

They sat down at a table in the shade. The little Algerian came rushing over. Moss ordered a Saint Raphael. "I say, John, have you heard the latest? It's too fantastic."

"I've heard two or three fantastic things today so far. What's yours?"

"It all has to do with a wild man the Istiqlal had been coaching to excite the mob—one of those poor demented things in rags who go about waving their arms, you know? The police fell directly into the trap." He proceeded to tell what was substantially Rhaissa's story, but with the added element of premeditated provocation on the part of the Nationalists. "It's not very sporting of them, to sacrifice the poor old fool so cold-bloodedly, I must say. In any case, Hugh went dashing off in the car to investigate, and was promptly arrested. He telephoned a while ago, in a complete rage, because they won't let him go until he produces his passport, which means that I've got to take it in to him. It's rather curious how he manages always to botch things, isn't it? All so unnecessary."

"But why are you sitting here calmly having a drink, if he's waiting?"

"Oh, I've ordered a cab," Moss said wearily. "It'll be here in a moment. But I really can't take it too seriously, or feel too sorry for Hugh, you know, because he's an idiot. His whole attitude is that of a boy at a cricket match. And of course it's not a cricket match, is it? One doesn't sit back and cheer when people are being killed. My feeling is that unless one can be of help in some way, one stays out of it entirely, don't you think?"

Stenham agreed. Moss had finished his drink, wiped his mustache with a handkerchief; now he stood up. "Well, my boy, I'll see you anon. And do stay here in the hotel. They may arrest me too, who knows, and I'll need you to get me out. Of course the blasted Consul has gone off somewhere for the day. I think it's deliberate on his part. Be on the lookout for a telephone call."

CHAPTER   20

When he got to his room, slightly out of breath, for the day was not only hot but unaccountably sultry and oppressive, his door was open and Rhaissa was scrubbing the floor. She had taken up the rugs and hung them over the balconies in the windows. The room smelled of the creosote solution in her pail. Pillows and bedclothes were piled on the chairs; his presence in the room at the moment was clearly redundant. However, he stepped inside and said to her: "Any more news?" She looked up, startled, and motioned for him to close the door behind him, which he did. Then, standing up and rolling her eyes in a way meant to imply conspiracy, she said: "There's not going to be any feast."

"Feast? What feast?" He had quite forgotten the advent of the Aïd el Kebir.

"Why, the Feast of the Sheep, the great feast! We've had our sheep on the roof for three weeks. Now he is very fat. But they will kill anyone who makes the sacrifice."

"Who will? What are you talking about?" He was in an unpleasant humor, he realized now, but he felt that it was partly her fault. Besides that, he wanted to sit down, and there was no place.

"The Moslems. The friends of freedom. They say anyone who sacrifices his sheep is a traitor to the Sultan."

One more step toward death, he thought bitterly. Whether the rumor were true or not, the fact that they were saying such things, that such an inconceivable heresy should even occur to them, was indicative of the direction in which they were moving.

"*B'sah?*" He said harshly. "Really? And I suppose everyone is going to listen to them and obey them? Politics is more important than religion? Allal al Fassi is greater than Allah? Why don't they call him Allah el Fassi and have done with it?" The pun seemed rather good to him.

She could not follow his reasoning; she understood only enough of what he had said to be profoundly shocked. "No one is greater than Allah," she replied gravely, considering what punishment was going to be meted out by God to this ignorant Nazarene for his outrageous utterances.

"Are you going to sacrifice your sheep or not?" he demanded.

She shook her head slowly from side to side, keeping her eyes on his. "*Mamelouah*," she said. "It's forbidden."

He was exasperated with her. "It's not forbidden!" he shouted. "On the contrary, it's forbidden not to! Allah demands it. Has there ever been a year when there was no sacrifice?"

She continued to shake her head. "Last year," she said, "there was no feast."

"Of course there was! Didn't Abdelmjid kill a sheep last year?"

"His father killed it. We were not married until afterward, just before Mouloud."

"But he did kill it."

"Oh, yes. But it was wasted, because the Sultan was taken away that very day."

"Ah," said Stenham thoughtfully. "I see. Of course." The French had chosen the holiest day of the year to whisk the Sultan away, and it had been the false Sultan who had performed the sacrifice. Therefore there had been no sacrifice. He was silent a moment. Presently he asked her: "Why can't you sacrifice your sheep in the name of the true Sultan?"

"The Istiqlal doesn't want any feast," she said patiently. "It's a sin to make a feast when everyone is unhappy."

"You mean the people might forget they were unhappy if they had their feast, and that's what the Istiqlal doesn't want. It wants them to remember they're unhappy. Isn't that it?"

"Yes," she said, a little uncertainly.

"But can't you see?" he cried, shouting in spite of himself, aware that she couldn't see at all, never would see. "Can't you see that they're trying to take your religion away from you so they can have all the power? They want to close the mosques forever and make slaves out of all the Moslems. Slaves!"

"My mother was a slave in the Pacha's house," said Rhaissa in a matter-of-fact tone. "She used to have chicken every day, and she had four bracelets of heavy gold and a silk kaftan."

As people have a way of doing when they know they are lost. Stenham resorted to sarcasm. "And I suppose she loved being a slave," he said.

"It was written." Rhaissa shrugged.

"Yes. Of course," he said, wondering how he had happened once again to allow himself to fall into the error of engaging in an argument with one of these people, since it was manifestly impossible to keep control of any discussion, and since the discussion's inevitable failure to remain on the road of logic always gave him a depressing sense of his own futility. After all, if they were rational beings, he thought, the country would have no interest; its charm was a direct result of the people's lack of mental development. However, one could scarcely hope for them to be consciously and militantly backward. Once they had got hold of even the smallest fragment of the trappings of European culture they clung to it with an absurd desperation, but they were able to make it their own solely to the extent that the fragment was isolated from its context, and therefore meaningless. But after so many centuries in the deep-freeze of isolation, it was to be expected that, having been brought out of it, the culture should now undergo a very rapid decomposition. "It was written," she had told him, and he had agreed with her; that was the final and all-embracing truth about Morocco—about the world, for that matter. Discussion was nothing more than the clash of personalities.

"*Mektoub.*" She was standing there, still looking at him inquiringly. He did not know what she was expecting him to add, and since he had nothing to say, he smiled at her, opened the door and went back downstairs. She would never finish the room if he stayed there.

For a while he sat in a dark corner of the lobby looking at old numbers of magazines dealing with the commercial aspects of the French colonies; they were illustrated with what were to him inconceivably dull photographs of factories, warehouses, bridges and dams under construction, housing projects and native workers. It all reminded him of the old Soviet publications he had used to study. After all, he reflected, Communism was merely a more virulent form of the same disease that was everywhere in the world. The world was indivisible and homogeneous; what happened in one place happened in another, political protestations to the contrary. Or perhaps the great difference was that the West was humane; it allowed its patients to be anesthetized, whereas the East took suffering for granted, plunged ahead toward the grisly future with supreme indifference to pain.

"The trouble with you, John," Moss had declared, "is that you have no faith in the human race." He had admitted it, but his argument had been that for him it was necessary first to have faith in God. "And have you the faith?" Moss had asked him. He said he had not. Moss was triumphant. "And you never will have!" he had cried. "The two are inseparable." Stenham had qualified this as specious reasoning, typical of the lack of humility of modern man. "Don't give me that," he had said. "I don't want it. It's exactly where all the trouble has come from." It was little scenes such as this one which he dreaded most when he was with Moss, and Moss was always provoking them; they would be in the midst of one before he realized it. Moss was so sure of himself, so comfortably anchored and so untroubled by the surges of existence; his facile homilies were meaningless.

He slapped the magazines down on the table and went to eat lunch. The silence of the dining-room was disturbing. The waiters came and went on tiptoe, and their conversation with each other was carried on in whispers. For the first time he heard orders being given in the kitchen. And then from the open window came the long, slowly rising note of a muezzin calling the prayer of the *loulli*. Immediately it was joined by another, until it became a great ascending chorus of clear tenor voices. Just as there was always the first lone voice, there was also the last, after the others had finished. He listened to the way it drew out the final syllable of its *Allah akbar!* Having called to the east and south and west, the man was now facing the north, and the voice came floating over the city clear as the sound of an oboe. Then a rooster's crowing on some nearby roof covered it, and the waiter arrived with a large *vol au vent* and set it before him. All at once he was conscious of the absurdity of the moment. This entire mechanism, the kitchen with its chef, the busboys in the pantry, the hierarchy of waiters, the assortments of china, glassware and cutlery, the wagon with its rotating display of hors d'oeuvres, the trays on wheels with their aluminum ovens and flickering blue alcohol flames, all of it was for him, was functioning for him alone. It was not as though there were a possibility that someone else might come in and lift the weight of responsibility from his shoulders. No one would come, and when he finished, the whole array would be cleared away and the tables set for dinner that night, and then even he might not be there, if he decided to go and eat in the city. Suddenly, aloud, he said: "Oh, my God!" He had just remembered that he was expected at Si Jaffar's for dinner.

It would certainly be rude to call and ask whether under the circumstances he ought still to come, for although he knew the family well enough to be aware that they would never admit the existence of any political situation, he had no idea on which side their sympathies lay. On several occasions in the house he had met officers in the French army with their wives, and the atmosphere had been one of complete cordiality. Furthermore, two of Si Jaffar's sons worked as functionaries with the French administration; the chances were pretty good, he thought, that the family was pro-French. And yet, every one of them had at some time or another voiced the strongest criticism of the French. He had used to join in, but lately he had thought it wiser merely to laugh and let them do the excoriating. If they were indeed on the side of the French, his own police dossier must have grown by leaps and bounds as a result of the evenings he had spent with them, for they would have had no choice but to report everything. There was no way of collaborating halfway with the French; if you were with them you had their complete protection, at least until such time as they decided you were no longer useful, and if you were not with them you were against them. To telephone Si Jaffar and say to him: "I wondered if you still wanted me to come, in view of what is going on at the moment," would have yielded no result at all, for he would have claimed absolute ignorance. Besides, just what was going on? Stenham himself did not know. The man in the antique store had been very kind to tender him his cryptic warning (he had not thought him capable of such a disinterested gesture), but he was going to disregard it, all the same. When he had finished his lunch he would go out the gate and down into the Medina on a little inspection tour of his own.

But the long meal and the heavy heat, and perhaps the silence of the dining-room, had their effect, and when he had eaten his fruit he rose and went upstairs to stretch out on the bed for a few minutes. First he drew the curtains so that the room was protected from the afternoon's yellow glare. A few flies buzzed in circles over the table; he directed a short blast at them from an aerosol bomb and took off his shoes and trousers. Then he lay down. The air was clogged with heat, and the gloom in the room was so deep that he could not see the painted arabesques on the beams of the high ceiling above his head. Somewhere off in the mountains, down in the Middle Atlas, there was the triumphant rolling of thunder, muted and gentle at this great distance. The sound came at regular intervals, enfolding him in its softness. Nothing lay between him and sleep.

And there he was suddenly, a century later, sitting up, blinking at a hostile unreal room invaded by lavender emptiness. The thunder crashed again in the garden, and he swung himself out of bed and ran to the windows. The rain was just arriving, angry and violent, and the city glowed in an unnatural twilight. It was quarter past five. He went back to the bed and lay down, reaching over his head for the bell. The sound of its ringing in the maids' room on the floor below was covered by the storm, but it had rung, for a moment later there was a loud knocking at the door.

"*Trhol!*" he shouted.

Rhaissa's head appeared, her eyes looking very white in the dimness. Surely she was eager to discuss the weather, but he was still paralyzed by sleep. "Bring me my tea, please," he told her, and she closed the door.

A moment later there was another knock. He thought he must have dozed again, for it was always at least a quarter of an hour before the tea arrived. "*Trhol!*" he cried, and then, since there was no response, he said it louder. The door opened, and a man stepped in. Stenham snapped on the light and saw Moss, his suit irregularly splashed with water, his cane under his arm.

"Come in, come in," he told him.

"I don't disturb you?"

"Not at all. I'm just about to have tea. I'll have her bring an extra cup."

"No, no. I must go down and change. I'm quite wet. I shan't even sit down. I merely wanted to report to you. It's been an incredible day. Details later." He wiped his forehead, blew his nose. "Hugh's in his room, so at least I accomplished my mission. I must say my opinion of the French has altered somewhat since this morning. Shall I see you at dinner?"

"Yes," Stenham said. "If the hotel's still standing, and hasn't been washed down into the river. Listen." He held up a finger: the rain roared. Moss smiled and went out.

Before Rhaissa brought the tea, the rain stopped with dramatic suddenness. It was now dark. He opened the windows, heard the water still clamoring in the drainpipes and spattering from the trees onto the terrace. But the air was quiet and chill. He stood awhile leaning out, listening and taking deep breaths.

Later, while he was drinking the tea, he again remembered his appointment at Si Jaffar's. There was no remedy for it; he would merely put on an old suit and splash through the mud to the house. By taking a series of short-cuts that he had worked out over the years, he could arrive in about a half hour. He gulped down the last of the tea, dressed quickly, put his flashlight in his hip pocket, and telephoned Moss.

It took a long time to get him, and when he answered, his voice sounded gruff. "*Oui? Qu'est-ce qu'il y a?*" he demanded.

"Have I waked you up?" Stenham began.

"No, John, but I'm dripping water all over the rug. I was in the bath."

Stenham apologized, explained why he would not be at dinner. Moss hesitated before saying: "John? I'm not sure I'd go if I were you. I don't think it's wise at this point."

"I've got to go," said Stenham flatly. "Get back into your tub and I'll see you tomorrow."

The streets were deserted. He walked at the side, keeping against the walls to avoid the brooks that ran down the middle. As he approached the river there was much more water; he was forced eventually to turn back and take a higher point at which to cross. Had he kept to his original course, he would have been in rushing water up to his knees by the time he had got to the bottom. The few men who passed were too much occupied with the business of walking to pay him any attention.

It was a difficult climb up the steep streets of the Zekak er Roumane; the mud was as bad as the water, and he kept sliding back. Behind the wet walls of the dwellings and from the terraces above, cocks were crowing senselessly, and small bats swooped in the air around the infrequent street lights. When he came out into the Talâa he found it almost as unpopulated as the side streets: the stalls were boarded up, and it was only now and then he passed a lone man sitting silently beside a donkey or a load of charcoal or a roll of matting. Even the beggars who usually crouched by the fountain below the turn-off to Si Jaffar's alley were gone tonight. He glanced at his watch and saw that it was almost eight o'clock. If only it were eleven, he thought, and he were on his way back to the hotel, the ordeal behind him. These endless evenings at Si Jaffar's were excruciating; he dreaded them with almost the intensity most people dread an appointment with the dentist. The conversation was of necessity highly superficial, and it went without saying that nothing which was said had even a trace of sincerity; if a truth happened to be uttered, it was a matter of sheer accident. Sometimes he tried to get the family on the subject of native customs, but even here on various occasions he had discovered them in the act of lying to him, purposely misinforming him, doubtless in order to enjoy a good laugh at his expense after he had gone. All the members of the family were most amiable, however, even if their friendliness was expressed in an arbitrary and usually ceremonious manner, and he felt that it did him good to tax his patience by sitting among them and learning to chat and joke with them on their level. Had anyone asked him why he thought it beneficial to make this strenuous effort regularly, his answer would have been that theory without practice was worthless. Si Jaffar and his family were typical middle-class Moroccans who had offered him the unusual honor of throwing their home open to him. (He had even met the wife, the daughters, unveiled, the aunts and the grandmother, an ancient lady who crawled everywhere through the house on her hands and knees.) It seemed to him that he could scarcely afford to miss any opportunity of seeing them.

Moss had once said to him: "For you Moslems can do no wrong," and Stenham had laughed sourly, agreed, and reflected that if that were so, neither could they do any right. They did what they did; he found it all touching and wholly ridiculous. The only ones he judged, and therefore hated, were those who showed an inclination to ally themselves with the course of Western thought. Those renegades who prated of education and progress, who had forsaken the concept of a static world to embrace that of a dynamic one—he would gladly have seen them all quietly executed, so that the power of Islam might continue without danger of interruption. If Si Jaffar and his sons had sold their services to the French, that still did not invalidate their purity in his eyes, so long as they continued to live the way they lived: sitting on the floor, eating with their fingers, cooking and sleeping first in one room, then in another, or in the vast patio with its fountains, or on the roof, leading the existence of nomads inside the beautiful shell which was the house. If he had felt that they were capable of discarding their utter preoccupation with the present, in order to consider the time not yet arrived, he would straightway have lost interest in them and condemned them as corrupt. To please him the Moslems had to tread a narrow path; no deviation was tolerated. In conversation with them he never lost an opportunity to revile Christianity and its concomitants. It was the greatest pleasure for him when they looked at one another with wonder and said, shaking their heads: "This one understands the world. Here is a Nazarene who sees the evil in his own people." A question which often came up at this point in such discussions was: "And have you never wanted to become a Moslem?" This embarrassed him profoundly, for it seemed to him that he was less equipped to embrace their faith than any other faith: it demanded a humility and submission that he could not conceive himself as feeling. He admired it in them, but he could never accept it for himself. Discipline for the sake of discipline, mindless and joyous obedience to arbitrary laws, that was an element of their religion which, praiseworthy though it might be, he knew was not for him. It was too late; even his ancestors of several centuries ago would have said it was too late. Who was wrong and who was right he did not know or care, but he knew he could not be a Moslem.

Still, it seemed to him that it was this very fact which made contact with them so desirable and therapeutic. Certainly it was this which lent the obsessive character to his preoccupation with them. They embodied the mystery of man at peace with himself, satisfied with his solution of the problem of life; their complacence came from asking no questions, accepting existence as it arrived to their senses fresh each morning, seeking to understand no more than that which was directly useful for the day's simple living, and trusting implicitly in the ultimate and absolute inevitability of all things, including the behavior of men. And this satisfaction they felt in life was to him the mystery, the dark, precious and unforgivable stain which blotted out comprehension of them, and touched everything they touched, making their simplest action as fascinating as a serpent's eye. He knew that the attempt to fathom the mystery was an endless task, because the further one advanced into their world, the more conscious one became that it was necessary to change oneself fundamentally in order to know them. For it was not enough to understand them; one had to be able to think as they thought, to feel as they felt, and without effort. It was a lifetime's work, and one of which he was aware he would some day suddenly tire. However, he considered it the first step in establishing an awareness of people; when he had told Moss that, Moss had exploded in laughter.

"Morally you're still a totalitarian." Sometimes it seemed impossible that Moss had been serious in confronting him with such an accusation; surely he had said it out of pure perverseness, knowing it was the antithesis of what was true about him. But if that were so certain, why then did the idea stick there, embedded like a burr in his mind? He tried to think back, to recall whether one day he might have used an inconsidered word which could have led Moss to misunderstand later remarks, but of course it was useless; he could remember no such occurrence. "Maybe I am," he said to himself once again, listening to his footsteps echo in the covered passageway. If it was "totalitarian" to estimate the worth of an individual according to what he produced, or to evaluate any segment of humanity using as a scale its culture, then Moss was right. There was no other criterion to use in determining the right of an organism to exist (and in the end any judgment one passed on another human being was reducible to the consideration of that right). If, for instance, he deplored the violence that resulted in the daily bombings and shootings in the streets of Casablanca, it obviously was not because he felt pity for the victims, who, however pathetic, were still anonymous, but because he knew that each sanguinary incident, by awakening the political consciousness of the survivors, brought the moribund culture nearer to its end. Now he recalled an occasion when they had been talking about war, and he had said: "People can be replaced, but not works of art." Moss had been indignant, called him selfish and inhuman. Perhaps it was a few careless phrases such as this that Moss had stored in his memory and used as a springboard for making his accusation. He would bring up the subject again at the right moment. This was the door to Si Jaffar's house. Seizing the knocker, he banged the iron ring against the wood, twice.

The youngest son had led him into the patio where the orange trees still let fall drops of rain onto the mosaic beneath. There he stood for a minute or two, alone by the central fountain, waiting for Si Jaffar. The wrought-iron balustrade around the basin was hung with cleaning rags. Some were even looped around the lower branches of one of the trees. From somewhere in the house there came the insistent pounding of a pestle in a mortar: one of the women was grinding spices. When Si Jaffar appeared, he was wearing striped pajamas, a loosely wound turban was around his head, and he was wringing his hands and smiling his eternal smile.

"We have had a little accident, with slight damage," he said. "I hope you will forgive the inconvenience." He led him into the large reception room. Several tons of rubble lay piled up at one end: stones, earth and plaster. The wall of the house across the street was visible through the gaping hole. The family had retrieved most of the mattresses and cushions, and ranged them in the center of the room. "The rain," Si Jaffar said apologetically. "This is an old house. One is afraid the entire wall may crumble."

Stenham glanced nervously up at the ceiling. Si Jaffar noticed his movement and laughed indulgently. "No, no, Monsieur Jean! The roof is not going to fall. The house is strong." Stenham was not reassured, but he smiled and sat down on the mattress indicated for him, against the opposite wall.

"You must forgive my informality. I am late," said his host, touching his pajama-top and his turban with a forefinger. "With all this disturbance I had not found the time to dress. But now with your permission I shall go and change. I have arranged for my cousin, Si Boufelja, to amuse you on the *oud* while you wait.

One can't have one's guests sitting idle. Just a small moment, please." He went out across the patio, bent forward like an old man with his hands folded against his chest. Immediately afterward he reentered the room in company with a tall bearded man in a navy blue *djellaba*, who carried a very large lute in front of him as if it were a tray. Si Jaffar, beaming, neglected to introduce the two men, watched his cousin only long enough to see that he sat down and began to tune the strings, and then he excused himself.

The man continued to test the pitch of the strings, listening intently, never once glancing in Stenham's direction. A cat went by in the street outside, wailing raucously; it was as though the animal were in the room with them. The man disregarded the noise, soon began to play what sounded like a wandering improvisation that consisted of short breathless phrases separated from each other by long silences. Stenham listened carefully, thinking how much pleasanter his other evenings might have been if only the cousin's aid had been enlisted. One by one the other male members of the family came in, greeted him discreetly, and sat down to pay attention to the music. A good deal later Si Jaffar made his entrance, resplendent in white silk robes, with a dark red *tarbouche* stuck at a saucy angle on the top of his head. As if there were no music at all going on, he began to speak in a normal voice. This was obviously a signal for the volume of sound to be reduced, to pass to the background. The cousin now played softly, but he seemed to have lost interest: his expression of intentness relaxed, his gaze wandered from face to face, and he nodded his head absently in rhythm with his notes. When the servants brought in the dinner tables, they placed one in front of Si Jaffar and Stenham, who ate in uncrowded comfort while the six others sat surrounded by debris at the second table in the center of the room. Stenham presently made the bold suggestion that perhaps the cousin would be more comfortable at their table with them, where there was more space. Si Jaffar, smiling blandly, said: "We will all be happier this way."

"I didn't mean to be indiscreet," began Stenham.

Si Jaffar, licking his fingers one by one, did not reply. Now he clapped his hands for the servant; when the latter had come in, gone out again, Si Jaffar grinned widely, showing a whole set of gold teeth, and remarked complacently: "My cousin is very timid."

In the middle of the meal the electric light bulbs, which hung naked from the ceiling, went out. The room was absolutely dark; a husky voice from the other table muttered: "*Bismil'lah rahman er rahim*," and there was silence for an instant. Then Si Jaffar called very loudly to the servant for candles.

"In a moment the light will be back again," he assured Stenham, as the man came in, a burning candle in each hand. But they went on eating, and the power remained off.

The room was now mysterious and huge, with a theatre of shadows above, on the distant ceiling. During dessert the servant entered triumphantly with an old oil lamp which smoked abominably; everyone but Stenham greeted its arrival with murmurs of delight. Two or three times there was a flurry of conversation at the other table; on each occasion Si Jaffar tried to distract his guest's attention by beginning a pointless story. Stenham, annoyed by the clumsiness of these attempts to keep him from hearing what the members of the family were saying, pointedly turned his face toward the other table now and then while Si Jaffar talked.

After they all had finished eating, washing their hands, rinsing their mouths and drinking tea, they sat back and launched into the telling of a series of comic anecdotes. As usual, Stenham found it impossible to follow these stories; he understood the words, but he never got the point. However, he enjoyed watching the family during their telling, and hearing the loud laughter that followed each tale. The only member of the family who enjoyed the prerogative of smoking was Si Jaffar; to emphasize his privilege he chain-smoked, plying Stenham with a fresh cigarette every five minutes, occasionally while Stenham was still puffing on the previous one. The others did not have the right to light up in his presence.

"Do you understand our nonsense?" he asked Stenham.

"I understand the words, yes. But—"

"I shall explain the story Ahmed just told. The legionnaire liked the lantern, but he imagined he could buy it for a hundred rial. You know what figs are?"

"Yes."

"Well, the Filali had filled the lantern with figs, and his wife had hidden her bracelet at the bottom of the basket, so that the figs covered it up. That was why the Jew didn't see it when he put his head under the bed. You see? If he had had time before the legionnaire knocked at the door he would have taken all the figs out, but of course there was no time. That's what the Filali meant when he said: 'A young eucalyptus tree cannot be expected to give the shade of an old fig tree.' You follow this?"

"Yes," Stenham said uncertainly; he was expecting some further clue which might connect all the parts.

Si Jaffar looked pleased. "And that's the reason the Filali's wife had to dress up as a slave of the Khalifa. If she had allowed the Jew to guess her identity, he would have told the legionnaire, of course, and made his commission, which as you remember was fifty percent. I don't know whether you are acquainted with young eucalyptus trees? Their leaves are very narrow and small. So that what the Jew said to the Filali's wife was a compliment of a high order. But it was really only flattery, not sincere, you understand?"

By now Stenham understood absolutely nothing of the story, but he smiled and nodded his head. The others were still repeating the important line about the shade of the young eucalyptus tree, savoring its nuances at length, chuckling appreciatively. "I'm not certain you have understood," Si Jaffar told him after a moment. "There are too many things to explain. Some of our stories are very difficult. Even the people from Rabat and Casablanca often must have them explained, because the stories are meant only for the people of Fez. But that's what gives them their perfume. They wouldn't be amusing if everyone could follow them. Also some of them are very impolite, but we shan't tell any of those tonight, because you are here." He closed his eyes, apparently remembering one of the improper stories, and presently giggled with delight. Then he opened one eye and looked at Stenham. "I think the shocking stories are the most delicious," he said coyly.

"Tell one," urged Stenham. He was very sleepy, and he felt that if he should close his eyes for a moment like Si Jaffar, he would fall asleep directly. At his suggestion everyone laughed uproariously. Then the oldest son began to relate an involved tale about a hunchback with a sack of barley and a jackal. Before it had gone on for very long there was a lion in it, and then a French general who had lost a kilo of almonds. Whether or not the story was of the improper variety it was impossible for Stenham to guess; however, when it was finished he laughed with the others. A good deal later the cousin was called upon to play once again. This time he sang as well, in a tiny falsetto that was sometimes barely audible under the plucking of the strings. In the middle of the selection Si Jaffar seemed to become impatient: he pulled out his snuffbox and meticulously sniffed a pinch through each nostril. Then he took off his *tarbouche* and scratched his bald head, put it back on, tapped indolently with his fingertips on the snuffbox, and finally clapped his hands for the servant, bidding him bring a brazier. The cousin continued his piece imperturbably, even when the servant arrived carrying the vessel full of hot coals and set it in front of his master. Si Jaffar rubbed his hands in happy anticipation, and produced from the folds of his garments a packet containing small strips of sandalwood. With a spoon which had been brought for that purpose he poked the coals until he had uncovered the brightest ones, and placed the pieces of wood among them. Next he squatted over the brazier, so that it was completely covered by his garments, and remained that way for a minute or so, his eyes closed and an expression of beatitude on his face. When he rose, a cloud of sweet smoke billowed out from beneath his *djellaba,* and he murmured reverently: "*Al-lah! Al-lah!*" Then he sat down and picked his ears with a small silver earpick. The music continued. Stenham, comfortably ensconced in a mound of pillows, closed his eyes, and for a time did actually doze. Then he sat up straight, looking around guiltily to see who had noticed. Probably all of them, he thought, although no one was looking at him. Some-one drove a squeaking wheelbarrow along the street on the other side of the open wall; the noise was so loud that the musi-cian stopped to wait for it to pass. "Aha!" cried Si Jaffar. "That was very beautiful. Enough music for tonight, no?" He looked significantly at his cousin, who set the *oud* on the mattress and lay back against the cushions.

Stenham decided to seize this opportunity to announce his de-parture. Si Jaffar replied what he always replied at this point, re-gardless of the hour: "Already?" Then he continued: "Come and let me show you the damage. It is interesting." Now everyone got up and began to move around the room distractedly. With the lamp in one hand—its chimney was by now black with soot—one of the sons led the way across the stricken room.

They examined the wall and the composition of the rubble, discussed the relative costs of trying to repair the present wall and tearing it down to build a new one, inquired of Stenham whether American houses often caved in when it rained, and when he told them that was not the case, wanted to know in detail why it was not. Nearly an hour later they moved slowly in a group out through the patio to the antechamber by the front door, where in the dimness a ragged Berber sat waiting.

"This man will take you to your hotel," said Si Jaffar.

The man got slowly to his feet. He was tall and powerfully built; his inexpressive face could have been that of a cutthroat or a saint.

"No, no," Stenham protested. "You're very kind, but I don't need anyone."

"It's nothing," Si Jaffar said gently, with the modest gesture of a sultan who has just presented a subject with a bag of dia-monds.

It was useless to offer objections; the man was going with him whether he liked it or not, and so he thanked them all together, separately, and together once more, and stepped through the doorway into the street. "*Allah imsik bekhir*," "*B'slemah*," "*Bon soir, monsieur*," "*A bientôt, incha'Allah*," they choroused, and one of the sons said shyly: "*Gude-bye, sair*," a phrase with which he had been planning for some time to surprise Stenham, only now finding the courage to utter it.

CHAPTER 21

He was tired after his long walk back through the darkness of the Medina, and he did not feel like going downstairs again. Standing before the mirror of the armoire, putting his necktie back on, he reflected that this was the first time Moss had ever sent him a message at night. He looked at his watch: it was twenty minutes past one. From the doorway he cast a brief, longing glance at his bed; then he stepped out and locked the door behind him. The key had a heavy nickel tag attached to it; it felt like ice in his pocket.

In the lower garden it was very dark; the lanterns outside Moss's door had not been turned on, but slivers of light came through the closed blinds. A stranger opened the door in answer to his knock, stepped aside stiffly to let him pass, and closed it again after him. Moss had been standing in the center of the room, directly under the big chandelier, but now he began to pace slowly back and forth, his hands locked behind him. Stenham turned and saw a second stranger standing by the wall beside the door.

Moss did not bother to introduce the two to Stenham. He merely said: *"Enfin. Voici Monsieur Stenham."*

The two murmured, inclining their heads ever so slightly.

"Vous m'excusez si je parle anglais, n'est-ce pas?" said Moss to his two guests. It was only Stenham who detected the acid tones of mockery in his politeness, and he thought: It's unlike Moss to be rude. He must have had provocation. Now he looked at the

two men. One was short and plump, with round pink cheeks and large eyes; the taller one, who wore spectacles, was gaunt and yellow-skinned. Neither could have been more than twenty-five years old, and, he reflected, neither could have laughed if his life depended on it. It was obvious that for years they had insisted upon being serious, and the intensity of their effort had left its indelible mark; their common obsession showed in their faces and in the movements of their bodies. Immediately Stenham identified them as Nationalists. They were unmistakable.

"These two gentlemen have been kind enough," Moss went on, "to come and warn us that we should leave the hotel at once. It seems the situation has suddenly become very grave indeed."

"Ah," said Stenham. The two young men stood watching them with alert eyes. He felt sure they understood English perfectly. "Well, I suppose there's nothing to do but thank them. Tomorrow we can look into the matter and see what's what."

"But—at once, John! That means this minute."

"That's ridiculous," Stenham snapped. He turned to the taller Moslem, and said to him in Arabic: "Why? What's happened?"

The other looked first surprised and then pained, to hear his own tongue being spoken. With dignity he replied in French: "Things are going very badly. I can scarcely give you details, but I assure you there will be unpleasant events here in the Medina within twenty-four hours—very likely much sooner. The French will not be in a position to offer the hotel any protection whatever."

"Why should we want the protection of the French?" demanded Stenham. "And why should anyone bother us? We're not French."

The young man looked at him with the searching stare of the extremely myopic, but his expression revealed the depths of his hatred and scorn. "You are foreigners, Christians," he said. The plump young man broke in, with an attempt at affability; he had a rather strong Arab accent. "For the people in the street the enemy is the non-Moslem," he explained.

"Why?" demanded Stenham angrily. "This isn't a religious war. It's a fight purely against the French."

The near-sighted man's face had assumed a frozen expression, the mouth slightly twisted. He breathed more quickly. "A religious war is precisely what it threatens to become. *C'est malheureux, mais c'est comme ça.*"

Stenham turned to Moss; he did not want to look at the grimacing face. Then he turned back and said: "You mean, that's what you want to make it."

"Easy, John," Moss said quietly. "These gentlemen came as friends, you know, after all."

"I doubt it," Stenham muttered.

"The movement," pursued the man with glasses, "is as you say, directed above all against the French imperialists. Likewise it is against all those who assist the French. *Je vous demande pardon, monsieur,* but the arms used against the Moroccan people were largely supplied by your government. They do not consider America a nation friendly to their cause."

"Of course she is not an enemy either," said the other in a conciliatory tone. "Had you been Frenchmen we should not have given ourselves the trouble of coming here tonight. What would have happened to you would have been your own lookout. But, as you see, we are here."

"It's very kind of you," said Moss. He had begun to pace back and forth thoughtfully. A sudden flurry of rain spattered on the tiles outside the door.

"*Oui, nous vous sommes bien reconnaissants,*" Stenham said. He offered them each a cigarette; they both refused curtly. "These are English, not American," he informed them lightly. They did not bother to reply. He lighted a cigarette and stood considering them.

"*Enfin,*" said Moss, "we are all very tired, I'm sure. I think the time of our departure will have to be left for us to decide. It's impossible for us to leave tonight. Where could we go at this hour?"

"Go to the station in the Ville Nouvelle. There will be a train to Rabat at half past seven in the morning."

"Half past eight," corrected the shorter one.

The other made an impatient movement with his head, as

though a fly had alighted on his face. "The station is under the protection of the French at present," he continued.

"*Non, merci!*" Stenham laughed. "There's a train blown up every other day. I'd rather walk. You take the train."

The young man with glasses lowered his head and thrust it forward aggressively. "We have not come here to amuse ourselves, monsieur. I see that it was a great waste of effort. Perhaps you would like to telephone the police and inform them of our visit." He pointed to the telephone. "*Yallah,*" he said gruffly to the other, and started toward the door. Before he reached it he stopped, turned, and said furiously: "Your frivolity and stubbornness may easily cost you your lives. *On ne badine pas avec la volonté du peuple.*"

Stenham snorted. The man continued to the door and opened it. Without offering him his hand the other bowed slightly to Moss, and followed.

"The will of the people! What people?" Stenham shouted. "You mean the leaders of your party?"

"John!" said Moss sharply.

The two young men went out, leaving the door open behind them. Moss stepped across the room, closed it and locked it.

"I must say, John, that was a most unpolitic performance on your part. There was no need to antagonize them. I'd been doing my best to keep on their good side, and I'd managed quite well until you came. They left in a jolly ugly mood, you know."

Stenham sat down, waited a moment before he spoke. "Do you think it matters what kind of a mood they're in?"

"I think common courtesy matters, yes. Always."

"Were they courteous with me, would you say?" Stenham demanded.

"Oh, my dear man, one can scarcely put oneself on their level," Moss said impatiently. "That's a feeble excuse, my boy, most feeble. After all, they're only patriots trying to help their country. One must look at the thing in that light. See their behavior in its proper perspective. No one is himself under the stress of passion, you know."

Stenham laughed shortly. "The only passion those cold fish

know is hatred; I can tell you that. And they're not *patriots*, anyway. I object."

"We won't go into it," Moss said hastily. "I'm far too exhausted to argue. I was almost asleep when the office telephoned to say those two were here to see me. I hadn't a clue as to who they were, and of course I had to dress before having them down, and it was a bloody nuisance, I can tell you. Coming on the heels of my day with the police it was almost too much."

"You should be glad I got rid of them so quickly. Now you can get some sleep."

"Oh, I'm delighted with that side of it. But I do feel they have a right to their point of view. Then there's another thing." Moss's face became thoughtful. "If there *is* to be the kind of trouble they predict, it's quite obvious that we should be better off here if we were on friendly terms with them."

Stenham looked at him. "Friendly terms!" he repeated. "And the French?"

Moss laughed indulgently. "I think my connections at the Résidence in Rabat are sufficient to place me above suspicion. You know as well as I that the French are not fools, whatever else they may be. They'd understand perfectly, no matter what I did, that I'd done it purely as a matter of tactics. Don't be absurd."

"Well, I'm afraid I've got no such guarantee," Stenham said.

"You?" said Moss, and he waited a moment. "No," he said finally, "I'm afraid you haven't."

"And I don't want one, either. The French can go to Hell, and so can the Nationalists. It's as simple as that."

Moss smiled wryly. "Now that you've disposed of them all, what about us? Have you a helpful suggestion as to where we might go? Hugh, I meant to tell you, has gone to Tangier. He left directly after dinner."

"What?" Stenham cried; for some reason he felt that this was a desertion. "You mean he just suddenly packed up and left? But he was so determined not to let them scare him off. I don't get it."

Now Moss sat down on the bed, removed his glasses wearily.

Without them his face took on an expression of sadness. Stenham regarded him with vague curiosity.

"My dear John," Moss said, twirling the glasses by a stem, "I
think if you had seen the things we saw today you'd understand
better why he no longer cared. As he himself said at dinner, up
until then he'd thought of the whole show as a kind of game and
it was a part of the game to stick it out, obviously. But this afternoon—" he shook his head deliberately and paused—"I must
confess I had never expected to be that close to brutality and
suffering. One reads about such things in the newspapers and is
horrified by them, but even with the most active imagination
one falls far short of the actuality. It's all the unexpected details,
the expressions on the faces, the helpless little gestures, the senseless and unrelated words that come out of their mouths, things
that one would never be able to invent, those are what does one
in, when one is actually there."

"What did you see, for God's sake?" Stenham demanded.
Without Kenzie's car available, the situation was different; he
felt less easy in his mind, although he told himself it was
illogical.

"We merely saw hundreds of Arabs at the police station being
brought in, being beaten, knocked down, kicked in the places
where it would do the most damage, and tortured. Yes, tortured," Moss repeated, raising his voice. "That's the only word
for it. When one says torture, one's inclined to picture something refined and slow and diabolical, but I assure you, it can
also be swift and brutal. If you'd merely seen the floor, slippery
with blood, and with teeth lying here and there, I think you'd
find it easier to understand why Hugh suddenly felt no desire to
go on playing his game with the French. He couldn't think of
it in those terms any longer."

Moss was silent for a moment, listening to the wind in the
poplars. "At first they had him locked up, and it took me about
two hours of ranting even to get to see him. Then we had to wait
on a bench in the corridor until almost four o'clock to see some
monstrous little functionary who was to give the final official
word that he was to be released. That was when we saw them be-

THE HOUR OF THE SWALLOWS 231

ing dragged in. But, John, the French have lost their minds! Those people had simply been taken in off the streets! Old men who hadn't the slightest idea what was happening to them, boys of ten screaming for their mothers. The police simply clubbed them all without discrimination. They pounded them, kicked them in the face with their boots when they fell. I don't know. It's useless to think about it, and still more useless to talk about it, and I'm going to stop. But don't judge Hugh too harshly for beating a retreat. I personally think he's shown very good sense, and I can't imagine what I'm doing staying on, as a matter of fact, except that with all my paraphernalia I couldn't very well get packed in time to go with him, and in any case I don't want to go to Tangier." He put his spectacles on and stood up. "How curious the world is," he said, as if to himself; then he turned and walked toward Stenham's chair. "There's no end to violence and bloodshed, is there? I had a peculiar presentiment today as I sat there speechless, watching it all, that it was only a prologue to a whole long period of suffering that hasn't even begun. But I hope I shan't see it."

"I hope not," said Stenham.

"Good night, John. I'm sorry to have dragged you down here at this hour, but they did ask for you, you know, and anyway, I needed a bit of moral support. Let's see what tomorrow brings forth, and plan accordingly."

"Right," said Stenham.

The garden lay in darkness, bathed by a mild, damp wind. When he got to his room he opened the table drawer and stood a moment looking down at the pages of typescript lying there; he had a sudden desire to pick them up, crumple them into a ball, and throw them out the window. Instead, he undressed, brushed his teeth, and got into bed. But he could not sleep.

CHAPTER 22

And yet, he thought, when he entered again into the world, becoming conscious of the daylight out there beyond the window, he must have slept, because the ritual he was in the act of performing at the moment was the accustomed one of awakening. In his mind he had planted firmly the idea that he was not sleeping, had not slept, would not sleep, and he became aware only now that each time he had reminded himself: "I am still awake," he had actually had to come back from sleep to do it. In spite of the long journey he had made through fantasy when he first lay down—"What if," his mind had asked, and then the screen had lighted up and the projections had begun—at some point there had been a halt and sudden darkness, and, although he had not slept very long, because it was still scarcely later than dawn, he felt surprisingly lively. It could of course be the false energy that sometimes manifests itself at the moment of awakening after a short night's sleep, only to change to lassitude after the first hot cup of coffee. As he stretched and yawned voluptuously, he suddenly remembered that he had slept all yesterday afternoon; the idea of this encouraged him to think that perhaps he had had enough sleep after all, and could risk looking at his watch, which in effect meant getting up, since once he knew the hour he almost never fell asleep again.

It was a few minutes before ten; the gray, unaccustomed light above the Medina was that of a dark day—not of dawn. He sat up and rang the bell. It was Abdelmjid who knocked in answer. He ordered his breakfast by shouting from bed, without opening the door. Then he crossed the room to the washstand, dashed cold water over his face, and combed his hair. On his return to the bed he unlocked the door. He lay back against the pillows, waiting, looking out over the further edges of the city to the dim hills behind. The light rain falling blurred the air and removed the color from the landscape, giving it instead a gray luminosity which blotted out the familiar landmarks.

Abdelmjid was a long time coming with the tray. When he entered, his face was set in a rigid mask which announced as well as words could have that he did not want to talk. And Stenham realized, when he looked at him, that as a matter of fact neither did he. They exchanged the brief commonplaces appropriate to the time of day, and Abdelmjid went out.

It was as he was finishing his breakfast that Stenham always began to plot the course of his work for the morning. Today it was not even to be considered. It was impossible to spin fantasies about the past when the present was like a bomb lying outside the window, perhaps ready to explode any minute. This was the most cogent argument for leaving the place—not the warnings of the Nationalists or the threats of the French. If all prospects for work were withdrawn there was no point in staying; the only sensible thing was to move on to another place, in the Spanish Zone this time, where he would still be in Morocco, but in a Morocco not yet assailed by the poison of the present. He did not want to leave; he dreaded going to Moss and discussing it, but there was the undeniable fact in front of him. This was the moment of the day when he saw things most clearly, while his breakfast tray was still across his lap. A judgment reached later in the day could go wide of the mark because then he had the use of his equipment for self-deception, whereas at this hour it had not begun to function.

"Good. Then it's decided. I get out." Moss could stay or go as he liked; his own mind was at rest. When, as he was dressing, he looked out the window at the grayness, he was thankful for the rain, for it made his decision seem less painful. It was easier to renounce the city when it was colorless and wet, and the outer hills were hidden from view, and he knew that the mud was in the streets.

He packed methodically for about an hour, putting the filled valises one by one at the door, ready to be carried downstairs. Instead of notifying the desk to prepare his bill he decided to demand it in person at the last possible moment: they would have less time to work out the false extras with which they so loved to pad their *factures*. As he was stuffing some soiled shirts into a duffle bag full of books, the telephone rang.

"Hi," said a lively, matter-of-fact voice.

He opened his mouth to speak, but said nothing—merely held the receiver in his hand and looked at the wall a few inches in front of him.

Then the voice said: "Hello?"

"Lee?" he asked, although there was no need for that.

"Good morning."

"Well, my God! Where have you been? Where are you now?"

"I've been everywhere, and I'm in my room here at the hotel, this hotel, your hotel, the Mérinides Palace, Fez, Morocco."

"You're here in the hotel?" he said. "When did you come?" He had almost said: "Why did you come?" turning his head to look at the row of valises by the door. "When can I see you? I want to see you right away. We can't talk on the phone."

Her answer was a short, satisfied laugh. Then she said: "I'd love to see you. Suppose I meet you in the writing room, that room upstairs with the big window."

"When?"

"Any time. Now, if you like."

"I'll be right down."

He got there first, but she came in half a minute later, looking just as he had remembered her, only better. She was deeply tanned, and in places the sun had lightened the brown of her hair to gold. They sat down on the cushions against the window. He made her do most of the talking. She had simply decided to go to Meknès, she said, and from there she had gone on to Rabat, and then she had wired a friend of hers from Paris, a French girl who had married an army man, stationed down in Foum el Kheneg, on the edge of the Sahara, and they had invited her down there, and so she had gone, and everything had been marvelous. Why she had left Fez, and above all, why she had returned—when he came to ask her those two questions, he found he could not.

"You know," he told her, "I nearly went to Meknès after you did."

"You did?" she said curiously. "Why?"

He brought out his wallet and pulled the folded telegram from it. "Look at this wire you sent me," he said, spreading it on the cushion in front of her. "Look. Doesn't it say: JOING MEKNES? For a while I was sure it was the final 'G' that was the mistake. Wistful thinking."

She laughed. "It's lucky you didn't come. You'd never have found me."

"I'll bet I would. Weren't you at the Transatlantique?"

"I was not. I was in a little native hotel called the Régina. It was pretty grim, too."

He looked at her incredulously, and felt all the uncomfortable suspicions surge again in him. This time, even if it destroyed their friendship, he would find out.

"I don't know," he said unhappily. "I think you're crazy."

Apparently she was aware that something was amiss with him, for she was studying his face with an expression of curiosity. "Why, do you think it's improper or something for me to put up at cheap hotels? Moving around costs money, you know. We can't all stay in the Mérinides Palaces and Transatlantiques *all* the time."

It was not good enough. "Lee, you know damned well what I mean." But of course he could not go all the way. "There's an undeclared war on here, people are being shot and blown up every day all over the place, and you calmly wander around in a way nobody would do, even in normal times. What's the answer?"

Again she laughed. "The answer is that you only live once."

"Haven't you got a better one than that? I mean, a more truthful one?" he said, staring at her intently.

"More truthful?" she repeated, puzzled.

He was assailed by doubt, decided to laugh. "Now I'm in deep," he said ruefully. "I mean, are you sure you're not snooping around down here for somebody?"

"What a peculiar thing to say!" she exclaimed, drawing her head up and back in surprise. "What a funny man you are!"

His laughter continued, lame and unconvincing. "Just skip it. It was just an idea that came to me."

But now she was indignant; her eyes blazed. "I certainly won't skip it! What did you mean? You must have meant something. Why would such an idea just 'come' to you?"

"Consider it unsaid and accept my sincere and profound apologies," he suggested with mock contrition. And before she could answer again: "Look!" he cried, pointing out the window, "the rain has stopped. The sun's coming out. Let's hope it's a good omen."

"For what?" Her voice sounded angry still, and instead of heeding his exhortation to look out into the garden, she had opened her compact and was studying herself in its mirror.

"For today. For the trouble here."

"Why? Is it so much worse now? Is it really bad?"

"What do you mean, is it bad? It's terrible! Didn't you see anything at the station when you came in? Soldiers or crowds?"

"I didn't come by train. I hired a car in Rabat and came straight through."

He was delighted to have found a way out of the impasse of an instant ago, and he went ahead to recount the story Moss had told him last night, leaving out the visit of the two young men to the hotel. She listened, an increasingly horrified expression on her face. When he had finished, she said: "I wondered why Hugh had suddenly left like that. It wasn't like him not to leave at least a note."

"You mean for you? But how would he know you were coming back to Fez?"

"I wired him from Marrakech," she said.

"Oh. I see." For the moment he had forgotten that she was Kenzie's friend, that it was he who had introduced them. "Yes." After a pause he said: "Are you sure he didn't leave some word for you? They might easily have mislaid it in the office."

"No, he didn't."

"Are you very much upset to have missed him?"

"Oh, it's too bad. But perhaps I'll see him in Tangier on my way up. I'm only going to stay a day or so here. I've got to get back to Paris."

He was thinking: You may not find it that easy. She seemed still not to have envisaged the possible effects of the conflict should it break out into violence, and this puzzled him; however, he did not feel that it was his duty to try to make her aware by alarming her.

They went down to lunch. The empty dining-room astonished her. "You mean there's not a soul in the hotel but you and Mr. Moss?" she exclaimed.

"And you and the staff. That's right."

Their table was by the window; they watched the sun slowly devour the mist that steamed upward from the Medina.

"This may be a historic day in the annals of Fez," he said. "I'm damned if I'm going to sit here in the hotel all afternoon. I'd like to get out and see something. At least see if there's anything to see."

"Well, then, let's go out."

"Fine. Let's. But first I've got to leave a note for Mr. Moss. We'd been more or less planning on leaving if things got bad" (he thought with surprise, almost with disbelief, of the luggage stacked inside his door upstairs) "and we were going to have a sort of council of war today at some point."

"Don't you think you ought to go and see him?" she suggested.

"I'll drop in later, when we get back. I don't think he's all that eager to go. He's very conscious of the whole situation, as far as any outsider can be, and I don't think he thinks it's too dangerous. The trouble is, nobody really knows anything except a handful of Arabs and maybe a still smaller handful of French."

She told him about her trip to Foum el Kheneg—the difficulties of getting there, the unbelievable heat, the desolation of the landscape, the delightful home that Captain Hamelle and his wife had made for themselves in the hostile wilderness, and the trips they had taken in a jeep through the mountains to the Berber *casbahs* roundabout.

"I've never been in that particular valley," he said, "but I've been in country like it. It's magnificent."

"Magnificent country," she agreed, "but a pretty terrifying civilization, completely feudal. Those *caïds* have the power of life and death over their subjects, you know. Think of the gap those people have got to get across before they can hope to be anything."

He felt the anger rising to his lips; fighting it back, he said: "I don't think I know what you mean. What would you like them to be, other than what they are, which is perfectly happy?"

She looked at him carefully, as if she were measuring his intelligence. "Will you please tell me what makes you think those helpless serfs are *happy*? Or haven't you ever given it a thought? Are they just happy by definition because they're absolutely isolated from the world? They're slaves, living in ignorance and superstition and sickness and filth, and you can sit there and calmly tell me they're happy! Don't you think that's going a little far?"

"It's not going nearly as far as you. I say leave them alone. You say they've *got* to change, they've got to *be* something." He was excited; this was what had been standing between them. Perhaps they could get to it this time.

She tossed her head in a gesture of impatience. "They'll change," she said, with the air of a person who has access to private sources of information.

"You and the Istiqlal," he murmured.

"Look, Mr. Stenham. I don't think we know each other well enough to get into an argument. Do you?"

He was silent; the *Mister Stenham* had indicated the distance between them which doubtless had been there all along, only he had not been conscious of it. She was infinitely less approachable than he had thought; indeed, at the moment it was difficult to imagine what it would be like to be on intimate terms with her. He looked away from the table: the two rows of waiters, Moroccan and European, stood against their respective walls watching them discreetly.

"Smile," he told her.

THE HOUR OF THE SWALLOWS 239

She hesitated, drew back her upper lip in a tentative momentary grimace that was a sketch of a smile.

"Your teeth are too sharp," he said. "When I was a kid I once had a baby fox. It had fluffy fur and a big bushy tail and everyone who saw it used to make a dash for it and try to pet it. You can imagine the rest."

Now she smiled. "As far as I know, Mr. Stenham, I haven't got either a big bushy tail or fluffy fur."

"Don't you think it might help our struggling friendship if you called me John, instead of Mister Stenham?"

"It might," she admitted. "I'll try to remember. I'll also try to remember that you're a hopeless romantic without a *shred* of confidence in the human race." She was staring at him fixedly, and he resented the deep sensation of uneasiness her expression was able to awaken in him.

"You're a bright girl," he said with irony.

"You remind me so much of a friend of mine," she went on, still watching him. "A nice enough boy, but all tied up in knots by his own theories about life. You even look a little like him, I swear! He wrote pretty good poetry, too. At least, it seemed all right until you took time off and suddenly asked yourself what it meant."

"I'm not a poet." His voice was sour, but he smiled at her.

She continued, impervious. "And I'll bet your life histories have a lot in common. Did you ever join the Communist Party? *He* did; he used to put on a special outfit and go and stand on corners and sell the *Daily Worker*. Later he went in for Yoga, and the last I knew he'd become a Roman Catholic. That didn't stop him, though, from getting to be an alcoholic."

Stenham, whose face had briefly shown traces of alarm, now smiled. "Well," he said, "I think you've drawn a pretty complete picture of somebody who's about as different from me as he could get."

"I don't believe it," she announced in a firm voice. "I can *feel* the similarity. Intuition," she added, as if to keep him from saying it with sarcasm.

"Have it your own way. Maybe I am like him. Maybe the first

thing I know I'll be standing on my head or going to Mass or joining Alcoholics Anonymous, or all of them at once. Who knows?"

"And another thing," she pursued. "Now that I think of it— of course!—it was after he left the Party that he began to have delusions. He suspected everybody else of belonging to it. You had to be practically a Swami for him not to challenge whatever you said. He smelled propaganda everywhere."

"I see," Stenham said.

"You may be unconscious of it, but twice since we've been sitting here *you've* practically accused *me*. You think back a minute."

He sat quietly until the waiter had left the table. Then he leaned forward, speaking intensely. "But, Lee, I don't make any bones of the fact. Of course I was in the Party. Exactly sixteen years ago. And I stayed in, officially, exactly twenty months and attended exactly twenty-four meetings and so what? I wasn't even in the United States most of the time—"

She was laughing. "But you don't have to defend yourself! I don't care how long you were in the Party or why you joined or what you did in it. I'm just delighted to see I was right, that's all."

"Do you want coffee?"

"No, thanks."

"I think we'd better go, don't you? The mud'll be pretty well dried by now."

"Just a minute," she said with mock sternness. "You *did* accuse me, didn't you?"

"All right, I did. But you brought it on yourself with your re- marks."

"I think you're crazy."

"No, I mean it."

"Let's go," she said, rising.

The head waiter bowed them out and closed the door after them. Stenham walked behind her along the damp corridor with its straw-paneled walls, thinking that the conversation had been completely unsatisfactory. What he had wanted to say was: You brought it on yourself with your half-baked, pseudo-democratic idealism. But he knew she would not accept criticism from him; she was an American woman, and an American woman always knew best. She assumed the role of a patient and amused mother, and with gentle ridicule reduced you to the status of a small boy. But if you spoke up in your own defense, which necessarily meant attacking the falseness of her position, she swiftly invoked the unwritten laws of chivalry. Too, he envied Lee for being able to speak in so jaunty and offhand a manner of a thing about which he felt such a profound, if irrational, guilt.

The mud had been dried into an inoffensive paste that crumbled underfoot, the sky was clear, and the glare that had accompanied the rising of the mist had been dissipated. For Stenham the act of stepping out into the street constituted an automatic leaving behind of rancor; he observed this and rejoiced, for it would have been an ordeal to wander through the town carrying the weight of his bad humor. As they followed the zigzagging street between the walls, he wondered whether coming out here had performed the same catharsis for her, or whether she even needed such a thing, seeing that she could not very well consider herself in any light save that of victor in the recent verbal bout. Apparently she had nothing at all on her mind save the things she was seeing around her. Every little while she hummed a tune to herself as she carefully picked her way around the places that might still be slippery. He listened: it was *On the Sunny Side of the Street*, phrased arbitrarily, according to her breathing.

They came to the pigeon market below the old mosque at Bab el Guissa. There was certainly something abnormal about the day, but he could not discover what it was that made him think so. Work was going on as always in the quarter, which was devoted largely to oil presses and carpenters' workshops. There were the usual numbers of donkeys being driven and ridden back and forth, of small children bearing trays of unbaked and baked bread on their heads going to and from the ovens, of girls and old women carrying vessels of water from the public fountains. At the same time there was a definite if subtle difference between today and other days, one which he was convinced was not imaginary, and yet he could not tell where the difference lay. Could it be in the expressions on the faces? He decided not; they were inscrutable as always.

They got to the blind passageway just beyond the Lemtiyine school, a long narrow alley leading downward to an arched door whose gate was always open. Split banana-leaves waved across the top of the wall like the battered paper decorations of a festival long past. Suddenly he knew what was amiss; seeing this empty corridor had told him.

"Ah!" he said with satisfaction.

"What is it?"

"I'd been thinking that there was something strange about the place today, but I couldn't put my finger on it. Now I know what it is. All the boys and young men are missing. We haven't seen a boy over twelve or a man under thirty since we left the hotel."

"Is that bad?" she asked.

"Well, it's been known to be bad, all right. The crazy French think if they can get that age group behind bars they automatically remove most of the sources of trouble. But probably today it's a case of something big going on down in the town, and they're all there to see it. What's going on is anybody's guess."

"I don't want to get into any crowds," she declared. "It's all right with me where we go and what we do, as long as we steer clear of the mob. I have a thing about getting caught in a crowd. I don't think there's anything more terrifying."

They walked more slowly. "I'm inclined to agree with you," he said. Suddenly he stopped. "I'll tell you what. If you don't mind walking a little more, it might be the better part of valor to go back and out Bab el Guissa, and do the whole thing outside the walls. That way we're sure of avoiding getting hemmed in down in the Talâa. We'll get to Bou Jeloud a little later, that's all."

She looked at him as if she were wondering why he had not suggested this in the beginning, but all she said was: "Fine."

For ten minutes or so they retraced their steps, until they came to the mosque. The massive arch of Bab el Guissa was behind, a short distance up the hill, a small fortress in itself, the interior of which had been rebuilt by the French to house a police office. They went through the first gate into the cool darkness. The passage made a turn to the left, then to the right, and they saw the trees and hills ahead. As they walked through the outer arch, two French policemen standing along the wall conferred briefly, and then one of them called out.

"Where are you going, monsieur?"

Stenham said they were taking a walk.

"You are from the Mérinides Palace?"

Stenham said they were.

"When you go back into the Medina to return to your hotel, you will use the other gate, not this one," the policeman told him.

Stenham said they would.

"And when you have finished your walk, you will take no more walks until you are told. They should have warned you at the hotel. There are disorders in the native quarter."

Stenham thanked him and they walked on.

"We'll have to go a little out of our way now," he told her presently, "or they'll see we're turning in the wrong direction and call us back."

They walked straight ahead toward the hills until they came to the main road. Then they stopped and looked back. Behind them stretched the blank face of the ramparts, broken only by the single arch of Bab el Guissa. The two policemen were still visible, tiny blue spots against the darkness of its opening.

When the road curved, they set off across the cemetery, cutting back toward a path that ran more or less parallel to the ramparts, but along extremely uneven terrain. First they were at a level with the top of the ramparts, and could see the further side of the Medina, then they were in a deep hollow where the path wound between rows of cactus and aloes, with nothing beyond but the steep dust-colored slopes rising on both sides toward the sky. Then the land dropped away, and the narrow lane which had been at the bottom of a ravine followed the spine of a twisting hill. Goats wandered and cropped the dwarf thistles under the olive trees on the hillside below. They skirted the bases of per-

pendicular cliffs, where dogs barked to protect the caves that
men had dug with their hands out of the clay, and where babies
now squalled and occasionally a drum was being beaten. Then
they were in a dried-up meadow where the earth was veined with
wide dark cracks.

"Whew! It's like walking inside an oven," she said.

"We'll take a cab back."

"If we ever get there. How much further is it?"

"Not far. But you're going to have to hold your nose pretty
soon. I warn you."

From the top of an absurd little crest of land across which the
path led them, they could see over the ramparts into the Casbah
en Nouar near by; its roofs and gardens hid the center of the
Medina. They stood still a moment and looked at the panorama
of strange formations around them. The earth's configurations
here were like those of an unruly head of hair. The land whirled
up into senseless peaks and dropped off vertically into mysterious
pits and hollows.

"Listen," Stenham told her. Like the shrilling of insects came
the distant sound of prolonged shouting from many throats.
"There's whatever's going on," he said.

"Well, thank heavens we turned around. I wouldn't be down
in there for anything in the world."

The stench began before the village came into view. Then
they passed the first dwellings, made with packing cases, thorn
bushes and oil cans, tied together with rope and strips of rags. A
more intense squalor would have been inconceivable. Children,
naked or with mud-colored pieces of cloth hanging to them,
played on the refuse-strewn waste land between the huts, where
the ground glittered with tin and broken glass.

"This is all new," he told her. "None of this existed a few years
ago."

"God," she said with feeling.

The mud had not dried here; they were obliged to walk at the
sides of the path. The ground crawled with countless flies; at
each step a small swarm rose a few inches into the air, only to settle again immediately. As they passed through the village the peo-

ple stared at them, but with no expression beyond that of mild curiosity. The way now led up a steep hill toward the ramparts. Tons of garbage and refuse had been dumped at the top and, sliding down the long slope, threatened now to engulf the improvised dwellings below; along the side of this encroaching mountain half-starved dogs wandered like hopeless ghosts, feebly nosing the objects, occasionally dislodging a tin can which rolled a bit further down. There were people here, too, carefully examining the waste, and from time to time putting something into the sacks they carried slung over their shoulders.

When they reached the top of the hill, panting, they did not stop and turn to see the village behind them, but continued to walk until the stink had been left behind and they had gone through Bab Mahrouk's two portals. Then, beyond the shadow of the ramparts, in the wicker market, they stood still a moment to catch their breath.

"I'm going to say something that's almost worthy of a John Stenham," she told him. "And that is, that I wish you hadn't taken me through there. It somehow spoils the rest of the place for me."

"That's about one twentieth of what there is outside the walls," he said. "Don't you take slums for granted, yet? Have you ever seen a city that didn't have them?"

"Oh, but not that kind! Not quite that hopeless. My God, no!"

"I should think you'd be glad to have seen it. It's one more thing to be changed."

Ignoring his sarcasm, "That much it certainly is," she said grimly.

He pointed back at Bab Mahrouk's wide arch. "One reform they've made recently," he went on in the same mock-innocent fashion, "is that now there are no heads decorating that beautiful gate. They used to have a row of them on pikes for people to admire as they went out. Enemies of the Pacha and other evildoers. Not in the Middle Ages, I mean, but in the twentieth century, just a few years ago. Don't you think it's an improvement without them?"

"Yes," she said with exasperation. "It's an improvement without them."

It was a pleasure to walk in the shade of the plane trees along the avenue that led back toward Bou Jeloud. When they got to the square where the buses waited, policemen were lined up in front of the gaudy blue gate; it looked like a scene in a lavish musical comedy. They waited at the far end of the open space, studying the array of men in uniform. Framed by the arch of Bab Bou Jeloud among the squat mud buildings was a low minaret with a huge mass of straw atop it, and in the middle of the straw stood a stork with one leg raised and bent against its body; it looked very white in the strong sunlight.

"I think this is the end of our excursion," he said to her. "If we go through the gate we'll be in the Medina, and we don't want that. And anyway, it doesn't look to me as though they'd let us through. There's a nice little café here. Are you game for a mint tea?"

"I'm game for anything as long as I can sit myself down," she said. "Just to sit would be a terrific luxury at this point. But let's make it inside, out of the glare."

CHAPTER   23

There were four cafés on the square, and each one had a large space in front of it which was ordinarily full of tables and chairs. Today, these had prudently not been set out, so that the sides of the square presented a deserted aspect which was emphasized by the fact that the center also was empty, for no one was walking in it. True, it was hot, and there would have been few strollers at this hour in any case, but the absence of people was so complete that the scene—even if the line of police could have been disregarded—had no element of the casualness which ordinarily gave the place its character.

"*Very* strange," Stenham muttered.

"Am I wrong," she said, "or does this look sort of sinister?"

"Come on." He took her arm and they hurried across to the café nearest the waiting buses. One of the *mokhaznia* standing by the footbridge across the stream looked at them dubiously, but did not stop them from passing. In the café, a group of thirty or forty men sat and stood quietly near the windows, peering out through the hanging fronds of the pepper trees at the emptiness of the sunny square. More than by the unusual tenseness of these faces, Stenham was at once struck by the silence of the place, by the realization that no one was talking, or, if someone did speak, it was in a low voice scarcely pitched above a whisper. Of course, without the radio there was no need to shout as they ordinarily had to do, but he felt that even had the radio been playing, together with all its extra amplifiers for the smaller rooms, they still would only have murmured. And he did not like the expressions on their faces when they looked up and saw him. It was the first time in many years that he had read enmity in Moroccan faces. Once more than twenty years ago he had ventured alone inside the *horm* of Moulay Idriss—not the sanctuary itself, but the streets surrounding it—and then he had seen hatred on a few faces; he had never forgotten the feeling it had given him. It was a physical thing that those fierce faces had confronted him with, and his reaction to it had likewise been purely physical; he had felt his spine stiffen and the hair at the back of his neck bristle.

He began to speak with Lee in a loud voice, not paying much attention to what he was saying, but using what he thought would be an unmistakably American intonation. He saw her glance at him once with surprise.

"There are a lot of little rooms out in the back," he went on. "Let's get one that's not so crowded." She was annoyed; he could see that. He could also see that the only result his bit of play-acting had brought him was that a good many more of the bearded, turbaned and *tarbouched* individuals had looked away from the window and were staring at them with equally hostile countenances.

"Let's just sit anywhere and stop being so conspicuous," she said nervously; at the same time she took several steps toward an unoccupied table by the wall opposite the entrance. But Stenham wanted, if it were possible, to get out of the range of these unfriendly faces. In the next room they found a party of elderly men from the country sprawled out, smoking kif and eating. A boy stood in the doorway to a further room. Behind him the room appeared to be empty. Stenham stepped across and peered in; the boy did not move. There was no one in there at all. Through a back window he caught sight of a sheet of water shining in the sun.

"Lee!" he called. She slipped through the doorway and they sat down.

"Are you yelling so they'll think you're an American? Is that it?" she demanded.

"It's very important they shouldn't think we're French, at least."

"But you sounded so funny!" She began to laugh. "It would have been so much more effective if you'd just roared: 'O. K., give money, twenty dollar, very good, yes, no, get outa here, god damned son of a bitch!' Perhaps they'd have gotten the point then. The way you did it, I don't think you got it across to them for a minute."

"Well, I did my best." Now that he was in the inner room out of sight of the inimical faces, he felt better.

Presently the waiter came in with a glass of tea for the boy at the other table. Stenham ordered tea and pastries.

"Damnation!" he said. "I forgot to leave a note for Moss."

"It's my fault," she declared.

"Very sweet of you, but completely untrue."

"You could phone him."

"No. There's no phone here. I don't know. Sometimes I wonder what's wrong with me. I know just how to behave, but only before or after the fact. When the moment's there in front of me, I don't seem to function."

"You're no different from anybody else," she said.

He suspected that she was waiting for an adverse reaction to this statement, so he said nothing. They were both silent for a minute. The Arab boy was sipping his tea with the customary Moslem noisiness. Stenham, in good spirits, did not mind his presence; he was a bit of native decoration. He would not have objected even if the boy had begun to make the loud belches that polite Moroccans make when they wish to show their appreciation of what they have eaten or drunk. The boy however did not belch; instead he rose from his table and taking up a good-sized stone from the floor, started to pound on the bolt of the door that led to the little garden outside. Stenham leaned across the table and took Lee's hand. He had never noticed the wedding ring until this minute—a simple gold band. "It's good to see you," he told her, and then immediately wished he had sat still and said nothing, for at the contact of his hand her face had clouded. "It's always good to see you," he added with less buoyancy, watching her closely. For a time she seemed to be trying to decide whether or not to speak. Then she said: "Why do you do that?"

"Why shouldn't I?" He spoke quietly because he wanted to avoid stirring up another argument.

Her expression was one of utter candor. "Because it puts me in a false position," she told him. "It makes me so uncomfortable. I can't help feeling that something's expected of me. I feel I should either go coquettish or prudish on you, and I don't want to be either one."

"Why don't you just be natural?" he suggested gently.

"I'm *trying* to be natural now," she said with impatience, "but you don't seem to understand. You put me in a position where it's next to impossible to be natural."

"Is it that bad?" he said, smiling sadly.

"They say you can't tell any man that you don't find him sexually attractive, that a woman's whole success in life is based on the principle of making every man feel that given the right circumstances she'd rush to bed with him. But I think there must be a few men bright enough to hear the news without going into

a fit of depression. Don't you think so?" She smiled provoca-
tively.

He said slowly: "I think you know that isn't true. What's
being bright got to do with it? You might as well say an intelligent man won't mind being hungry as much as a slow-witted
one will."

"Well, maybe that's true," she said gaily. "Who knows?"

He was hurt; to keep her from knowing it he held her hand
tighter. "I'm not that easy to discourage," he assured her lightly.
She shrugged and looked down at the table. "I was just being
friendly," she pouted. "Because I really like you. I like just being
with you. If that isn't enough—" she shrugged again— "well,
then, the hell with it."

"Fine, fine. Maybe you'll change."

"Maybe I will. I like to think I have an open mind."

He did not answer, but sat back and looked out the window.
The boy had taken off his shoes and was wading in the pool, a
sight which, because of his state of mind, did not at once strike
him as peculiar. When he saw him bend over and fish a large,
bedraggled insect out of the water, he became interested. Now
the boy held his hand very close to his face, studying his prey,
smiling at it; he even moved his lips a few times, as though he
were talking to it.

"What is it? What are you staring at?" she asked.

"Trying to make out what that kid's doing out there, standing
in the middle of the water."

Suddenly the insect had flown away. The boy stood looking
after it, his face expressing satisfaction rather than the disappointment Stenham had expected to see. He climbed out of the
pool and sat down at its edge where he had been before.

Stenham shook his head. "Now, that was a strange bit of behavior. The boy made a special trip into the water just to pull
out some kind of insect."

"Well, he's kind-hearted."

"I know, but they're not. That's the whole point. In all my
time here I've never seen anyone do a thing like that."

He looked at the boy's round face, heavy, regular features, and curly black hair.

"He could be a Sicilian, or a Greek," he said as if to himself. "If he's not a Moroccan, there's nothing surprising about his deed. But if he is, then I give up. Moroccans just don't do things like that."

Lee stood up briefly and looked out the window; then she sat down again. "He looks like the model for all the worst paintings foreigners did in Italy a hundred years ago. *Boy at Fountain, Gipsy Carrying Water Jar;* you know?"

"You want another tea?"

"No!" she said. "One's plenty. It's so sweet. But anyway, I don't believe you can make such hard and fast general rules about people."

"You can in this case. I've watched them for years. I know what they're like."

"That doesn't mean you know what each one is like individually, after all."

"But the whole point is, they're not individuals in the sense you mean," he said.

"You're on dangerous ground," she warned him.

For fear that she might take exception to his words, he was quiet, did not attempt to explain to her how living among a less evolved people enabled him to see his own culture from the outside, and thus to understand it better. It was her express desire that all races and all individuals be "equal," and she would accept no demonstration which did not make use of that axiom. In truth, he decided, it was impossible to discuss anything at all with her, because instead of seeing each part of total reality as a complement to the other parts, with dogged insistence she forged ahead seeing only those things which she could twist into the semblance of an illustration for her beliefs.

From somewhere outside there came a faint sound which, if he had not known it was being made by human voices, he might have imagined sounded like the wind soughing through pine branches. The boy, who sat by the pool as though he were the express reason for the sun's existence at that moment, seemed to hear the sound, too. Stenham glanced at Lee: apparently she heard nothing. There were only two bits of stage business, he reflected, of which she was capable. One was to pull out her compact and occupy herself by looking into its mirror, and the other was to light a cigarette. On this occasion she used the compact.

He watched her. For her the Moroccans were backward on-lookers standing on the sidelines of the parade of progress; they must be exhorted to join, if necessary pulled by force into the march. Hers was the attitude of the missionary, but whereas the missionary offered a complete if unusable code of thought and behavior, the modernizer offered nothing at all, save a place in the ranks. And the Moslems, who with their blind intuitive wisdom had triumphantly withstood the missionaries' cajoleries, now were going to be duped into joining the senseless march of universal brotherhood; for the privilege each man would have to give up only a small part of himself—just enough to make him incomplete, so that instead of looking into his own heart, to Allah, for reassurance, he would have to look to the others. The new world would be a triumph of frustration, where all human-ity would be lifting itself by its own bootstraps—the equality of the damned. No wonder the religious leaders of Islam identi-fied Western culture with the works of Satan: they had seen the truth and were expressing it in the simplest terms.

The sound of shouting suddenly increased in volume; it was obviously coming from a moving column of men. How many thousand throats did it take, he wondered, to make a sound like that?

"Listen," said Lee.

The progress through the streets was slow, and the acoustics, changing from moment to moment, brought the sound nearer, then removed it to a more distant plane. But it was clear that the crowd was on its way up toward Bou Jeloud.

"Here comes your trouble," he said to her.

She bit her upper lip for a second, and looked at him dis-traughtly. "What do you think we ought to do? Get out?"

"Sure, if you like."

The boy came through the door, glanced shyly at them, and turned to sit down at his table. Stenham called out to him: "*Qu'est-ce qui se passe dehors?*" The boy stared at him, uncomprehending. So he was a Moroccan, after all. "*Smahli,*" Stenham said. "*Chnou hadek el haraj?*"

The other looked at him with wide eyes, clearly wondering how anyone could be so stupid. "That's people yelling," he said.

"Are they happy or angry?" Stenham wanted to know.

The boy struggled to keep his sudden suspiciousness from becoming visible in his face. He smiled, and said: "Maybe some are happy, some are angry. Each man knows what is in his own heart."

"A philosopher," Stenham laughed in an aside to Lee.

"What does he say? What is it?" she asked impatiently.

"He's being cagey. *Egless.*" He indicated the third chair at their table, and the boy sat down carefully, never taking his eyes from Stenham's face. "I'd better offer him a cigarette," Stenham said, and did so. The boy refused, smiling. "Tea?" asked Stenham. "I've drunk it. Thank you," said the boy.

"Ask him what he thinks about staying here," Lee said nervously.

"You can't hurry these people," he told her. "You get nothing out of them if you do."

"I know, but if we're going to go we should go, don't you think?"

"Well, yes, if we are. But I'm not sure it's such a good idea to go out there running around looking for a cab now, do you think?"

"You're the expert. How should I know? But for God's sake try and make sense at this point. I don't feel like being massacred."

He laughed, then turned his head to face her completely. "Lee, if I thought there were any serious danger you don't think I'd have suggested coming here, do you?"

"How do I know what you'd have suggested? I'm just telling you that if there's any question of a mob smashing into this café I want to get out now, and not wait until it's too late."

"What's this sudden hysteria?" he demanded. "I don't understand."

"Hysteria!" She laughed scornfully. "I don't think you've ever seen a hysterical woman in your life."

"Listen. If you want to go, we'll go now."

"That's just what I *didn't* say. I merely asked you to be serious and realize that you've got the responsibility for us both, and act accordingly. That's all."

What a schoolmarm, he thought angrily. "All right," he said. "Let's sit right here. This is an Arab café. There are about fifty police outside and there's a *poste de garde* right across the square. I don't know where we could be safer, except in the Ville Nouvelle. Certainly not in the hotel."

She did not answer. The noise of the crowd had become much louder; it sounded now like prolonged cheering. He turned to the boy again.

"The people are coming this way."

"Yes," said the boy; it was evident that he did not want to discuss the subject. Another tack, a different approach, thought Stenham, but not a personal one, either. "Do you like this café?" he said after a moment, remembering too late that statements were better than questions in the task of trying to establish contact with the Moroccans.

The boy hesitated. "I like it," he said grudgingly, "but it's not a good café."

"I thought it was a good café. I like it. It has water on both sides."

"Yes," the boy admitted. "I like to come and sit. But it's not a good café." He lowered his voice. "The owner has buried something outside the door. That's not good."

Stenham, bewildered, said: "I see."

The noise now could not be disregarded; its rhythmical chanting had grown into a gigantic roar, unmistakably of anger, and it was at last possible to hear details in its pattern. It had ceased being a unified wall of sound, and become instead a great, turbulent mass of innumerable separate human cries.

"*Smahli*," said the boy. "I'm going to look." Quickly he rose and went out of the room.

"Are you nervous?" Stenham asked her.

"Well, I'm not exactly relaxed. Give me a cigarette. I've run out."

While he was lighting her cigarette there came the sound of one lone shot—a small dull pop which nevertheless carried above the roar of voices. They both froze; the roar subsided for a second or two, then rose to a chaos of frenzy. Their wide eyes met, but only by accident. Then from what they would have said was the front of the café there was a phrase of machine-gun fire, a short sequence of rapidly repeated, shattering explosions.

They both jumped up and ran to the door. The other room was empty now, Stenham noticed as they went through it, save for one old man sitting on the floor in the corner, holding a kif pipe in his hand. They went only as far as the doorway of the large front room. There men were still falling over each other in their haste to get to the windows. Two waiters were sliding enormous bolts across the closed entrance door. When they had finished doing that they hurriedly pushed a large chest in front of the door, and wedged tables between it and a pillar near by. They did the work automatically, as though it were the only reaction conceivable in such a situation. Then they went behind a wall of bottle cases and peered worriedly out a small window there. From where they stood in the inner doorway Lee and Stenham could see, through the florid designs of the grillwork in the windows, only a series of senseless vignettes which had as their background the hard earth of the square. Occasionally part of a running figure passed through one of the frames. The noise at the moment was largely one of screaming; there was also the tinkle of shattering glass at intervals. Suddenly, like so many huge motors starting up, machine-guns fired from all around the square. When they had finished, there was relative silence, broken by a few single revolver shots from further away. A police whistle sounded, and it was even possible to hear individual voices shouting commands in French. A man standing in one of the windows in front of them began to beat on the grillwork like a caged animal, shrieking imprecations; hands reached out from beside him and pulled him back, and a brief struggle ensued as he was forced to the floor by his companions. Stenham seized Lee by the wrist and wheeled her around, saying: "Come on." They returned to their little room.

"Sit down," said Stenham. Then he stepped out into the sunlight, looked up at the walls around the patio, sighed, and went back in. "No way out there," he said. "We'll just have to sit here."

Lee did not reply; she sat looking down at the table, her chin cupped in her hands. He observed her: he could not be certain, but it seemed to him that she was shivering. He put his hand on her shoulder, felt it tremble.

"Wouldn't you like some hot tea, without the sugar?" he asked her.

"It's all right," she said after a pause, without glancing up. "I'm all right."

He stood there helplessly, looking down at her. "Maybe—"

"Please sit down."

Automatically he obeyed. Then he lighted a cigarette. Presently she raised her head. "Give me one," she said. Her teeth were chattering. "I might as well smoke. I can't do anything else."

Someone was standing in the doorway. Swiftly Stenham turned his head. It was the boy, staring at them. Stenham rose and went over, pulling him with him out into the next room. The old man still sprawled in the corner in a cloud of kif smoke.

"Try and get a glass of tea for the *mra*," he told the boy, who did not appear to understand. "The lady wants some tea." He's looking at me as though I were a talking tree, thought Stenham. He took the boy's arm and squeezed it, but there was no reaction. The eyes were wide, and there was nothing in them. He looked back into the room and saw Lee hunched over the table, sobbing. Pulling the boy by the arm, he led him to the chair beside her and made him sit down. Then he went out to the main room to the alcove where the fire was, and ordered three teas from the *qaouaji*; he too seemed to be in a state bordering on catalepsy. "Three teas, three teas," Stenham repeated. "One

with only a little sugar." It'll give him something to do, he
thought.

The feeble chaos outside was now almost covered by the
voices of the onlookers within the café. They were not talking
loud, but they spoke with frantic intensity, and all together, so
that no one was listening to anyone else. Happily, this occupied
them; they paid him no attention. He felt that if he left the
qaouaji to prepare the tea and bring it by himself, he would be
likely to fall back into his lethargy; he determined to remain with
him until it was ready. From where he stood, through the small
window in front of him, he could see only a part of the center
of the square. Usually it was empty, but when a figure appeared,
moving across the space made by the window's frame, it was
always a policeman or a *mokhazni*. What had happened was
fairly clear: the crowd had attempted to pass out of the Medina
through Bab Bou Jeloud, and had been stopped at the gate itself. Now there were small skirmishes taking place well within
the gate as the marchers retreated. When he heard a cavalcade of
trucks begin to arrive, he knew it would be safe to go and look
out the window, and so he squeezed himself into the narrow
corridor between the piles of cases of empty bottles and the
wall, and went to peer out. There were four big army trucks
and they had drawn up in a line behind the two abandoned
buses. Berber soldiers in uniform, their rifles in their hands,
were still leaping out of the backs of the trucks, running toward
the gate. There must be about two hundred of them, he calculated.

Now a slow massacre would begin, inside the walls, in the
streets and alleys, until every city-dweller who was able had
reached some sort of shelter and no one was left outside but the
soldiers. Even as he was thinking this, the pattern of the shooting
changed from single, desultory shots to whole volleys of them,
like strings of fire-crackers exploding. He stood there watching
tensely, although there was nothing to see; it was like seeing a
newsreel of the event, where what is presented is the cast of
characters and the situation before and afterward, but never
the action itself. Even the gunfire might as well have been a

sound-track; it was hard to believe that the rifles he had seen two minutes before were at this moment being used to kill people; were firing the shots that he was hearing. If you had had no previous contact with this sort of violence, he reflected, even when it was happening where you were, it remained unreal.

He went back to the alcove where the fire was, and was pleasantly surprised to see that the *qaouaji* had nearly finished making the tea. When it was done, he followed the man as unobtrusively as he could to the back room. When he looked at the table he did not know whether he was annoyed or delighted to find Lee and the boy engaged in a mysterious bilingual dialogue.

"Have some hot tea," he told her.

She looked up; there was no sign on her face that she had been crying. "Oh, that's sweet of you," she said, lifting the glass, finding it too hot, and putting it down again. "These people are really amazing. It took this child about two minutes to get me over feeling sorry for myself. The first thing I knew he was tugging at my sleeve and turning on the most irresistible smile and saying things in his funny language, but with such gentleness and sweetness that there I was, feeling better, that's all."

"That *is* strange," Stenham said, thinking of the state the boy himself had been in when he had left him. He turned to him and said: "*O deba labès enta?* You feel better? You were a little sick."

"No, I wasn't sick," the boy said firmly, but his face showed three consecutive expressions: shame, resentment, and finally a certain trusting humility, as if by the last he meant that he threw himself upon Stenham's mercy not to tell Lee of his weakness.

"When can we get out of here? We want to go home," Stenham said to him.

The boy shook his head. "This isn't the time to go into the street."

"But the lady wants to go to the hotel."

"Of course." The boy laughed, as though Lee's desires were those of an unreasoning animal, and were to be taken no more seriously. "This café is a very good place for her. The soldiers won't know she's in here."

"The soldiers won't know?" echoed Stenham sharply, his intuition warning him that there was more import to the words than his mind had yet grasped. "What do you mean? *Chnou bghitsi ts'qoulli?*"

"Didn't you see the soldiers? I heard them come when you were getting the tea. If they know she's in here they'll break the door and come in."

"But why?" demanded Stenham idiotically.

The boy replied succinctly and in unequivocal terms.

"No, no." Stenham was incredulous. "They couldn't. The French."

"What French?" said the boy bitterly. "The French aren't with them. They send them out alone, so they can break the houses and kill the men and take the girls and steal what they want. The Berbers don't fight for the French just for those few francs a day they give them. You didn't know that? This way the French don't have to spend any money, and the city people are kept poor, and the Berbers are happy in their heads, and the people hate the Berbers more than they hate the French. Because if everybody hated the French they couldn't stay here. They'd have to go back to France."

"I see. And how do you know all that?" Stenham asked, impressed by the clarity of the boy's simple analysis.

"I know it because everybody knows it. Even the donkeys and mules know that. And the birds," he added with complete seriousness.

"If you know all that, maybe you know what's going to happen next," Stenham suggested, half in earnest.

"There will be more and more poison in the hearts of the Moslems, and more and more and more"—his face screwed itself up into a painful grimace—"until they all burst, just from hating. They'll set everything on fire and kill each other."

"I mean today. What's going to happen now? Because we want to go home."

"You must look out the window and wait until the only men

there are French and *mokhaznia*—no partisans at all. Then you make the man open the door and let you out, and go to a policeman, and he'll take you home."

"But we don't like the French," objected Stenham, thinking this was as good a moment as any to reassure the boy as to where their sympathies lay; he did not want him to regret his candor when the excitement of the instant had passed.

A cynical smile appeared on the young face. "*Binatzkoum.* That's between you and them," he said impassively. "How did you get to Fez?"

"On the train."

"And where do you live?"

"At the Mérinides Palace."

"*Binatzkoum, binatzkoum.* You came with the French and you live with the French. What difference does it make whether you like them or not? If they weren't here you couldn't be here. Go to a French policeman. But don't tell him you don't like him."

"Look!" said Lee suddenly. "I don't feel like sitting here while you take an Arab lesson. I want to get out of here. Has he given you any information at all?"

"If you'll just have a little patience," said Stenham, nettled, "I'll get all the details. You can't hurry these people; I've told you that."

"I'm sorry. But it *is* going to be dark soon and we *have* got to get all the way back to the hotel. What I meant was, I hope you're not just having an ordinary conversation."

"We're not," Stenham assured her. He looked at his watch. "It's only four-twenty," he said. "It won't be dark for a long time. The boy doesn't think we ought to go outside quite yet. I'm inclined to think he's right."

"He probably doesn't know as much about it as you do, if you come down to that," she said. "But go ahead and talk."

The sounds of shooting had retreated into the distance. "Why don't you go and look out the window?" Stenham suggested to the boy, "and see what's happening."

Obediently the boy rose and went out.

"He's a good kid," said Stenham. "Bright as they come."

"Oh, he's a darling. I think we should each give him something when we go."

It was a long while before he returned, and when he came in they saw immediately that he was in a completely different state of mind. He walked slowly to his chair and sat down, looking ready to burst into tears.

"*Chnou?* What is it?" Stenham demanded impatiently.

The boy looked straight ahead of him, a picture of despair.

"Now *you* be patient," Lee said.

"You can go," the boy said finally in a toneless voice. "The man will open the door for you. There's nothing to be afraid of."

Stenham waited a moment for the boy to say more, but he merely sat there, his hands in his lap, his head bent forward, looking at the air. "What is it?" he finally asked him, conscious that both his experience and his Arabic were inadequate for dealing with a situation which demanded tact and delicacy. The boy shook his head very slowly without moving his eyes. "Did you see something bad?"

The boy heaved a deep sigh. "The city is closed," he said. "All the gates are closed. No one can go in. No one can come out."

Stenham relayed the information to Lee, adding: "I suppose that means going through hell to get into the hotel. Officially it's inside the walls."

She clicked her tongue with annoyance. "We'll get in. But what about him? Where does he live?"

Stenham talked with the boy for a bit, drawing only the briefest answers from him. At the end of a minute or so, he said to Lee: "He doesn't know where he's going to eat or sleep. That's the trouble. His family lives way down in the Medina. It's a mess, isn't it? And of course he has no money. They never have any. I think I'll give him a thousand. That ought to help some."

Lee shook her head. "Money's not what the poor kid needs. What good's money going to be to him?"

"What good is it!" exclaimed Stenham. "What else can you give him?"

Lee reached over and tapped the boy's shoulder. "Look!" she said, pointing at him. "You. Come." She waggled her fingers like two legs. "Him." She indicated Stenham. "Me." She pointed her thumb at herself. "Hotel." She described a wide arc with her hand. "Yes? *Oui?*"

"You're crazy," Stenham told her. A flicker of hope had appeared in the boy's eyes. Warming to her game, Lee bent forward and went on with her dumb-show. Stenham rose, saying: "Why get him all worked up? It's cruel." She paid him no attention.

"I'm going to take a look into the other room," he said, and he left them there, leaning toward each other intently, Lee gesticulating and uttering single words with exaggeratedly clear enunciation—like a schoolteacher, he thought again.

"What does she want? Gratitude?" He knew how it would end: the boy would disappear, and afterward it would be discovered that something was missing—a camera, a watch, a fountain pen. She would be indignant, and he would patiently explain that it had been inevitable from the start, that such behavior was merely an integral part of "their" ethical code.

The other room was quiet. Only a few men stood in the windows looking out. Of the rest, some talked and the others merely sat. He went to the little window where he had gone before, and peered out. In the square there was activity: the soldiers were piling sandbags in a curved line across the lower end, just outside the gate. A large calendar hung on the wall beside the window; its text written in Arabic characters, it showed an unmistakably American girl lifting a bottle of Coca-Cola to her lips. As he went back across the room two or three men turned angry faces toward him, and he heard the word *mericani*, as well as a few unflattering epithets. He was relieved: at least they all knew he was not French. It was unlikely that there would be any trouble.

In the middle room the old man had slumped to one side and closed his eyes: so many pipes of kif in one afternoon had proven more than he could manage. When Stenham stepped through the further doorway Lee stood up, smoothed her skirt, and said:

"Well, it's all settled. Amar's coming with us. They can find somewhere for him to sleep, and if they won't, I'll simply take a room for him tonight."

Stenham smiled pityingly. "Well, your intentions are good, anyway. Is that his name? Amar?"

"Ask him. That's what he told me. He can say my name, but he pronounces it Bali. It's rather nice—certainly prettier than Polly."

"I see," said Stenham. "It means old, applied to objects. If you want to lug him along it's all right with me."

The boy was still seated, looking up at them anxiously, from her face to his and back again.

"Suppose he hadn't happened to meet us," Stenham suggested. "What would he have done then?"

"He'd probably have gone back into the town before the trouble started and gotten home somehow. Don't forget it was you who spoke to him and asked him to sit down with us."

"You're sure you wouldn't just like to give him some money and let it go at that?"

"Yes, I'm sure," she said flatly.

"All right. Then I guess we'd better go."

He handed the boy five hundred francs. "*Chouf.* Pay for the tea and *cabrhozels*, and ask the *qaouaji* to open the door for us." Amar went out. It was perfectly possible, thought Stenham, that the proprietor of the café would refuse to run the risk of opening the door; they had no one's word but the boy's to the contrary. He stepped to the back door and looked out once again at the pool. The sun had gone behind the walls; in the afternoon shade the patio had taken on an austere charm. The surface of the water was smooth, but the plants along the edges, trembling regularly, betrayed the current beneath. A swallow came careening down from the ramparts toward the pool, obviously with the intention of touching the water. Seeing Stenham, it changed its direction violently, and went off in blind haste toward the sky. He listened: the shooting was not audible at the moment, there were no street-vendors' shouts, no water-sellers' bells jangling, and the high murmur of human voices that formed the city's usual backdrop of sound was missing. What he heard was the sharp confusion of bird-cries. It was the hour of the swallows. Each evening at this time they set to wheeling and darting by the tens of thousands, in swift, wide circles above the walls and gardens and alleys and bridges, their shrill screams presaging the advent of twilight.

So, he thought, it's happened. They've done it. Whatever came to pass now, the city would never be the same again. That much he knew. He heard Lee's voice behind him.

"Amar says they've unlocked the door for us. Shall we go?"

BOOK 4

THE ASCENDING STAIRWAYS

A questioner questioned concerning the doom about to fall upon the disbelievers, which none can repel, from Allah, Lord of the Ascending Stairways.

—THE KORAN

CHAPTER   24

The man and the woman stood there for a moment while the
qaouaji closed and bolted the door behind them. A pall of dust
lay over the square, raised by the boots of the soldiers as they
hurried back and forth from the trucks to the barricade they
were building at the foot of the gate. In his head Amar was
thinking: "Allah is all-powerful." Once more He had intervened
in his favor. Now that he reviewed the events of the past two or
three hours, it seemed to him that at the first moment when the
man had come into the café he remembered having noticed a
strange light around his head. A second later he had seen that it
was only the glint in his blond hair. But now that their two
fates were indissolubly linked, he recalled the brightness that

had moved in the air where the man's head was, and preferred to interpret it as a sign given him by Allah to indicate the course he must follow. It was his own secret power, he told himself, which had made it possible for him to recognize the sign and behave accordingly. From the moment he had seen the man's grave face looking out the window at him as he sat by the pool he had known that he could, if he wanted, count on his protection. It was even possible that in addition he might be able to add enough to his savings to buy a pair of shoes. But that was a secondary consideration of which he was ashamed as soon as it occurred to him. "I don't want the shoes," he told Allah, while they were crossing the square. "All I want is to stay with the Nesrani and obey his commands until I can go home again."

The fact that it was the woman who had made the actual suggestion of taking him to the hotel counted for nothing: the pattern of life was such that women were on earth only to carry out the bidding of men, and however it might look as though a woman were imposing her desires, it was always the will of men that was done, since Allah worked only through men. And how rightly, he thought, gazing with distaste at this woman's scanty clothing and her shameless way of walking along jauntily beside the man, as though she thought it perfectly proper for her to be out in the street dressed in such a fashion.

They had come to a row of policemen who stood in the way of the exit from the square. The man was talking to them. One of them designated Amar. He supposed the man was explaining that this was his servant, for presently whatever difficulties had existed appeared to have been smoothed out, and the Frenchmen seemed satisfied. Two of the uniformed men began to walk with them, so that they were now a party of five, going up the long avenue between the walls toward the sunset.

There were soldiers everywhere; they walked in the public gardens under the orange trees, leaned against the wall along the river, strutted among the overturned deck-chairs of the cafés in the park, and stood glowering at attention on either side of the high portal that led into the old Sultan's palace. A few were French, but most of them were grim-faced Berbers with shaved heads and narrow slanting eyes. They had helped the French in Indochina, and now they were helping them once more in their own land, and against their own countrymen. Amar felt his heart swell with hatred as he walked past them, but then he tried to think of something else, for fear the Frenchmen going along beside him would feel the force of his hatred. The man and the woman were talking together in a lively fashion as they turned into the long street of Fez-Djedid, and occasionally they even laughed, as though it had not occurred to them that death was everywhere around them, behind the walls of the houses and in the twilit alleys to their left, to their right. Perhaps they did not even know what was happening: they belonged to another world, and the French had respect for them.

About halfway to Bab Semmarine the street took on a somewhat more usual aspect. Here the large Algerian cafés were full, the flames of the lamps flickered on the tea-drinkers' faces, certain clothing shops were open, throngs of men and boys walked back and forth talking excitedly, being prevented from stopping by the police who constantly prodded them, saying gruffly: "Allez! Zid! Zid! Vas-y!" It was along here that Amar suddenly became aware of someone walking behind him, softly saying his name: "Amar! Yah, Amar!" The voice was deep, mellow, resonant; it was Benani. But remembering Benani's warning of the night before, that he must not step outside the walls of the Medina, he decided to pretend to hear nothing, and walked along as close to the Christian man as he was able. Still the voice continued to call his name discreetly, perhaps two meters behind him, through the hubbub and chaos of the crowd, never increasing in volume or changing its inflection.

"So that's what they're like," he thought cynically. Amar was supposed to stay inside the Medina and wait for the French to shoot him or carry him off to jail, while the members of the Party, once they had made the trouble, took care to remain outside, so that they might enjoy complete freedom.

In a café on their right several Algerians were singing, grouped around a young man playing an *oud*. The two tourists wanted to stand still a moment and listen, but the police would

not let them, and instead hurried them along toward Bab Semmarine. It was only when they had gone beneath the first arch,
and were holding their breaths against the onslaught of the
urinal's stench inside, that the insistent voice became more
pressing. "Amar!" it said. "Don't turn around. It's all right; I
know you hear me." (Amar glanced slyly first at the policeman
on his left, then at the other. Apparently neither one of them
understood Arabic, and even if they had, it was unlikely that
they would have been able to notice and single out that one
voice in the tumult around them.) "Amar! Remember you have
no tongue. We—" The echoing sound of a carriage passing
through the vaulted tunnel covered the rest of the message.
When they had come beneath the further arch out into the
open once more, the voice was gone. The bad dream had been
dispersed by the admonition to keep silence; Benani imagined
that he and the two foreigners were under arrest.

The Rue Bou Khessissate was virtually deserted, the shop-
fronts had been battened down, and the windows of the apartments in the upper stories, where the more fortunate Jewish
families lived, were hidden behind their shutters. Here and
there, as they went briskly down the long, curving street, Amar
saw, in back of a blind partly ajar, a stout matron in her fringed
headdress, holding a lamp and peering anxiously out, doubtless
asking herself vaguely if the thing which every Jew feared in
times of stress might come to pass—if the infuriated Moslems,
frustrated by their powerlessness to retaliate against the Christians, might not vent at least a part of their rage in a traditional
attack upon the Mellah. For there was certainly nothing to stop
them, if the desire came to them: a token detachment of police,
most of them Jewish themselves, and one little radio patrol car,
stationed just inside Bab Chorfa, which the mob could have
turned over with one hand if it had felt like it. He wondered
whether the young Arabs would be coming tonight to kill the
men and violate the girls (for although it was not a very great
triumph to have a Jewish girl, still it was a fact that a good many
of them were actually virgins, and this was an undeniable at-
traction in itself); his intuition told him that this time would

not be like the other times, that the Istiqlal would issue special
directives forbidding such useless excesses. For the moment he
felt magnificently superior: he was walking with four Nazarenes, and he could count on their protection. Then he thought
of the old adage: "You can share the meal of a Jew, but not his
bed. You can share the bed of a Christian, but not his meal,"
and he wondered if he would have to share the man's bed. It
was well known that many Christians liked young Arab boys. If
the Christian attacked him, he would fight; of that he was certain. But he did not really believe in the likelihood of such a
thing.

When they came to the Place du Commerce, he saw that the
fair which had filled the square the night before was now almost
entirely dismantled. Even in the dark, with the aid of flashlights
and carbide flares, workmen were hastily folding the flimsy
partitions, crating the mechanical apparatuses, and piling everything into the trucks that had been standing behind the booths.
There were several taxis at the far end of the square. The
policemen led them to the first car, and when Amar and the two
tourists were inside, one of them got in front beside the driver.
The other stepped back, saluted, and told the man at the wheel
to go to the Mérinides Palace. Amar was elated. He had never
before been in a taxi, nor, indeed, in any ordinary automobile—
only in buses and trucks, and there was no denying that these
small vehicles went much faster. The little suburban villas sped
past, then the stadium and the railway crossing, and then there
were, on one side, the long unbroken ramparts enclosing the
Sultan's orchards, and the open desolate plain on the other.

So far, the man had studiously avoided speaking at all to
Amar, and Amar guessed that he did not want the police to
know he understood Arabic. Occasionally the woman flung an
encouraging smile at him, as if she thought he might be afraid
to be with strangers. Each time she did this he smiled back
politely. They were talking about him now, he knew, but it was
in their own language, and that was all right.

Outside Bab Segma there was great activity. In the dust
raised by moving vehicles the beams of several powerful search-

lights crossed each other, making a design that was complicated
by the headlights of trucks and camionettes. As the taxi approached the gate, Amar saw a row of small tanks lined up
against the wall. A sudden, enormous doubt surged within
him. It was perfectly useless, this absurd flight he was making
from his own people into a foreign precinct, with foreigners.
Even if the police did not pull him out of the car here at Bab
Segma, or further along the road, or at Bab Jamaï, they would
surely take him from the hotel. And even if the kind lady and
gentleman managed to protect him for a certain length of time,
sooner or later there would come an hour when he would be
alone momentarily, and that was all the French needed. Certainly in their eyes he would be more suspect for having been
with these two outsiders.

The taxi swerved to the left, climbed the hill that led past
the entrance to the Casbah Cherarda where the Senegalese
troops were quartered. There were tanks there, too, and it was
evident that tonight the guards were not the customary tall
black men with their faces decorated by knife-scar designs,
stiffly holding their bayonets at their sides; in their place stood
red-faced Frenchmen with tommy-guns. At the top of the hill
the car turned right, and went along the barren stretch where
the cattle market was held on Thursdays. The policeman lolled
beside the driver, one arm over the back of the seat, smoking a
cigarette. Now that they were out in the country, and Amar's
fear had subsided somewhat, he was again able to view things
rationally, and to be ashamed of his emotions of a minute ago.
Allah had provided him with a means of escape from the café,
without which he would no doubt have remained in there
indefinitely, for no one else would have stirred outside, with all
those soldiers in the square. And it was probable that he would
eat tonight, and sleep quietly until morning. No man could
righteously ask for more than that. When morning came, it
would be a new day with new problems and possibilities, but of
course it was sinful to think about a day that had not yet
arrived. Man was meant to consider only the present; to be
preoccupied with the future, either pleasantly or with anxiety,

implied a lack of humility in the face of Providence, and was unforgivable.

All at once the car was filled with a sweet smell, like flowers, as the lady opened a small bag she carried with her, and pulled out a pack of cigarettes. Fez lay far below, wrapped in darkness, its presence betrayed only here and there by a feeble reddish gleam—a lamp in some window or a fire in a courtyard, visible for the fraction of a second as the taxi moved ahead, following the sinuous course of the road along the edge of the cliffs.

They came to the summit, where the ruined tombs of the Merinide royal family looked down across the olive groves and the eastern end of the city. The broken domes stood out black and jagged against the limpid night sky. Amar recalled the last time he had come down these slopes and rounded these curves: he had been on his way home to a beating. He smiled as he remembered how the boy steering the bicycle had misunderstood his query about the brakes, had imagined Amar was afraid it might go off the road, when actually he had been hoping that it would do just that, catapulting them both into a ravine. And he smiled again when he thought of how very seriously he had taken the prospect of that beating, whereas now, he decided, it would mean nothing to him, save the sadness he would feel at being the object of his father's displeasure, for he had grown up a good deal since then. But had he grown up entirely? For an instant he was sufficiently detached to be able to pose the question. In his pocket was a paper of kif, part of a long-term project of vengeance against Mustapha, in retaliation for that very beating. Would it not be pleasing to Allah if he should suddenly toss it out the window at this moment? But Bab Jamaï then appeared below in a confusion of moving lights, and the thought slipped out of his head to be replaced by the more real preoccupation with what might happen if the police should insist on pulling him from the taxi. This was the most dangerous spot, because it was here that they had to go into the Medina. They had arrived at the gate. The driver came to a halt and shut off the motor. A flashlight was played into their faces and then around the interior of the taxi, and a French soldier poked his head through the back window, exchanging a few words with the man and the woman. "*Et cet arabe-là*," he said, indicating Amar with the faintly contemptuous familiarity of proprietorship, "he is your personal servant?" And although Amar did not understand the words, he knew perfectly well what the soldier had said. Both the foreigners replied yes, that was the case. "*Vous pouvez continuer à l'hôtel*," he told them, and the car started up and went ahead the hundred yards to the hotel gateway.

And then began for Amar a strange series of confused impressions. Led by his new friends, he passed through two small courtyards and up two flights of carpeted stairs to an endless corridor, also carpeted, so that their footsteps made no sound. And there was expensive reed matting covering the walls all along the way, and lanterns overhead such as were found only in the Karouine Mosque or the Zaouia of Moulay Idriss. And then they opened two great doors of glass and went down a few steps into a room which was like nothing he had ever seen, but which, he decided, could not have been made for anyone but a sultan. The intricacies of the high domed ceiling were only faintly illuminated by the many-colored rays of light that streamed from the colossal lanterns overhead; it was like being in a vast and perfect cave. He had only a short moment to look around as they crossed the room, and then they were out in another corridor climbing another flight of stairs, this time very old ones of mosaic, and without carpeting—rather like the stairs in his own house, except that the edges of the steps were of white marble instead of wood. The man and woman spoke in low voices as they climbed, Amar behind them. At the top of the stairs there was another corridor, less beautiful than the one below.

Then the man opened a door and they were in the room. "Go in," he said to Amar, breaking the long silence that had been between them. He spoke to the woman, urging her to enter, too. After some hesitation she finally agreed, and she and the man sat down in two large chairs. Amar remained standing by the door, looking at the magnificent room. "Sit down," the

man said to him. He obeyed, seating himself on the floor at the
spot where he had been standing, and continued his careful
examination of the carvings on the beams overhead and the
fancy painted plaster frieze of geometric designs. The rugs were
thick, the heavy curtains hid the windows, and on the bed the
covers had been pulled back to reveal the whiteness of clean
sheets.

Now the man looked at him closely for the first time, took out
a pack of cigarettes, and after offering the woman one, tossed
the pack to Amar. "What's the matter with your nose and eyes?"
he asked him. "Have you had a fight?" Amar laughed and said:
"Yes." He was embarrassed, and he longed to get up and look
into the mirror over the washstand, but he sat still and smoked.
The man's manner of casual familiarity with him was assuredly
designed to put him at his ease, and he was grateful to him for
it; however, the presence of the woman made him nervous. She
kept looking at him and smiling in a way that he found disconcerting. It was the way a mother smiles at her small child in
a public place when many people are watching and she hopes
that it will continue to behave properly. He supposed she meant
it to be friendly and reassuring, perhaps even an encourage-
ment, a promise of future intimacy if ever they should find
themselves alone. But to him it was a shameless and indecent
way for her to behave in front of the man, now that they were
all three seated in his bedroom, and he felt that out of defer-
ence to his host he should pretend to ignore her smiles. Unfortunately she would have none of this; the less attention he
paid her, the more determinedly she kept at him, grimacing,
wrinkling her nose at him like a rabbit, blowing smoke toward
him as she laughed at things the man said, and generally behaving in an increasingly shocking fashion. And the man went on
talking, as if he were completely unaware of what she was
doing—not pretending, not indifferent, either, but truly unaware.

Amar was embarrassed for them all, but particularly for
the man. He disapproved likewise of the fact that the man and
the woman presently embarked on a long and occasionally

276 THE SPIDER'S HOUSE

stormy conversation regarding him; he knew he was the subject by the glances they gave him while they were talking. Being with them was going to be difficult, he could see that, but he was determined to show a maximum of patience. It was the least he could do in return for having been offered protection, shelter and food in this time of hardship. The discussion appeared to be one concerning food, for suddenly without any pause or transition the man said to him: "Would you mind eating alone in this room?" He answered that he would not mind at all—that, indeed, he thought it the best idea. The man seemed relieved upon hearing his reply, but the woman began to make silly gestures meaning that he ought to go downstairs and eat with them. While she did this the man glowered. Amar had no intention of accompanying them to any public room where he would be on view to the French and the Moroccans who worked in the hotel. He smiled amiably and said: "This is a good room for eating." For a while the conversation between the two became more animated; then the woman got up petulantly and walked to the door, where she turned and waved coyly at Amar before she went out. The man stepped into the corridor with her for a moment, came back in, and shut the door. His expression was one of annoyance as he took up the telephone and spoke briefly into it.

Amar had been studying the patterns in the rug beside him; he had decided it was the most beautiful object in the room.

When he had hung up the receiver, the man sat down again, heaved a deep sigh, and lit another cigarette. Amar looked up at him.

"Why do you talk so much with that woman?" he said, the expression of his voice a mixture of shyness and curiosity. "Words are for people, not for women."

The man laughed. "Aren't women people?" he asked.

"People are people," Amar said stolidly. "Women are women. It's not the same thing."

The man looked very surprised, and laughed more loudly. Then his face became serious; he leaned forward in the chair. "If women aren't people," he said slowly, "how does it happen they can go to Paradise?"

Amar looked at him suspiciously: the man could scarcely be that ignorant. But he could discern no mockery in his face. "*El hassil,*" he began, "they have their own place in Heaven. They don't go inside where the men are."

"I see," the man said gravely. "It's like the mosques, is that it?"

"That's it," said Amar, still wondering if the man might not be making fun of him.

"You must know a lot about your religion," the man said dreamily. "I wish you'd tell me something about it."

Now Amar was convinced that he was being baited. He gave a short, bitter laugh. "I don't know anything," he said. "I'm like an animal."

The man raised his eyebrows. "Nothing at all? But you should. It's a very good religion."

Amar was displeased. He studied the face of this patronizing infidel for a moment. "It's the *only* one," he said evenly. Then he smiled. "But now we are all like animals. Just look in the streets, see what's happening here. Don't you think it's the Moslems' fault?"

The man's swift glance told him that he was awakening some sort of respect. "The Moslems have some blame," he said quietly, "but I think the great blame goes to the French. You don't judge a man too harshly for what he does to an intruder he finds in his house, do you?"

Now Amar was about to reply: "Allah sees everything," but a voice in his head was whispering to him that it was not the sort of remark the Nazarene would really hear. If he wanted to keep alive the spark of respect he felt he had kindled, he must work hard inside himself. "The French are thieves in our house, you're right," he agreed. "We invited them in because we wanted to take lessons from them. We thought they'd teach us. They haven't taught us anything—not even how to be good thieves. So we want to put them out. But now they think the house is theirs, and that we're only servants in it. What can we do except fight? It is written."

"Do you hate them?" the man asked; he was leaning forward, looking at Amar with intensity. There was no one there but the two of them; if the man turned out to be a spy he would at least have no witnesses. But that was an extreme consideration: Amar was positive he was only an onlooker. "Yes, I hate them," he said simply. "That's written, too."

"You have to hate them, you mean? You can't decide: I will or I won't hate them?"

Amar did not completely understand. "But I hate them *now*," he explained. "The day Allah wants me to stop hating them, He'll change my heart."

The man was smiling, as if to himself. "If the world's really like that, it's very easy to be in it," he said.

"It will never be easy to be in the world," Amar said firmly. "*Er rabi mabrhach.* God doesn't want it easy."

The man did not answer. Soon he rose, went to the open window, and stood looking down at the dark Medina below. When he turned back into the room, he began to speak as though there had been no break in the conversation. "So you hate them," he mused. "Would you like to kill them?"

This immediately put Amar on his guard. "Why do you ask me all these questions?" he said aggrievedly. "Why do you want to know about me? That's not good at a time like now." He tried to keep his face empty of expression, so that it would not look as though he were indignant, but apparently his effort was not completely successful, for the man sat back and launched into a long apology, making a good many errors in Arabic, so that Amar often was not certain what it was he was trying to tell him. The recurrent motif of this speech, however, was that the Nazarene was not attempting to pry into Amar's life in any way, but only to learn about what was happening in the city. To Amar this was a most implausible explanation; if it were the truth, why did the man keep asking him for his personal opinion?

"What I think about the trouble is less than the wind," he finally said with a certain bitterness. "I can't even read or write my own name. What good could I be to anybody?" But even this confession, with all it cost him to make it, seemed not to convince the man, who, rather than accepting it and letting the matter drop, seemed positively delighted to learn of Amar's shame. "Aha!" he cried. "I see! I see! Very good! Then you have nothing to fear from anyone."

This remark Amar found particularly disturbing, for it must mean that he was going to send him away. The Nazarene had understood nothing at all; Amar's spirits sank as he perceived the gap that lay between them. If a Nazarene with so much good will and such a knowledge of Arabic was unable to grasp even the basic facts of such a simple state of affairs, then was there any hope that any Nazarene would ever aid any Moslem? And yet a part of his mind kept repeating to him that the man could be counted on, that he could be a true friend and protector if only he would let himself be shown how.

They continued to talk, but the conversation was now like a game in which the players, through fatigue or lack of interest, have ceased to keep the score, or even to pay attention to the sequence of plays. The point of contact was gone; they seemed to be looking in different directions, trying to say separate things, giving different meanings to words. Mercifully, a knock came at the door, and the man sprang to open it. The woman stood there, dressed in a more seemly manner this time, and looking very pleased with herself. In she came, down she sat, and then on and on she talked, while Amar's boredom and hunger grew. When there was another knock at the door, he rose, swiftly crossed the room, and managed to be at the window, leaning over the balcony, when the servant came in carrying his tray, and he remained there until he had heard him go out and shut the door behind him. His eyes having grown used to the dark as he stood there, he was able to find, among the thousands of cubes which were the houses in the dimness below, the mosque that stood on the hill at the back of his house. And

off in the east, behind the barren mountains, there was a glow
in the clear sky which meant that the moon would shortly be
arriving.

In the room the man and the woman made clinking sounds
with their glasses, and talked, and went on talking. He wondered how the man found the patience to go on making conversation with her. After all, he reflected, if Allah had meant
women to talk to men, He would have made them men, and
given them intelligence and discernment. But in His infinite
wisdom He had created them to serve men and be commanded
by them. The man who, forgetting this, allowed one of them to
addle his brain to such an extent that he was willing to meet her
on equal terms, sooner or later would bitterly regret his weakness. For women, no matter how delightful they might seem,
were basically evil, savage creatures who desired nothing better
than to pull men down to their own low state, merely to watch
them suffer. In Fez it was often said, half jokingly, that if the
Moroccans had been really civilized men, they would have devised cages in which to keep their women. As it was, the women
enjoyed far too much freedom of movement; and yet the Nationalists actually wanted to give them more, wanted to allow
them to walk alone in the street, go to the cinema, sit in cafés,
even swim in public places. And most unthinkable of all, they
hoped to induce them to discard the *litham*, and show their
faces openly, like Jewesses or Christians. Of course this could
never really happen; even the prostitutes wore veils when they
went out to shop, but it was characteristic of the times that
some Nationalists dared speak openly of such things.

Soon the man called: "*Fik ej jeuhor?* Hungry?" Amar turned.
On the tray there was a plate with pieces of white bread on it.
"These are for you," the man said. "That's your dinner."

Determined not to show his disappointment at finding that
the man held him in such low esteem as to offer him nothing
but these few mouthfuls of bread, he smiled, went over to the
table, and took a piece. Then he discovered that each one was
two pieces, and that they had butter and chicken inside. This
was partly consoling. The tray also held a bottle of Coca-Cola.

He sipped a little, but it was too cold. "We're going down and eat," the man said. "This is enough for you?"

Amar said it would be. He was now terrified that someone might come to the room while he was in it alone. "Please lock the door," he said.

"Lock the door?"

"Lock the door, please, and take the key with you."

The man repeated this to the woman; he seemed to think it an amusing request. When she heard the words her face assumed a bewildered expression, as though it were an unheard-of idea to lock anyone into a room. Then the man, in passing him, tousled his hair, saying: "*Nchoufou menbad.*" Amar's mouth was full of bread and chicken, but he nodded his head vigorously. After the man had shut the door, he went over and tried the knob, just to be sure. Then he set the tray on the floor, sat down beside it, and began to eat in earnest.

CHAPTER   25

They sat opposite each other at a small table in the farthest corner of the bright dining-room. Lee was thinking: How white the French waiters look, and how dark the Moroccans. But it was more than that. The French stood in apathetic postures, without even whispering among themselves, staring morosely or self-consciously at the floor, and the Moroccans were stiffer than usual, with set, inexpressive faces. The room seethed with an abnormal silence; it was difficult to talk above it.

Suddenly she laughed. Stenham looked inquiringly at her. "This is really very funny, I think," she said, aware that it was a lame explanation; but she could find no other immediate one.

She knew he was going to say: "What is?" which was exactly what he did say. And then of course she had nothing to answer, because if he didn't see it, nothing could make him see it.

"You know you never called Mr. Moss," she told him, as though she had just thought of it, although it had occurred to her nearly an hour before, while they were having soup.

"There's no point in calling him now, because he's out."

This was typical of Stenham; she was faintly piqued without knowing exactly why.

"He is! But how do you know?"

"They gave me a message from him when I phoned down for the drinks."

"Oh? You didn't tell me."

"I didn't think you'd be interested."

"But what's he doing out, tonight of all nights?"

"He could get in and out of the Medina during a full-scale war, that one. He could see the leader of the Istiqlal for tea and have the Résident for dinner."

She was amused at his evident resentment. "You don't like that, do you?" she said.

"What man does like to see another enjoying privileges he'll never have?"

"Well!" She laughed. "You'd better be careful with that subversive talk! You sound almost like me."

"After all," he continued, pretending to ignore her sarcasm, "he's got millions, so his motives are above suspicion. While who knows what we might be up to? We might be seeing the wrong kind of native. Like the kid upstairs, who'd never join any group, but would do anything at all if the right person gave the order. And that right person could be anybody he chanced to meet and admire. Those are the dangerous ones—not the joiners. You can keep tabs on the joiners easily enough. I can see why the French are going crazy. The only natives under control are the few thousand party members. The other nine million fanatics are anybody's guess."

Now Lee's voice became thin and sharp, her accent a parody of the accent of the typical New York stenographer: "Is there any comment on Comrade Stenham's report? If not, we will proceed to the next point on the agenda. In the absence of Comrade Lipschitz—" He stopped her with a well-aimed snap of his napkin in her face. The Moroccans stared in astonishment; the French remained sunk in their collective lethargy. Lee snickered. She was in a good mood. The day had not been without its adventure, and the future was just unpredictable enough to be exciting. Then, the dinner had been better than usual, since, with only two guests to cook for, the chef had not bothered to attempt any of his more complex creations. In addition, she was just a little tipsy from the wine, to which she had kept helping herself because it was so good, being chilled to exactly the right temperature. She had just ordered another half bottle, and was looking forward to having coffee on the terrace.

"I don't know what I'll do when I leave Morocco and have to give up this marvelous Algerian rosé," she said.

"You can get it in France," he told her.

It was at that instant that the lower garden sneezed. They looked at each other as the echoes shuddered from wall to wall; in another second there was only the sound of a fine rain of earth and stones falling. Now they were on their feet, running to the window, but there was nothing to see below save the dark interlacing of branches and the tile walks reflecting the early moonlight.

"Why would they do that?" Stenham said, his voice sounding unrecognizable after that racket; or perhaps it was his imagination.

"It's a French hotel," she answered, her teeth together, as though she had a gun in her hands and were saying it over her shoulder between shots.

He laughed briefly. "Let's go back and finish dinner." The waiters had rushed out onto the balcony and were peering over the railing down into the garden, French first, and Moroccans craning to see over their heads.

The rest of the meal was not a success. In some indefinable manner one would have said that the air had changed in density, that the room had altered its proportions. The acoustics seemed different, the lights shone too brightly and the shadows were too dark. And the mechanism of the service appeared to have been thrown hopelessly out of order. They were each brought two custards by mistake, but no spoons with which to eat them. The waiters gave the impression of being in a great hurry, but they had forgotten where things were.

"Did it upset you?" he asked her.

"No more than any other sudden noise would have," she said. "I hate sudden noises. You're always waiting for them to repeat themselves."

"I know. Why don't we have coffee in the bar? I think it'd be a little *too* reckless to have it on the terrace at this point."

"Let's have it up in your room. We ought to get back to that poor kid."

They found him sitting in the middle of the floor facing a semicircle of shoes; he had a shoe in his hand, and was examining it.

"These are good shoes," he announced, pointing to the one he held. "You should always give them polish. The leather is going to crack, and then they'll be finished. *Safi!*"

"If I'm not mistaken, he's found my shoeshine and rag, and polished all these shoes before he put them out to admire," Stenham said. "It's the sort of thing I never have time to do, and would never remember if I had."

"Ask him what he thought of all the noise."

A moment later, Stenham told her: "He doesn't seem to have given it much thought. He says the boys in Casablanca make the bombs, and they're not much good, and they throw them haphazardly. What the French call *des bombes de fabrication domestique.* In any case, he says it's a new thing here in Fez. It's been mostly individual stabbings and shootings."

Even as Stenham spoke, there was another loud explosion below in the Medina, not very far away. Amar ran to the window, stood there awhile looking down. When he turned his head back toward the room he said: "I think that was at the bank."

"He's so calm about it," said Lee. "You'd think it happened every day of the year."

"It's all a game to them."

The coffee came, Stenham taking the tray from the waiter's hands in the doorway to prevent his entering the room. Then they sat discussing the trouble, while from time to time Stenham, in a manner slightly more oblique, made further efforts to elicit information and personal reactions from Amar. But it was clear even to Lee, on the outside of all this, that the boy was not in a confiding mood. Under his mask of polite reserve he was hesitant and reluctant to answer Stenham's questions, and, she thought, at times even outraged by them. Finally she decided to interrupt, for the boy was looking increasingly confused and unhappy.

"Oh, let the poor kid alone!" she exclaimed. "He'll end up thinking we're as bad as the French. I don't think it's right to grill him that way."

Stenham did not seem to have heard her. "This kid is split right down the middle," he said. "You've got all Morocco right here in him. He says one thing one minute and the opposite the next, and doesn't even realize he's contradicted himself. He can't even tell you where his sympathies are."

Lee snorted. "Don't be ridiculous. I never saw a face with more character. If he doesn't talk, it's only because he's decided not to."

"What's character got to do with it? He's in a situation. He's on the spot. It has nothing to do with him. Whether he manages it one way or another, it'll be the same for him."

She got up, walked to the window, and walked back again. "I'm awfully fed up with that kind of mysticism," she declared. "It's such a bore, and it's so false. Every little thing makes a difference, whether you decide it yourself or whether it's pure accident. So many people have had the whole course of their lives changed by something perfectly simple like, let's say, crossing the street at one point instead of another."

"Yes, yes, yes, I know," Stenham said with exaggerated weariness. "As far as I'm concerned that's just as boring, and a lot

more false, by the way. The point I'm trying to make is that he
loves his world of Koranic law because it's his, and at the same
time he hates it because his intuition tells him it's at the end
of its rope. He can't expect anything more from it. And our
world, he hates that too, just on general principles, and yet it's
his only hope, the only way out—if there is one for him personally, which I doubt."

Lee poured herself half a cup of coffee, sipped it, and finding
it cold, set it down. "You talk as though it were his own private
little set of circumstances, something that had to do with him
as a person. My God! I'd like to know how many millions of
people there are in that identical situation at this minute, all
over the world. And they're all going to do the same thing, too.
They're all going to throw over their old way of thinking and
adopt ours, without any hesitation. It's not even a problem.
There's simply no question about it in their minds. And they're
right, right, right, because our way happens to work, and they
know it."

For an instant his anger was so great that he could not trust
himself to speak.

"My dear little friend," he finally said, and his voice grated
unpleasantly, "the worst fate I can wish for you is that you'll
still be around when the horror you want is here."

"I'll be around," she said calmly, "because it's not going to
take long."

It was too bad she had to have opinions; she had been so
agreeable to be with before she had started to express them.
And then, the terrible truth was that neither she nor he was
right. It would not help the Moslems or the Hindus or anyone
else to go ahead, nor, even if it were possible, would it do them
any good to stay as they were. It did not really matter whether
they worshipped Allah or carburetors—they were lost in any
case. In the end, it was his own preferences which concerned
him. He would have liked to prolong the status quo because the
décor that went with it suited his personal taste.

There was not much more conversation that evening. When
the moment came for Lee to go to her room, the question of

Amar's sleeping-place arose. She wanted to call downstairs and arrange for the management to give him a servant's room or a bed in some corner, but Amar, when Stenham relayed this idea to him, began a frenzied plea to be allowed to remain where he was and simply stretch out on the rug.

Lee shrugged. "The only thing is," she told Stenham, "I don't want you to be bothered. I brought him, and now you seem to be getting stuck with him. I'm afraid he may interfere with your work."

"It makes no difference at all," he said brusquely; he was still exceedingly angry. When she had gone, and he had heard her lock her door, he took the boy down the stairs to the lavatory, and waited in the big, dark ballroom to show him the way back.

A cricket had installed itself somewhere in the matting, and was singing happily. Its repeated silvery note was like a tiny bell being tolled there in the darkness. The huge moon was high in the sky, and its light entered the room through the shifting screen made by the leaves of the poplars in the garden. He stood there listening and looking, wondering whether he would ever see the big room again by moonlight, as he had seen it night after night for so many years, passing through on the way to his room in the tower. Perhaps never again moonlight after this minute, he thought, as he heard the flushing of the toilet behind him, and the opening of the door. The boy came out, and in a penetrating stage-whisper began to call: *"M'sieu! M'sieu!"* "My God! I can't have him calling me that," he said to himself, glad for something to seize upon, to take his mind away from its melancholy speculations. Saying "Shh!" he led the way back up the stairs to his room, pushed him inside, and locked the door.

Immediately the boy seized a cushion from the seat of a chair and tossed it onto the rug in the center of the room. Then he took the spread from the foot of the bed, and wrapping it around him, lay down on the floor. "*'Lah imsikh bekhir,*" he said dutifully to Stenham, whereupon he whispered a few words of prayer and was quiet.

Stenham read for a half hour or so before turning off his bed-lamp. He was in an unpleasant frame of mind over the way the evening had turned out. It was getting mixed up with this boy that had done it all; without him there would have been a way, in spite of Lee's coolness and candor at the café. He even suspected her motives in insisting upon bringing the boy along to the hotel: mightn't she have guessed that he would prove useful by providing a convenient obstruction to any possible intimacy? Twice in the night he awoke and saw the shrouded form lying there in the moonlight.

The next time he opened his eyes, the sun was very bright, and the boy stood in one of the windows looking out. One thing he did not want was to get involved in talk before he had had coffee. Surreptitiously he felt around behind the pillows for the bell, pushed the button, and pretended to be sleeping. The ruse worked so well that he was actually almost asleep again by the time there was a knock at the door. As he opened his eyes, he realized that the boy was trapped, in full sight of whoever was to come into the room. He jumped out of bed and opened the large mirror door of the armoire, signaling to the boy to step behind it. The knocking was repeated with added force.

A stout Frenchman stood there with his breakfast tray. "I'll take it," he said nonchalantly, reaching out for it. It was not until he had the tray in his hands that he felt free to go on talking. "What's happened to the Arabs?" he asked; no one but Rhaissa or Abdelmjid had ever brought him his breakfast. "*Tous les indigènes sont en tôle.*" The man was grinning. "The major domo has locked them all in their rooms and put the keys in the office safe. That way we're sure of *those* natives, at least." Changing his tone, he went on: "It's very serious, what's happening, you know."

"I know," said Stenham.

"I'm surprised you stay."

"And you?"

The big man shrugged. "*C'est mon gagne-pain, quoi!* We all have to earn our living."

"Ah, you see?" Stenham exclaimed. "That's why I stay, too."

The man nodded, making it obvious that he did not believe

this for a moment. Stenham shut the door, and the boy's head appeared around the side of the wardrobe, his eyes large with excitement. Probably his imagination was still ablaze with images of police tortures.

"*Sbalkheir.* Good morning."

"*Sbalkheir, m'sieu.*"

Stenham poured half the coffee and half the hot milk into a tumbler, sweetened it, and handed it down to the foot of the bed where the boy stood. It was this gesture, together with the consciousness of exactly how many francs it represented, which made him smile at the absurdity of having this primitive youth, whose name he did not even know, sharing his room and breakfast with him. The mechanics of ridding himself of him were nothing; on the other hand, the moral responsibility involved was enormous, or so it seemed to him. And each hour that the boy spent with him would increase its weight.

Suddenly he asked the boy his name. "Of course, now I remember." He took another swallow of coffee and finished eating a slice of toast. "What would you do, Amar, if I should put you out?" The boy focused his piercing gaze upon him. His eyes were those of a wild animal, but at the same time they were human, compelling and extraordinarily expressive.

"I am in Allah's hands. If I go, that will be His will."

"Then you're not afraid?"

"Yes, I'm afraid. And I want very much to see my father and mother." He seemed about to say more, then to think better of it.

There was a knock at the door, and the stout waiter came in. "*Ah, pardon!*" he exclaimed, looking at Amar in surprise. "I thought monsieur had finished."

"Bring the same order again, will you? I'm still hungry. I've shared my breakfast." It was a moment that demanded brazenness.

The waiter smiled. "*Une petite causerie matinale?* A little morning chat over the coffee cups is always agreeable." Still smiling, he went out.

I suppose he's on his way down to the manager to report the

presence of the enemy in the fort, thought Stenham, but he said nothing. A few minutes later the waiter reappeared with another tray, which he set on the bed between them. *"Et voilà!"* He stepped back, flourishing his napkin. *"Votre serviteur discret!"* His pink face beaming, he stood an instant looking at them. Then he went out.

"More coffee?" Stenham held the spout of the pot over the boy's cup. But Amar had once more fallen into a state of frightened melancholy. It took Stenham a half hour to convince him that the waiter almost certainly was not going to report his presence to the police.

Outside the window the burning sun climbed slowly to a higher position over the city. It was a cloudless day, so clear that each ravine on the distant mountain-slopes was visible in painstakingly etched detail. And the ten thousand flat rooftops below were beginning to collect the heat and to send it back up into the air, where it would gradually take on intensity and substance, and remain until long after dusk.

It was about nine o'clock when the disorders began. Stenham was standing before the washbasin, shaving, and in the mirror he saw the boy move soundlessly to the window. At first there was only shouting, from one part of the town directly below, and then from a more distant quarter to the west. But shortly there came the nervous and formless phrases of gunfire, and this seemed to issue from all regions of the city, more or less at the same time. Stenham made no comment, continued to shave, imagining the conflict that must be going on inside the watching head at the window. On and off, all morning long, the shooting continued. Occasionally Stenham tried to engage the boy in conversation, but his replies were monosyllabic.

The packed valises still stood by the door. "Am I staying or leaving?" The answer seemed to be that he certainly was not leaving at the moment, in any case. Yesterday he had been ready to get out; her arrival had made him willing to stay, even without the possibility of work. There was the point at which he had gone off the track; that was clear enough, now that he was no longer free to go, now that nearly twenty-four hours later he was still there. But this morning he did not feel that he *was* here; he could have been anywhere. The room was not the same room that it had been, nor was the hotel the place that had been his home for so many seasons. It was all vaguely like an innocuous dream whose only meaning lies in the sleeper's awareness that at any moment it can become a nightmare. Of course there was no question of working again; the idea was ludicrous. Nor would he be able to sit and read. All he could do was to wait for the drama to play itself out, except that because he had no part in it, it would not even do that—at least, not in a way that could be satisfactory to him.

The boy did have a part in it; there he was, fingering the curtain at the window, looking out through the heat at the city where he had been born, listening to his people being murdered, feeling God only knew what emotions as he stood there. Inextricably involved, he still could do nothing which might conceivably change the smallest detail—perhaps not even within himself.

If he had any character, Stenham reflected, he would give the boy some money and turn him out, letting him take his chances in the street like the rest of his countrymen. Then he would telephone Moss and see if he wanted to leave, do the same with Lee, and just start going, with or without the other two. That would make a kind of sense that no other action could. And now he wondered why he had ever expected it to be anything but overwhelmingly depressing to watch the city being destroyed. Perhaps (he could no longer remember) he had imagined that somehow an occasion would present itself in which he could perform some positive act, could be of help. But of help to whom? The two adversaries shooting one another down there were equally hateful to him; he hoped each side would kill as many of the other as possible.

When it was about eleven, the telephone rang: Moss was speaking from his room.

"I say, John, I'm frightfully sorry about yesterday. I had some business that needed attending to. I couldn't let it go on any longer. You know, this thing has got quite out of hand. I think the time has come to take action."

"What action?" Stenham's inflection was more derisive than interrogatory.

"Could we meet shortly for a little talk?"

"That'd be fine. That's just what I feel like, myself."

Moss came to Stenham's room a quarter of an hour later. Seeing Amar standing at the window, "Who's that?" he demanded, as if he had discovered him in his own room.

"It's a long story. I'll tell you in a minute. Sit down."

Moss sat in the large easy chair, folded his hands in front of him, and looked up at the ceiling. "This is all so distressing," he said.

Stenham regarded him suspiciously. "You look very pleased with yourself," he told him. "My guess is that you made some money yesterday."

Moss showed astonishment; then a veiled smile spread across his face. "I made a small profit. Yes. Not nearly so much as I'd counted on, naturally. By waiting I might have doubled it, and then again it's possible I'd have found no market at all. My personal feeling is that it's time to move on to calmer waters. Which is what I wanted to discuss with you. Don't you think we could organize a joint exodus between us, rent a car, I mean, this afternoon, and go?"

"Go where?" said Stenham, immediately suspicious at hearing the words: "we could rent." If such a mode of travel was to be used, he did not intend to share in its expense.

"Practically anywhere. I'd thought of Rabat, because I have friends there" ("And probably a garage to sell," Stenham added mentally) "but it could just as easily be Meknès or Ouezzane, if you like, I suppose. I'm very keen on not being in Fez tomorrow. It's the Aïd, and practically anything may happen. Surely you agree there's no point in having trouble if we can avoid it."

"Madame Veyron's back, you know."

"Oh, no! How really extraordinary! What on earth for?"

"I think it's just inquisitiveness."

"Ah, your great plot proved not to have her in it?"

Stenham frowned. "No, I'm afraid she's innocent." But he was thinking: Where's the difference between innocence and guilt, in cases like hers?

"I'm delighted to hear you admit it," Moss was saying patronizingly.

"And then there's Amar." He pointed to the window.

"So I see. But who is he? What's he doing here?"

When Stenham had finished telling him, Moss exclaimed: "Oh, come! Now what's this nonsense? I haven't understood a word of what you've said. It's all very commendable and romantic to take in a waif, but surely you don't intend to keep him."

"No, no, no!" Stenham cried. "Of course not! I don't know what I intend. I don't intend anything. I've just got to have time to think a little, that's all."

"Time! There isn't much of that at the moment, you know. I suggest you turn the institution of oriental cupidity to your advantage for once, hand the young man a five-thousand-franc note, and then set him free. It's astonishing what an excellent safe-conduct money can be."

"Yes, I've thought of that," Stenham replied distraughtly. "I don't know."

"Really, John! I can only look at you and marvel at the inscrutability of the human soul."

He's warming up for a round of the old game, thought Stenham. But I haven't got the energy to play. He did not answer.

Moss was silent for a moment. Now and then, in the confusion of rifle and machine-gun fire, there came the heavier sound of a grenade bursting. "With or without waifs and Americans," he resumed, "I have my eye set upon being far from Fez before tomorrow's dawn. And I'm dead serious about this, John. It's not a little fantasy of mine."

"You think tomorrow's the bad day, and after that it'll be better?"

"I think tomorrow will be the climax. It's going to be a thwarted Aïd el Kebir, don't forget. After that I think passions will slowly subside. Nothing can stay at fever pitch indefinitely."

Stenham, without replying, had begun to talk with Amar.

"Oh, that accursèd dead language that refuses to die!" Moss wailed, raising his eyes heavenward. "In order to say good morning one must use eighty-three separate words, each one with more hideous sounds in it than the last. Now, John, stop being difficult and talk to me, will you, please?" For a time he sat silent, in an attitude of mock resignation, looking very sorry for himself.

Presently Stenham looked up. "I've found a solution," he announced. "Amar will take us to Sidi Bou Chta."

"Very kind of him, I'm sure. If anyone wants to go. And would you like to tell me where this place is, and why we should go there, instead of somewhere that we've heard of?"

"It's a pilgrimage spot in the mountains, miles from anywhere. The great advantage is that there are no French. That means there's no trouble, either for them or for us. And they'll really observe the feast. I'd like to see it."

"Hotel?" said Moss.

"We'd sleep on mats, in the shelters."

Now Moss stood up and recited the lengthy tirade he had evidently been preparing. Its organization, phrasing and delivery were all admirable. When he had finished, "I enjoyed that," Stenham told him. "You're still *en forme*. I suppose you mean you won't come."

Moss yawned and stretched, reassumed his normal voice. "I'm afraid not, John. It's just not my cup of tea. You should know me well enough to understand that. What would you do: stay a day or two, and then come back here?"

Wearily Stenham said he did not know, that the idea had only now occurred to him, that how it was carried out would depend upon the boy, and whether it were put into effect at all would probably be decided by Madame Veyron. "It doesn't matter to me one way or the other," he concluded. "But I think you're right about not being here tomorrow."

"Well, John, it looks like the parting of the ways for a time."

"It's awful," said Stenham, for whom any leavetaking had a faint savor of the deathbed. "So sudden."

"I shall miss our expeditions. Into the Medina, I mean. Not those into the labyrinths of polemics."

Stenham smiled feebly. "Where will you be?"

"I think I'll visit some friends in Cintra. It's very charming there. I don't think you'd like it. You can reach me at the British Consulate in Lisbon. Three or four days ought to see me through my business and out of Morocco. I must say I hope so. All this excitement is fatal for my painting. And you, how can you concentrate on your work in a place that's like an overturned anthill?"

Stenham heard the phrases and understood them, but a part of his consciousness was perversely working to distract his attention. Morocco, Moss, motor, moustache, moving, mow, sometimes my mind runs away with me like this, but it's usually only in moments of stress. So, this must be a moment of stress. He's the last link with the way things used to be. Moxie, it went on, Moylan ("That's not allowed; nobody ever heard of it." "It's where the Hedgerow Theatre is, outside Philadelphia. Objection overruled.") *Mozo.* ("This is *my* game. No holds barred. Foreign languages accepted.") *Mozo* was certainly the boy in the window. But thank God that's the end of the alphabet. Thank God his name was Moss, and not Moab. Now he looked at Moss, and thought how sallow his complexion was, and how unusually long his eyelashes were; he had never noticed either of those details before. Perhaps it was the angle at which the thick lenses of his glasses struck the lashes, but he doubted it.

"Or probably the idea appeals to you, staying on here and seeing it all with your own eyes."

"No, it doesn't," he said simply.

Moss shifted his feet with impatience. He sighed. "Oh, well, John, it's all too mysterious and complicated. We do what makes us happy, and there's no point in going further into it."

"That's right." It was a completely erroneous summing-up of all the understandings they thought they had reached in the years they had known each other, but the world was the way it was. "That's absolutely right," Stenham said again, with more feeling.

After a few more exchanges of words, they shook hands, and Moss left.

CHAPTER 26

When Polly Burroughs arrived back in her room, she put on a clean pair of shantung pajamas, got into bed with her tiny typewriter, and set to work writing letters. Her correspondence was a lusty one; most days she sent off a dozen or so missives, some short and some surprisingly lengthy, all of which she typed with great speed and gusto. It often happened that she could not be sure what she thought about a thing until she had written a letter to someone about it; in the spontaneous sentences that flowed from her fingertips as she ran them over the keyboard, her ideas were crystallized, became visible to her. She was not one to be concerned with profundities, for she was well aware that there are too many different angles, all of them more or less equally valid, from which to look at a simple truth; what she strove for was a neat arrangement of her own personal opinions and reactions to outward phenomena, and she possessed an over-all formula which greatly facilitated the achievement of this. By keeping in her mind's eye the face, the sound of the voice, and the temperament of the individual to whom she was writing, she managed to speak directly to that person and to no one else. She had no one mode of expression, no style, which could properly be identified as hers. The letters were considered breezy and original, and were much admired (and carefully collected) by almost everyone who received them; the steady production of them had come to be one of her principal *raisons d'être.* "Wonderful? I don't know what you mean. And anyway, I don't write them; they write themselves. It's just a state of mind you have to get into."

Polly belonged wholly to her time. Alert to its defects and dangers, she nevertheless had reached what she herself called an "adjustment," and she was very firm in her belief that without the attainment of a state of conscious harmony with the society in which he functioned, no individual could hope to accomplish much of anything.

She had understated the facts in telling Kenzie that she had "heard of" Stenham. Actually she had read all his books and was something of a fan of his. She liked his style, an important by-product of what seemed to her an unusually vigorous mind in a healthy state of controlled, and therefore constructive, rebellion. Particularly the way he wrote about love pleased her: the passages had a militant detachment that bordered on the clinical, and yet were saved from that kind of shallowness by what she felt to be an underlying and ever present sense of inevitability. These sections of his books were the very antithesis of what commonly is considered "romantic," yet to her they were all of that and much more: she had gone so far as to call them "sheer poetry." She had even known he was in Morocco when she had decided to come. There were Marrakech and the political situation and the Grand Atlas and native festivals, certain of which would take place during her stay, and Fez and Stenham and the Sahara, plus whatever might present itself in between. For Polly Burroughs had the makings of a good journalist. She believed that, assuming one had open eyes and an open mind, one needed only to be on the spot in order to capture the truth. If anyone had discussed it with her, she would have maintained that a photograph was nearer to reality than a painting, because it was objective. For her there was either the garden of facts or the wilderness of fantasy, and because Stenham's florid ramblings appealed to her imagination, she had decided they were actually a variety of fact—symbolic fact, it was true, but still fact.

"... I finally met your favorite writer," she had written
weeks back, the day they had all had lunch at the Zitoun,
"or isn't John Stenham your favorite? It seems to me I remember words to that effect from you, one day when we were sitting
on the Brevoort terrace, at least five years ago. I'm a little
disappointed because he's not in the least as I had expected.
Probably that's my fault, because he's a true writer, and the best
of any true writer is in his books, where it belongs. There were
also some real British drips present. They were useful as atmosphere, of course, along with the storks and Arab waiters in
costume, but at least the last two didn't try to make conversation, thank God."

To a different friend the next night she had written: "As
you probably know, John Stenham lives here in Fez. We went
for a long carriage drive together today. I don't recommend
ever meeting an author whose books you admire. It spoils everything, but everything. I had imagined someone so utterly
different, someone more decided and less neurotic, more understanding and less petulant. I feel terribly let down. You
could say he means well, I suppose, but he's so clumsy and
moody and calculating, all at the same time, that a little of him
goes a long way. The most embarrassing moment came when
it got dark and he decided that I expected him to take an interest in me. It was all very sad. He does know the country and
speak the language, *mais à quoi bon?*, I keep thinking, since he
couldn't be more apathetic regarding the struggle for independence. That of course is the big thing here. You feel it in the air,
something colossal and heroic and potentially tragic, and in any
case very exciting. ..."

Tonight her work was cut out for her: to report to as many
stay-at-homes as possible the events of the afternoon. "... I
only got back to Fez last night, and during my absence things
have moved swiftly to a crisis. ..." "... The city is without
electricity, and in a virtual state of siege. ..." "Today there
was a wholesale massacre of demonstrators at one of the gates.
God knows how many hundred were slaughtered. ..." "...
Here I am, in the middle of a real war. You won't read about

it, or if you do, it will be a perfunctory and watered-down version, since all news is strictly censored by the French. (As a matter of fact, you may never even get this, but anyway, I'm doing my best.)"

It was only in her fourth letter of the evening, which was to a friend in Paris, and therefore, she thought, less likely to be destroyed by the French authorities than those going to America, that she allowed herself to divagate sufficiently from her theme to reach the subject of Stenham. ". . . One person who could if he wanted give me a satisfactory breakdown on the whole situation is John Stenham, but God forbid that I should have to go to him for it. If he were standing in the middle of the railroad track and the crack express were coming around the curve, he would begin to ask himself which side of the tracks it would be better to stand on while the train passed. It's that kind of mind, a little like Dr. Halsey, but even more ineffectual and soft. At the same time he's the most reactionary and opinionated man I've ever met, bar none—a typical disillusioned liberal. (I might add I just had an argument with him, so you won't think we're on quite such bad terms as this might sound.) The mystery to me is where the books come from. It's hard to believe they could have come out of that flabby, selfish mind. If I had several lives I'd read them again out of curiosity, just to try and tie them up with the man, and see what ever made me think they were alive, because *he* certainly isn't. . . ."

When she reread this passage, it seemed a little excessive, because she did not feel so strong an antipathy to Stenham as its words suggested, and so she immediately added: "At the same time, there's something vaguely saintlike about the man, but it's as though he had only the mind of a saint and not the soul, and were quite conscious of the fact that he could never come any nearer to it than that. Very unsatisfactory for him, I should think. The awful thing is, and this is confidential, he's definitely interested in *me*, and as far as I'm concerned it's like having a two-toed sloth interested. *Rien à faire.* But one of these days, if I get out of this country in one piece, I'll be back at the *rue* St. Didier, and I'll call Élysée 53-28 and tell you everything. . . ."

When she had finished her letter-writing, she set the type-writer on the night table, turned out the light, and at the end of five minutes of darkness, during which she was conscious of the mildewed smell of the bed and the intense silence around her, a silence changed only by the sound of a few leaves rustling outside her window when a faint breeze moved them, she fell asleep. There were almost no interstices in her life. When she was awake she was busy, and when she ceased being busy she went to sleep. It was seldom that she made room in her day for thought or conjecture: anything of an indefinite nature, not immediately soluble, made her uneasy. And so, untroubled by interior difficulties, she slept well; it was a habit of long standing.

The following morning about nine o'clock she began to expect a telephone call from Stenham. The hysteria in the city below had irrupted then, and she thought it unlikely that he would be either sleeping or working through such an uproar. When time passed and he did not call her, she felt neglected and consequently resentful, although she told herself that she had every reason to rejoice at being left to her own devices. As the commotion down in the Medina increased, even though only slightly, she grew unaccountably nervous, her letter-writing mechanism jammed, and then she furiously typed: "Can't go on now. The noise is too much." She hesitated as to whether to add: "It sounds as though the mob had started up the hill toward the hotel," decided it would look melodramatic (and in any case the noise did not really sound any nearer—merely louder and more general). She finished: "In haste and with love," and signed her name with a fountain pen.

Downstairs in the office she stood at the desk awhile, waiting for someone to come to sell her stamps. Here the sounds of disorder were almost shut out by the high walls that surrounded the garden, and in an adjacent room a subdued radio played Hungarian gypsy music.

It was the manager himself who finally appeared. "*Bon jour, madame,*" he said ceremoniously. Then, abruptly changing his tone, he continued. "I meant to ask you, have you made arrangements for leaving Fez? We have received orders to close the hotel."

She was shocked. "You're going to close? When? I don't understand. Of course I haven't made any arrangements." Her voice sounded indignant and querulous, in spite of her efforts to keep it normal.

"*Ah, mais il faut faire des démarches,*" he announced, as if she had told him she had known it all the time, but hadn't bothered to do anything.

"But what steps?" she cried. "You can't put me out until I have somewhere to go."

The manager's eyebrows went up. "You are not being *put out,* madame," he said, enunciating with great clarity. "These are circumstances beyond our control."

She looked at his immaculate clothing, his supercilious face, and hated him. "And where am I supposed to go?" she demanded, knowing in advance that he would have an answer to everything, that she could not possibly win.

"I can scarcely be of use to you on that score, madame. But if my personal opinion interests you, I should advise you to leave Morocco altogether. One can expect to encounter disorders of this kind in every city. Shall I order a car for you at three, after you have had lunch?"

"*Mais c'est inouï,*" she protested feebly, "it's unheard-of to send a woman off alone like this. . . ."

"The police will see to it that you are in no danger," he said wearily. "You will be escorted."

She decided to temporize. "What about Monsieur Stenham? What time is *he* going?"

"One moment. I have not yet apprised him of the official decision." And while she stood there, drumming her fingers on the desk, he turned and in funereal tones telephoned Monsieur Stenham and informed him that he too must prepare for an immediate departure.

Apparently the recipient of this news was no more pleased to get it than she had been; she heard insect-like buzzings issuing from the earphone, and the man's face assumed a martyred expression. "Let me speak to him," she said, reaching out for the instrument.

"Good morning!" she cried, her eyes on the wall clock above: it was ten minutes to noon. "Isn't this incredible?"

His voice sounded like the first phonograph record. "I guess it is." This insufficient reply disappointed her; she felt somehow betrayed. "Would you mind coming down so we can talk about it?"

"Be right down."

When he arrived, he said: "*Bon jour*," in a peremptory fashion to the manager, took her arm and led her out and across the terrace to the court where the high banana plants grew. The sunlight burned the skin of her bare arm like an acid, and she took a step in order to be completely in the shade. He described his project for going to Sidi Bou Chta. She listened patiently, feeling all the time that it was a harebrained idea, but without a counter-proposition with which to meet it. "I see," she said from time to time. "Oh."

"And afterward?" she finally asked. "When we've finished there and seen the festival. Where do we go?"

"Well, we come back here and start out fresh from here, wherever we're going. I'm going to the Spanish Zone."

"Why not just go to the Spanish Zone today and have done with it?"

"Because I'd like to see what goes on up there at their festival."

"That's ridiculous," she said nervously. "It's much more important to get out while it's still possible."

"Well, there's no point in arguing about it," he sighed, seeing that they were on the verge of doing just that. "I'll be going in a native bus anyway. I don't think it would be very comfortable for you."

"You don't know anything about me," she declared, snapping up the bait. "But the point has nothing to do with whether you go in a bus or on a mule."

Then they did enter into a long argument from which they

both emerged hot and ill-tempered. "Let's go and sit down," he suggested finally.

"I've got to see the manager about getting a car. And I'm not packed. Perhaps I'll see you at lunch." She stepped back into the searing sun and strode across the terrace, furious at herself for having displayed even a little emotion. He would think it mattered to her whether he was with her or not. And to be perfectly honest, she admitted to herself, it did matter quite a lot. In a crisis like this she would expect any American man to do his utmost to see that she got out in comparative safety. And any other American man *would* have done his utmost. Each step she took across the terrace's blistering mosaic floor was like another note in a long crescendo passage of rising fury, so that by the time she got to the office she was nearly beside herself with anger. "Selfish, egotistical, conceited monster," she thought, vaguely eying a travel poster that showed a nearly naked Berber with a pigtail holding up a huge black cobra toward the cobalt sky, through which rushed a quadri-motored plane. MOROCCO, LAND OF CONTRASTS, ran the legend beneath. When she had ordered a car for three o'clock she went up to her room and packed. It seemed to her that the heat had increased to a fantastic degree in the past half hour. When she breathed she had the impression that she was not breathing at all, because the air was so warm she could not feel it entering her lungs, or even her nostrils. Then she breathed too deeply and violently, and that made her dizzy. And all the objects she touched seemed to be warmer than her hands, which was disconcerting. "How can it be so hot?" she thought. It was half past one when she finished her packing, and she telephoned down for a porter.

"Ah, madame, I regret. There are no porters," said the manager.

"I don't know what you mean," she shrilled. "It's absurd. There must be someone who can carry my things down."

The noise in the town still continued; she had forgotten about it for at least an hour, but there it was.

"I regret."

"And lunch. I suppose there's no one to serve lunch, either?"

"The *maître d'hôtel* will prepare you an omelette and an *assiette anglaise,* madame."

"Why can't one of the waiters carry my luggage?"

The manager seemed to be losing patience. "He cannot, madame, because all the native servants, including the waiters, are locked in their dormitories, and Europeans do not carry luggage in Morocco. V*ous avez compris?* The hotel regrets profoundly that it is unable to accommodate you, but as I pointed out to you earlier, these are circumstances which go beyond us. I suggest you ask Monsieur Stenham to assist in transporting your valises to the taxi." He hung up.

She sat on the bed and looked out at the glaring, barren hills. A little fire of cosmic hatred had begun to burn inside her, a hatred directed at everyone and everything, at the idiotic poplar trees in the garden, whose leaves were stirring when there was not a breath of air, at the hideous satiny tenor of the manager's voice on the telephone, at her rumpled linen dress, already soaked at the armpits, at the evasive geometrical designs so carefully painted on the beams over her head, at her red fingernails, at the popping of the deadly fireworks out there, and directed above all at her own weakness and carelessness in allowing herself to fall into such a state. Then she decided to blame it all on the heat. "It's suffocating in here," she thought. She took a deep breath and stood up. By herself she carried the bags out into the corridor. But then she realized that she would never be able to lug them through the hotel and out to the taxi. Perhaps when it arrived if she described her plight to the driver he would offer to help. However, long association with the French had taught her that they could be the least chivalrous of men when they chose, and so she did not have too much hope. "I *won't* ask that son of a bitch," she kept telling herself, as if it were a consolation, looking down the hall toward Stenham's door.

Suddenly she thought of Amar. If she could get to the boy without seeing Stenham, he would surely help her. It occurred to her that perhaps Stenham had already put him out; they had not mentioned him during their conversation. She decided to go down to lunch now; possibly then she could leave the dining-room while Stenham still was eating. Outside his door she stopped to listen; she heard nothing. The windowless hall was very still. No sounds came up from the hotel. Then she did hear an exchange of mumblings from the room. She passed silently along and down the stairs.

The omelette came in almost cold, and the *assiette anglaise* consisted of two very thin slices of ham, a piece of cold liver and some extremely tough roast beef, which she suspected of being horsemeat. When she had nearly finished, Stenham came into the dining-room, saw her, and approached the table. "Sit down," she said, giving a ring to her voice that would make it sound as though she were trying, against great odds, to be pleasant.

He sat opposite her. "This is the worst meal I've ever eaten, I think," she told him. He was staring beyond her head, out the window into the sky, and did not seem to have heard her. However, an instant afterward he said: "Is it?" The *maître d'hôtel* approached. "A bottle of beer," she announced. "Tuborg." When he had moved off, she said: "What's happened to our orphan? Is he still upstairs or is he gone?"

Stenham looked at her almost as if he were surprised that she knew of the boy's existence. "Why, no. He's up there. He's having his lunch."

They made perfunctory conversation while she drank her beer, avoiding the topic which, proclaiming its presence afresh each instant with a new burst of bullets, filled their minds completely with itself and its corollaries. It could not be discussed because she hoped for an Istiqlal victory, and he did not.

"I've ordered a car for three o'clock. Did you say you were coming back here after your festival? How can you? I don't understand."

"Back here to Fez, to the French town, I mean."

"Oh." She laid her napkin on the table and got to her feet. "Will you excuse me? I've got a few more things to finish up."

Climbing the stairs she wondered why she had gone to the trouble of such elaborate subterfuge in order to ask the boy to carry her bags. It would have been simple enough to go and knock on the door and say to him: "Come with me," Stenham or no Stenham. But then Stenham very likely would have insisted on helping, which, since she wanted to keep her image of his supreme selfishness intact, was not at all desirable.

Unfortunately she had not counted on Stenham's small appetite. He had found the food so bad that he had not bothered to eat it, and was back upstairs standing in the doorway while she was still trying to explain to Amar what it was she wanted.

"Is there something wrong?"

She jumped, startled, hoped she did not look as guilty as she felt, and turned to face him. "Nothing at all," she said, flushing with annoyance. He was really incredible, to have followed her upstairs this way. "I'm just trying to get some help with my luggage. There's no one in the hotel to carry it. I thought Amar might be willing."

"We'll have it out there for you in two minutes. Where is it?" He glanced down the corridor, saw the bags, and calling: "*Amar! Agi! Agi ts'awouni!*" started in the direction of her door.

"You go back and finish your lunch," she said coldly. "He can do it perfectly well." The boy ran past her.

Stenham laughed without turning his head. "What lunch?"

At that moment she heard someone coming up the stairs, and she stepped to the door so she would not actually be in Stenham's room when the person passed. It was the fat waiter who had brought her breakfast. He smiled, said: "*Pardon, madame,*" and pushed by her into the room. As he returned, bearing Amar's empty tray, he said: "It's really hot, isn't it?"

"*Affreux,*" she agreed.

"Ah, yes," he said philosophically. "*La chaleur complique la vie.*"

She stared after him, feeling that he had been insolent, that he had somehow had his mysterious joke at her expense. This was what she so hated about the French: when they wanted to be subtle it made no difference to them whether they were understood or not. The mere voluptuous pleasure they got from making their hermetic little phrases seemed to suffice; they imagined they became superior by shutting you out. It could be perfectly true that, as the waiter had said, the heat complicated people's lives; it had even complicated hers this morning, but why should he make the observation to her at that particular moment?

By the time she had ceased trying to define the insult, all her luggage had been carried out. Stenham joined her in her room; Amar had remained at the back entrance with the bags.

"The hotel's empty, deserted," he informed her. "I was a little worried that somebody might see the kid and ask questions, but there's not a soul, there's nobody at all."

The telephone rang. "*Oui?*" she said. Once again the manager's doleful voice spoke. "We have been requested by the authorities to inform our guests" (Even as he talked, *Now* what's coming? she thought.) "that vehicles will be permitted to circulate only along the highway to Meknès-Rabat-Casablanca, where adequate protection will be afforded them."

"What?" she cried. "And if one wants to leave the country?"

"It is no longer possible, madame."

"But you yourself advised me this morning to leave."

"The frontier has been temporarily closed, madame."

"But where will I go? What hotel can I find?"

"The Transatlantique in Meknès is not operating as of today. In Rabat the Balima and the Tour Hassan are full, of course. However, there are many hotels in Casa, as you know."

"Yes, and I know they're always full too, unless one has a reservation."

"Perhaps madame has influence at the American Consulate. Otherwise I should advise her to stay here in Fez, in the Ville Nouvelle."

She was shouting now. "*Mais ça c'est le comble!* This is the last straw!"

"Doubtless it is most disagreeable for you, madame. I have communicated to you the orders issued by the police. Your bill has been prepared. You will pass by the office to settle it?"

"I usually do," she said furiously, and slammed the telephone into its cradle. She turned to Stenham. "It's really too much." She repeated the manager's message.

Stenham's face assumed a pensive expression. (If she had not been there, she decided, he would have been as indignant as she.) His mind raced ahead through likelihoods and possibilities. "The border's closed. That's bad," he said slowly. "But they'll probably reopen it in a day or two. It's obviously to keep the Nationalists from getting out. They've been combing all the cities, street by street and house by house. It's a *ratissage*."

She had gone to the window. "I just hope the Arabs raise holy hell with them, and make them wish they'd never set foot here." She walked back toward him. "Why, if I spoke the language I'd be down there day and night working for independence. Nothing would give me greater pleasure at this point." Without transition she continued. "Where am I supposed to go? Where am I supposed to sleep tonight? In the street?"

"There's only one place for you to go, and that's the Ville Nouvelle here in Fez. There are hotels."

"Well, *that* I *refuse* to do. After all, the whole point of being here is to be where the natives are."

He was about to tell her not to be childish, but he decided not to. "Then come with me," he said, smiling and shrugging. "I'm going to be where natives are."

"All right, damn it, I will!" she exclaimed. "And it had better be good."

CHAPTER 27

Almost from the outset she found herself in a better humor. Perhaps it was the fact that upon leaving the city the bus had begun at once to climb, threading its way back and forth across the southern slope of Djebel Zalagh, and the air was growing increasingly fresher. Or perhaps it was purely emotional: the bus without glass in its windows, the excited chatter of the people in their mountain clothing, and the relief she felt that no policeman or soldier had prevented their departure at the last moment before the crazy old vehicle finally had moved out of the shabby side street in the Ville Nouvelle.

They had used her taxi only to transport their luggage to a sad little hotel where they had engaged one desperate room, piled it all in, and locked the door. The proprietress, sour-faced but not really unpleasant, had demanded to see their passports, and upon examining them had insisted Stenham pay her three days in advance.

The passengers were almost all country folk from the mountains to the south who had gone to Fez solely because the road passed through and they had to change buses there. They were beautiful people, clean and with radiant faces, and she wondered vaguely if it were possible that they had heard nothing about the disturbances. She would have asked Stenham his opinion if he had been sitting near enough to her, but although they were occupying the same bench, they were separated from each other by three women, he near the left end of the bench and she at the extreme right, beside the glassless window.

And Amar, mysterious youth, had brought along a friend—or, rather, an enemy, she would have sworn, judging from his expression when the other had accosted him on the sidewalk beside the bus. She had happened to be near the scene, and was positive she had noticed a grimace of distaste or even some stronger emotion when Amar had turned to see who had tapped on his shoulder. Why then had he presently sought out Stenham and asked his permission to invite the newcomer to accompany them on the journey? She did not know, but she was not averse to his presence: he was well brought up, polite, a good deal cleaner than Amar (whose clothes were in a shocking state), and he spoke French fluently. The two boys had managed to get a small strip of seat together in the back of the bus; the last time she had looked around they had appeared to be conversing amiably.

The late afternoon light illumined the countryside. It was a characteristic of Moroccan mountain roads that they very seldom passed through a village; the villages could be seen, cowering against the flanks of distant side-hills, or standing like crest-feathers at the tops of cliffs, or spread out sparsely along the sinuous ridges of lesser mountains, always with a valley lying between the road and them. In spite of the heat the air was pungent with the scent of mountain plants, and its utter dryness, after the vapors of the ubiquitous river-waters of Fez, was a tonic in the nostrils. Whenever the bus passed through a wooded spot, the frantic shriek of the cicadas came in from both sides of the road. A curve, a bank of pink clay, the swaying and rattling of the chassis, the ceaseless sound of the heated motor laboring in second, a green-gray cactus at the edge of the abyss ahead, a curve, a hundred miles of granite mountaintops against the enamel sky, the explosive shifting of gears and the altered sound and speed that came after it, the sleepy sobbing of a baby somewhere behind her in the bus, a curve, a savage ravine below, with the twilight already welling up from its depths. And on a slope beside her, still glowing in the calm late sunlight, a grove of ancient olive trees, their great twisted trunks as if frozen in the attitudes of some forgotten ceremonial dance. She remembered what Stenham had told her before they had started out: that they would be going through a region where the cult of Pan was still alive, its rites still observed with flutes and drums and masks. She had neither believed nor disbelieved it; at the time it had sounded merely like a rather improbable statistic. But now as she looked, it seemed for no good reason entirely credible. The wild land lent itself to such extravagances.

What she found astonishing about these people was the impression of cleanliness they gave her. It was not only their bodies and clothing that seemed clean (the interior of the bus smelled like laundry drying in the sun); it was as much the expressions on their faces, the aura of their collective spirit; they made her think of the purity of mountain streams, untouched regions. She determined not to discuss any of her reactions with Stenham, because he would make analytical remarks which, false or correct, would only end by infuriating her.

Yesterday afternoon in the café, for instance, he had said: "The intellect is the soul's pimp." She had not wanted to know what he meant, but of course he had gone on and explained that the intellect was constantly seducing the soul with knowledge, when all the soul needed was its own wisdom. The only way to enjoy this excursion, she decided, was to refuse to discuss anything at all with him, and not even to comment on what was before their eyes, save perhaps to exclaim now and then if an exclamation seemed in order. She knew that such a plan would prove at least partially unenforceable, but if she persevered, she thought, it was just conceivable that he might become aware of what she was doing and follow suit.

They stopped at a spring for water. The sudden lack of motion and the silence broken only by occasional murmurs (for most of the voyagers had long ago fallen asleep) made her feel faintly nauseated; she longed for the bus to start again. A few people wanted to get down, but the driver, who had stayed at the wheel while his assistant filled the radiator, objected. Stenham leaned forward, looked across the three white bundles who slept between him and her, said: "It's a relief to be up here, isn't it?"

"It's marvelous!" she agreed, startled by the unnaturally heartfelt enthusiasm in her own voice. Her ears sang, and she was a little giddy from the altitude. But now she knew, as the door slammed shut and the comforting sound and motion re-

sumed, *why* it was a relief. It was not only the pure air and the
slowly increasing coolness; much more than those things it was
being away from the vaguely sinister sense of expectancy and
apprehension with which she had been living for the past two
days. Those two days had been endless. The city had been there,
right under her eyes the whole time, and she had been able to
stand in her window and examine it roof by roof, but it might
as well have been invisible, like a snake hidden in the bushes,
waiting. At the moment she felt she never wanted to see Fez
again. However, it was extremely important to keep *that* from
Stenham: if he guessed how she felt he would make capital
of it, taunt her with her inability to accept the physical concomitants of the social change she advocated. "Ah!" he would
say triumphantly, "at last you're beginning to understand what
it means, this business of destroying faith." And she would only
become querulous and invent a series of bad-tempered rejoinders, instead of telling him simply that even though every detail of the transition were hateful to her, she would still wish it
wholeheartedly because it meant life, whereas if the metamor-
phosis failed to take place, there were only decay and death
ahead. So she would be very careful about it, and if she could
not keep him from noting an added glint of health in her eyes
which had not been there before (for he was observant), she
would tell him that Fez had been damper than she had realized, because now upon having left it her sinus pains had completely vanished.

At first she dozed, as if exploring that first ledge of non-
being; then she slipped and fell into the chasm of sleep. The
early night came, blue and not dark under the clear sky. The
bus had turned on to a side road and was navigating the edge
of a precipice. Only the driver and his helper could appreciate
the skill that was required to keep its shuddering old carcass upright, out of the ditch on the one side and yet at a safe number
of inches from the brink on the other. Far ahead and below,
Stenham caught sight of a pair of headlights rounding a curve,
and he thought: There's going to be trouble when that car gets
here; one of us will have to back up. But the other car never ar-

rived, and he realized that it was moving ahead of them, another bus filled with pilgrims, very likely.

When they had come to the bottom of the descent they crossed a rushing stream, and set off in another direction over a plain. Here it was warmer, and they raised clouds of dust, some of which came up between the floorboards and set people to sneezing. Then once again they began to climb, this time on a trail which was so bad that several sleeping forms rolled off their seats. Lee had awakened and was holding on to the bench ahead for support. He caught her eye and grinned. She shook her head, but she did not look unhappy. The score or so of men traveling on the top of the bus began to pound violently on the metal roof. At first he thought that someone might have bounced off, but presently he heard them singing, and the banging resolved itself into a rhythm. The mad climb with its incredible jolting and swaying lasted for nearly an hour. Then what looked like a city of pink lights came into view ahead. A moment later the bus drew to a halt. The city was several thousand tentlike shelters improvised of sheets and blankets that had been stretched between the trunks of a vast olive grove covering the slopes of two hills, and against each square of cloth the flames that flickered inside threw shadows. That much they saw while they were still in their seats. In the confusion of getting down (for each passenger had innumerable bundles of food and cooking utensils, and there were loose babies and live fowls scattered about among the bundles) they forgot about it, and it was only an hour or so later, when they had climbed up out of the hollow where the trucks and buses were ranged, and sat, all four of them, on a log watching the moon rise, that Stenham commented on the strange aspect of the place.

"It's wonderful," she answered in a low voice, hoping to keep him from saying more. He appeared to have understood, for he began to talk to the two boys, leaving her to think her thoughts. Of course it was wonderful, with the shadows and the flames and the great circles of men, hundreds of them, dancing arm in arm, and the orchestras of drums like giant engines pulsing. But it was wonderful only as a spectacle, since it meant nothing.

That was what she must remember, she told herself, because she felt that the place represented an undefinable but very real danger. It meant nothing, never could mean anything, to Polly Burroughs. For that to happen, she would have to go back, back, she did not know how many thousands of years, but back far enough for it to denote some sort of truth. If she possessed any sort of religion at all, it consisted in remaining faithful to her convictions, and one of the basic beliefs upon which her life rested was the certainty that no one must ever go back. All living things were in process of evolution, a concept which to her meant but one thing: an unfolding, an endless journey from the undifferentiated toward the precise, from the simple toward the complex, and in the final analysis from the darkness toward the light. What she was looking down upon here tonight, the immense theatre full of human beings still unformed and unconscious, bathed in sweat, stamping and shrieking, falling into the dust and writhing and twitching and panting, all belonged unmistakably to the darkness, and therefore it had to be wholly outside her and she outside it. There could be no temporizing or mediation. It was down there, spread out before her, a segment of the original night, and she was up here observing it, actively conscious of who she was, and very intent on remaining that person, determined to let nothing occur that might cause her, even for an instant, to forget her identity.

As time passed, she could feel Stenham growing restless, but it had not occurred to her that he might be hungry until he suddenly rose and announced that he was going down to see what sort of food was on sale at the stands. "Anything special you want?" he asked her. She replied that she was not very hungry. "I'll bring back something. *Nimchiou?* Shall we go?" he said, turning to Amar, who jumped to his feet.

When she and the other youth were alone, she asked him his name. "Mohammed," he answered, flattered by her question, but particularly because she had said *vous* to him instead of *tu*. "And have you known Amar for a long time?" "*Oui*," he said vaguely, as if the subject were of no possible interest. They were silent for a while. Then he asked her where her husband had gone; she burst into laughter and immediately felt a wave of disapproval emanate from him. Bending toward him, she saw his stern young face in the moonlight; swiftly she grew very serious, and committed the even graver error of telling him that Stenham was just a friend. "A very old friend," she added, hoping that this might in some way save her from worse opprobrium. Apparently it was not a mitigating circumstance in his eyes, for he merely grunted, and soon burst out indignantly: "You shouldn't have come here with him if he's not your husband. Where is your husband?"

"He's dead," she told him, not being sure of the Moslem attitude toward divorce.

"How long ago did he die?" he wanted to hear. Now she began to improvise wildly. He had been killed in the War, leaving her with three children. (She did know that they approved of a woman's bearing as many children as possible.) This was not well received, either; he obviously thought she should be with them, and not consorting with a strange man. "This is a holy place, you know," he informed her; his words were a reproach and a warning. "*Ah, oui, je sais,*" she agreed feebly.

The music and dancing went on; it must go on without a break for at least twenty-four hours, Stenham had told her. Occasionally the singing in one circle or another would disintegrate for a time into a series of savage rhythmical cries, vomited from a hundred throats at the same split second, with a simultaneity which gave the sound an extraordinary solidity. She sat listening to the senseless noise rather in the way one looks down into a tank full of crocodiles, her principal emotion one of thankfulness at being where she was, at not having accompanied Stenham to the food-stands, which were in the center of a constant throng. To her it seemed that he had been gone for well over an hour; she could not understand how buying a little food could take so long. In the tent nearest to where she and the silent Mohammed sat, the flames were unusually bright, women were laughing behind its slightly waving walls, and outside, a few paces higher up the hill, a tethered horse stamped its hoof on the earth. The astringent smoke from the number-

less fires of thuya branches curled lazily upward, sometimes
sweeping suddenly back down and making a flat screen above
the hillside as a breeze gave chase to it. Then the screen would
move out over the furthest fires into the deserted countryside
and be dissipated, and again the casual spirals would form. Each
turban, donkey, and olive branch was needle-clear in the powerful moonlight. (If she had had a newspaper she could have read
it easily, she was certain—even the fine print.) The moonlight
was hard; it gave the impression of having converted all the
elements of the landscape into one substance, not blue, not
black, not green, not white, but a new color whose thousand
gradations partook of the essences of all those colors. And everywhere in this world made soft by the hard light from above,
the fires burned, looking redder than fire should look.

Out of the shadows beside her Stenham appeared, startling
her. A second later Amar was there behind him. "Did you get
anything?" she asked.

"I did. Two dozen skewers of lamb. Shish kebab. Amar's got
the whole lot. Sorry to be so long. The crush was terrific."

They sat eating, the two Moroccans at one end of the log
and the two Americans at the other. The meat had a peculiar
flavor, not spicy but herbal. "We can't drink the water," Stenham said, "so we'll have to go down and have tea afterward
in one of the cafés."

She was surprised that there should be cafés here, but her
mouth was full and she said nothing. Presently, "It seems I
ought by all rights to be your wife," she told him, laughing.
"Mohammed thinks it's indecent of me to be here, an unattached woman."

"It is," he agreed. "Very indecent. If you're unattached, it
can only mean you're potentially attached to anyone and everyone. You shouldn't have told him."

"I don't think it would have helped much not to. Amar certainly knows we're not married."

"Oh, Amar! He's different."

She reached for another skewer. "I can feel that, but I don't
quite know where the difference lies."

"It's everywhere, everywhere," Stenham said absently.

"And anyway," she pursued, making her voice jovial again, "I believe you already have a wife in some part of this world, haven't you?"

"*Yes*, I have a wife." He laughed shortly. "What part of this world she's in, though, I couldn't tell you. Last I heard she was in Brazil. But that was quite a while ago."

"If I were your wife and I heard you talk about me in that offhand manner, I think I'd kill you. Assuming, of course, that I were and you did. If and if."

"My dear Lee," he said with mock courtesy, "those two ifs are mutually exclusive. But in the case of my true wife—I was almost going to say her name aloud and risk seeing Sidi Bou Chta vanish in a puff of smoke—she knows damned well how I talk about her, and I hear that when she mentions me it's a lot worse. There's no love lost, I can tell you."

"I don't know whether to sympathize with you or with her. What's she like? Not that a description coming from you would—"

He cut her short, rather rudely, she thought, saying: "There are two more skewers. You want one? The two kids have eaten sixteen between them. I've counted."

"No, I don't. I'm finished."

"Well, then, if you'll excuse me, I'm going to eat both of them. I had no lunch. And then let's go down and have our tea and see something. The whole thing is magnificent."

"Good," she said, rising and making a silent resolution to be amenable here; even if it proved terribly difficult, it would be more satisfying in the end than finding objections at every turn. She wanted to take the maximum of remembered trophies back to Paris with her, and she knew herself well enough to realize that her shell of recalcitrance, if she indulged herself to the point of donning it, would impede her receptivity.

When they had stumbled down the hill over stones and bushes that lay hidden in the shadow of olive leaves, they stopped for a while on the fringe of the nearest ring of spectators, and gradually wedged their way in toward a position from which they could see the dancing. Well over a hundred men participated, all of them in white *djellabas* and turbans, chanting breathlessly as they heaved and dipped. Their movements were rather like those of horses, she decided. Sometimes they pawed the earth with a certain spiritedness and nobility; then they went back to being work-horses, straining to pull their invisible loads as they all bent in one direction and then in another. "How strange," she said to Stenham, because it was like nothing she had ever seen or imagined. She could not see his face, but he pushed her toward the fore, saying nothing, and stationed Amar on her left and Mohammed on her right, he standing directly behind her. This solicitousness annoyed her: it made her feel like a piece of property being guarded against thieves, and, which was worse, she suspected it to be a maneuver, very probably unconscious, aimed at influencing her reactions to what she was seeing—an attempt, as it were, to establish a sort of mesmeric control. And, in any case, there was an extremely tall man directly in front of her. She moved ahead, the men politely yielded and allowed her to step into the front ranks facing the circle of dancers. Now she was able to see that the circle was really an ellipse; at one end of the enclosed space was a huge bonfire whose flames shot up to the height of her face, and at the other was a smaller ring of a dozen or so seated men playing drums. "It's quite a show," she said to herself contentedly, and she became interested in the pattern of the dance. From time to time she looked back to be sure Stenham and the boys were there. Once Amar waved to her, his face beaming with delight.

It was not long before she became aware that something absurd had begun to happen inside her. It was a little as though she were living her life ahead of time. It had started, she thought, while she was sitting up there with Mohammed. Observing the phenomenon from the outside, she came to the conclusion that it might be because no one had ever before made her feel quite so unwanted. She had seen herself back in Fez in the horrible little Hôtel des Ambassades, separating her valises from those of Stenham, alone in a cab riding to the station (as if there were trains running now, she thought with a sudden wry grimace). She was in the train with the new issue of *Time* and a copy of the Paris *Herald* on her lap; she was on the Algeciras ferry watching the gray, lumpy mountains of the African coast slowly fade into the distance; she was eating shrimps under an awning in a waterfront café, being brushed against by the newsboys passing among the tables; she was sitting with the Stuarts at Horcher's in Madrid with the treasure of her Moroccan trip stored away in her memory, a treasure which would seem the richer for being kept hidden, with only a piquant detail divulged here and there—just enough to suggest the solid mass beneath the surface. "I have so many things to tell you, but I don't know where to begin. My mind is so disorderly." "Don't be silly, Polly. I've never known anyone with a clearer mind, or such a gift for telling experiences."

The insistent drums were an unwelcome reminder of the existence of another world, wholly autonomous, with its own necessities and patterns. The message they were beating out, over and over, was for her; it was saying, not precisely that she did not exist but rather that it did not matter whether she existed or not, that her presence was of no consequence to the rest of the cosmos. It was a sensation that suddenly paralyzed her with dread. There had never been any question of her "mattering"; it went without saying that she mattered, because she was important to herself. But what was the part of her to which she mattered?

She pulled out a cigarette and lighted it with impatient gestures. Unreasonably enough, she felt that she had already seen whatever the festival might have to offer. If one man went into a trance and beat his breast and tore out handfuls of hair during his seizure, as was now happening in front of her, it was the same as if a score of men were to do it, one after the other or all together. There could be no progression: she refused to slip into the hypnotic design. If all the members of this particular circle of leaping figures became possessed, took out their souls and threw them onto the pile in the middle (they were doing it; she knew it) so that there was only one undifferentiable writhing mass in there and no one was sure of getting his own back when it was finished, and, moreover, no one cared, then she had seen that, too, and she did not need to go on to another group to see the same thing done again, this time to a slightly different drum rhythm and with the addition of oboes and occasional gunfire. But Stenham was succumbing, she was positive of that; certainly he never had intended any resistance. He was going to let his enthusiasm for the *idea* of the thing carry him off into a realm whose atmosphere was too thin for rationality to exist in it, and where consequently everything could be confused with everything else—a state of false ecstasy, false because self-induced. That was why she would have none of it, she insisted to herself; she wanted no counterfeit emotions.

The glare of fire before her face, the long white robes catching its redness in their folds as the men crouched and leapt, and the darkness pressing in from left and right! But it was not darkness, since darkness has no breath and hands. "Mr. Stenham," she called, looking back past the bearded faces, the tightly wound turbans, the shining black eyes, and mouths stretched (in a monkey-like, frozen smile that had nothing to do with smiling) to reveal the rows of white teeth ("wild animals"), heads tilted upward to see over other heads, and panic began to pour in upon her from all sides. "Mr. Stenham!" She was with her back to the fire now, her eyes running over the rows of fascinated faces, looking desperately for the lighter face. "Nonsense," she said aloud, horrified that the panic had been able to get in so easily. It simply wasn't possible; she knew herself too well. But there were her knees, feeling like paper tubes. She turned around and called his name again into the uproar, like a pebble being tossed against an onrushing locomotive. And then she caught sight of him for a flash, between two cavorting figures as they gyrated. He had moved all the way around to the other side of the circle. Rage exploded in her; she could feel its heat just beneath the skin of her throat and cheeks and forehead. But now at least she knew where he was, and she turned and pushed her way toward the outer edges until she was free to walk normally. It was dark here after the fire's glare, and she bumped blindly into several astonished strollers before she regained her vision.

"Well, that was an unpleasant experience," she thought, to help her to believe it was over. When she had worked her way around to what she thought was the place where she had seen Stenham, she had to look for rather a long time before she located him. Then she took up a position behind him and concentrated on regaining complete command of herself. To do this she tried to get back into the stream of fantasy in which she had been swimming a while ago, but it was no good—the sober brown interior of Horcher's would not come alive. It might as well have been the Hanging Gardens of Babylon she was striving to evoke. The act of walking had partly calmed her, and rather than risk losing the solace of even that meager control, she decided to speak to him now. She called his name as loud as she dared, and, miraculously, he heard and turned. Now she smiled, put on as natural an expression as she could muster. He came slowly back toward her, pushing his way past the transfixed onlookers. "It's better from this side," he remarked. "Yes," she said, then after waiting what she thought was a normal interval, she suggested they go and have their tea. "Ah, of course!" he cried. "Amar! Mohammed!" he called. They appeared from different sides, and together the four wandered away from the light, into the dark.

The café consisted of several strips of matting placed on uneven ground, fenced in by bunches of green branches wired together. Long stakes had been driven into the earth at arbitrary points and blankets suspended by their corners from them, but in a completely haphazard fashion. Near the entrance, behind a little counter of rocks, the qaouaji and his assistants crouched; the remainder of the space was fairly well filled with seated and reclining men. Even beside the center pole the draped ceiling was not high enough to stand up under; they had to advance with their heads bent far forward.

Once they were installed on the mat and had been given

glasses of tea, she said to Stenham: "You know, I thought I'd lost you for a while."

"Oh, no," he said lightly. "I had my eye on you. I knew just where you were."

"Oh, you did!" She wanted to ask him why he had gone around to the other side and left her alone, but she suspected she could not go into the subject without losing her temper.

"Anyway, this'll be our headquarters, this café," he went on. "We can always find each other back here. When we want to sleep, they'll clear out the people from this whole end, and we'll have it to ourselves. The *qaouaji* seems all right."

When they had drunk the tea, Stenham suggested they go out again. Amar and Mohammed had already risen and were standing outside the entrance.

"Why don't you go, and I'll stay here and rest," she said. "Come back in a half hour or so and maybe I'll feel like going out with you again. I'm a little tired." What she meant was: "Stay here with me awhile," and she thought surely he would interpret her words thus.

"But how can you stay alone?" he exclaimed. "I don't like to leave you here all by yourself."

"Why not?" she demanded sourly. "At least I can't get lost in here."

"I'll be back in a few minutes." His voice sounded uncertain. "Shall I order you another tea before I go?"

"No, thanks. I'll order one if I want it."

He glanced at her oddly. "Well, so long." Then he stooped and said a few words to the *qaouaji*. When he had gone out, she counted to ten slowly, then sprang up, ramming her head against the blankets above, which she had forgotten. Quickly she stepped across the café and out through the opening, turning in the opposite direction to the one Stenham had taken. The wind had come up stronger. She looked back for a second, to fix the place in her mind; the shape of the olive tree above the café was unmistakable. Then, in a turmoil of rage and self-pity, she strode ahead up the hill, at first oblivious and afterward indifferent to the men who gazed at her.

The women in the tents were cooking the evening *tajine;* the smell of the hot olive oil mingled with the wood smoke. She kept on climbing, telling herself that she should have expected all this to happen, that it was her own fault for having come, since she had known from the start that he was a selfish clod. Her initial reaction had been the correct one. "I won't go," she had said, and then her anger with the French had blunted the edge of her common sense.

Up here the tents were sparsely strewn among the trees, and ahead there was only the empty countryside. The sound of the drums still came up from below, but it was mixed with the hissing of the olive leaves in the rising wind. Some distance away a native dog barked; the high sound was like the hysterical laughter of a woman. When she had gone beyond the last tent and its light was no longer visible, she stopped, a little sobered by the solitude, and stood leaning against a low-swung bough. The wind's force increased by the minute. She was out of breath, and she would have liked to sit down, but memories of scorpion and snake stories she had heard kept her standing, and she remained as she was, breathing hard of the pure air that came rushing across the hillside toward her. It was a strange wind, she decided; it blew as if it were determined not to allow itself to abate for a single second. It was not like a wind at all, but like the breeze from a monstrous stationary fan, or like a huge draught steadily increasing in force. The noise it made in the trees was like the ocean now, or like the sound of an approaching storm. Instinctively she looked up into the sky: the calm, coldly burning moon stood above, and no cloud existed. But that was what it was; the noise like the sea out there on the mountain was a windstorm that had not yet arrived, a crazy nocturnal gale on its way. She listened for a trace of the festivities behind her and could hear none. Still, she knew she had only to go over the hummock beyond that fat-trunked tree to see the flickering pink walls of the last tent.

When the full force of the wind struck, she flung out her arms and let it push her against the tree, and she breathed deeply of it until she was giddy and would have had to sit down had

she not been pinioned there by it. It had an amazing smell, like
the smell of life itself, she thought; but after a moment it reminded her of sun-baked rocks and secret places in the forest.
Then it grew very strong indeed, and she decided she would
have to go back. A few more breaths, she said, filling her lungs
completely with it, breathing out, and in.

Her head swam. Cataracts of wind rushed down the polished
channels they had gouged across the sky, spilling out against
the mountainside. Dust and dry bits of plants dancing upward
in spirals smote her face. Carefully she sat down on the ground
and leaned against the tree. Now she felt momentarily ill, but
much happier. The wind roared; something touched her shoulder. She looked up, catching her breath, frightened for one instant, relieved for the next, and vexed immediately afterward.
It was Stenham, standing over her, saying nothing, about to
crouch down beside her. She made a great effort and got to her
feet.

"Hello," she said, feeling like a guilty child, but only because
he would not say anything. Now he did speak. "What's the
idea?" His voice was angry.

"What idea?" she asked, and spat out the dust that had
blown into her mouth.

He seized her arm. "Come on," he said, trying to pull her
along.

"Stop. Wait." She was not ready to leave the hilltop.

"How'd you get way up here?"

"I walked. Would you mind letting go of me?"

"Not at all. That's quite all right with me."

"Do you have to be insulting, too?"

"What's the matter with you?" He took her arm again, impatiently.

"Please. I can walk perfectly well. Let go of me!"

"Oh, well, God damn it, *fall* down, then, if that's what you
want."

It was like a command: she stumbled against a rock, tried to
go on, and sank to the ground. He stooped, was beside her,
trying to comfort her, being ineffectual, saying: "Where does it

hurt?" and "I'm terribly sorry" and "I feel as though it were my fault," at which she made a silent gesture of denial, although he probably did not interpret it as such. "Do you think you can walk?" he inquired. She said nothing; all she wanted to do was push against the pain. If she relaxed the pressure an instant she would burst into tears, and that could not happen, must not happen. But after he had grown used to her muteness, sitting back helplessly to watch her, he came nearer again and put his arm around her, caressed her shoulder tentatively. It was not what she wanted. She shivered, and moaned inaudibly once. Then he tried to draw her to him, both of them squatting there in that ludicrous position.

At all costs this must be stopped, she told herself, even at the risk of having him see her weep, which she felt would certainly happen if she moved or spoke. And anyway, she thought, as she felt his hands moving softly along her flesh (as if she were a tree and they were the tendrils of a creeping parasitic plant), what sort of man was it who would take such a blatantly unfair advantage? With this pain how could she be expected to defend herself against his unjust tactics? The tears began to flow; it had required only that last reflection to loose them. She sobbed, and with all her might tore his hands away.

She was free, but now she was in the grip of her tears, and the shame of having him see her this way, even in the moonlight and with the vast wind sweeping by, increased them. Hatred for him welled up within her; if she had had the strength she would have hurled herself upon him and tried to kill him. But she did not move, doubled up there on the earth, pressing and rubbing her ankle as she wept. "What a *fool* you are! What a *fool* you are!" she heard her own voice repeating inside her head, and she did not know whether she was saying that to him or to herself. He had risen, and remained aloof now, looking down at her. After a long time, she slowly got to her feet, and with his help (it made no difference, now that she hated him) limped painfully all the way back down to the café.

And then she sat there in the smoke and dimness, with the hubbub of voices and music around her, and began to live the

next hours of her own bland hell. Stenham sat near by, breaking
his silence only now and then to say a few words to the two
boys, both of whom looked exceedingly glum and sullen. Once
she found herself thinking: Thank God nothing happened up
there, and was furious that she should have such a thought;
there had been no question of it. But she could not look at
Stenham. She passed the time massaging her ankle and smoking
furiously, not planning the details of her vengeance, but rein-
forcing her determination to have it, one way or another. About
midnight, when the pain had subsided somewhat and she was
beginning to feel exhausted and a little sleepy, perhaps because
of the pall of kif smoke that lay in the tent, he turned and said
to her: "The wind has died down." She did not answer for a
moment; then she said: "Yes." That was all. Then he began to
talk seriously and at great length in Arabic with the boys. Once
again, a good deal later, he spoke to her, his voice enthusiastic,
almost tremulous, as if he had for the moment completely
forgotten that a state of hostility existed between them. "This
boy sees an untainted world," he exclaimed. "Do you realize
that?" Her mumbled reply apparently was inaudible to him.
"What'd you say?" he asked.

   "I said I couldn't say," she replied, raising her voice. She did
not know whether the world that Amar saw was still in a
pristine state or far advanced in decay; she suspected it was the
latter, but in either case, the speculation was one of distinctly
minor interest to her at the moment. Her mind was occupied
with thoughts of herself and her mistreatment; because she felt
she had been humiliated, she also believed that Stenham must
be triumphant, must imagine he had gained some perverse sort
of victory over her. For the time being she saw her whole
Moroccan adventure as a ghastly fiasco, and she herself as having
failed in some mysterious but profound manner.

   In the first place, she argued, getting back to inessentials,
which were the only things she could manipulate in her present
state, her first meeting with him should have persuaded her that
he was not a man she could ever want to know, for he was not
physically attractive to her. Of that she had been aware in a

flash. She could tell immediately what was for her and what was not, and Stenham had straightway fallen into the latter category: he had failed the test. (The test consisted of imagining a man lying in bed asleep in the morning; if the thought of his inert form sprawled out there among the sheets in their disorder could be entertained without revulsion, then she knew there was a possibility, otherwise he simply was not for her.) The test had always worked, and she had always sidestepped getting to know too well those who had failed to pass it, precisely in order to avoid just such circumstances as these. But her weakness and carelessness this time by no means excused a jot of his behavior, nor, when the moment of reckoning came, would she even consider her own shortcomings.

She dozed, awoke, dropped off again, returned to hear always the same eternal conversation: Stenham, Amar and the other boy, whose voice came in only now and then, like a *compère*, with the chorus of tea-drinkers and kif-smokers in the background. Tomorrow would be unbearable from all points of view; she contemplated its confusion and endlessness with dread. But she would escape in the first bus or truck that moved out of Sidi Bou Chta, even if it meant spending a day, two days, in the filthy little room at the Hôtel des Ambassades.

Again, a long time afterward, she awoke to find all three of them gone. "So much the better," she thought grimly. The chaos of drums and shouting still went on, with added vigor, if anything, and guns were being fired into the sky at short intervals. In an hour or two it would be light; the dawn of the Aïd el Kebir would have broken, and the already sharpened knife-blades would be thoughtfully thumbed once again in anticipation of the mid-morning hour of sacrifice.

CHAPTER 28

They sprawled on the matting, Stenham, Amar and Mohammed, involved in a discussion which had been going on for at
least two hours. As far as Stenham was concerned, its subject
was religion, and Amar seemed content to let it remain on that
plane. Mohammed, however, felt constantly impelled to give it a
political direction; indeed, one would have said he was incapable of keeping the two things separate. Religion to him was a
purely social institution, and the details of its practice were a
matter of governmental interest. Stenham was irked by the boy's
thick-headedness; he wondered why Amar had wanted to bring
him along.

Most of the men who were not asleep had by now gone out to
pray and to be present when the dawn came. A few still engaged
in aimless conversation; the rest slept. Lying on this ground,
thought Stenham, was like being astride a starved horse: no
matter what position he took, he could not make himself comfortable. There seemed to be rocks everywhere under the
smooth mat. Lee at last lay unmoving. For a long time she had
been in a half-sleep, turning repeatedly from one side to the
other. The two boys had been upset when she had come limping in, leaning on Stenham's arm, but she had looked at them
with such animosity that their expressions of sympathy had died
on their lips. As the time had passed and she had refused to
address even a word to any of them, Amar had remarked to
Stenham that the lady was unhappy. "Of course. She's in pain,"
Stenham told him. "No, I mean she's always unhappy. She's
always going to be unhappy in her head, that lady." "Why?"
Stenham had asked, amused. "Do you know why?" "Of course I
know why," Amar had replied confidently. "It's because she
doesn't know anything about the world."

This had seemed a pointless enough reply, and Stenham had let the subject drop. But during this long discussion, which had provided him with his first true opportunity for going even a little below the top of Amar's mind, he had been struck again and again by the boy's unerring judgment in separating primary factors from subsidiary ones. It was a faculty which had nothing to do with mental alertness, but derived its strength rather from an unusually powerful and smoothly functioning set of moral convictions. To have come upon this natural wisdom in an adult would have been extraordinary enough, but in an individual who was little more than a child, and illiterate as well, it was incredible. He sat watching the changes of expression on Amar's countenance as he spoke, and began to feel a little like the prospector for gold who in spite of his own prolonged lack of hope suddenly finds himself face to face with the first nugget. And he marveled at the mysterious way in which the pieces of the world were tied together, that it should have been a purely sentimental detail like a dragonfly struggling in a pool of water, a thing exterior to any conceivable interpretation of Moslem dogma, which had made it possible for him to suspect, even unconsciously, the presence of hidden riches.

When a silence arrived, he said to Amar: "So the lady knows nothing about the world? What makes you think that?"

"*Hada echouf.* You can see she wants to be something powerful in the world. She thinks she can, but that's because she's never surrendered."

"Surrendered? What do you mean?"

"Of course. What is the first duty of everyone in the world? To surrender. *Al Islam! Al Islam!*" He thrust his arms forward (the mud of the Medina was still on his sleeves from his encounter with the police) and bent his head downward in the beginning of a gesture of prostration. Then, continuing, he sketched a series of imaginary instances where the persons involved had or had not submitted to divine authority. In each illustration the accursed person—that is, the unhappy one—saw himself as a being of importance, whereas the blessed and joyous ones had understood that they were nothing at all, that whatever strength they were able to wield existed only in direct proportion to the degree of their obedience to the inexorable laws of Allah.

To be happy, cease striving and admit you are powerless. Islam, the religion of surrender. It had never occurred to Stenham that the word "Islam" actually meant "surrender." "I see," he said aloud.

"Every man you see in the street thinks his life is important," pursued Amar, warming to his subject, for his own life still seemed terribly important to him, "and he doesn't want it to stop. But Allah has decreed that each one must lose his life. O *allèche?* Why? To convince men that life isn't worth anything. No man's life is worth anything. It's like the wind." He blew his breath into the air and made a single clutching motion with his outstretched hand.

"Now, wait," said Stenham. "You say—"

But Amar would not wait. "Why are we in the world?" he demanded.

Stenham smiled. "I'm afraid I can't answer that."

"You don't know why?" asked Amar sadly.

"No."

Mohammed yawned ostentatiously. "I'll tell you," he volunteered. "To talk all night long, while real men are being shot."

Stenham would have said that a shadow of pain flickered across Amar's face, but in an instant it was gone, and he continued. "We're in the world for only one reason, and that's to act out what was written for us. The man whose destiny is bad, he's lucky, because all he has to do is give thanks. But the man whose destiny is good— Ay! That's much harder, because unless he is a very very good man he'll begin to think he had something to do with his good luck. Don't you understand?"

"Yes, but perhaps he *did* have something to do with it." (In such arguments Stenham often found himself unexpectedly extolling the bourgeois virtues.) "If he was good himself, and worked hard—"

"Never!" cried Amar, his eyes blazing. "You're a Nazarene, a Christian. That's why you talk that way. If you were a Moslem and said such things, you'd be killed or struck blind here, this minute. Christians have good hearts, but they don't know anything. They think they can change what has been written. They're afraid to die because they don't understand what death is for. And if you're afraid to die, then you don't know what life is for. How can you live?"

"I don't know, I don't know, I don't know," Stenham droned amiably. "And I don't think I ever will know."

"And the day you do know you'll come to me and tell me you want to be a Moslem, and we shall all have a great festival for you, because a Nazarene who has become a Moslem is worth more to Allah than a Moslem who was always a Moslem."

Stenham sighed. "Thank you," he said. He always thanked them when this point had been reached, for it was a proof of friendship when someone broached the subject of conversion. "I hope some day all that may happen."

"*Incha'Allah.*"

"Let's go out and watch the dancing," suggested Stenham, who suddenly felt like cutting the conversation short. It would be a good way, since the noise of the drums and chanting was so loud that talking became an impossibility once one had pushed one's way into a circle. The two boys jumped up and slipped into their sandals. Stenham rose, stretched, and glancing quickly at Lee to be sure she was still asleep, took his shoes in his hand and tiptoed over to the opening in the tent. "*Nimchi o nji,* I'll be back," he told the *qaouaji.*

It was the coldest hour of the night. The moon had gone behind the mountain that lay to the west, but a part of the sky there was still bright, and the more distant parts of the countryside continued to bathe in its radiance. The two boys stamped their feet and kicked up their heels in the steps of an improvised dance; this took them along the ground more quickly than Stenham could walk. When they had got ahead some distance he saw Mohammed glance swiftly back, and then put his hand on Amar's shoulder and say a few words into his ear. He watched Amar to see his reaction, but as far as he could tell there was none. However, he did reply briefly. When they reached a more crowded crosspath they stood still and waited for Stenham to come abreast of them. He turned his face toward the eastern sky, hunting for a sign of daybreak, but it was not yet due.

"What are they up to?" he wondered with a faint uneasiness. He could not believe that Amar would take part in any sort of craftiness directed at him, but of course Mohammed was an unknown quantity, probably a typical *harami* of Fez, and he did not know the extent of his influence over the other.

It was as if the night, in her death agony, were making a final, desperate effort to assert herself by creating as much darkness as she could. The fires and flares in most of the circles had died, and the sound of the drums coming out of the gloom seemed much louder. Down here in the crease between the two hills, the chill in the air was intense; those who walked had the hoods of their *djellabas* up, so that the principal thoroughfare looked like a dim procession of monks. The smoldering fires gave forth much more smoke than when they had been blazing; one heard constant coughing.

Several smaller circles had formed since he had last come this way. It was difficult to tell what was going on in their midst, or why people crowded in to watch. In one a woman stood perfectly still, her long hair almost completely covering her, making a faint and rhythmical moaning sound; occasionally she seemed to shiver imperceptibly, but Stenham could not be sure. In another, there was an old Negro leaning far forward, his chest propped against a stake that had been driven into the ground. Beside him lay an earthen pot of coals from which rose a sluggish smoke with a foul stench. "What is it?" asked Stenham in a scandalized whisper. "*Fasoukh.* Very good," Amar told him. "If you wear that in your shoe, even though there's something buried at the entrance of a house or a café, you're safe." "But why do they burn it?" he insisted. "This is a bad hour," said Amar.

He looked at the old man, and found him vaguely obscene. "What's he doing?" he whispered. "He's trying to remember," Amar whispered back. The man's eyelids were half open, but his pupils had rolled quite out of sight, and from time to time his ancient, soft lips moved very slightly to form a word which never came out; instead, a bubble of saliva would slowly form and break. In the front row of spectators, seated, was another very black man wearing a jacket and skullcap entirely sewn with white cowrie-shells. The sounds that came from the flat drum he was languidly beating were his only interest; he listened with complete attention, his eyes closed, his head to one side. "*Nimchiou*," Stenham muttered, eager to escape the fantastic odor of the smudge rising from the pot of coals. There was a sweet aromatic gum in the substance, but there was also a greasy smell as of burning hair; it was the mixture that was offensive. Even when they had gone well out of its range, the membrane of his throat and nose seemed still coated with the viscid fumes. He spat ferociously. "You don't like *fasoukh*," said Amar accusingly. "That means you're in the power of an evil spirit. No! By Allah!" he cried, as Stenham protested laughingly. "I swear that's what it means." "All right," said Stenham. "A *djinn* lives in me."

They had come upon another small circle. Here two girls spun silently round and round, their heads and shoulders entirely hidden by pieces of cloth which had been laid over them. No grace was in their movements, no music accompanied them. One would have said that two children had taken it into their heads to see how many times they could turn before they dropped, and that the people had gathered to watch out of sheer inanition. "What is this?" Stenham inquired. "*Zouamel*," said Amar softly. So they were not girls at all; they were merely dressed as girls.

They turned to go back to the flatter part of the valley where the large groups were gathered. The exhibits had left Stenham with a faint nausea. The combination of meaninglessness and ugliness bothered him. There had been something definitely repulsive about those little rings of unmoving people. It was not the long-haired woman herself, nor yet the old Negro, and certainly it was not the spectators; the mindless watching of a thing which he felt should have been going on in the strictest privacy, that was what was upsetting. The world had suddenly seemed very small, cold, and still.

Amar raised his arm and pointed. "The day's coming," he said. Stenham could see no light in the sky, but Amar was insistent that it was there. They edged into what looked like the largest of all the circles. In the center, by the light of what remained of a fire, stood a woman all in white, singing. And the chorus of men surrounded her, their arms interlocked, answering at the end of each strophe with a cry like a great gush of water, but one which ended miraculously each time in the same long channel of accurate musical sound, that led to the first note of her next strophe. At this moment it seemed always that they were about to rush in upon her and crush her. Lowering their heads, they would push forward like charging bulls, take three long steps, so that the circle, receding inward from the spectators, became very small; then, while the woman slowly turned like a stately object on a revolving pedestal, they would catch themselves up and pull backward and outward. The very repetitiousness and violence of the dance gave it a hieratic character. The woman's song, however, could have been a signal called by one mountain wayfarer to another on a distant hill. In certain long notes which lay outside the passage of time because the rhythm was suspended, there was the immeasurable melancholy of mountain twilights. Telling himself it was a beautiful song, he decided to stand still and let it work upon him whatever spell it could. With this music it was senseless to say, because the same thing happened over and over within a piece, that once you knew what was coming next you did not need to listen to the end. Unless you listened to it all, there was no way of knowing what effect it was going to have on you. It might take ten minutes or it might take an hour, but any judgment you passed on the music before it came to its end was likely to be erroneous. And so he stood there, his mind occupied with uncommon, half-formed thoughts. At moments the music made it possible for him to look directly into the center of himself and see the black spot there which was the eternal; at least, that was the way he diagnosed the sensation. *Cogito, ergo sum* is nonsense. I think *in spite of* being, and I *am* in spite of thinking.

The dark died slowly, fighting to remain, and the light came, at first gray and hideous, and then suddenly, once the sky existed, beautiful and new, and people began surreptitiously to look at one another, to see who had been standing next to them, and the lone woman in the middle became a real woman, but somehow less real for being more than a mask made red by the fire's light. And as all these things came about, and the sum of the drumming grew less urgent (because so many of the drummers, suddenly realizing that something had changed, and it was daylight now, had ceased pounding on their drums), a strange new sound rose up on all sides to meet the dawn. It was like cockcrow, but it was the voices of the thousands of sheep roundabout, inside the tents, calling to each other, greeting the day on which they were to die for the glory of Allah.

The piece had finished, although there was never any clear-cut end, because the drumming always went on in a desultory fashion through the interlude, until a new piece had begun and had swept it along with it, back into the stream. The woman quietly stepped through the circle of men and disappeared. Stenham glanced at Amar, looked away, and then looked again carefully. There was no doubt about it: tears had wet his cheeks. Out of the corner of his eye he watched the boy become conscious of his surroundings, rub his face with his sleeve, harden his expression, turn a quick hostile glance at Mohammed to reassure himself that the other had not noticed his weakness, and then spit loudly on the ground behind him.

Inwardly Stenham sighed. Even here there existed the unspoken agreement that to be touched by beauty was shameful; one must fight to keep oneself beyond its reach. Nothing was really what he had imagined it to be. In the beginning the Moroccans had been for him an objective force, unrelieved and monolithic. All of them put together made a *thing*, an element both less and more than human; but any one of them alone existed only in so far as he was an anonymous part or a recognizable symbol of that indivisible and undifferentiable total. They were something almost as basic as the sun or the wind, subject to no moods or impulses started by the mirror of the intellect. They did not know they were there; they merely were there, at one with existence. Nothing could be the result of one individual's desire, since one was the equivalent of another. Whatever they were and whatever came about was what they all desired. But now, perhaps as a result of having seen this boy, he found himself beginning to doubt the correctness of his whole theoretical edifice.

It was not that what Amar said was different from what so many others had said before him. Probably it was that he said it with such a degree of certainty, and had been so unaffected by the presence of the other culture, rational and deadly, at his side. Stenham had always taken it for granted that the dichotomy of belief and behavior was the cornerstone of the Moslem world. It was too deep to be called hypocrisy; it was merely custom. They said one thing and they did something else. They affirmed their adherence to Islam in formulated phrases, but they behaved as though they believed, and actually did believe, something quite different. Still, the unchanging profession of faith was there, and to him it was this eternal contradiction which made them Moslems. But Amar's relationship to his religion was far more robust: he believed it possible to practice literally what the Koran enjoined him to profess. He kept the precepts constantly in his hand, and applied them on every occasion, at every moment. The fact that such a person as Amar could be produced by this society rather upset Stenham's calculations. For Stenham, the exception invalidated the rule instead of proving it: if there were one Amar, there could be others. Then the Moroccans were not the known quantity he had thought they were, inexorably conditioned by the pressure of their own rigid society; his entire construction was false in consequence, because it was too simple and did not make allowances for individual variations. But in that case the Moroccans were much like anyone else, and very little of value would be lost in the destruction of their present culture, because its design would be worth less than the sum of the individuals who composed it— the same as in any Western country. That, however, he could

not allow himself even to consider; it required too much effort
to go on from there, and he had not slept at all during the
night.

Now he had to go back and face Lee. If I know her at all, he
thought, she'll still be angry. She was not the sort to wake up in
the morning having decided to forget the night before. "*Yallah!*" he said roughly, and the two boys followed him. On the
way back to the café he turned to see if they were in his wake,
and again he found Mohammed engaged in surreptitious conversation with Amar; its conspiratorial nature was confirmed
when they saw Stenham looking back at them and quickly
drew apart. He stopped walking, to wait for them to catch up
with him. Mohammed immediately slowed his pace, obviously
in the hope he would go on, but he stood still and waited. Amar
came first; his face wore a determined expression. Before Stenham had an opportunity to speak, he said: "M'sieu! Mohammed
and I want to go back to Fez."

Stenham was both relieved that Amar should have spoken
out, and troubled by his request. "Oh," he said. "That's what
you've been whispering about together all night."

"*Sa'a, sa'a.* Once in a while. Mohammed says the French let
everyone come here so it would be easier for them to kill the
ones who stayed behind."

Mohammed, guessing the subject of their dialogue, loitered
even more shamelessly.

"I thought you had some brains," Stenham told Amar disgustedly. "How many people do you think have come here from
Fez? Probably about fifty. How are the others going to get out
of the Medina and come here when it's all closed and the
soldiers are at every gate? Tell me that."

Amar did not reply. At last Mohammed had arrived within
speaking distance.

"What's this about going to Fez? Why do you want to go?"

Assuming an aggrieved air, Mohammed enumerated a list of
utterly unconvincing arguments for their being in Fez that day,
rather than here in the mountains. At first Stenham had intended to reply to each point, demolishing them one by one,

but as the number and absurdity of Mohammed's reasons increased, he despaired, and then grew angry. "Just tell me one thing," he finally demanded. "Why did you come?"

This question presented no difficulties to Mohammed. "My friend asked me." He pointed at Amar.

"You can go back again if you want to. It has nothing to do with me."

"The bus ticket." He looked reproachfully at Amar.

"None of it has anything to do with me. I'm not going to buy your bus ticket. I invited you both here, and you're here. I haven't invited you back to Fez yet. When I do, I'll buy your bus tickets. But it won't be today. You're lucky to be here out of trouble. If you had any heads, you'd both know that." As he spoke he watched Amar, whose changing countenance convinced him that he was voicing what were more or less Amar's opinions, and that it was only Mohammed who was bored and wanted to get back to the city. Mohammed was a troublemaker; there was no doubt of it. But it was out of the question that he should be sent back alone: he would not have gone without Amar, nor would Amar have allowed him to go by himself. The shame attached to such behavior would be overwhelming. If Amar had invited Mohammed to Sidi Bou Chta, Mohammed was Amar's guest, and Amar was responsible for his well-being and contentment while he was there. Now Mohammed wanted to go to Fez, therefore Amar must take him to Fez.

"If Amar wants to buy your bus ticket, that's all right." But Amar looked woebegone upon hearing this. Now I'm in the act of becoming the wicked Nazarene, Stenham thought. They always have to have one around, and I might as well be it. He began to walk again.

In the café Lee was sitting up, smoking, and looking even more dour than he had expected. "Good morning," he said jovially. "Good morning," she said quickly, like a machine, and without glancing at him.

A wave of rage swept over him; he wanted to say, with the same pleasant heartiness: "How's the martyr this morning?" but of course he said nothing. The two boys came in, removed their sandals, and sat down, still muttering to each other. Then Amar remembered Lee and looked toward her, saying: "*Bon jour, madame,*" and Mohammed followed suit. Her acknowledgment of their greeting was slightly more cordial.

Most of the men in the café were the same ones who had been there the night before, but there were also two or three new faces among them, noticeable because they were obviously from the city. Having nothing else to do, he watched them, comparing their city gestures and postures with the noble bearing of the country folk. Decadence, decadence, he said to himself. They've lost everything and gained nothing. The French had merely daubed on the finishing touches at the end of a process which had begun five hundred years ago, at least. Their intuitive moral desires coincided with the ideals embodied in the formulas of their religion, yet they could live in accordance neither with those deepest impulses nor with the precepts of the religion, because society came in between with all the pressure of its tradition. No one could afford to be honest or generous or merciful because every one of them distrusted all the others; often they had more confidence in a Christian they were meeting for the first time than in a Moslem they had known for years.

Now, that foxy-looking one there in seedy European clothes, he thought, with the thick lips and the heavy fuzz on his cheeks and the boil on his neck, talking so secretively to the enormous mountain man with his silver-handled dagger stuck in its scabbard at his hip—what could a miserable young purveyor of the *souks* like that have of interest to tell a man who looked like a benevolent king? Something of vital concern, to judge from the way in which the man presently reacted, for his eyes gradually opened very wide, as an expression of consternation spread across his face. The younger one sat with narrowed eyes, rubbing his hand over his unshaven chin, and leaned even closer, whispering urgently.

Seized with a sudden suspicion, Stenham rose and left the tent. At random he chose another café a little further down the hill, went in, and ordered a glass of tea, disregarding the glances of suspicion that were leveled at him. Such glances were an old

story and he was used to them. This café differed very little from
the other, save that it was somewhat larger, and had a second
room, more symbolic than actual, the division being marked by
a length of matting tacked onto some upright poles. In the larger
space where he had seated himself very little seemed to be
going on: the men smoked their kif pipes and sipped their tea.
Soon he rose and entered the second room, where he chose a
corner and sat down to wait for his tea. Here again were the
same peculiar and unexpected circumstances, only more strik-
ingly presented than in the other café, in that here the city
youth, this one wearing glasses, was speaking to six important-
looking rustics, instead of only one. It was difficult for him to
feign nonchalance in the face of the sudden silence and the
frankly hostile glares that followed his entry into this little chamber. He decided to play the innocent tourist, in search of
atmosphere; not that they would recognize the part he was
playing, but it was the only way he could be sure of being able to
carry it off. He smiled fatuously at them all, and said: "Good
morning. *Bong jour. Avez-vous kif? Kif foumer bong.*" I hope I
haven't overdone it, he thought. Two of the men had begun to
smile; the others looked confused. The city man sneered, said
contemptuously: "*Non, monsieur, on n'a pas de kif.*" Then he
turned and said to the mountain men: "How did that foreign
pig find his way to Sidi Bou Chta? Even here, and on the Aïd,
we have to look at these sons of dogs." One of the men smiled
philosophically, remarking that last year there had been three
Frenchmen at the Moussem of Moulay Idriss, and they had
taken photographs. "This one's not even French," the young
man told him disgustedly. "He's some other kind of filth from
England or Switzerland." Again he let his gaze of hatred play
over Stenham's face for a moment; then he turned away with an
air of finality and resumed his monologue, but now in a very
low voice which kept Stenham from hearing all but an occasional isolated word or phrase. However, the young man, forgetting, soon raised his voice a shade, and this difference made it
possible for Stenham to hear most of the words. When the tea
came he drank it as quickly as he could without the risk of

attracting attention to himself, then, bidding a clumsy good-bye to the men in the room, he went outside once more. There was no possible way of believing that one or two stray young men from Fez had come up and happened to be telling friends of the recent turn of events there, but he wanted the pleasure of knowing, instead of merely entertaining a suspicion. He determined to try a half dozen more cafés, to see on how large a scale the campaign was being waged. In the event anyone asked him what he was doing, he would pretend to be looking for Amar. And so, one after the other, he stopped and went in, glancing about in a preoccupied manner, and retiring after scanning the faces of the occupants.

Only in one did the *qaouaji* ask him what he wanted. The man's voice was unpleasant, and he did not give himself the time to look with care. In one other he could not be sure: the type he had singled out was not well enough defined. But in the other four there was not the least doubt. The Istiqlal had sent an entire committee up here to make contact with the *cheikhs, caïds* and other notables, and attempt to dissuade them from carrying out the sacrifice. Furthermore, they were spreading the story, very likely true in its general outlines, that the girls and women of the Medina in Fez were being systematically raped by the tens of thousands of native soldiers the French had turned loose inside the city. Houses and shops were being looted, great numbers of men and boys had been shot, and fires had started all over the city. That much he had heard in the second café while he waited for his tea, and the expressions on the faces of the listeners in the other places had been identical in each case.

He stood in the hot morning sun, hearing the chorus of bleating sheep all around him, and because he was tired and hungry, had a little imaginary conversation inside himself. Well, now are you satisfied, or do you have to see another ten cafés? No, there's no need. And now that you know, what are you going to do about it? Nothing. I just wanted to know. You thought there was a place that might still be pure. Are you satisfied?

But he did not want to go back to the café and see the two

boys, and be forced to feel that he was standing in judgment before them. For, absurd as it might sound, it was inevitable that he should feel a certain guilt when he thought of the disparity between their childish hopes and his own, which were scarcely to be formulated because they were purely negative. He did not want the French to keep Morocco, nor did he want to see the Nationalists take it. He could not choose sides because the part of his consciousness which dealt with the choosing of sides had long ago been paralyzed by having chosen that which was designed to suspend all possibility of choice. And that was perhaps fortunate, he told himself, because it enabled him to remain at a distance from both evils, and thus to keep in mind the fact of the evil.

He stopped at the food stalls and got himself half a disk of bread and some skewers of lamb. Then, eating as he went, he set out for the hill that lay behind the eminence where the sanctuary was built. There was a constant coming and going of people on their way down from and up to the shrine, but the route they used was to his left, and his path, made by goats most likely, was unfrequented. For the only permanent building in the region was the little *marabout* which had been constructed around the tomb of Sidi Bou Chta himself. When there was no pilgrimage, no one happened by but individuals who had come to fulfill their vows, plus whatever shepherd chanced to stray within the precinct with his goats.

From the very top he looked down upon the whole bright panorama, the barren ochre earth to the south, the rows of mountain ranges to the north, and in front of him to the west the wooded gray-green slopes with the open spaces, where the thousands of tiny white figures were. Whatever movement these last made was so dwarfed from this height that they seemed frozen and stationary objects in the landscape; it was only if he watched carefully for a while that he could convince himself that they were actually moving about. Here in the joyous morning sun he felt very remote, and he wondered vaguely if it might not be better to witness the sacrifice from here—see it while not seeing it. The Istiqlal agents could never succeed in preventing

all the people from killing their sheep; that was not their purpose, in any case. They would manage just well enough to see
that the elements of confusion, uncertainty and suspicion were
injected into the proceedings, in such a way as to divide the people among themselves and ruin any sense of satisfaction which
could have resulted from a well-performed ritual. This sort of
destruction had to be carefully planned, and then allowed to
work by itself. If the young men were clever, the people would
go away from Sidi Bou Chta this year in a disgruntled mood,
and many of them would fail to come back next year. One
break, one year without the ritual, and the chain was sundered;
the young men knew that. Any kind of change in their rhythm
disorientated the people, because their lives were entirely a
matter of rhythmic repetition, and failure to observe a pre-
scribed ritual brought its own terrible psychological consequences, for then the people felt they were no longer in Allah's
grace, and if they felt that, very little mattered to them—they
would do whatever was suggested to them. He wondered if all
the young Istiqlal agents had come up in one bus. If they had, he
thought, what a blessing it would have been for it to have
plunged off the road over a cliff on its way up! The people would
have carried out the directions of Allah with rejoicing, and
happiness during the coming year would have been assured for
the countryside roundabout. A little sentence he had once read
came into his head: *Happy is the man who believes he is happy.*
Yes, he thought, and more accursed than the murderer is the
man who works to destroy that belief. It was the unhappy little
busybodies who were the scourge of mankind, the pestilence on
the face of the earth. "You dare sit there and tell me they're
happy," Lee had said to him, the self-righteous glow in her eyes.
Surely the intellectuals who had made the French Revolution
had had the same expression, like the hideous young men of the
Istiqlal, like the inhuman functionaries of the Communist Party
the world over.

In the mouth of any but the most profound man the words:
"All men are created equal" were an abomination, a clear
invitation to destroy the hierarchies of Nature. But even his

closest friends, when he suggested this to them as one of the reasons why the world became worse each successive year, smiled and said: "You know, John, you should be careful. One of these days you're going to grow into a real crank." The lie had been too firmly planted in their minds for them to be able to question it. Besides, he had no compulsion to save the world, he told himself, lying back to see only the sky. He merely wanted to save himself. That was more than enough work for one lifetime.

The morning wind had come up from the east behind him; it carried off the faint thumps of the drums down there, so that he heard only the light whistling sound it made in the thorn bushes as it passed. He fell gradually into a mindless reverie, a vegetative state in which the balance between the heat of the sun and the cool of the wind on his skin became his entire consciousness. His last clear thought was that there would be many more mornings somewhere on the earth for him to lie thus, spread out under the sky, considering these meaningless problems.

CHAPTER   29

For a long time Polly Burroughs had been banging along the rough roadbed of her dreams, vaguely aware that something was wrong, but without the power to know that she was only desperately uncomfortable, her body twisted there in one tortured position after another, all of them dictated by the bumpy contours of the matting beneath her. And little by little, painfully, through a world of dust and Arabic words, her mind began to climb up from the place where it lay. Eventually a loud burst of laughter from the qaouaji's corner roused her, and she sat up suddenly, feeling as though every muscle in her body were about to snap in two. A few boys looked at her with curiosity; she refrained from stretching, which was what she desired more than anything. Foregoing that voluptuous pleasure made her sorry for herself; it would have been so satisfying. However, she did push forth her arms, wriggling her fingers, and yawn discreetly, and even this was agreeable enough to remind her that she had scored a victory.

It was almost like a dream now, that short interval between two sleeps when she had been so wide awake. The boy had come into the tent with his friend, had had the audacity to wake her, and in her anger she had seen him in his true light, clearly. Clearly, that is to say, in that for the first time she had understood just what he signified to Stenham. (What the boy meant to himself she did not assume the possibility of knowing, nor was she interested.) She sat there, momentarily incapacitated by fury, and stared at him. A boy with smooth, weather-tanned skin, huge eyes and black hair, and with the basic assurance of a man but not by any means the manner of one. A complete young barbarian, she thought, the antithesis of that for which she could have admiration. Looking at him she felt she knew what the people of antiquity had been like. Thirty centuries or more were effaced, and there he was, the alert and predatory sub-human, further from what she believed man should be like than the naked savage, because the savage was tractable, while this creature, wearing the armor of his own rigid barbaric culture, consciously defied progress. And that was what Stenham saw, too; to him the boy was a perfect symbol of human backwardness, and excited his praise precisely because he was "pure": there was no room in his personality for anything that mankind had not already fully developed long ago. To him he was a consolation, a living proof that today's triumph was not yet total; he personified Stenham's infantile hope that time might still be halted and man sent back to his origins.

The other youth crouched near by, gnawing on a stick, surveying her with a calm and detached air of amusement.

"What is it?" she said evenly to Amar, quite forgetting that he could not understand her.

346 THE SPIDER'S HOUSE

"He wants to say good-bye to you," the other explained.

(He's not going to get away that easily, her mind remarked, but by "he" she meant Stenham.)

"Mohammed," she said, "*tu ne veux pas faire quelque chose pour moi?*"

He sat up straight.

"I wonder if you'd go down and buy me a pack of Casa Sport?"

She opened her handbag and took out some change. He was on his feet, his head bending forward so it would not rub against the blanket above. He took the money and went out. She waited half a minute to be sure he had really gone. Then she turned to Amar and without hesitation handed him all the banknotes that were in her purse. They were neatly folded.

"Of course, he doesn't understand anything," she thought, as she saw his eyes become even larger, opening wide at the sight of the money in his hand. And even as she started to sketch the gestures of explanation he was trying to give it back to her. "Boom," she whispered in his ear. "*Révolver, pistolet.*" She did not know whether he understood or not; she glanced around the tent. So far, no one was looking at them. She directed his attention to her right hand in her lap, and carefully raising it to the level of her face, crooked her index finger and shut her left eye, sighting with the other along an imaginary barrel. Then she pulled the trigger and pointed swiftly to the bills he held.

"Thank God," she thought: he did understand. She could tell that by the new expression on his face. She frowned and looked worried, indicating that he must quickly hide the money. He slipped it into his pocket. All was well.

When Mohammed returned, she was lying back, her arms folded behind her head, staring vacantly upward. To be civil, she talked awhile with him, and then the two boys rose to take their leave. When Amar shook hands with her, she looked meaningfully at him, as if to warn him against displaying any sign of gratitude, and merely said: "*Bonne chance,*" as she released his hand. They went out, and she lay back, wondering why she felt that she had accomplished a particularly difficult piece of work.

Suddenly she smiled ruefully. Until now, she had had the firm intention of returning to Fez in the first vehicle that moved out of Sidi Bou Chta. That way she would not have to see Stenham again, unless he happened to come back and catch her in the act of leaving. But now it occurred to her that she had not finished with him. It was absurd, but unthinkingly she had made seeing him again a necessity. She had no money, and it was not likely that any bus-driver could be persuaded to take her to the city for nothing, merely because she gave him the address of the little hotel where she had left her luggage. The situation was more than absurd, she told herself; it was abject. "What the hell could have been in my subconscious?" she asked herself with astonishment and indignation.

She sent the *qaouaji's* assistant out for some skewers of lamb, and paid for them with her last coins. Then, feeling tired again, she stretched out and promptly fell asleep.

All that had surely been several hours ago. Now she sat blinking, staring out through the flap of the tent at the trunks of the olive trees in the hot light of what must be mid-afternoon. She glanced at her watch. "Ten past three," she murmured with a qualm of uneasiness. The drums still continued; they had not stopped once since she had got out of the bus the night before.

And the faces in the tent were new; she did not recognize any of them. With relief she saw that the *qaouaji* had not changed. She beckoned him over and asked him if Stenham had returned and gone out again, but his French was so rudimentary that it took a good deal of gesturing to get him to say that he had not seen the Nazarene gentleman all day. She thanked him and began to feel a little apprehensive.

She lay back, thinking that maybe she could lose herself in sleep once again: it was such a convenient way of making time pass. But there seemed to be no possibility of it, and she realized that she wanted to go outside and walk about. Her muscles ached, she felt nervous; to lie still any longer would be agony.

The dry, dust-laden air smelled of the horses and donkeys that stood among the tents, and the sun shining on the millions of tiny silvery olive leaves made her long for a drink of cool water. Down below, half-hidden by the curtain of white dust they were raising as they stamped, the dancers still moved mechanically, and the watchers still crowded around them. She turned and climbed upward in the direction of the open country.

It was easy to walk up here in the sunlight, and it had been so difficult in the dark. She went much further than she had gone the night before, until the trees had all been left behind and there were only wiry, stunted bushes and great rocks. She felt better: the muscular pains were nearly gone now, and the pure air had washed away her uneasiness. She leaned against a big boulder, first scrutinizing it for scorpions, and looked across the valley at the hill opposite. A tiny, lone figure was making its way slowly downward across the curved tawny expanse of countryside. A shepherd? She strained her eyes to sight the goats or sheep, but there were none.

She watched it awhile, and all at once she decided that it was Stenham: no Moroccan would wander so far alone. She stood a long time staring across the valley as the figure came lower and lower, finally leaving the sunlight and entering into the shadow thrown by the heights behind her. She could not be certain that it was actually Stenham, nor, she told herself, did she care in the least, but still, she was almost sure it was he, and she felt a pang of eagerness at the prospect of breaking her triumphant news, of announcing to him the manner and extent of his defeat. She took her time in going back down to the café, dallying where she wished, stopping to snap off the leaves from plants, sometimes leaping from rock to rock, and, when she got within sight of the outer tents, even sitting down to smoke a cigarette.

When she reached the café, she looked in and found he had not yet returned. She decided to walk among the trees to a place from which she could see the entrance, so that when he went in he would not find her; that would give her an immediate moral advantage. Over toward the left she went, through the wood smoke and dust, and stood like a conspirator, leaning against a tree, watching around its trunk for his arrival. People came out of the tents and stared at her with surprise and distrust, but not, as far as she could tell, with hostility. It seemed to her that he was very long in coming; he must have stopped to watch the dancing. But suddenly she saw him trudging up the hill toward the café. When he had gone in, she began to walk.

This morning she had been surly and uncommunicative, and she felt she must go on with it, take it up where she had left off. At the same time, such behavior did not suit her present purpose. She entered the tent.

He was sitting in the corner, looking rather glum, she thought. When he saw her his face brightened.

"Hello," she said without expression. "I was outside."

"How are you?" he asked, looking up at her, and then he moved over so she could sit down.

"All right," she said noncommittally; too obvious a show of truculence might stifle the conversation altogether. He held out a pack of cigarettes to her; she shook her head.

"I was afraid you might have gone," he said uncertainly.

"I intended to. But I was so sleepy. Besides," she added, as if it were an afterthought, "I haven't a penny. You'll have to lend me some money, I'm afraid. I gave all mine to Amar to buy a pistol with."

"You did what?" he said, as if she had been speaking a language he scarcely understood.

"I simply gave him all the money in my purse, and told him to go and buy a gun. And the important thing is, he took it. What he does with it's immaterial." She was about to add: "So there's your purity," but then suddenly she was no longer sure of the extent of her own intelligence. Everything she had said sounded absurd; she had done it all wrong. She closed her mouth and waited.

He had passed his hand over his eyes as though to shield them from too bright a light, and now he held it there loosely. There was no decipherable expression on his face. When he finally spoke, he said slowly: "Let me get this straight." Then he continued to sit without speaking. Finally his hand came down, and looking away from her, he said: "I don't think I understand, Lee. It's too complicated for me."

"Don't be silly," she said gaily. "You're just *making* it complicated. If you had even a grain of poetry in you, you'd understand. The boy wanted action. At his age he has to have it. This is the crucial point of his whole life. He'd never have forgiven himself later if he'd sat around moping now. Can't you see that?"

Stenham looked at her, but not as though he were listening to her. The mask of preoccupation he wore contrasted strangely with his violence in suddenly crying: "Leave all that!" Now he turned to face her. "I'm not thinking of him. He's gone. One little life, another little life. What's the difference?" (She studied his face briefly, and found that she was unable to tell whether this last was irony or whether he was speaking sincerely. Now he seemed to be waiting for her to answer, but she said nothing.) "What I don't understand is you." He stopped, hesitated. "As a matter of fact, I do understand it. I just want to hear you say it in your own words. What did you think you were doing? What in the name of God would make you decide to do a thing like that?"

She was disappointed: where was the rage? "It's *something* to make a person happy," she began tentatively.

"Agh!" His voice was harsh. "There's a four-letter word for that. You guess which one and tell me. It'd mean more coming from your lips. You could give it its money's worth."

She had been lighting a cigarette to cover her nervousness, and she had discovered that her hand was trembling. Of course, she told herself, he would show his anger in this icy, abstract fashion. She had been foolish to expect a normal, simple quarrel.

"Your venom isn't really insulting, you know," she told him. "It has no focus. If you want to be really nasty, at least you've got to be conscious of the other person."

At this point she thought he was going to say: "I'm sorry," but he merely looked at her.

"I believe in what I did," she went on. "There's no reason—"

"I know," he interrupted. "That's the tragic part of it. You have no sense of moral responsibility. As long as you get your vicarious thrill you're fine. This time you had two thrills. The little one was Amar and the big one was me."

She laughed uncomfortably. "It could be. I haven't an analytical mind."

He glanced toward the entrance of the tent. The light outside was fading, the drums still went on, and the café was being slowly filled by older men who talked quietly.

"What does it feel like to have the power of life or death over another human being?" he asked her suddenly. "Can you describe it?" And because he looked truly angry now for the first time, she felt her heart leap up and light a corresponding flame within her.

"It must be exhausting to see everything in terms of cheap melodrama," she said with feigned solicitousness. "I wonder you have the vitality."

Now he said the four-letter word he had not said a few minutes earlier, got to his feet, and stalked out of the tent. She sat on, smoking, but she did not feel calm.

Almost immediately he came back in, clearly having been debating with himself outside the entrance; his expression was determined, a little embarrassed, and he was shaking his head. He walked over to her. "God damn it," he said, sitting down again beside her, "why do we have to act like two six-year-olds? I'm sorry if I've behaved badly." He waited for her to speak.

She could feel herself growing more nervous by the second. "If you mean just now—" she began. Then she stopped; she had been going to refer to his behavior last night, but she was quiet an instant.

"Oh, it doesn't matter," she heard herself saying with a vast, incomprehensible relief, as if this were solving everything.

He was looking at her with great seriousness. "After all, we got on all right with our differences of opinion before we saddled ourselves with that kid. I don't know why we shouldn't be able to pick up where we left off. Nothing's changed, has it?"

"That's true," she said thoughtfully. But in her mind she was aware that something *had* changed, and because she did not know what had made this difference or in what it consisted, she postponed complete agreement with his thesis until some later time. Then she said, with a sudden vehemence which made him look at her curiously: "I don't know. I don't think the boy had that much to do with it. I think it's this place that's got us down. I know if I have to sleep here again tonight, I'll go into a decline, that's all. Can't you find *some* way out of here?"

She had spoken without thinking, and now she expected resistance. But all he said was: "It won't be easy. And don't forget, we came up here so as not to be in Fez today. It's still the big day."

"I haven't forgotten," she protested. "They can come and murder me in my bed, but at least it'll be a *bed*, and not a pile of rocks." She patted the matting beside her, and glanced up quickly to catch his expression; did he understand, or was he merely disgusted with her? ("Nothing's changed," he had said an instant ago.) And now, when she saw his smile, she knew in a flash what had changed; she knew that even though she still thought that smile faintly fatuous, it did not repel her. With her gesture of hostility she had brought herself within his orbit. But it was not only she who had changed, for, otherwise, why was he smiling?

"We can't do more than try," he said, still smiling, and got up to go out.

Later, when the passage back was all arranged, and the truck would be leaving in an hour or so, and they had finished their evening meal of soup, bread, lamb and tea, they took a stroll, climbing to the top of the hill behind, to watch the panorama once again. "Back to the scene of the crime," she thought, feeling the pressure of Stenham's fingers on her arm as he guided her between the dim bushes, around the dark rocks, to a spot from which the valley of flame, smoke and moonlight was entirely visible. Up there they sat quietly, and when he drew her to him, implanting a kiss first on her forehead, then on each cheek, and finally (so beautifully), on her lips, she knew it was decided, and she realized with some surprise that however eagerly he might be looking forward to the intimacies of love, she herself hoped for that moment with no less impatience.

She stretched out her hand, wonderingly touched first the hard stubble on his chin, and then the smoothness of his lips, and thinking: "Why now, and not before?" pulled him to her again.

CHAPTER   30

The convoy of buses sped around the curves, each one bathing in the dust raised by the one ahead. In the first vehicle sat all the young men from the Istiqlal, who had planned with the drivers of the other buses that as part of the strategy they would stop at a certain point on the road before they arrived back at the junction of the main highway, and rearrange the seating in such a way that when they drew near to Fez there would be two or three party members in each bus. They were also not to drive into the town all together, of course, but were to time the entry of each vehicle at alternate ten- and fifteen-minute intervals. From the first moment when he had heard the terrible news, Amar had begun to tremble; they must be halfway to Fez now, and he was still trembling. An image haunted his mind: he stood just inside the door of the large room in his house, seeing his mother pinned to the floor by the point of a bayonet, but struggling to rise, while a shadowy form engaged in the deflowering of Halima on the cushions in the corner. Doubtless his father and Mustapha lay dead outside in the courtyard, which explained the fact that they did not figure in the fantasy.

Mohammed sat beside him trying to make conversation, but

Amar could not hear what he was saying. Surely this was the day of reckoning, the day of vengeance—perhaps his last day on earth! The other men in the bus sat stiff and grim, without speaking, some of them with their faces covered against the dust. Suddenly there was a loud report, above the clanking and rattling. Hands went to daggers as the bus slowed and stopped, but it was a punctured tire. Everyone got out and wandered up and down the road, while the other buses went by one by one, leaving storms of white dust in the air behind them. Ordinarily the men in the buses passing would have called and waved with glee, because it was always amusing to see one's friends suffer a slight misfortune, but today they scarcely looked out. Mohammed was disgusted. "The sons of whores!" he grumbled. "Suppose we need something to change the tire with. Who's going to give it to us? Nobody! They've all gone by."

Amar returned slowly from his scenes of carnage. He and Mohammed were sitting on a boulder looking down at the bus; he was surprised to find himself nibbling sunflower seeds. It seemed to him that Mohammed had been talking for hours, and he had heard scarcely a word. Now he was again on the subject of the money he thought Amar should have given him for the bicycle three days ago. When he had taken it back to the Frenchman, he had not been able to pay for its rental; with great luck he had managed to borrow enough from a friend who worked in the lumberyard down the street. But now it was the Aïd and the friend wanted to be repaid, and anyway, whose fault was it that they had gone to Aïn Malqa, and who had promised to pay for both the bicycles?

Amar had every intention of giving him the money, but he found Mohammed's insistence annoying, above all at this moment. "With everyone dying you're worried about a few francs," he said scornfully. The Nazarene lady had given him an enormous amount of money; how much, he did not know, because he had not yet had an instant's privacy in which to count it. At all events, now he was very rich, and the little he owed Mohammed did not trouble him. However, he thought it shameful on Mohammed's part to keep talking about it. Suddenly he turned his

THE ASCENDING STAIRWAYS 355

entire attention to what Mohammed was saying. "And the thirty
rial I had to spend for medicine after you hit me, let them go;
they don't matter." His apology had thus counted for nothing,
or Mohammed would not be reminding him of their fight.
What was the good of trying to make a friendship with a boy like
this? "*Yah*, Mohammed," he said. "You don't trust me, but
that's only because you think everybody's like you." He wanted
very much to take out his money and hand over every franc
he owed him, just to have done with it, but of course it was out
of the question to let him see how much money he had. Mohammed turned a withering glance upon him, saying in disgust:
"You have a head like an owl, or a scorpion, or a stone. I don't
know what kind of a head you have." "*Majabekfia*," retorted
Amar. "Don't worry about me." They sat a long time, perhaps
an hour, without speaking, before the tire was finally changed
and the bus ready to leave.

Now that theirs was the last bus, once they had started up,
the driver felt impelled to go like the wind. They skirted the
edges of the abyss at terrific speed, the brakes squealing as they
rounded curves, the old motor roaring like a demon when they
were not coasting. If Allah had not been with them, Amar
thought, on several occasions the bus would surely have hurtled
into space. When they approached the place where it had been
agreed that they would all stop so that the Istiqlal men could
spread out, there was nothing but the empty road. This seemed
a bad omen; the men shook their heads and grumbled. For
they wanted the learned young men to be with them when they
arrived in the city. All the other buses had their quotas of them
by now; only this one, through the stupidity of the driver (for
they now held him responsible for the delay occasioned by
the blowout), remained without its commanders. But as they
came almost in sight of the paved road, a small truck loaded high
with watermelons appeared around a curve, coming toward
them, blowing its horn in an imperative manner; dark arms
emerged from both sides and wigwagged furiously. The bus
driver slowed, stopped, and everyone stared at the wild faces of
the four men in the truck.

"Brother! Brother!" all four cried at once. "Don't go! They got them all! They killed them!" The four men jumped up and down on the seat, waved their arms and struck each other in their excitement, and the truck driver sketched a dramatic, sweeping semicircle to suggest a machine-gun firing. "By the railroad crossing!" At this news there were groans and curses in the bus, together with the uttering of the names of unfortunate relatives and friends who had left Sidi Bou Chta in the other buses. As the first explosion of frenzy died down and words began to be spoken in more nearly normal tones, it appeared that only a few men had actually been killed by gunfire, the others having been carted off to jail in military trucks; as each bus had arrived, its occupants had been transferred under guard to trucks manned by French soldiers, and had been driven away. The important thing now, if they wanted to get to the Ville Nouvelle, cried the four men, was to bypass the road where the trouble had occurred, take the Meknès road and double back, stopping at a point which they would indicate, having just come from there.

"It's a police trap," murmured Mohammed into Amar's ear; this was the first word to pass between them since the disagreement on the boulder. "Who knows? Maybe they're *chkama*. Maybe the others all got through."

Amar had studied the faces of the men in the truck, and he would have staked his entire future on the veracity of their story. "You're dizzy," he told Mohammed, reflecting at the same time that there was one so crafty that he distrusted everyone, which was almost as foolish as trusting everyone.

At all events, the bus driver seemed not to doubt the truth of their account. He waited while the truck backed and turned, and then he began to follow it at a distance of about fifty meters. This was a terrain closed in by steep slopes of bare earth; in the midday sun it had become a little inferno. When they got onto the highway the truck increased its speed, as did the bus, and so there was some breeze inside. The driver shouted to the men sitting silent behind him: "Pray! You're coming from Sidi Bou Chta!" This seemed an excellent idea. If they passed

a police car at Bab el Guissa a pilgrims' prayer might possibly
allay suspicion.

> "*Oua-a-l ach f'n nebbi,*
> *selliou alih.*
> *Oual'la-a-ah m'selli alih,*
> *karrasou'llah!*"

they chanted, as the bus sped along the flat highway across the
bridge, frightening two white herons in the river below, and
then started to wind its way upward through the tangles of canebrake. This was scarcely the usual moment to invoke divine
protection for the voyage, when everyone had returned safely
from the pilgrimage, and the bus driver was fully aware of it;
the cynicism of his suggestion resided in the fact that he also
knew there were probably not more than two Frenchmen in all
of Fez who would be aware of it, and neither of them was a
policeman. The Moroccans could count on a certain degree of
obtuseness in the observational powers of the French.

Since the servant always gains more knowledge of the master
than the master can hope to gain of him, the Moroccans knew
they could afford imprecisions without being detected, while the
French had no such advantages; it was virtually impossible for
them to deceive anyone. The Moroccans who had any contact
at all with the French knew where their masters went, whom
they saw, what they said, how they felt, what they ate, when and
with whom they drank and slept, and why they did all these
things, whereas the French had only the most sketchy, mechanical and inflexible understanding of the tastes, customs and
daily life of the natives in whose land they lived. If an officer in
the cavalry showed less skill than usual one day in mounting his
horse, his orderly saw it, began to speculate as to the reason, and
secretly spied on him. If a functionary were smoking a cigarette
which was not one of his accustomed brand, the shoeshine boy
noticed it and commented upon it to his colleagues. If the mis-
tress of the house drank only one cup of *café au lait* when on

other mornings she habitually drank two, the maid's curiosity was aroused, and she mentioned it to the scrubwoman and the laundress. The only way the French could preserve even the illusion of privacy was simply to pretend the natives did not exist, and this automatically gave the natives an enormous advantage. Thus it did not seem likely that the police would see anything strange in their chanting at this moment; on the contrary, it might give the bus an inoffensive air, for they had found that if they appeared to be occupied with religious matters, the French generally let them alone.

Where were they going and what did they intend to do when they got there? Not one of them could have answered the question, nor could the question have been posed; it would not have been in key with the prevailing temper, more suited to the chanting of prayers than to the elaboration of projects. They knew that if an angel were to appear suddenly in the sky above the fruit orchards they were passing, and were to give them the clear choice between renouncing their vows of vengeance and dying, they would gladly give up their lives then and there, rather than betray their brothers in Islam. But no angel came, and they were not far from the city walls.

Alone among all the passengers Amar was working out a plan of action: no one but he had a mother and sister in the Medina. The mountain men's vested interest in the holiness of the city provided them with excitement, but it was excitement of the sort that comes when many people make a common decision to defend a cause, and it awakened none of the desperate intelligence of the individual who finds himself in extremities. Mohammed's family had gone to Casablanca to pass the Aïd there with relatives, and he was staying with a married sister in Fez-Djedid outside the walls, which meant that not only was he free from worries about the possible fate of his mother and sisters at the hands of the partisans, but could come and go as he pleased. This explained, even if it did not excuse, his obvious lack of interest in Amar's predicament. All he wanted was his bicycle money, and that Amar intended to give him as soon as he had a minute to hide himself and count it out; he would hand it to him and say good-bye, for he wanted to get rid of him before he set to work.

They were approaching the big curve by Bab Jamaï, which brought the road up out of the orchards to within a few meters of the walls, and then swung it immediately away again, out onto the stony mountainside. Several hundred soldiers were there, moving about among the tents that had been hastily set up along the outside of the ramparts. But the pilgrims looked straight ahead, chanting with ferocity, and pounded the sides of the bus and the seats. On up the hill they went, their clear voices floating out over the empty cemeteries. When they got to the top, Amar could not keep from stealing a glance down at the Medina. No columns of smoke rose from its midst; it looked the same as every other day. The Nazarene gentleman had told him that the Istiqlal spread many lies. He knew that; everyone told lies. It was for the intelligent man to distinguish truth from lies, just as it was only the intelligent man who knew how to lie in a way that made it next to impossible for others to find his lies and identify them as such. As he looked at the Medina stretched out down there in the glaring sun, unchanged, it occurred to him to question the truth of what they had said, but only for an instant. If it were not yet true, it soon would be. His problem was to get home, if possible before it was too late, but in any case to get there.

The road now straightened out; the little truck ahead with its load of watermelons went faster. Again there were tents along the walls, between Casbah Cherarda and Bab Segma. The men from the mountains sang out into the surprised, slow faces of the Senegalese soldiers. No one halted the bus, and it sped ahead toward the west, along the Meknès road.

They stopped a few meters off the side road in a lane with high cane on either side. Quickly everyone got out. The four men of the truck were in a frenzy of anxiety. "Hurry! Hurry!" they cried, suddenly having exhausted the courage which had made it possible for them to go to the rescue of the lost bus. Without thinking, they had driven into the lane to show the way; now they were obliged to wait until the bus had backed out

360 THE SPIDER'S HOUSE

to the road, before they themselves could get out. "Quick!" And it was a bad moment when an old man fell flat on his face and had to be helped up, dusted off and set straight.

When Amar's feet touched the ground and he became aware of the familiar odor of the river, he felt all at once as though he had been away from home a very long time, and his sense of urgency redoubled. It was as if he had been asleep, and had awakened. His patience with the pilgrims was at an end; they were moving ineffectually around the bus in a dazed fashion because the chanting was over and their minds were still in it, but at any moment someone might come along the road and turn into the lane. "Come on," he said to Mohammed, and they started back to the road.

"But where are we going?" Mohammed wanted to know.

"I'm going to see a friend of mine, and I'm going alone."

"And my money?" cried Mohammed.

Amar was delighted. It was exactly the reaction he had been hoping for. This would make it easy to pay him off and dismiss him without ceremony. "Ah, khlass!" he said, making a show of disgust. "Your money! All you have in your head is your money." He was looking for a stretch of wall or cactus fence, something to go behind for a moment, and until he found it he would have to improvise a critical lecture on Mohammed's cupidity. Finally he caught sight of an abandoned hut ahead; when they had reached it, he said: "Wait a second." He could see that Mohammed was loath to let him out of his sight, for fear he would bolt without paying him, but he could scarcely follow him into the hut, where he was going ostensibly to relieve himself. There was daylight inside: long ago the roof had fallen. He pulled out his money and counted it. The Nazarene lady had been generous even beyond his expectations: there were eight thousand-franc and two five-hundred-franc notes. He looked down at them with love. "Mine," he thought, and then he corrected himself. "*Jiaou.* They came. It was written." It was for this that Allah had decreed the man should take him away from the café, feed him and protect him. True, there was another part to it somewhere, that had to do with friendship and the man's own understanding of him, but it was too difficult to reach with his mind now, and he did not insist upon it. He folded the money carefully and put it away again. Then he took two hundred francs out of the handkerchief in which his own money was tied and put it loose into his other pocket. When he came out, Mohammed was standing there, looking anxiously toward the door, as if he were afraid Amar might simply vanish. This was a mystery Amar had never been able to fathom. The rich were not ashamed to let it be seen that they cared about money. Where a man with only twenty rial in the world would as a matter of course use those twenty rial to pay for all the teas at the table, another with a thousand rial in his wallet, when the time came to leave the café, would begin to fumble inside his clothing and murmur aloud: "Let's see, there are six people at fifteen francs each, that's eighteen rial. I have only fifteen francs change, which is exactly my share. Each one had better pay his own." For the poor man such behavior was unthinkable: his shame would be so great he could never face his friends again. But the rich gave it no importance. "That will all change when the French leave," Amar was fond of thinking. The concept of independence was easily confused with that of social equity.

They walked along briskly, Amar apparently having forgotten the monologue he had been delivering. To Mohammed this meant he had forgotten the money once more, and he was rash enough to mention it. Amar stopped walking, reached into his pocket, and pulled out the two hundred francs. Without saying anything he put it into Mohammed's hand. They took a few more steps. "Happy?" asked Amar with what he considered delicate irony. Mohammed seemed shamed into silence.

When they came to a dirt road leading off across the fields to the south, Amar stood still again and said firmly: "I'll see you some day soon. *B'slemah.*" Mohammed merely looked at him. That was the world, Amar thought as he walked away. He had been willing to make him his friend, and Mohammed lacked the sense to realize it. He had even given him a second chance, which Mohammed had likewise disregarded. It was all really very fortunate, he reflected, for now he had complete freedom of movement, whereas Mohammed's presence would surely have hampered him.

He looked back twice, just to be sure Mohammed had really continued along the other road; the first time he was still standing there, as if he were debating whether to follow him and try to get more money, but the second time he had already gone some distance down the road toward the city.

The fields were parched; only a dead yellow stubble covered their cracked earth. But insects whirred and buzzed in the weeds that edged the lane, and where there was a tree there were birds. When a man was extremely thirsty the sound of a bird singing was like a little stream of water trickling from the sky. His father had told him that, but he could not see that the birds were of any help now. Or perhaps they were; perhaps his thirst would have been stronger without them.

An hour or so later he came upon the cut-off he had been looking for—a path that led straight across the open plain between stiff-speared agaves, to the Aïn Malqa road. The distances were big out here; things looked near and small, but they were always larger and further away than one thought. It was the golden hour of the afternoon where he reached the olive grove. This time no motorcycle appeared, and he arrived at the house without disturbing the fabric of cricket-songs through which he walked. For a moment he stood by the door doing nothing, reluctant to bang the knocker. But having come all the way here, he was unable to think of anything else to do, and so he lifted the iron ring and let it fall, twice. The sound was surprisingly loud, but immediately after it the calm was there again, unchanged. He listened intently for voices inside. The crickets were too loud.

He waited a long time. If no one answered, he was prepared to sit at some distance from the house in the bushes and go on waiting there, until Moulay Ali returned. From where he stood, he surveyed the overgrown garden, selecting and rejecting vantage points. There was a click behind him, and he wheeled about. The door was open just far enough to let a nose and mouth be seen in the aperture. "Mahmoud?" he asked hesitantly, his voice breaking on the second syllable, as it still did sometimes when he put insufficient force behind it. The name had come to him that instant, as he had said it. But whoever it was softly closed the door, and he was alone again. And now he waited even longer, but with the knowledge that at least someone was in, even though there was no more sound inside or out of the house than as if it had been a ruin. In the grove a bird called repeatedly, two clear notes, a silence, two clear notes.

CHAPTER   31

This time the door really opened, very quickly, and a tall man with a gray *tarbouche* and one white eye stood there, holding a large, bright revolver which was leveled straight at Amar's chest.

"Good afternoon," said the man, and on hearing the deep voice Amar remembered his name, too.

"*Yah, Lahcen, chkhbarek?* How are you?" he began, a little too familiarly, he realized, as the big man's expressionless face did not alter.

"Come in," Lahcen said, stepping aside, following Amar's movements with the gun. "I wonder if he thinks I'm afraid of that," Amar was asking himself. He heard Lahcen bolting the door as he started up the stairs. When they were up on the gallery they did not go into the large room where he had been before, but walked its battered length, the droning of bees above their heads, to a small door at the far end. "Open it," said Lahcen.

There were three steps leading down onto another gallery which ran at right angles with the first. This part of the house was even more dilapidated than the other: the floor tiles were almost all missing, the walls had partially crumbled and fallen, and some of the ceiling beams, rotted away at the outer edge, sagged so low that they had to bend their heads as they passed. Now Lahcen stepped ahead and opened a door on the right. It was dim inside; there was only one small window which had been covered over with a sheet of yellowed newspaper, and in the air was the still heat of a closed-up room in summer, the dry, blind smell of slowly accumulating dust. Lahcen shut the door and Amar heard his slightly labored breathing as he brushed past him.

Suddenly there was light. A door directly in front of Amar had opened. Moulay Ali stood there in a green silk dressing gown, his hand on the doorknob. Behind him was a flight of narrow wooden stairs leading up, or so it looked, to the sky.

"*El aidek mebrouk.* Holiday greetings," said Moulay Ali pleasantly, with no trace of irony. "Come up." He turned and mounted the stairs ahead of Amar, and Lahcen came behind him.

It was the sky that Amar had seen; the sky was all the way around the room, because the walls were made entirely of windows. Some were open and some were shut, and there in the dying sunlight were the mountains, the plain, the tops of the olive trees below, and on the front side only the roof of the house, which was built up higher than the room. Amar looked around delightedly, very much impressed. Moulay Ali watched him. The only furnishings were a large table and some heavy leather hassocks to sit on. The table was littered at one end with books, magazines and newspapers; at the other end there was a typewriter.

"Sit down. How do you like my workroom?"

"Never in the world have I seen such a room," Amar told him, glancing sideways toward Lahcen, who had sat leaning against the door, his revolver still in his hand. Moulay Ali noticed his wandering gaze and laughed.

"Lahcen's my bodyguard this afternoon. For once I think I

have one I can trust." Lahcen grunted complacently. "The others all went singing their little songs to their friends."

"You mean to the police?" said Amar, scandalized.

Still Moulay Ali studied him, his head slightly to one side. He smiled. "No," he said calmly. "But they talked too much, and that's almost as bad. You see, I'm not here today. You think you see me, but I'm really in Rabat." Suddenly he changed the tone of his voice and said, somewhat menacingly, Amar thought: "But what's all this about the police? Why would anyone go to the police? Why did you say that? You'll have to explain that to me, I'm afraid. I don't understand."

The fresh twilight breeze was beginning to move across the plain from the mountains; it came through the open window and touched Amar's cheek. If Moulay Ali had really intended to play the game of innocence with him, he would not have told him what he had just told him about Rabat. "I don't know," he said simply. "I suppose the French would like to catch you. Wouldn't they like to catch everyone who works for freedom?"

Moulay Ali narrowed his eyes. "I think you're right," he said, gazing out across the countryside. "I think they would like to catch me. That's why it's not good to have people know where I live." He turned back and looked thoughtfully at Amar.

Amar was silent, wondering whether he should explain to him now why he had come, or wait a bit. So long as they spoke at cross purposes, he decided, with Moulay Ali wondering how much he knew, and he wondering what Moulay Ali was suspecting about him, it was hopeless. And he had an uncomfortable feeling that each minute which passed without the situation's being clarified held the danger of bringing forth some irreparable decision on Moulay Ali's part.

"I saw Benani," he said suddenly.

"I see," replied Moulay Ali; he seemed to be waiting for Amar to go on. (At least he had not said: "Who's Benani?")

After a pause, Moulay Ali said evenly: "Who else did you see?"

"I don't know their names, the ones who were with him."

"I'm not talking about them," Moulay Ali said quietly. "I know who they were. I meant who else have you seen since you were here three days ago?"

Only three days, thought Amar; it seemed a month. In the pink light that came from the setting sun a large round sore on Lahcen's leg looked as though it were full of fire. He sighed. This was going to be like Benani's grilling, all over again. "I saw my family, and Mohammed Lalami."

"Who?" said Moulay Ali sharply. Amar repeated the name. "Who's that?" he wanted to know. "A *derri* who lives in the Medina. The one who hit me in the nose the other day," he added brightly. "Who went to Aïn Malqa with me."

"Who else?" pursued Moulay Ali.

It simply did not occur to Amar to mention the two tourists; they and the time he had spent with them were part of another world far away, that had nothing to do with the world they were living in and discussing at the moment. "Well, I didn't see anybody else," he said.

"I see." All at once Moulay Ali's face became extremely unpleasant to look at. It twisted itself up into a knot and twitched, like a snake that is dying, and then for the fraction of an instant he seemed to be about to shed tears, but instead he took a deep breath and his eyes opened very wide, and Amar was frightened, because he realized that Moulay Ali was exceedingly angry. He exploded into a yell of rage, jumped to his feet, and began to talk very fast.

"Why haven't you any respect for me?" he shouted. "Respect! Respect! Just simple respect! Only a little respect would put enough sense into your donkey's head so you'd know you can't lie to me. Where'd you sleep last night?"

He towered above Amar, his body shaking slightly as he spoke. Instinctively Amar got to his feet and stood a little further away on the other side of the hassock.

"I didn't sleep at all," he said with an air of wounded dignity. "I was at Sidi Bou Chta watching the *fraja*."

Moulay Ali looked to the ceiling for support; the thought passed through Amar's head that the angrier he got, the less respect he inspired, because he became just like any other man. "The master of lies! Listen to him!" He turned and thrust his head forward at Amar. "Do you want to know where you slept?" he roared. "You slept at the *Commissariat de Police*. That's where you slept; I can tell you, since you've got such a bad memory." He reached out and yanked Amar roughly to him, felt in his pockets until he had found all his money; then he let go of him, and with the packet of banknotes slapped his cheek smartly. It certainly did not hurt, but as an insult it was unbearable. Without any regard for the possible consequences Amar drew back and delivered a good blow with his fist to Moulay Ali's prominent chin. Lahcen was on his feet; the pistol was suddenly waving in front of Amar's face, and at that moment Moulay Ali dealt him a blow which sent him to the floor. Now he sprawled there, leaning obliquely against the hassock where he had been sitting, and rubbing his face automatically, but watching Lahcen.

Moulay Ali counted the money, threw it on the table. The handkerchief with Amar's own money in it he still held in his hand, winging it around and around.

"Nine thousand francs! I didn't know I was worth so much to them," he said with quiet sarcasm and a faint air of surprise.

Amar was beside himself. To be innocent and to be treated as though he were guilty, that was something he could not accept. This man was not his father; he owed him nothing. Lahcen could shoot if he wanted. It did not matter. "You mean you didn't know *I* was worth so much to them!" he cried.

Lahcen growled menacingly, but Moulay Ali pushed him back toward the door. "Sit down," he said. "I can manage this *ouild*. He's very interesting. I've never seen an animal quite like him." He began to walk back and forth, a few steps one way and a few the other.

"I've seen a lot of *chkama* in my life, practically nothing but *chkama*. Most of the *drari* like you end up by turning informer; that's not unusual," he added with a short laugh. "But I admit I've never yet seen one anything like you."

"Then look carefully," Amar retorted, nearly weeping with emotion (what emotion he did not know); "because you'll never see another. A man like you who's used to blacksmiths doesn't meet spice-sellers. May Allah give you some brains. I swear I'm sorry for you."

Moulay Ali snorted, turned to Lahcen. "But listen to him!" he shouted, astounded. "Have you ever heard anything like that?" To Amar he said: "I think I can manage with the brains I have, without Allah's further help."

These last words were sheer blasphemy. Amar looked at Moulay Ali, turned his head away and spat ferociously. Then he turned back and spoke in a low, intense voice. "I came here happy in my head to see you, even though I know you're not a Moslem." Moulay Ali opened his mouth, closed it again. "I did have respect for you, much respect, because I thought you had a head and were working for the Moslems. But whatever you make for us will be a spiderweb, an *ankabutz*, and may God who forgives all hear my words, because it's the truth." He sobbed, and having done it that once, buried his face in the hassock and continued.

At one point Moulay Ali had ceased pacing the floor, to stand merely looking at Amar in fascination; now he resumed walking back and forth, perplexedly rubbing his chin. The sunset was over; the light in the room was swiftly fading. "Tell Mahmoud to bring a lamp," he said to Lahcen, who rose and handed him the revolver before he went out. Moulay Ali laid it quietly on the table beside the typewriter and stood watching Amar. He picked up the money and flicked it several times with his fingernails. Then, apparently having made a decision, he crossed to where Amar was, knelt, and touched his shoulder. Amar lifted his head, but turned away miserably and remained silent.

"When you feel like talking," Moulay Ali told him gently, "tell me the whole story."

Amar sighed deeply and shook his head. "What good will it do?" he murmured.

"That's for me to decide when I hear it," said Moulay Ali somewhat less gently. "I want to hear everything, everything you've done since you left my house."

Still sighing, Amar picked himself off the floor and sat again

on the hassock. He described his trip back to the Ville Nouvelle, the storm, the bus ride, the fair, the sailor doll, and all the
other details of that evening. Once or twice he heard Moulay
Ali chuckle; this gave him a little incentive to continue. The part
about his meeting with the two tourists seemed to interest his
listener considerably; he asked a good many questions about
them, but finally let the story get on to hearing Benani's voice
behind him in the street when he was walking with the tourists
and the police. At this point the door opened, and Mahmoud
came in carrying a large oil lamp which he set on the table. He
was about to go out again, but Moulay Ali stopped him.

The light of the lamp shone into Amar's face. "I think you
want something to eat," said Moulay Ali, looking at him carefully. To Amar it seemed a long time ago that hunger, and even
thirst, had existed in the world. And so if he said yes, it was only
out of politeness toward his host.

Mahmoud shut the door behind him. "Go on," prompted
Moulay Ali. "Did you know Benani thought you had been arrested, or didn't you?"

"Yes, I knew it," Amar answered, and he went on with his recital, too tired to choose between relevant and extraneous detail
and thus including everything that came into his head—the carv-
ing on the beams in the tourist's room, the lady's loquaciousness,
the mechanism of the flush toilet, the fat French waiter who,
once the tourist was out of the room, would keep bringing him
more food every two minutes and pinch his cheek while he ate it,
how he had manged to persuade Mohammed Lalami to go with
him to Sidi Bou Chta by telling him the Nazarene lady was eager
for love and had slept with him the night before, and how Mohammed, once he was alone with her, had been so nervous that
he had said all the wrong things. "And then we watched the
Aïssaoua and the Haddaoua and the Jilala and the Hamacha
and the Derqaoua and the Guennaoua and all that filth, because
the Nazarene liked to see the dancing." He made a wry face at
the memory. "It makes you sick to your stomach to look at it, all
those people jumping up and down like monkeys."

"Yes," agreed Moulay Ali. "And then?"

"Then I heard what they were all saying about the partisans in the Medina, and I wanted to go home."

"So you came to me instead. Why? Did you think I could get you into the Medina?"

Amar admitted he had thought that, and Moulay Ali laughed, amused and a little flattered by his ingenuousness. "My friend," he told him, "if I could get you into the Medina I could make every Frenchman leave Morocco tomorrow morning. Go on."

But Amar seemed not to hear. The full import of what the other had said was only now reaching him; he looked into Moulay Ali's face desperately. It was useless to say: "My sister, my mother." There were thousands of sisters and mothers. But he said it anyway. Moulay Ali smiled sadly.

The tray that Mahmoud brought had bread and soup on it. "Bismil'lah," murmured Amar, and he began to chew a piece of bread mechanically. Moulay Ali, his bowl of soup tilted in front of his face, observed him carefully over its rim, saw hunger slowly fill the boy's consciousness as he tasted food. He said nothing until Mahmoud had returned with a second tray, this time with a large earthenware *tajine* of lamb, eggplant and noodles.

"Perhaps I can help you," he said finally. "I have a few contacts at different spots. I might be able to get news from your house."

Amar stared. The idea of finding out about his family without going home himself had not occurred to him.

"Would you like that?" said Moulay Ali. Amar did not answer. What good was hearing about his family if he could not be there to see them with his own eyes? And how could he believe whatever news came to him, good or bad? But he saw that Moulay Ali was doing his best, was trying to be helpful, and so he said: "I'd be very happy, Sidi."

"I'll see what I can do. Now tell me the rest."

There was not very much more to tell, said Amar. Mohammed and the lady had been talking in French about the fighting in the Medina. He had been too unhappy to listen to what they were saying. The lady had waited until Mohammed had stepped outside, and then she had called Amar over to her, opened her pocketbook and, making sure that no one was looking, put the folded bills into his hand. When he described the gestures she made to indicate an imaginary gun, Moulay Ali interrupted, exclaiming delightedly: "Ah, a woman with a head!" And when he came to the episode of the buses and the carrying off to jail of all the mountain men, Moulay Ali, looking very grim, said: "Good! Good! The more the better." Amar was startled, because he had expected quite the opposite reaction from him. Perhaps his mystification showed in his face, for a moment later Moulay Ali elaborated. "When they get back to the mountains not one of them will be able to hear the word *France* without feeling his heart ready to burst with hatred." Amar thought a bit. "That's true," he agreed. "But some of them were killed."

"They died for freedom," said Moulay Ali shortly. "Remember that."

They did not speak for a moment. Through the open windows, along with the constantly increasing night wind, came the sound of a dog howling, from some distance away. Amar looked up, and saw in the shining glass panes distorted reflections of their movements against the blackness beyond. Mahmoud had brought a big bowl of sliced oranges prepared with strips of cinnamon bark and rose water. When they had finished Moulay Ali sat back, wiped his face with his napkin, and said: "Yes. They died for freedom. And that's why I'm not going to ask your pardon for being rough with you. It would be an insult to them. I was suspicious, and I was wrong, but I wasn't wrong to be suspicious. Do you understand? At first I thought: No, he couldn't have gone to the French, because if he had, he certainly wouldn't come back here."

"Ah, you see?" Amar said, pleased.

"But then I thought: Wait. They've used him as a guide, and sent him in alone, and they're outside waiting."

"Oh!" said Amar. He was thinking that now if by some terrible misfortune the French did manage to find Moulay Ali, he would be certain to suspect that Amar had had something to do with it; he decided to let Moulay Ali know what was in his mind.

"No, no, no," replied Moulay Ali consolingly. "They'd have been in the house long before this if they'd come with you. The day a Frenchman learns patience the camels will pray in the Karouine."

These reassuring words set off a whole series of mechanisms inside Amar which resulted almost immediately in an overpowering desire to close his eyes; he could feel his head being turned to stone, and his body being rapidly immured in the paralysis of sleep. Moulay Ali was talking, but he heard only the sound of his voice.

"Come, come," the voice said sharply. "You can't just fall asleep like that."

Moulay Ali had risen, and was standing above him. "Get up, and come with me," he said. With a flashlight in one hand he led him down the stairs through the hot little room, to the back gallery, where a man lying on a mat in front of the door grunted and sat up as Moulay Ali stepped over him, saying softly: "*Yah, Aziz.*" They picked their way along the uneven floor.

Another door was opened; the inquisitive beam of the flashlight played briefly around its walls. There was the mattress. "I think that will take you through to morning," said Moulay Ali. "*Incha 'Allah,*" Amar replied. Then he thanked Moulay Ali with what sense and force he had left, and let himself drop onto the mattress. "*'Lah imsik bekhir,*" said Moulay Ali as he closed the door. The crickets were singing outside the window.

CHAPTER   32

There are mornings when, from the first ray of light seized upon by the eye, and the first simple sounds that get inside the head, the heart is convinced that it is existing in rhythm to a kind of unheard music, familiar but forgotten because long ago it was interrupted and only now has suddenly resumed playing. The silent melodies pass through the fabric of the consciousness like the wind through the meshes of a net, without moving it, but at the same time unmistakably there, all around it. For one who has never lived such a morning, its advent can be a paralyzing experience.

Amar awoke, heard the cackling of geese against a soft background of bird song, listened for a moment to the unfamiliar sounds about the house—the closing of a door, words exchanged between servants and the noises they made in their work—and without even bothering to open his eyes, sank into a melancholy but comfortable state of nostalgia for his childhood, that other lifetime finished so long ago at Kherib Jerad. He remembered little events that he had not thought of since the day they had happened, and one big event: the time he had got into a fight with Smaïl, his only friend among the boys of the place, who instead of hitting him had all at once sunk his teeth in the back of Amar's neck and refused to open his jaws until the men had come and beaten him. He still had the marks of those sharp white teeth; if the barber shaved his neck a little too high they were visible. And that night a delegation of the elders of the village had come with lanterns and torches to see his father, to apologize, and, which was much more important to them, to try and exact a word of forgiveness from Amar, for if Amar refused, everything would go badly for them until they brought an offering to the young Cherif who had been wronged by one of their number. And Amar did refuse, being still in a good deal of pain, so that the next day they came again with a beautiful white sheep which they gave his father in order that their crops and homes might be spared the displeasure of Allah. His father had been unhappy about it. "Why wouldn't you forgive Smaïl?" he asked him. "I hate him," Amar had replied heatedly, and there was no more to be said about it.

He remembered the river and the coves between its high clay banks where he had played; and the fine clothes he always had worn on the bus trip to Kherib Jerad, for in those days there had been money, and his mother had spent a great deal of it keeping Amar in capes and trousers and vests and slippers made for him by the best tailors and cobblers in Fez. He remembered, and he listened to the birds singing near by and farther away, and it seemed to him that the sweet sadness he felt would never stop as long as he lived, because it was he; he had ceased being himself by having been cut off from his home. Now he was no one, lying on a mattress nowhere, and there was no reason to do anything more than simply continue to be that no one. Occasionally he slept for a moment, dipping softly downward, so that the horizon of being disappeared; then he came up again. It was like floating on a gentle ocean, following the will of the waves.

At one point, toward mid-morning, the door opened quietly and Moulay Ali looked in at him, on his way to his office in the tower, but it happened to be a moment when he slumbered; Moulay Ali shut the door and left him alone. Again when it was nearly noon he returned, and seeing him still lying there, decided to awaken him. Unceremoniously he shook him by the shoulder and told him it was very late; then he went and called Mahmoud, who came and led him, still more asleep than otherwise, to a room where there was a pail of cold water and a cake of soap. By the time he had washed thoroughly he was wide awake. When he re-emerged onto the gallery Mahmoud was just arriving with a huge copper tray which he set on its legs outside the bathroom door. "Eat here," said Mahmoud. "It's cooler."

While Amar was eating his breakfast Moulay Ali came along the gallery. He looked weary and unhappy. "Good morning. How did you awaken?" he inquired, and without waiting for a reply he walked on toward his office. At the door he turned and said: "I may have news for you later." Then Mahmoud came by to see if Amar had finished; since he had not, he stood looking down at him, watching him eat. "You can't go out of the house, you know," he told him suddenly. This information was not a surprise to Amar, nor did it interest him. There was nothing he wanted to do outside, in any case, no one to see, nowhere to go—

only the olive trees, the hot sunlight and the cicadas shrilling. He was quite content to sit in the house and bask in the listlessness that the day had brought.

Apparently Mahmoud sensed the apathy in which he was submerged, for when he lifted the tray to carry it away he said: "Come," and led him to the big room where he had sat with the boys the other day. Now it was in even greater disorder, with newspapers lying open on the cushions, unemptied ashtrays here and there in the middle of the floor, and in a corner a small table holding a disemboweled radio, its parts spread out in confusion around its empty case. On one couch there were several copies of an Egyptian illustrated review. He sat down and began to thumb through them; in each one there were some pictures of Morocco. French policemen pointed to a long table laden with pistols and daggers, wounded Moslems were helped along a street by their countrymen, a child wandered in the ruins of a bombed-out building, five Moslems lay in the twisted postures of death in a Casablanca street, the traffic going by at only a step from their bodies, while a French soldier delicately indicated them for the photographer with the tip of his boot. It was hard to understand why these publications should be so strictly prohibited, when they had exactly the same photographs in them as the French magazines that were on sale outside the shops of the Ville Nouvelle. But then, was there any way of comprehending the laws made by the French, save to assume that they all had been made with the same express purpose, that of confusing, harassing, insulting and torturing the Moslems? On other pages there were pictures of Egyptian soldiers in smart uniforms driving tanks, inspecting machine guns, demonstrating to students the technique of throwing hand grenades, watching army maneuvers in the desert, and marching through the magnificent streets of Cairo in their khaki shorts. Everyone looked happy and healthy; the women and girls waved from the windows of the apartment houses. He turned back to the pictures of Morocco and studied them, taking a masochistic pleasure in remarking the contrast between the scenes of wreckage and death and the platoons of triumphant young soldiers.

He looked around the room; it seemed to him the very essence of the sadness and remoteness of Morocco. *Maghreb-al-Aqsa,* that was the name of his country—the Farthest West. Exactly, the extremity, the limit of Islam, beyond which there was nothing but the empty sea. Those who lived in Morocco could only look on with wistfulness and envy at the glorious events which were transfiguring the other Moslem nations. Their country was like a vast prison whose inmates had almost relinquished all hope of freedom, and yet Amar's father had known it when it was the richest and most beautiful land in all Islam. And even Amar could remember the pears and peaches that had grown in the orchards outside the walls of Fez near Bab Sidi bou Jida before the French had diverted the flow of water to their own lands and left the trees to wither and perish in the summer heat.

The room smelled strongly of kerosene: someone had been careless in filling the lamps. He got up and wandered about listlessly. Yes, the room was Morocco itself; there was not even any way of seeing out, because the windows were all high above the level of anyone's head. He walked to the door and stood listening to the long sound of the bees, wondering vaguely whether, if a man were to smash their nests and be stung, their poison would be powerful enough to kill him.

Presently Moulay Ali appeared in the doorway coming from the back gallery, and seeing Amar, approached and took him by the arm. "You shouldn't have come here," he told him. "I can't let you go, and you'll get very tired of being shut up here." He led him back into the room and closed the door. "But the world's very bad this day, very bad." From his pocket he took Amar's handkerchief with the money in it, the packet of notes the Nazarene lady had given him, and the little paper of kif he had bought for Mustapha at the Café Berkane. This last he dropped into Amar's hand quickly and with great distaste. "What are you doing with that filth?" he demanded. "I thought you were a *derri* with some sense."

Amar, who had forgotten the existence of the tiny bundle, was horrified to see it lying there in his own hand. "That's not mine," he exclaimed, looking down at it.

"It was in your pocket."

"I mean, it's for my brother. I got it for him."

"If you loved your brother you wouldn't put chains on his legs, would you?"

Amar had no answer. Moulay Ali had just put into clear words what he had only vaguely hoped: that the kif might indeed be a chain to bind Mustapha. If he pretended innocence he would seem abysmally stupid in the eyes of Moulay Ali; if he did not, he would probably think him incredibly wicked. Moulay Ali stood looking at him expectantly.

"We don't get on very well," Amar finally murmured.

But now Moulay Ali's face was rapidly changing. "You mean," he said incredulously, "that he likes kif and you give it to him to ruin his health and weaken his mind, so he'll never be worth anything? Is that it?"

Amar admitted miserably that such had been his intention. Since he had told Moulay Ali the truth about everything else, he might as well tell it here too. "But he's already not worth anything," he added by way of explanation, "and besides I didn't give it to him."

Moulay Ali whistled, a long low sound. "Well, my friend, you're just a young Satan. That's all I can say. Satan a hundred percent. But here's your money. Otherwise I may forget it."

As he was about to go out, he spun around and raised his forefinger threateningly. "And don't buy a gun with it, *smatsi?* Unless you want to spend the rest of your life in Aït Baza." Seeing Amar's forlorn expression, he turned all the way around. "Some friends will probably be coming tonight, if they don't get killed or arrested first, and they'll sing you a song. Do you know the one about Aïcha bent Aïssa?"

"No," said Amar, for whom the prospect of arrivals gave the day a sudden slight glow.

"It's a very important song for you to hear." Moulay Ali went out and shut the door.

Somewhat later an unkempt-looking boy brought in a tray of fruit and bread and honey, grinned at Amar, and went away again. Amar ate without appetite. *"Ed dounia mamzianache,"*

Moulay Ali had said—the world was very bad today. It could scarcely be worse than yesterday, he told himself, yet forebodings of gloom filled his mind, and he was afraid. After he had eaten, he removed all the newspapers and magazines from the most comfortable mattress, and curled up there, staring for a long time at the blue sky through the window opposite, and finally closing his eyes. He stayed there all afternoon, sunk in a melancholy whose only antidote was the occasional memory of Moulay Ali's promise that the evening would bring company and there would be someone to talk to.

And at the end of the afternoon, as the light faded from the squares of sky above, and life ebbed from the airless room, his sadness grew, became a physical pain in his heart and throat, and he felt that nothing could ever mitigate it—not whole days of weeping, and not even death. One day, years ago, when he and his father had been walking in the Zekak al Hajar where the beggars sat chanting, holding up their stumps of arms and displaying their disfigured bodies, his father had said to him: "When a man dies and is buried, he is finished with this world, and his friends give thanks that he has had the good luck to escape. But when a man crawls in the street without friends, without clothes, without a mat to lie on, without a piece of bread, alive but not really alive, dead but not even dead, that is Allah's most terrible punishment this side of the fires of Jehennam. Look, so you will understand why charity is one of the five duties." They had stopped walking and Amar had looked, but really only with fascinated repulsion at a man whose lips had grown out into an enormous purplish pouch as big as his whole head, and he had thought in his childish brain what a strange being Allah must be, to play such odd tricks on people.

Now he remembered what his father had said. This misery was what would soon be happening to him and to everyone else, but there would not be between them even the bond forged by suffering which made the beggars help one another to get through the streets (the ones with twisted legs creeping ahead like sick dogs, leading the blind ones), because each one would hate and fear his fellow, and no one would know which were the spies and which were not, for the simple reason that any one of them, given the appropriate inducement, or subjected to the proper torture, was capable of betraying the others.

For a while the objects in the room remained visible, held together by the lingering light, then the texture of things disintegrated, turned to ash, darkened, and finally dropped into total obscurity. Amar lay still, devoured by self-pity. To be a prisoner in a lonely house in the country was bad enough for anyone used to the Medina and its crowds, but to be left alone in the darkness without even the possibility of making a light, that was really too much. But now he heard footsteps approaching along the gallery, and an instant later someone opened the door. A flashlight played across the mattresses, picking him out where he lay. There was an exclamation of surprise from Moulay Ali. "Are you asleep in there?" he cried. Amar said very clearly that he was not. "But what are you doing in the dark? Where's Mahmoud? Hasn't he brought a lamp?" Amar, for whose wounded ego this solicitousness was balm, replied that he had not seen Mahmoud for several hours—not since his breakfast, to be exact.

"You must forgive him," Moulay Ali said, still standing in the doorway. "He's been very busy today. Everyone in the house has been very busy."

"Of course," said Amar.

It was Moulay Ali's suggestion that they go up to the office and watch for the arrival of the guests, who would be coming by a back lane from the Ras el Ma road. As they went through the dusty little antechamber toward the foot of the stairs he told Amar: "This will be just a small gathering of a few friends. Even in the middle of a war one must laugh." It was the first time Amar had heard the trouble referred to as a war; the word excited him. Perhaps among those who were to arrive there would be men who that very day had killed Frenchmen with their own hands—heroes such as one sees only in the cinema or in magazines.

The shaded lamp on the table had been turned down so that it gave only a dull yellow glow. They sat on the hassocks and talked, Moulay Ali running his eyes unceasingly over that particular region of the blackness outside in which he expected to see lights appear. "It's very bad to be impatient," he remarked at one point, "but tonight I'm more than that. In this work, at times like this, every day is like a year. You know the situation in the morning; by evening it's all different, and you have to learn it all over again. But the one who wins is the one who studies it most."

Amar looked at the well-nourished flesh of Moulay Ali's face. He was talking because he was nervous, that much was evident. It was also clear that he thought of himself as a kind of general in this struggle he called a war, and the men who surrounded him accepted him as such. But a general does not live in a comfortable house attended by servants, nor spend his time sitting at a table typing and reading, Amar reflected; he has the finest horse and sword of all, and he rides at the head of his troops, spurring them on to greater daring and more complete disregard of life. That was what generals were for; they were to set the example. However, instead of giving voice to the things that were on his mind he merely sat quietly, until he heard Moulay Ali give a little grunt of satisfaction. "Aha, at last," he said, sitting up straight and peering out into the night. Amar looked, saw nothing, continued to look, and eventually did see some small lights moving along irregularly, disappearing, re-emerging and gradually coming nearer. "It's not an automobile," he said in surprise. "Of course not," said Moulay Ali. "They're coming on donkeys. It's a very narrow path." He rose to his feet. "Excuse me a moment. They'll be here in a little while. I want to be sure the big room is ready."

In the dim room, sitting alone, Amar felt his doubt grow more intense. Moulay Ali might be a very good man, but he was not a Moslem. He never said either *"Inchâ'Allah"* or *"Bismil'lah,"* and he drank alcohol and almost certainly did not pray, and Amar would not have been at all astonished to hear that on occasion he had eaten pork or neglected to observe Ramadan. How could such a man take it upon himself to lead Moslems in their fight against the injustices of the infidels?

As he was thinking about this, there came to him the un-formulated memory of another personality; it was only a flavor, a suggestion, a shadow, like the premonition of a presence that had been with him and mysteriously still was with him, and a part of his mind compared it to the flavor of Moulay Ali, and found it better. All this taking place in the lightless depths of himself, he was aware only of a troubled feeling whose source he would not attempt to locate. But, as a whiff of smoke can whisper of danger to a man buried in the depths of sleep, this other presence, which he felt only as an unquiet place within him, was murmuring a message of warning—against what, he did not know.

C H A P T E R   33

The dinner had been very good. They sprawled on the mat-tresses around the sides of the big room, talking and laughing. There were ten of them, including Lahcen, who had arrived late, having come by the main road on a bicycle. At the begin-ning of the meal, when one of the guests, a student from the Medersa Bou Anania, had tried to bring politics into the con-versation, Moulay Ali had turned to him and announced loudly that he for one wanted to forget work and trouble for a while, and that he thought it would be a good idea to shelve the issues of the day while they ate. Everyone had approved vehemently; as a result the student had adopted a sour expression and refused to say a word to anyone during the remainder of the meal. Several bottles of wine had already been emptied, and more were on the way.

"That lamp," said Moulay Ali suddenly to Amar, who sat

next to him. "Turn it down. It's smoking." Ever since the arrival
of the guests he had been using Amar as a sort of orderly, a position which Amar was not at all loath to occupy, since it implied
a certain intimacy between them. And then, he had noticed that
it annoyed Lahcen, which gave him great pleasure, for he had no
friendly feeling left for him, after all the gun-waving the big
man had done in his face last night. Lahcen kept glowering in his
direction, making it obvious that he disapproved of the whole
game. Having heard Amar's denunciation of his idol, he had
decided once and for all that the boy was an enemy, and that it
was very unwise of Moulay Ali to keep him in the house; in his
uncomplicated mind there were no mitigating circumstances for
behavior such as Amar's.

Occasionally, as if they all had decided beforehand at what
instant it should be, there would come a silence, a gap in the
sound of talking through which the hostile night around them
was clearly perceptible, and they heard only the deceptively reassuring music of the crickets outside. Then swiftly, a little reck-
lessly, someone would begin to talk, about anything at all—it
did not seem to matter—and his words would be welcomed with
an enthusiasm completely disproportionate to the interest they
had evoked.

Mahmoud now brought a tray of bottles, most of which contained beer. But there was also the same decanter of green chartreuse from which Amar had been served the other day. Moulay
Ali tried to give him a bottle of beer. When he refused it, he
offered to pour him a little of the liqueur. Amar wanted to
say: "I'm a Moslem," but all he said was: "I don't drink." "But
you drank some of this the other afternoon," said Moulay Ali,
looking at him in astonishment. "That was a mistake," Amar
told him.

When everyone had been served, Moulay Ali leaned toward
him and said in a low voice: "The news I promised to try and
get for you is good." Amar's heart leapt. "Don't talk about
this," he went on. "I don't want all the others to hear. You have
an older sister?" Without letting Amar reply, he continued.
"Your mother and young sister went to Meknès three days ago

to stay with her and her husband. That's all I know." Raising his voice, he called across to a thin little man with glasses and a tiny moustache: "*Eh! Monsieur le docteur!*" (Amar stared at him in horror at the sound of the hated language.) "Come and sit here and tell me a few things." To Amar he said: "You don't mind moving down that way." Amar walked to the other end of the room and sat on a fat cushion by himself, facing the whole assemblage. The two young men nearest him, seated at the end of the mattress, sipped beer and discussed the party newspaper.

Presently one of them shouted to Moulay Ali: "Felicitations, master! I hear your bubonic plague story made the placards in the students' manifestation in Rabat yesterday. 'Moroccans in the Concentration Camps Aren't Dying Fast Enough to Suit the French. What's the Remedy? Introduce Bubonic Plague into the Camps, and Make Room for More Prisoners.' That was what they said. It made a number one scandal."

Moulay Ali smiled. "I should hope it would," he said.

Amar paid no attention to the talk, which seemed to grow louder as it progressed. He was occupied in giving repeated thanks to Allah for having saved Halima and his mother. As he began to listen once more to the words being said around him, he realized that this time Moulay Ali must have told his friends that it was safe to speak in front of him, for they were making no attempt to veil the meaning of anything they said. He could afford to feel delight over this, now that the worst tension was eased. Three days ago, Moulay Ali had said. That was the day he had gone to the Café Berkane and met the two Nazarenes, the very day he had walked out of his house to take a stroll, and his mother had said: "I'm afraid." They would have had to leave the house very shortly after he had, to have got out of the Medina before the shooting had closed it entirely. What could have decided his father to get them out so suddenly? Perhaps Allah had simply sent him a message.

"No chance of negotiation," said the doctor. "They can send a new Résident from Paris every morning if they like. It won't get them anywhere. It would still have been possible last week.

Even yesterday, perhaps. Now, never." He seemed to be speaking to the room at large; everyone was listening. "It was a master stroke to get them all in there at once."

"But will the people really take it as hard as we imagine?" This was said rapidly in a high voice by a young man in a blue business suit. "Is the *horm* really so important to them? That's very necessary to know."

"*Sksé huwa*," said Moulay Ali shortly, pointing at Amar. "There's your people. Ask him."

Everyone but Lahcen turned and looked at Amar eagerly, with a strange expression almost of greed, he thought, as if he were a new kind of food which they were about to try for the first time. Moulay Ali merely smiled like a contented cat, while the doctor said to Amar: "Do you know what happened today in the Medina?"

"No, *sidi*," Amar replied, new dread being born within him.

"The French swore they would put all the *ulema* of the Karouine in prison."

"They couldn't do that," said Amar. "The *ulema* are holy."

"Ah, but they could if they wanted! But the *ulema* went and took sanctuary in the *horm* of Moulay Idriss."

In spite of himself Amar was relieved. "*Hamdoul'lah*," he said with feeling. The others watched, fascinated.

The doctor then leaned forward a little as he said: "But the French broke into the *horm* and beat them and pulled every one of them out. By now they're all in Rabat."

Amar's eyes had grown huge. "*Kifach!*" he cried. No one spoke. "But what's going to happen? Haven't we begun yet to burn the Ville Nouvelle?"

"Not yet," said Moulay Ali. "We will."

"But we mustn't wait!"

"Remember that the only people who can move around at all are the ones who live in Fez-Djedid. Everyone else is locked into his house. Don't forget that." Now he turned back to the doctor. "Brahim's suggestion would be sound if it weren't unrealistic at the very beginning. A thing like that takes time." They talked, but Amar retired once more into himself, with a

faint feeling of having been tricked. Not that he did not believe what the doctor had told him, but he resented the way in
which they all had wanted to see how he took the tragic news;
it was as if they themselves did not really care at all what had
happened, as if they were outsiders in the whole affair.

"*B'sif*," a man with a black beard was saying. "The sooner
you begin, the better. And you have to keep at it. Over and
over. America sends France two hundred billion francs. America gives France a hundred billion more. France would like to
leave Morocco, but America insists on her staying, because of
the bases. Without America there would be no France. And so
on. *Sahel, sahel.* All we need is one good attack on each American base. That shouldn't be so hard to work up. Do you think
so, Ahmed?" The man turned to the student who had sulked at
dinner.

"I think it would be easy, at least among the students." He
was more out of sorts with Moulay Ali than with the others.

"Even with the faces of the French dogs in front of them
everywhere, and the Americans hidden?" said Moulay Ali with
delicate scorn. "*Soyez réaliste, monsieur.*"

"We're not all *djebala*, straight from the mountains," the
student retorted haughtily.

"And once we've had a few incidents directly involving American lives and property, maybe the Americans will know there's
such a country as Morocco in the world," went on Brahim of
the black beard. "Now they don't know the difference between
Morocco and the Sénégal. You can all sit there and say it's unrealistic. But I'll wager you that within a year it'll be an official
directive. The target will be shifted from the French to the
Americans." No one said anything; apparently they had been
impressed into silence. The crickets sang: "Ree, ree, ree, ree."

"Even if it's only for propaganda purposes," continued
Brahim, encouraged by their stillness and by the wine he
had drunk, "it would be useful. But it's also true, which makes
it much more powerful as propaganda."

"The value of propaganda has no relationship to the degree
of its truth," intoned the man in the blue business suit, pouring

himself another glass of beer. "Only with its credibility to the section of the people at which it is aimed."

Moulay Ali looked surreptitiously at the doctor and raised his eyebrows; the doctor winked. Brahim, not to be discouraged, paid no attention. "It's the truth that America furnishes France with money, and that some of that money is spent for arms which are used against us. That may not make propaganda—I don't know. But it's the truth."

Amar listened; this was something new. He had not known of the Americans' secret villainy. But then, of course, there were a great many things that he was hearing for the first time. This word propaganda that they all kept using—he had never heard that before, but obviously it was a very important thing. The story of the evil Americans fascinated him; he longed to see one, to know what they looked like, what color their skin was, what language they spoke, but everyone else in the room knew the answers to those questions, and so he could not ask them. Now there seemed to be three separate conversations going on at once among the guests; some of them were shouting in their excitement. The room had grown smaller with their obstreperousness. A fat man had pushed the doctor out of the way and sat beside Moulay Ali, reading him a newspaper clipping. Moulay Ali leaned back, his eyes closed, now and then opening them to take a puff on his cigarette, and watching the smoke curl upward for a moment before he closed them again. Only he, of all of them, appeared able to maintain a wholly calm exterior. But even he, Amar thought with sadness, was not a Moslem and thus could not be relied upon to lead the people. A half-emptied glass of beer lay at his feet, and soon he would bend forward to pick it up.

Gradually Amar fell into a contemplative state, just sitting and watching the men slowly become drunk. No one paid him any attention. Their voices grew louder constantly, and they had ceased to stop and listen to the crickets outside, even for an instant. There was no silence any more in their world. Each one talked to impress the others with his intelligence and erudition. Even Lahcen was arguing with a thin, bald young man who obviously had no desire to be talking to him, and kept trying to get into the conversation which was going on opposite him. These men had no understanding of, no love for, either Allah or the people they pretended to be helping. Whatever they might manage to build would be blown away very quickly. Allah would see to that, because it would have been built without His guidance.

He sat there alone, looking at them, and it was as if he were far away on the top of a mountain, seeing them from a great distance. Sins are finished, the potter had told him. That was what people believed now, and so there was nothing but sin. For if men dared take it upon themselves to decide what was sin and what was not, a thing which only Allah had the wisdom to do, then they committed the most terrible sin of all, the ultimate one, that of attempting to replace Him. He saw it very clearly, and he knew why he felt that they were all damned beyond hope of redemption.

Suddenly Moulay Ali had brought out an *oud* from behind the cushions stacked in the corner near him, and was tossing it across to the doctor, who removed his glasses and began to tune it. For a while he plucked at the strings tentatively, perhaps not wanting to start a song until the conversation had worn itself down a bit. This did not happen; almost everyone continued to talk. Finally Moulay Ali clapped his hands impatiently for silence, and little by little the words stopped flowing.

"Aïcha bent Aïssa," said Moulay Ali. "Now, listen to this, Amar. Listen carefully. This is for you. He wants to do big things," he confided jovially to the others. "I promised him this song."

It was not true, Amar thought. He wanted nothing. Not to do big things for the Party, not to hear music, not to speak to anyone. He felt absolutely alone in the room, alone in this alien world of Moslems who were not Moslems, but he would sit and listen, for the song had begun. It had a simple tune and simple words, and, he thought at first, a simple story about a woman whose son was sixteen years old and belonged to the Party. When his number came up, and it was his turn to go out and commit the murder assigned to him, and they came and knocked at the door of his house, the mother told the men to come into the house for a moment. They went in, and she said: "Where is the gun?" and they handed it to her. Then she shot her son. But with the advent of this brutal and unexpected act, the song passed beyond his comprehension. He still listened, but the song, having shocked him, had ceased thereby to make sense. Then, sang the doctor, she handed back the gun to them, saying: "Get a man for your work—not a boy." That was all there was to it.

"She really exists, you know," murmured the student. "She lives in Casablanca, and the story is perfectly true." Lahcen, greatly touched, sniffed and rubbed his eyes with his sleeve. "He'll cry at a song," thought Amar disdainfully, "but if he saw the woman shoot the boy, he'd just stand there like a stone."

"Well, what about it?" cried Moulay Ali to Amar. "What do you think of it?"

Amar was silent, not knowing what was expected of him. Still Moulay Ali waited; in the end Amar said exactly what he was thinking. "I don't understand why she killed her son."

Moulay Ali was triumphant. "I didn't think you would. That's why I wanted you to hear it. She shot him because she knew he wasn't ready, and the Party was more dear to her heart than her own son." Amar looked confused. "She saw that when the French caught him he wouldn't die like a man, his lips closed tight, but like a boy, crying and telling them whatever they wanted to know. That's why she shot him, my friend."

Now Amar understood, but still he did not feel the truth of it, or even believe it, for that matter. "And you say there really was such a woman?"

Everyone began to speak of friends who claimed to know the legendary Aïcha bent Aïssa. Some declared she lived in Fedala, the doctor insisted she ran a *bacal* in the quarter of Aïn Bouzia, and the bald young man seemed to think she had been made one of the leaders of the Party and sent, he believed, to Boujad or Settat or some such place. In any case, they all adhered firmly to the theory of her flesh-and-blood existence. All, save perhaps Moulay Ali, who merely said: "The Party used to have a lot of young boys in it. They won't take them any more, except very special ones, and the new policy's largely due to that song."

This time Mahmoud brought a tray of smaller glasses and two freshly opened bottles of cognac. His arrival was greeted by a certain amount of discreet applause by several of the guests; this in itself was proof to Amar, if any were needed, that they were no longer completely sober. The doctor sang several more songs, from which the attention of the others gradually strayed, so that in the end he was singing and strumming for his own pleasure. Amar sat for a long time watching them, not taking any part in their jokes and arguments, and feeling more and more solitary and miserable. At one point Moulay Ali called over to him, saying: "*Zduq*, Amar, it looks as though you'd be staying on awhile here with me."

Amar smiled feebly, hoping the other would not suspect what was passing through his mind as a result of that remark: a conscious determination to escape, in one way or another. Even the open fields, he thought, would be preferable to being shut into this house. He had money in his pocket now, and although he did not know his sister's address in Meknès, he was certain that he could find her house somehow. He put his hand into his pocket and felt the money there; the notes between his fingers excited him. He would buy a pair of real shoes, and some new trousers. For the first time, he thought of the money in terms of its buying power. But where would he buy the shoes? Perhaps in Meknès, *incha'Allah*. He was very sleepy; his eyes could scarcely stay open. Being near the door, he waited until the next time Mahmoud entered with more bottles and more glasses, and slipped out behind him just as he made his entrance. The gallery was dark, but the moon overhead shone down into the courtyard. Until he got to the back gallery he could hear the raucous laughter and the high thin notes of the *oud*, but once he was there the silence was complete, save for the countless little songs of the crickets. He felt his way cautiously to the door of

390 THE SPIDER'S HOUSE

the room where he had slept the night before, went in, and said a lengthy prayer because of the darkness. Then he lay down and instantly fell asleep.

He had been traveling great distances, and he did not want to come back, but a light shone in his face. He opened his eyes. A monster stood over him. He sprang up, crying out: "Ah!" but lost his balance and fell back down onto the mattress, and as he fell he knew it was only Moulay Ali standing there with a lantern. But the light shining from beneath made his face look like the face of a fat white devil, and his eyes were two round black holes. Amar laughed apologetically, and said: "*Khalatini!* You frightened me!"

Moulay Ali paid no attention, but held the lantern up higher, and whispered: "Come." The urgency with which he had uttered the one word did not strike Amar until he was already on his feet; then the relief he had felt after his initial fright began to give way to a new uneasiness, more rational but also very disturbing. "He's drunk," he told himself, as they went along the gallery, their shadows mingling on the ruined wall. Then he heard the voices of the others, and they all sounded like madmen. Some were whispering, some were laughing senselessly, in that their laughter had the sound but not the meaning of laughter, and some were talking, but about nothing at all. "Yes, very nice." "I thought that if she said it was like that we would go." "And do you like cigarettes?" "Oh, I, yes, I smoke. I like to smoke." "It would be better up there, if you knew what you have to know." "We came back, and, and, it was very hot." The intonations and rhythms were somehow wrong, too, and he had the impression that if the men had been asked what they had said, not one of them could have told, because the words had been merely the first words to come into their heads. Then someone—the doctor, he supposed—began to play on the *oud*, and these slight sounds, making a recognizable melody, mysteriously succeeded in giving the scene he had been listening to a semblance of sanity.

When they had reached the doorway to the large room, Amar saw that the guests were all standing. "My friends were about to go," explained Moulay Ali. (Where to, at this time of night, on the backs of donkeys? Amar wondered, but only in passing.) "And then I mentioned that you played the flute, and they all want to hear you."

"Oh!" Amar exclaimed, very much taken aback.

"Just one piece," urged Moulay Ali in a voice of velvet, pinching his arm. Amar stared at him: he seemed very odd indeed, and his eyes, even in this light, still looked like enormous black holes. He gazed around at the others in the room; they too had something extremely strange about them. Again he wondered if it could be the effect of alcohol, or hashish, perhaps, but he had seen plenty of men under the influence of one or the other, and their behavior had been completely different. The idea passed through his mind that Moulay Ali had not really come at all and wakened him. In that case he was still lying there in the comfortable dark of the little room; it was one of those dreams where all things—the people, the houses and trees, the sky and the earth—are doomed at the outset to be merged in one gigantic vortex of destruction. Doomed from the start, but unless the dreamer is on the lookout he may not realize what is going to happen, because it is a maelstrom which begins to move only after a long while, declaring its presence in its own good time. In the end, very likely, everything would begin going around, one thing becoming another, and they would all be sucked down into emptiness, silently screaming, and clawing at one another with gestures of the most exquisite delicacy. In the meantime he had to pretend to be Amar being awake.

"I have no *lirah*," he said, certain that Moulay Ali would produce one that very instant, which he did, taking it up from a hassock behind him.

"But I play very badly. Only a little," he protested. Moulay Ali stroked his arm eagerly. "*Baraka'llahoufik. Baraka'llahoufik*," he murmured. Was it really Moulay Ali, and was any one of these men the person he had been before? Or was it Amar who had changed while he slept, that now everything should be so different?

"*I'll* play a piece," said Moulay Ali. He lifted the little reed flute to his mouth. Straightway everyone was utterly silent; the words that had no meaning, the strained and vacant laughter, the frantic whispered monosyllables, which of all the sounds they had been making seemed the only valid ones, all were suspended in a flash, and only the small windy voice of the flute remained to take their place. Moulay Ali executed a few warming-up phrases, and then, walking alone out onto the gallery, began to play, without any particular virtuosity, a slightly altered version of a song called *Tanja Alia.* Amar watched the guests: they looked straight in front of them, as if they were not listening, but were imagining how they would look if they were really listening. "*Yah latif!*" he thought. "They're all bewitched." That was what was wrong with them; at least, it seemed a more reasonable hypothesis to Amar at this moment than any other he could invent. A moment before, they had been turning around and bumping into each other. Now they all stood completely still, close together, intent on the music that managed, weak as it was, to fill the emptiness of the night. When Moulay Ali had stopped, even before he reappeared in the doorway, they began to move around again distractedly, staying close together, as if no one of them could bear to think of being at more than an arm's length from at least two others.

"Here," said Moulay Ali, handing him the flute. "Now you've got to play. Come." He led him over to the cushions where they had sat together at dinner. "Now, make yourself comfortable, and show me how *you* play *Tanja Alia.*"

The more quickly he complied, thought Amar, the sooner he could go back to bed. He lay back on the cushions, put one leg up over the other, and began to play. After a few phrases, Moulay Ali smiled tautly, said: "Good. Beautiful," and walked back to the other end of the room. The guests had gone out the door onto the gallery. "Listen from there," he heard Moulay Ali murmur to them, while he breathed to start a new phrase. And a moment later he heard him whisper something else, something very curious indeed, that is, if he had not been mistaken. What he thought he had heard, behind and between the reedy sounds the flute made around his head, were the words: "It's Chemsi; don't forget. I know his walk. Don't forget."

Each time he opened his eyes he was aware of Moulay Ali's form standing over there beside the door, listening. It pleased him that he should want to hear him play, although he would rather have played for him alone than with all the others listening, too.

Chemsi. Who was Chemsi? Amar thought, as he brought to earth a long, slowly descending cadence that fluttered, quivered, tried to rise, and finally settled and lay still. Chemsi, of course, was the boy to whom Moulay Ali had handed all the newspaper clippings that first lost afternoon so long ago. But he was not interested in Chemsi, or in whether or not he had truly heard his name pronounced a few minutes back; he was bent on fashioning the most beautifully formed phrases of notes he could devise. Sometimes Allah helped him; sometimes He did not. Tonight he felt that there was a possibility of such help. When he himself became the music, so that he was no longer there, save as a single, advancing point on the long thread that the music spun as it moved across eternity, that was the moment when the music became a bridge from his heart to other people's hearts, and when he returned to himself he knew that Allah had lifted him up out of the world for an instant and that for that short space of time he had had the *h'dia*, the gift.

He played until he was alone in distant places. Allah did not help him, but it did not matter. The loneliness that was in his heart, the longing for someone who could understand him if he spoke, these came out in the fragile strings of sound he made with his breath and his fingers. Thinking of nothing, he played on, and slowly the person for whom he played ceased being the figure by the door, became that other presence he had become aware of back in the tower early in the evening, someone whose existence in the world meant the possibility of hope. He stopped for an instant, and in his head, indissolubly a part of that happiness liberated by the idea of the other being, he heard a second music—like singing coming from a far-off sunlit shore, infinitely

lovely and inexpressibly tender, a filament of song so tenuous
that it might be only the mind remembering a music it had
never heard save in dreams. He lay still, hearing it, unable to
draw the breath that would destroy it, perhaps forever. It was
not from Allah, it was here, and yet he had not known that this
world had anything so precious to offer. And when he finally had
to breathe, and the other music ceased, as he had known it
would, as naturally as if he had been thinking of him all the
time, he saw in his mind the Nazarene man, a puzzling smile on
his lips, the way he had looked in the hotel room the first evening.

At any moment Moulay Ali would say: "Go on," or "Thank
you," and Amar wanted to think of the Nazarene. He had been
a friend; perhaps with time they could even have understood one
another's hearts. And Amar had left him, sneaked away from
Sidi Bou Chta without even saying good-bye. He opened his
eyes and glanced toward the end of the room. The dark form
was still there, unmoving. He sat up suddenly and looked at it. It
was a jacket hanging on a nail in the shadows beyond the door.

CHAPTER   34

The *lirah* rolled down between two cushions where he had
dropped it. Almost as soon as he was off the mattress, he was at
the door, looking up and down the empty gallery. He knew
exactly what had hapened, and he went over it all in his mind
as he ran, checking each point. And he knew what would come
next, unless he was unbelievably lucky. It was to look for that
luck that he raced now to the stuffy little antechamber and up
the moonlit stairs to the tower room, deserted save for the night

wind that came through the open windows. There was only one side of the tower that interested him, and that was the side with the view of the roof; fortunately one of the windows on that side was ajar, so he would not have to run the risk of making a noise in pushing it open. He looked down, judged the distance to the top of the gable, a difficult calculation to make in the moonlight, for it seemed further as he sat on the window sill gauging it than it proved to be an instant later when he landed on it. He had thrust his sandals into his pocket, and his bare feet made almost no sound as he hit.

There was no place to hide on the roof where he could not be picked out by a flashlight either from below or from the tower; that he ascertained very quickly. What he wanted to know, however, was whether the tower itself, which he had never seen from the outside, had a flat roof or a dome, and now he saw, and gave thanks, for it was flat. The problem for the moment was to lift himself back up to the window sill and from there to the very top, managing on the way to close the window so as to put them off the scent as much as possible. They were looking first of all, of course, for Moulay Ali, a plump, unathletic middle-aged man, and it would not be reasonable to expect him to have climbed out the window and swung himself up to the top of the tower. In fact, Amar thought, as he worked at the feat, he did not know any boys of his age who could do it, either. The last part had to be done with faith that the tiny concrete cornice to which his fingers clung up there above his head would not detach itself as he hung his entire weight upon it. On his way up he had shut the window without being really able to shut it, since the only handle was on the inside. But if a strong gust of wind did not suddenly blow in through the tower from the west, it would stay as it was.

When he got to the top, he crawled on his belly to the center, flopped over onto his back, and lay looking up at the round moon almost directly above him. If he remained lying flat like this they could not catch him in any conceivable beam of light thrown from below. He wondered how many police there were down there with Chemsi, how much money they had given him, and whether Chemsi, as he stood hiding among the bushes with the French, and listening to the music of the flute, had been aware of any difference in the sound when Moulay Ali had ceased to play and Amar had begun. Very likely not, or there would have been a concerted attack on the house then and there; the police would have realized that this was the moment when Moulay Ali was getting away. He could very well imagine Chemsi standing out there, terrified, some petty grievance against Moulay Ali in his throat, so that all the friendship he had felt for him only a few days ago counted as nothing, whispering to the Frenchmen: "That's Moulay Ali playing now! He always plays that piece when he's drunk." And the extra few minutes that Moulay Ali had thus induced the French to take in making their preparations, those precious minutes that had saved him (for still there had been no sound, and a silent capture was inconceivable) had been supplied by Amar as he lay there like a donkey, making music which he hoped Moulay Ali might admire. He smiled, twisting his head around, trying to see the rabbit in the moon, wondering why he felt no hatred for Moulay Ali for having tricked him—only admiration for the psychological accuracy with which the idea had been conceived and executed, and extemporaneously, too. There was true Fassi cleverness. And then, he felt a little sorry for Moulay Ali, because he would surely be caught sooner or later, and that was not a pleasant thing to look forward to. Even if the present trouble died down, the French would never rest until they had brought him to earth. The idea of being hunted day and night, of never having a really peaceful moment, struck him as particularly terrible. And Chemsi! He would not want to be Chemsi for everything in the world. "Don't forget!" Moulay Ali had said as he went out, in case some were caught and some were not, in the flight they were about to make. Whoever was left free or could get a message to the outside would see to it that Chemsi was taken care of. For the Istiqlal was efficient above all at exterminating its own renegades. And they would find him eventually; he did not doubt that for a minute. The French would offer him only a token protection; they were at least sufficiently human to have only contempt for informers, even if it was merely because informers were so plentiful (and besides that, it was much more expedient to let the old ones be got out of the way and take on new ones whose identity was not yet suspected). It was not likely that Chemsi would live to see the Feast of Mouloud.

The moon was so bright that the stars were invisible. The warm wind carried the faint odor of summer flowers that open at night. Apart from the crickets, were there any other sounds to be heard? He thought so: vague stirrings below, on the other side of the house. Soon he was certain; a slight rasping noise came up, and then, unmistakably, a voice. A moment later, many voices: they had got into the house. He smiled, amused by the mental image he had of the rage that would be on the Frenchmen's faces when they discovered their quarry gone. They would run about like furious ants, along the galleries and into the rooms, up and down the stairs, shouting orders and curses, ripping open the mattresses and cushions, and smashing the tables—but carefully collecting all the papers. Not that it would do them any good, he thought; Moulay Ali was not the man to be careless with anything which could be compromising to members of the Party. If I'd been in the Party, he said to himself wistfully, he'd never have done this to me.

They were calling to each other in their harsh, hateful language, banging doors, stamping up and down. Now they had found Mahmoud and the other servants, and were bellowing at them in what they supposed was Arabic. "Which door did he go out?" roared one, and a second later, mimicking the inaudible reply: " 'I don't know, monsieur!' Maybe you'll know in the commissariat." He lay completely still, listening to each sound, wondering how far away Moulay Ali and the others had got by now. He hoped neither for their escape nor for their capture. It could not make much difference to Morocco one way or the other, nor could it be important how many other Moulay Alis there were and whether they failed or succeeded. By having lived with Christians they had been corrupted. They were no longer Moslems; how could it matter what they did, since they did it not for Allah but for themselves? The government and the laws they might make would be nothing but a spiderweb, built to last one night. His father had told him that the world of *politique* was a world of lies, and he in his ignorance and stubbornness, pretending to agree, privately had gone straight ahead believing that the old man, like all old men, was out of touch with everyday truths. Thinking of his father made him want to cry; he clenched his fists and hardened all the muscles of his face.

The sounds of shouting and banging had come very near. He heard the men climbing the stairs to the tower; he could even catch their little exclamations of satisfaction. Suddenly convinced that now they were going to find him, he abandoned precautions, and rolled over onto his side to press his ear against the concrete floor of the roof. The word *"machine"* figured in their comments. It was the typewriter whose discovery pleased them so much. Now he stared at the side from which they would appear. A thick hand, white in the moonlight, would come feeling its way up over the edge, then grasp the ridge, and then another hand would come up, and then a head with eyes.

All at once they were breaking the windows. In rapid succession they pushed out the panes. The sheets of glass hitting the ground below made a brittle music. He wondered if Moulay Ali were still within hearing distance, and if so, what were his reactions when these sounds reached his ears. Would he think that Amar had been caught and that a struggle was in progress? Above all, would he think that Amar was going to tell them what innocuous facts he knew? But then he sighed: Moulay Ali surely had gone so far by now that he could hear nothing. Such tiny tinkling crashes would die on the night breeze even before it had carried them as far as the olive grove.

It was only now that he discovered and verified an astonishing fact: with the police only three or four meters below him, he became aware that it was largely a matter of indifference to him whether they found him or not. He even had a crazy momentary impulse to bang on the roof and shout: "Here I am, you sons of dogs!" They would try to climb up to get him, and he would simply lie still and watch. And when they did have him finally, they would beat him and carry him off to the torture room in the police station where they would attach electrodes to his *qalaoui*, and the pain would be more terrible than anything he had ever known or imagined, but he would keep his lips closed tight. It would serve no purpose at all, beyond that of giving him at last the wonderful satisfaction of feeling a part of the struggle. Perhaps if he had had a secret to withhold, the temptation to announce his presence would have become too strong to resist. But he knew nothing; it would have been only a silly game. And it occurred to him that no one cared whether there was an Amar or not, that if anyone but his family should care, it would not be because he was he, but because, as he moved blindly along the orbit of his life, he had accidentally become the repository of some scrap of information.

He listened: they were going back down the stairs, back along the galleries, back through the house, and away. They had parked their jeeps somewhere far out in the fields, for he waited an interminable time before he heard the faint sound of doors being shut and motors starting up. When they were gone he turned over and sobbed a few times, whether with relief or loneliness he did not know. Lying up here on the cold concrete roof he felt supremely deserted, exquisitely conscious of his own weakness and insignificance. His gift meant nothing; he was not even sure that he had any gift, or ever had had one. The world was something different from what he had thought it. It had come nearer, but in coming nearer it had grown smaller. As if an enormous piece of the great puzzle had fallen unexpectedly into place, blocking the view of distant, beautiful countrysides which had been there until now, dimly he was aware that when everything had been understood, there would be only the solved puzzle before him, a black wall of certainty. He would know, but nothing would have meaning, because the knowing was itself the meaning; beyond that there was nothing to know.

After a long time he crawled over to the edge and climbed down into the tower, slipping his feet into his sandals to protect them from the slivers of shattered glass that reflected the moon's light. His silent passage through the dark house was not even

frightening: it was only infinitely sad, for now the house belonged completely to what had been and never would be again.
He went straight to the broken front door and stepped outside.
There were no sounds at all. The night had reached its furthest
point: no crickets strummed in the grass, no night birds stirred
in the bushes. In another few minutes, although it still was far
away, the dawn would arrive. Even before he reached the olive
trees, he heard the melancholy note of the first cockcrow behind
him.

CHAPTER   35

And here he was in the Ville Nouvelle, and it was the middle of
the morning. The sun hammered down upon the pavements that
covered the earth of the plain, and the pitiful little trees that
were meant to give shade slowly withered in its heat. He kept to
the quiet back streets where few people passed. It was a painfully
hot day. An old Frenchwoman was approaching, dressed all in
black, carrying her shopping bag full of food home from the
market. She looked at him with suspicion, and crossed the street
slowly before he got to her, so as not to have to meet him face to
face. Not a single child played outside the houses, no traffic
passed, and no radios played; possibly the electricity was still
cut off. The city seemed nearly deserted, but he knew that
behind the curtains of the windows were a thousand pairs of
eyes peering out into the empty streets, following the passage of
whoever ventured along them. Every sign was bad: when the
French were frightened there was no knowing what they might
do.
    Beyond the small park with the iron bandstand was the be-

ginning of the street that led to the hotel where he had gone with the Nazarene man and woman. He did not know how he was going to get to see the man (nor did it even occur to him that he might not yet be back from Sidi Bou Chta, or that he might already be gone); he knew only that he had to see him, to set things straight between them, to hear him talk a while in his halting but learned Arabic, saying things that he knew would in some way comfort him in his unhappiness.

He went around the end of the park instead of crossing it: often there were policemen in there walking along its paths. At the end of the long avenue on his right a few cars were parked, but no person was in the street; it was like a flat stretch of stony desert shimmering in the sunlight. Before he got to the hotel a truck laden with cuttings of rusty tin drove slowly past. A blond Frenchman at the wheel stared at him curiously and yawned. The gray façade of the hotel looked as if it had been boarded up and vacated a long time ago. Its six windows with their closed shutters were like eyes asleep. In a loud voice he said: *"Bismil'lah rahman er rahim,"* and pulled the bell.

The woman who answered the door had seen him before, the day he had come with the two tourists and had helped them in with their luggage, but now she did not appear to recognize him. Her face was like a stone as she asked him in French what he wanted. A few paces behind her stood a large red-faced man who stared over her shoulder at him threateningly. When she found Amar did not speak French, she was about to shut the door; then suddenly something in her face changed, and although her expression remained unfriendly, he knew she had remembered him. She said something to the man, and called in a shrill voice: "Fatima!" A Moslem girl appeared, dragging a broom behind her, and said to him: "What is it?" The French-woman seemed already to have known his answer, for she said nothing, and walked over to where some keys hung in a row against the wall. She examined them, exchanged a few words with the man, and spoke to the girl, who said to Amar: "Wait a-while," and shut the door. He walked to the curb and sat down. His knees were trembling.

After not too long a time he heard the door open behind him. Quickly he stood up, but the long walk in the sun and his stomach with no food in it had made him dizzy. He saw his friend in the doorway, his arm raised in a gesture of welcome; then a cloud came swiftly across the sun and the street shot into its dark shadow. He leaned against one of the small dead trees to keep from falling. From a distance he heard the Frenchwoman calling abusive words—whether at him or at the tourist, he did not know. But then the Nazarene was at his side, leading him into the cool shade of the hotel, and although he felt very weak and ill, he was happy. Nothing mattered, nothing terrible could happen to him when he was in this man's care.

The man eased him into a chair and in no time had wrapped a cold wet towel around his head. "*Rhir egless*," he said to him. "Just sit still." Amar did, breathing heavily. The room held the sweet smell of flowers that the woman had always had on her clothing. When he finally opened his eyes and sat up a little straighter, he expected to see her, but she was not in the room. The man was sitting on the bed near by, smoking a cigarette. When he saw that Amar's eyes were open, he smiled. "How are you?" he said.

Before Amar could answer, there was a knock at the door. It was the girl called Fatima, bringing a tray. She set it on the table, went out. The man poured him a cup of coffee with milk, and handed him a plate with two rolls and some butter on it. As Amar ate and drank and looked around the dim room with its closed shutters, the man wandered back and forth, eventually coming to stand near him. Then Amar told him his story. The man listened, but he seemed restless and distraught, and twice he glanced at his watch. Amar went on until he had come to the end of his story. "And thanks to Allah you were here," he added fervently. "Now everything is well."

The man looked at him curiously and said: "And you? What can I do for you?"

"Nothing," said Amar, smiling. "I'm happy now."

The man got up and walked to the window as if he were about

to open it, then changed his mind and went to the other. There was a crack in the shutter through which he peered briefly.

"You're lucky the police didn't see you here in the Ville Nouvelle today," he said suddenly. "Any Moslem in the street goes to jail. There's been big trouble."

"Worse than before?"

"Worse." The man went to the door. "Just a minute," he told him. "I'll be right back." He went out. Amar sat still for an instant. Then he stepped to the bed and carefully examined the pillow cases. Even in the half-light they were visible, the smears of red paint that whores and Nazarene women used on their lips, and the flower smell came up in a heavy invisible cloud from the bed. He went back and sat down.

The man opened the door, came in. It was only now that Amar saw the luggage stacked by the door.

"Well, I'm glad you came," said the man.

"I'm glad too."

"If you hadn't come now I wouldn't have seen you again. We're going to Casablanca."

It was all right, because the man was still there in front of him, and Amar could not really believe that having found him he would lose him so soon. If Allah had seen fit to bring them together once again, it was not so that they might talk for five minutes and then say good-bye. A car door slammed outside in the quiet street. "Here's the taxi," said the man nervously, without even going to peek through the shutter. "Amar, I hate to ask you again, but how about helping us once more with our luggage? This is the last time."

Amar jumped up. Whatever the man asked him to do, he would feel the same happiness in obeying; of that he was sure.

As he carried the valises downstairs one by one, the Frenchwoman and the big man stared out at him through a little window from where they sat in their room, observing a hostile silence. When all the luggage had been packed into the car, and Amar, a bit dizzy again from the exertion, stood on the curb with the man, the woman appeared in the doorway, looking prettier than Amar had ever seen her look, and walked toward them. She smiled at Amar and began to go through a pantomime of looking up and down the street fearfully, then pointed at him. Grinning back at her, he indicated that he was not afraid.

"Can I take you anywhere?" the man asked him. "We're going out the Meknès road. I don't suppose that will help you much—"

"Yes!" said Amar.

"It will?" said the man, surprised. "*Mezziane.* Get in front." Amar took the seat beside the driver, who was a Jew from the Mellah.

The woman was already sitting in the back, and the man got in beside her. When they had driven out to the end of the Avenue de France, the man said: "Do you want to get out here?"

"No!" said Amar.

They went on, past the service station and down the long road leading to the highway. The high eucalyptus trees went by quickly, one after the other, and in each one the insects were screaming the same tone. The man and the woman were silent. In the mirror before him, a little higher than his eyes, Amar could see the man's fingers caressing the woman's hand, lying inert in her lap.

As they approached the highway, the man leaned forward and told the driver to stop. Amar sat quite still. It was stifling in the car now that no breeze came in through the windows. The man touched his shoulder. "*El hassil, b'slemah, Amar,*" he said, holding his hand in front of Amar's face. Amar reached up slowly, grasped it, and turning his head around, looked at the man fixedly. In his head he formed the words: "*Incha'Allah rahman er rahim.*"

"I want to go to Meknès," he said in a low voice.

"No, no, no!" cried the man, laughing jovially and pumping Amar's hand up and down. "No, Amar, that won't do. Even here it's a long way for you to walk back, you know."

"Back to where?" said Amar evenly, neither shifting his gaze from the man's eyes nor letting go of his hand, which the man moved up and down again violently, trying to withdraw it. His face was changing: he was embarrassed, annoyed, growing angry. "Good-bye, Amar," he said firmly. "I can't take you to Meknès. There's no time." If he had said, "I won't take you with me," Amar would have understood.

Without the motor going, the one endless rasping note of the cicadas overhead was very loud.

"My mother's there," murmured Amar, scarcely knowing what he said.

The woman, who seemed not to understand anything, smiled at him, raised her arms, pretending to aim a gun, and cried: "Boom! Bam!" She shifted her position and was behind an imaginary machine-gun. "Dat-tat-tat-tat-tat!" she said very quickly. When she had finished, she pointed her forefinger at Amar. The man nudged her, raising an eyebrow at the back of the driver's head. Then he said something to the driver, who reached in front of Amar and opened the door for him, looking at him expectantly.

Amar let go of the man's hand and stepped into the road, his head lowered. He saw his sandals sinking slightly into the hot sticky tar, and he heard the door slam beside him.

"*B'slemah!*" called the man, but Amar could not look up at him.

"*B'slemah!*" echoed the woman. Still he could not raise his head. The motor started up.

"Amar!" the man cried.

The car moved ahead uncertainly, then it gathered speed. He knew they were looking out the rear window, waving to him, but he stood still, seeing only his feet in their sandals, and the black tar beside them. The driver turned into the highway, shifted gears.

Amar was running after the car. It was still there, ahead of him, going further away and faster. He could never catch it, but he ran because there was nothing else to do. And as he ran, his sandals made a terrible flapping noise on the hard surface of the highway, and he kicked them off, and ran silently and with freedom. Now for a moment he had the exultant feeling of flying along the road behind the car. It would surely stop. He could see the two heads in the window's rectangle, and it seemed to him that they were looking back.

The car had reached a curve in the road; it passed out of sight. He ran on. When he got to the curve the road was empty.

—*Taprobane, Weligama*
16/iii/55

These and other titles by Paul Bowles are available from ecco:

THE SHELTERING SKY

ISBN 0-880-01582-9 (paperback)
ISBN 0-06-019916-4 (50th anniversary hardcover edition)

In this classic work of psychological terror, Paul Bowles examines the ways in which Americans comprehend an alien culture—and the ways in which their incomprehension destroys them. The story of three American travelers adrift in the cities and deserts of North Africa after World War II, *The Sheltering Sky* is at once merciless and heartbreaking in its compassion.

"[*The Sheltering Sky*] is one of the most original, even visionary, works of fiction to appear in this century." —Tobias Wolff

THE STORIES OF PAUL BOWLES

Introduction by Robert Stone
ISBN 0-06-093784-X (paperback)

From "The Delicate Prey" to "A Distant Episode," the stories of Paul Bowles bear the mark of a master—a disconcerting and delicious tension where Fate plays itself out among characters cut adrift in menacingly exotic, unfamiliar places.

"His work is art. At his best, Bowles has no peer." —*Time*

THEIR HEADS ARE GREEN AND THEIR HANDS ARE BLUE

Scenes from the Non-Christian World
Introduction by Edmund White
ISBN 0-880-01301-X (paperback)

This engaging collection of travel essays deals largely with places in the world that few Westerners have ever heard of, much less seen—places as yet unencumbered by the trappings, luxuries, and corruptions of modern civilization. Bowles is a sympathetic and discerning observer of these alien cultures; his eyes and ears are especially alert both to what is bizarre and profound in these civilizations.